MW00466331

THE THIRD REVOLUTION II:
THE LONG
KNIVES

By Gregory Kay

Copyright by author, West Virginia 2006
All rights reserved

The Long Knives is a work of fiction, and any resemblance of any of the characters or organizations depicted in this book to any person, living or dead, or to any organization past or present, is purely coincidental.

THE LONG KNIVES is copyrighted by Gregory Kay, 2007, West Virginia; all rights reserved. No part of this book may be reproduced without permission.

Other books by Gregory Kay

THE THIRD REVOLUTION
THE THIRD REVOLUTION III: THE BLACK FLAG
DARK PATHS

A Note of Thanks

Again, I need to thank Jerry, Sam, and the usual cast of co-conspirators for making this book possible. Additionally, I'd like to extend my special thanks to Lynx and Lamb of *Prussian Blue*, to their mother April Gaede, and to their songwriter, Ken McLellen, for permission to use their lyrics, as well as for many hours of enjoyment and inspiration.

Obviously, above all else, I need to thank God for giving me what I needed. I'd be lost without you...literally.

DEDICATION

The Long Knives is dedicated to the late Dennis Wheeler, both a true Southern patriot and a truly wise man. You'll be missed; if we had a thousand more like you, we'd all be whistling *Dixie*!

"Death to every foe and traitor!
Forward! Strike the marching tune!
And our army fights for freedom!
Tis the rising of the Moon!"

~ *The Rising of the Moon* by John Casey
Kerrie O'Brien's version

DUTY ROSTER
1st COLUMBIA IRREGULARS

Confederate Army Provisional Supreme Commander:
Field Marshal Jonathon Edge

South Carolina Theater Commander:
Colonel Samuel Wirtz

1st Columbia Commanding Officer:
Captain Franklin Gore

Executive Officers:
Lieutenant Robert Johnson
Lieutenant Thomas Richardson

First Sergeant:
Basil Caffary

ALPHA SQUAD
SERGEANT: Ronald Hodges
CORPORAL: Mitchell Stanley
PRIVATES: Arnel Scot
            Casey Graham
            Jerry Smith
            Doug Long

BRAVO SQUAD
SERGEANT: Andy Buchanan
CORPORAL: Wayland Fowler
PRIVATES: Henry Toland
            David Worley
            Daniel Worley
            Marvin Connolly

CHARLIE SQUAD
SERGEANT: Marion Stock
CORPORAL: Jack Lewis
PRIVATES: Bill McGuire
Frank Godwin
David Snipes
Arnold Kessler

DELTA SQUAD
SERGEANT: John Thompson
CORPORAL: William Wilson
PRIVATES: Tim Matthews
Dean Yates
George Cox

ECHO SQUAD
SERGEANT: James Kowalski
CORPORAL: Jay Knott
PRIVATES: Daniel Drucci
Jack Davidson
Hubert Moore

PROLOGUE

The Third Revolution began in Columbia, South Carolina almost accidentally; its driving force was frustration, but its catalyst was something as simple as two people – Frank Gore and Samantha Norris – who doggedly insisted on telling the truth.

It didn't remain in Columbia long; within days there were actions in the cities and the countryside across the South ranging from more or less peaceful civil disobedience to fatal shootings and bombings. The war quickly began forcing people to take a side, and for most, once that side was chosen, there was no going back.

The Federal Government did its best to publicly minimize the impact of the guerrilla actions either as simple criminality or as isolated pockets of homegrown, right wing terrorism, but it was not quite as simple as that. Many Southerners fought as individuals, waging their own war for their own reasons, but the root of those reasons was preservation: of their ways, their faith, their liberties, their race, or simply their lives, and they fought hard. The Federal forces hit back even harder with torture, covert assassinations and middle-of-the-night raids that caused people to vanish without a trace, and then charged those who questioned where those people went with aiding terrorism under the auspices of the so-called 'Patriot Act.' The Confederates responded in kind, and the conflict became a game of grim one-upmanship, with each new act of brutality escalating in response to another, and Dixie began to bleed.

One reason the vastly outnumbered, outgunned, and highly disorganized guerrillas survived those earliest days was because the government was as of yet unwilling to bring the full might of the regular military, in the form of open occupation, against the 'Red State' conservative South during an election year. The Republican Administration knew that their already-slender chances of holding onto power wouldn't survive the alienation of their most reliable constituency. Conversely, the Southern forces themselves could not grow unless they risked the very destruction of just such an occupation, which would knock the fence sitters off onto their side.

The defacto leadership of the Southern forces – the Confederate Army Provisional under Field Marshal (or 'General' as he preferred to be called) Jonathon Edge and the Confederate Council – desperately tried to pull the independent forces together into something resembling an army so they would be ready when the hammer finally came down. It was not an easy job; any movement based on liberty tends to be resentful of authority, even when their own submission to that authority is necessary to secure those very liberties they seek. It didn't help matters that every member of the Council itself was suspicious of the motives of the others, usually with very good reason. Internal alliances shifted like the wind as they jockeyed for power, until no one could trust the man sitting next to him, all at the very point where everything rode on Southern unity. To the dedicated and opportunist alike, those were desperate times. Desperation, unfortunately, can lead to obsession and paranoia, which are every bit as fatal as the problems they arise in response to. They become an irresistible force, but occasionally that unstoppable energy collides with an immovable object; then things really get interesting because one or the other – or both – will break.

DAY 71

CHAPTER 1

Regional Federal Emergency Management Agency District Office
State Capital Building
Columbia, South Carolina
9:14 PM

"Just what the hell is going on down there?"

Even though he was alone in his office, Ronald Peters, the FEMA district chief kept his right hand firmly on the desktop, refusing to allow himself to squirm in his chair as he held the phone to his ear. He had been dreading this for a while, and it was no relief at all when it finally came.

"Sir, the situation is under control…"

"Under control? Do you know what I've had to deal with? Those damned squads of yours that we've managed to keep secret for years are all over the news now, do you realize that? There are right wing terrorists striking all across the South, reporters are surrounding the White House like Mexicans around the Alamo and everybody in Homeland Security is running around in a panic like their asses were on fire. Now, we've got half the resources of the Federal Government trying to figure out how the hell we can either discredit those accounts, or at least minimize their impact. This is bigger than Watergate!"

"Sir, I'm sure…"

"You're sure are you? You were sure when you brought in that squad of yours too; now look at it! What the hell are you sure about now?

"You've queered my chances for reelection; you know that don't you? Less than four months before November and you let this happen! Four months!"

11

"Sir, I have a plan…"

"Tell it to your boss. I don't want to hear about it, since I'll probably have to deny it under oath in an impeachment trial!

"Just understand one thing; if this screws up, I'll have your head on a plate! Do you understand me, you son of a bitch? On a plate!"
"I understand, Mr. President –" but he was suddenly talking to air and the annoying buzz of a dial tone. Carefully, with infinite self-control, he hung up the telephone, propped his elbows on the desk, and tented his fingers in front of his chin.

"That went well," he muttered sarcastically in the empty room to no one in particular.

Another meeting on the other side of town was going no better. This one was in person, in a vacant, boarded-up warehouse that stank of mice and mildew. At least the location was unknown to the authorities and thus fairly safe. As a bonus, the owner, a rebel sympathizer, had been allowing his church to store stuff in there, including folding chairs, so the men didn't have to sit on the floor.

Following the Confederate Army Provisional's successful raid on the Charleston Naval Base, militia leader Neil Larson was finally satisfied that the group was both competent and serious about fighting this war. He then bargained his way into a seat on the Confederate Council in exchange for his small private army consisting of thirty much-needed guerrilla fighters scattered across South Carolina. Since Jonathan Edge was CAP's overall commander, the men fell under his jurisdiction. Being in South Carolina put them under the charge of Edge's long-time friend and compatriot, Palmetto Colonel Samuel Wirtz, and his second in command, ex-cop, reluctant folk hero, and current Columbia Theater Commander, Captain Franklin Gore. The men were now their responsibility.

Actually, they were Frank's responsibility. Sam had seen him in combat, and now he wanted to see his organizational skills. The one-time hog farmer sat back and pretty well let the younger man run the show.

As the evening wore on, it became obvious that particular responsibility was going to be a strenuous one.

Larson's men were as tough a collection as could be found in South Carolina, at least since Frank, along with Edge and Sam and a tiny CAP force, had wiped out local FEMA Director Peters' death squad during the Charleston raid less than three months before. A mixed bag of militiamen, Klansmen, skinheads, and assorted anti-government activists, racialists and conspiracy theorists, they had only two things in common: an aversion to the direction the South was heading and a willingness to do whatever it took to save it. If there was ever any doubt, it quickly became obvious Neil Larson hadn't recruited them simply for their good manners and award-winning personalities.

Still, they had what was most important: the same belief in the dream of Southern independence that drove Frank, Sam, Edge, Larson, and all the rest, and a willingness to fight for it. That covered a multitude of sins...but not all. In every crowd there's at least one troublemaker, and in this one it was a personal sovereignty advocate named Larry Blair.

Blair, hailing from Anderson, down near the Georgia border, was an imposing figure in his late-twenties. Unkept dark hair, neither short nor quite long, framed a slightly olive complexion on a bulldog face, set off by a thin, mangy looking beard. Two inches taller than Frank's own six feet, he was heavier by more than half, very little of which was fat. His frame was that of a football lineman and dedicated power lifter, and his personality and raucous voice were as imposing as his size.

It seemed Blair was bound and determined to rudely call *everything* into question, from the location of the meeting to Larson's right to transfer his command. When his fellow guerrillas tried to calm him down in their own genteel fashion *("Why don't you shut the hell up so we can get this over with?")*, he raised just as much cane with them, claiming his *"sovereign right"* to do as he pleased. Frank didn't know if it was his sheer size that kept him from getting stomped, or whether the others were just used to him; as it

13

was, he had had some of his comrades so irritated it looked like they just might give it a shot anyway.

Sam looked at Frank. It was obvious they were going to have to get a handle on the situation, and quickly, or the command structure would be reduced to uselessness by chaos and lack of respect for authority. Frank raised an eyebrow in a question, and Sam gave an almost imperceptible nod. *Go for it!*

The ex-cop intended to do just that. After being framed for a crime he didn't commit, pursued halfway across South Carolina, having his wife kidnapped and tortured nearly to death, and fighting the police, regular Federal agents and covert death squads to get her back, Frank was a changed man, and those changes had gone far beyond the short, dark beard he had grown to help mask his identity from the casual glance. The alteration was not in his most basic nature but in his determination. In that brief period of time, the hammer of adversity had forged him on the anvil of necessity until he was like a razor-sharp, well-tempered blade, and woe betide whatever got in the way of the cutting edge. He had gone from being a firm man to one as hard as steel when the need was there, as it was now.

He walked over and planted himself in front of Larry Blair closer than convention and politeness dictated, deliberately invading his space.

"Mr. Blair, like it or not, you enlisted in Mr. Larson's unit. We are now at war. During times of war, units are transferred and commands change; that's just the way it is. Every man in this room, yourself included, voluntarily enlisted in a paramilitary unit and took an oath. You're in for the duration; *there is no going back.* Everyone here is going to do their jobs and obey their orders, and that includes you. You might as well get used to the idea, because that's the way it is. It's time you got on board instead of blocking the tracks."

He glared up at Frank, his big arms crossed defiantly. "Maybe I'll take orders from you and maybe I won't; I haven't decided yet!"

"*I've* decided, and you will. End of story." Frank's emotionless voice never rose.

Blair's mouth gaped with shock. Quickly glancing over his shoulder to gauge his comrades' reactions, he saw that he was alone in this. Most of them had the experience to recognize Frank's type, and they knew what was coming. The majority appeared expectant, and a couple of them were openly grinning at the prospect. Men like Blair didn't tend to make themselves popular.

He sneered at Frank. "And what're you gonna' do if I don't?"

Frank's tone never changed and he never broke eye contact. "Then I'm going to kick your ass all over this room."

If Blair had been shocked by Frank's forwardness before, he was stunned by it now. People just didn't talk to him that way. His face flushed with embarrassment and anger as the other men began laughing at the sight of him being put in his place. One of them, an older man with a leathery, rock-hard face and an iron-gray crew cut, gave him a piece of advice. "You better listen to him, boy; he means it."

"Let's see you try it!" Blair shouted before dropping his hands onto his knees to heave himself to his feet. The movement left his head wide open, and that was a bad mistake.

His rear was only six inches from the seat when Frank punched him in the face for all he was worth. The ex-cop had been an avid boxer and martial artist since childhood, and was in tremendous physical shape. His fist, with all his body torque and two hundred pounds of weight behind it, was no more than a faint blur, but it hit with the power and sound of a sledgehammer against a steer's skull.

Blood sprayed as Blair slammed back into the folding chair and kept going, tipping over backwards and landing in the floor with a crash. The back of his head bounced painfully off the concrete.

Several of the men in the room winced, a couple laughed, one loudly exclaimed, "*Damn!*" and the older man shook his head as he gave Blair a disgusted look and calmly mumbled around the unfiltered Camel he was smoking, *"I told you so"*.

"That's one," Frank told him calmly, still never raising his voice. "Don't try for two." He suddenly knew in his heart that he was going to have to kill this man. He hoped it wouldn't go that far, but this had to be nipped in the bud, even if a fatal example had to be made.

15

His life, the lives of the other twenty-nine men, the future of this unit, and quite possibly the future of the war, rested on his ability to command and have his orders obeyed.

Blair scrambled from the floor with a roar of rage, his broken nose literally mashed flat and spread across his face, streaming blood into his beard. Charging, he threw a hard overhead right at Frank's face with all of his considerable weight behind it. Frank stepped inside with his right leg, and whipped his right arm around Blair's neck while his left hand parried the punch and grabbed the arm. He bent his knees and continued to pivot until his back was to his opponent and Blair, carried by his own momentum, was literally wrapping around him. Frank snapped his legs straight while maintaining his pull, and drove Blair into the floor with a classic Judo *Tsuri-goshi* throw. Even the most hardened of the crowd cringed at the sound when the big man's body smacked the concrete. The nearer ones actually felt the vibration.

The calm tone of Frank's voice never altered, and he wasn't even breathing hard. "That's two, Mr. Blair. I strongly suggest you end this now, because if you try for three, I *will* kill you."

As the big man lay writhing, groaning and gasping for breath, Frank stepped away before turning back to the crowd and opening his mouth to speak. He heard Blair moving behind him, trying to get up. Frank felt the hairs on his neck prickle, and his hand began to stray towards his belt. The old Colt 1911 Mary had given him and Tommy had accurized hung there in it's holster, waiting.

Please, God, don't let him do this!

Larry Blair had never listened to God any more than he did to anyone else. He got to his feet, his huge right hand balled into a fist, and lunged.

Sam and the older man in the crowd yelled simultaneously, "Look" – *Bang!* – "out!"

Without looking back, Frank's instinct told him what was coming, and he had already closed his hand around the checkered grips of the cocked and locked slab-side .45 before the pair opened their mouths. Before they got the second word out, he had drawn, spun, and shot Larry Blair between the eyes at pointblank range with

16

a single hollow-nosed round. The larger man's head snapped back but his momentum kept him going, and Frank pirouetted gracefully on one foot like a matador to let the falling body pass. Blair collapsed in front of him, his shattered skull making a sound like a bag of wet gravel when he hit the floor. Blood immediately began forming a crimson pool. His right leg kicked twice.

Everyone was silent for a moment before the man who had joined Sam in warning him spoke up.

"I reckon that was three," he said in a deadpan voice.

Frank carefully kept his face blank. *Damn it! Why couldn't Blair have left well enough alone?*

Knowing what was necessary, what the men expected, even though it was the last thing he felt like doing, he deliberately stepped over the body and looked at the crowd.

"Now, if no one else has any objections, perhaps we can proceed with the integration of this unit." Everyone seemed satisfied to accept the recent event; at least no one spoke up.

"Good. Did Mr. Larson set up a chain of command or put any of you in charge?"

The older man chuckled dryly, apparently unaffected by the killing of his former comrade.

"Ol' Neil was too paranoid for that; he was afraid one of us would Jap him and take over."

Frank studied him carefully as he considered his words. He guessed the man was somewhere in his fifties, but his face was so hard and weathered it was difficult to say. He wasn't particularly tall – no more than five-nine – but there was an air of quiet competence and confidence about him that impressed the ex-cop. It was obvious he was the group's natural leader. He struck Frank as a 'tough nut'; far tougher than a larger and stronger blowhard like Blair.

Like Blair was, the voice inside him corrected.

He'd deal with that later...of that he had no doubt.

"What's your name, sir?"

"Basil Caffary, sir."

"Do you have any military experience?"

"I did twenty years in the Marine Corps – Gunnery Sergeant."

17

Frank had learned to trust his instincts, and he made his decision based on what they told him.

"Well, congratulations, Gunny Caffary; you just got yourself a promotion. You're the 1st Sergeant of the 1st Columbia Irregulars, effective as of now."

Frank looked around to see a very tall, powerfully built man with a shaven head raise his hand. He was in his late twenties and had the classic skinhead look, complete with Doc Marten boots and black suspenders over a white T-shirt that was stretched to its fullest capacity by his chiseled body builder's musculature. Swastikas, Iron Crosses, and other Teutonic symbols nearly covered his huge arms. He had evidently been slumped down in his chair, because Frank would have noticed him otherwise; he stood out, even in this unit.

"Yes sir? And you are?"

"Ron Hodges, sir," he declared, standing and straightening to his full height of six feet-four. He didn't seem to be unnerved by Frank, but the watching men also noted that if their new leader was the least bit intimidated by the giant, he showed no sign of it.

"Do you have an objection Mr. Hodges?"

"No sir," he said, breaking into a halfway smart-aleck grin and waving his hand toward Frank, "I just have a question: do you plan on shooting anyone else right now? If not, would you please put that thing away? You're making me nervous."

At his gesture, there was some general, uneasy laughter in the room, and Frank looked down to see the forgotten .45 still warm in his hand.

"Sorry," he said, returning it to his holster with a tight smile of his own. "I guess that does tend to put a damper on the conversation."

At Frank's direction, Sergeant Caffary had the men divide up into five six-man squads, with one squad being a man short due to Blair's sudden demise. Frank stayed out of it and allowed them to sort out who went where themselves under the career NCO's direction. He gave them fifteen minutes, while he and Sam used the time to access the situation.

"Frank, do you want my job?"

He was startled by the question.

"No! I didn't want this one. Why are you asking me something like that?"

"Because I know a leader when I see one. You're like General Forrest; you've got the charisma, the instinct, and the natural ability, more than I'll ever have. I'd feel more comfortable following you than having you follow me."

Frank shook his head.

"Sam, you've got the experience. You've been doing this a lot longer than I have."

"I've been doing it long enough to know I'll never be able to handle men like you do. You've already got 'em calling you 'sir' for goodness sakes – voluntarily!"

Frank sighed in frustration.

"Yeah, I handled them so well I've already had to shoot one of them. Besides, I know exactly jack about administration, and even if our *Field Marshal* would allow it, I still wouldn't do it. I got into this thing because I had to; I had no other choice. I didn't even think about Southern independence before that. I'm a 'true believer' now, of course, since I got my eyes opened, but I have no desire to do your job. That's just not me."

Sam chuckled dryly. "Well ol' hoss, I'm telling you as your commander that you're going to learn it anyway. You're going to rise in this man's army – such as it is – and assuming you live long enough, you're going to need the skills when you get there."

Frank gave him an exasperated look.

"Don't you think I'd better develop my direct command skills first?"

"Oh, you'll have plenty of time to do that. See, I've already spoken to Edge, and he's agreed and instructed me to put you directly in charge of this bunch; this company is now entirely your baby. All I'm going to do is act as liaison between you and General, help coordinate resources, keep you and him from killing each other, etcetera, etcetera. Nothing like on the job training, I always say."

Frank was as close as he ever got to panic. *I can't believe he's doing this to me!*

"You're *nuts!*"

Sam smiled like a mischievous Buddha with a silent but unusually smelly case of flatulence.

"It goes with the territory."

That wasn't all that went with the territory either, and Sam wasn't the least bit happy about the rest of it. What he told Frank was the truth, but a long way from the whole truth.

Jonathon Edge didn't exactly hate Frank Gore, but saw him as highly questionable in both the loyalty and reliability departments ever since Frank and Tommy Richardson had mutinied and forced Edge into mounting a hasty and extremely risky rescue operation that recovered not only Frank's wife Samantha and Tommy's partner Billy Sprouse from the clutches of a federal death squad, but managed to rescue the entire Confederate Council as well. The fact that the operation was successful and ended up putting Edge, both officially and in reality, in the catbird's seat was a moot point with him, blinding him to the simple truth: that Frank was not only not ambitious as far as his position in the movement, but had actually supported Edge when the others had their doubts. Edge had been in the Southern Nationalist Movement for much of his life, and the years of hard, bitter experience made even the possibility of anyone holding that attitude to be something utterly beyond his ken. All he could see as far as Frank was concerned, was here was a man who had mutinied, defied him, threatened to shoot him, was seen by the majority of those on both sides as the very symbol of the movement due to being the first one the Feds took an intensive interest in, and that he was highly capable to boot. This made the ex-cop not only a rival in Edge's book, but also a threat, and Edge was notoriously pragmatic in the matter of threats.

When Neil Larson – whom the General also saw as a rival and a threat, albeit with quite a bit more justification – turned over his militia to the Confederate Army Provisional, Edge was faced with a dilemma: what to do with thirty notoriously bellicose men from a faction he distrusted in the first place, and whose loyalty might still be to their former commander. His solution was simple; he put Frank Gore in charge of them. Sam had to agree that Frank was the only one with even a chance of handling the tough bunch and forging them into a unified fighting force, but he suspected that might be of secondary importance to his leader. What Edge was doing was gathering those he saw as potential enemies into one place. That way, he could keep an eye on them, and if there was something unusually difficult and dangerous to be done, they would be the ones called upon to do it. Just as importantly, when they royally screwed up – as Edge felt certain they eventually would, given their independent attitudes – he would simply put the blame directly on Frank and destroy him…perhaps literally.

The General didn't articulate these plans to Sam of course, but then again, he didn't have to. Sam had been Edge's friend for years – in fact, he was his only friend left alive – and he understood how the CAP leader thought, along with what lay between the lines of what he said. This left him in a quandary. He might have been friends with Edge, but now he was also friends with Frank Gore. In fact, it had been Frank who had saved his life from one of his own men gone berserk when they launched the raid that took their people back. Besides, the ex-cop was damned near impossible not to like. Whenever he was relaxed, he had a highly personable, 'good ol' boy' attitude, and was sometimes humble to a fault, something all too rare in a movement notorious for being full of out-sized egos. To go along with it, though, he had an extreme competence, a genius intellect, an ability to instantly slip into a cold, professional mode, and a strong, almost Medieval sense of honor. It was the intellect and the honor that worried Sam the most. Frank was intelligent enough that he would soon figure out what Edge was up to, assuming he didn't know already. What he would do if the General ever pushed him too far was anybody's guess. There was no question that Edge, with his vast experience, was the better overall leader, but if push ever came to shove, Frank was the better man.

Of course, all that didn't mean, despite his seeming openness, that Frank Gore might not have an agenda of his own that Sam didn't know about either. He had been known to play his cards pretty close to his vest on occasion. Sam had been with the movement a long time, long enough to know, just because he couldn't picture someone doing something, it didn't mean they weren't capable of doing it anyway.

His thoughts were interrupted when Caffary crossed the room to them.

"Excuse me, sirs. We have the squads organized."

"Excellent, Sergeant." Frank glanced at his watch. "You've finished four minutes ahead of time – good job!"

Frank went over and placed himself in front of the group.

"All right, gentlemen. After this meeting is over, I want each of you to go home and spend some quality time with your families; you won't be seeing them again for a while.

"Beginning approximately two weeks from today, you will reassemble – you'll be told where – and we will begin the training you need, both to survive and to win."

A low grumbling came from the crowd.

"Is there a problem here?" When he received no answer, he picked out one of the complainers, a tall, rail-thin militiaman. "You – what's your name?"

"John Thompson, sir."

"What's the problem, Thompson?"

Put on the spot, the man mumbled "No problem, sir."

"Horse manure. I asked you a question and I expect an answer – an *honest* answer. I'm going to ask you a second time; what is the problem?"

"That was two," Hodges advised him, only half jokingly. "If I were you, I think I'd answer the man."

Thompson's eyes widened as they strayed to Blair's body. Of course, Frank wouldn't actually shoot him for not answering, but he had no way of knowing that for sure.

"Well sir, it's just that we're already trained…"

"Are you?" Frank cut him off. He felt sorry for Thompson, but as before, a point needed to be made. "Are you qualified as a medic? Have you had advanced combat shooting? Demolitions? Hand to hand combat? Urban assault tactics? Are you intimately familiar with every military skill you may need?" He never gave him a chance to answer before going on. "Even if you are, have you trained in them with the other members of your squad *and* with this company until each and every man knows exactly what every one of the others will do in any given circumstance?" He gave Thompson a break and cut his eyes away toward the rest of the crowd. "Have any of you?"

When it was obvious that no one could answer in the affirmative, he continued.

"That is the purpose of this whole exercise, gentlemen: to make you work as a team. Every one of you is already a warrior, tough, ready, willing, and able to fight on his own, or you wouldn't be here; Mr. Larson wasn't the type to recruit a bunch of pansies. If we're going to win, however, it's not enough just to be a warrior. You've also got to be a soldier: part of a cohesive unit that functions like a single organism.

"Every squad here is a chain, and the chain is only as strong as its weakest link. There will be no weak links by the time you're done. We simply can't afford them.

"Sergeant Caffary knows you far better than I do, and has probably forgot more about the military than the rest of us will ever know. He will assist you in choosing a leader and a second – ranked sergeant and corporal respectively – for each squad. Bring your nominations to him. He will make the final decision and notify me of the result, but *his* decision *will* be final.

"Each and every one of you is literally your brother's keeper. Each squad, from the sergeants down to the privates, will be responsible for the proper conduct of the rest of that squad. Each squad will see to it that each and every one of its members, without exception, turns up for this training and for any future missions that you are assigned, or I *will* know the reason why."

He didn't point at Blair's corpse when he said that. He didn't have to.

"Resign yourselves to this, gentlemen; we are at war. We are at war with an enemy who will stop at nothing to destroy both you as individuals and the Southern race as a people. By the time this is over, the winning side will be the living side; the losers will either be driven out or they will be *dead*. Since we Southerners have no place else to go, that narrows down our options considerably. We will either win, or we will die, our families will die, and our people – our very race – will die. I intend for us to live, therefore, I intend for us to win."

He slowly swiveled his head, making eye contact with each one of the men, who were hanging on his every word.

"We all have different reasons for being here, and some of us have different ideas of exactly who the enemy is. For some, it's the United States Government; for others, it's pagan humanism. Some of you see the enemy as powerful Jews while others see it as Black agitators. For a few of you, it might be corporations, abortionists, global conspirators, or invaders from outer space, for all I know; frankly, I don't give a damn. That's your business, so long as you know who the *real* enemy is.

"The real enemy, gentlemen, is *anyone* or *anything* that stands between us and the sovereign independence of the Southern nation that we must establish in order to secure both our liberty and our people's very survival. Anyone, North or South, domestic or foreign, Black or White, who stands in the way of that *is* the enemy, and we will march across his *ashes.*

"God save the South!"

The room went wild. The men pumped their fists in the air, yelling at the top of their lungs. Hands clapped until the palms were red and chapped.

"Patton couldn't have done it better!" Sam whispered in his ear.

Frank looked back at the stiffening corpse. He wasn't so sure.

The door had no sooner closed behind the pair than the conversation started.

"Damn!" one of the younger skinheads exclaimed loudly. "Did you ever see anybody that fast?"

"Not me," another replied, shifting in his chair to gesture at the body on the floor. No one was overly bothered by its presence; they'd all seen dead men before, and none of them had particularly

24

liked Blair anyway. "I never even saw his hand move. Right between the eyes too! He sure doesn't put up with much in the way of bullshit, does he?"

First Sergeant Caffary's voice rose above them all to silence the chatter.

"All right boys; is everyone satisfied that this is a man we can follow? Hodges, you've usually got something to say; what do you think?"

The younger man thoughtfully rubbed his square chin for a moment before answering.

"Well, I admit I was skeptical before, but after seeing him in action, I'm inclined to believe everything we've heard about him. He's fast, he's tough, and there's no posing about him; he takes care of business. I respect that.

"What do you think, *Sarge?*"

Caffary's voice was serious.

"I think so too, but there's something I respect even more, and that's the way he treated us. It's his attitude: *'This is what I want. You make it happen.'* He let us divide our own company into squads, putting people where we see fit, rather than trying to micro-manage the whole thing himself when he didn't know his ass from a hole in the ground about any of us, or how we're used to doing things. He trusted us to make the best decision instead of trying to make it for us. He treated us like men instead of like cattle, like they do in the regular military.

"Of course," he pointedly looked at Blair's corpse, "he obviously understands the need for discipline too. From where I sit, I reckon he's the best of both worlds.

"I hate to say this boys, but I suspect we just might have a better leader here than our first one was, nothing against Neil."

"It'll be alright, Frank."

For some reason, people keep telling me that, like they really expect me to believe it.

He looked at Sam as they walked through the shadows of an alley, heading for their car. It was a relatively safe place due to the filth; there was so much trash and debris strewn around that a police car wouldn't be able to get down it if it had to, and cops who valued their lives didn't go on foot in Columbia anymore.

"Thanks, but I'm not sure how. It just seems to be getting worse."

"Some people, like Blair in there tonight, just have it coming, and they'll eventually get it in spite of hell. Nothing else will do them. It's just their destiny, I reckon; it's like they were born to do it." He paused, mulling over the idea. "Maybe it's some kind of Darwinian thing, where the chronically stupid develop an instinct to do everything they possibly can to get someone to give them a boost so they can climb out of the gene pool."

Frank stepped over a broken bottle and nearly set his boot on a startled rat that ran squealing for cover.

"Huh! I just wish they were getting the boost from someone else. Counting the raids, that's the fifth man I've killed in a little over a couple of months. It's not setting real well, if you know what I mean."

Sam was silent for so long Frank thought he wasn't going to answer.

"If it starts setting well, then let me know, because you've got a problem. Look, Frank; have you ever killed anybody you didn't have to?"

"No, but…"

"Alright then. We do what we have to, and at least the ones you've taken down have had it coming, as much as anybody does. I wish I could say the same."

"You were in Desert Storm, weren't you?"

"There and Panama. I tell you, Frank, I've seen some things and done some things that still wake me up at night. Still, I think that last one was the worst."

"Still thinking about that security guard when we rescued the prisoners?"

"I reckon I'll be thinking about him till I die. I intentionally and cold-bloodedly traded his life for the lives of six of our people. I looked him right in the eyes and shot him, and his crime was no

26

more than being in the wrong place at the wrong time, just trying to earn a living and feed his family."

Frank silently nodded his understanding.

There but for the grace of God go I, and I figure I'll end up going there more than once before this thing is over.

After glancing both ways, they emerged from the alley and turned left, walking along the cracked sidewalk. There were a few people here and there despite the curfew. Night people, as Frank thought of them: party animals and drunks, the insane, the transients, the hookers, hustlers, and predators, all on their mysterious nightly errands, and every last one of them a silent story of personal tragedy. Every day of an economy in the crapper seemed to bring more and more of them, until there were so many that the police couldn't begin to keep up, even during the restricted hours.

"Do you guys need a date?" a strained, frightened feminine voice called from behind them.

Both turned to see a starved, desperate looking White teenager in filthy clothes and a greasy tangle of auburn hair: just another of the growing army of homeless and hungry young prostitutes thronging the streets trying to make enough money to stay alive during the hard times. This one didn't look like she was doing too well at it, or smell like it either; on the street, places to wash were few and far between, and they caught a whiff of her body odor from six feet away. Frank sighed.

It's enough to break your heart.

They were about to wave away her offer when Frank realized she looked strangely familiar.

"Kerrie?" he asked, abruptly recognizing her despite her disheveled appearance. "Kerrie O'Brien?"

A look of recognition followed by a wave of horrified embarrassment flowed over her features. She sobbed once, very loudly, and threw both hands up to hide her face as she turned, stumbling away. Before she made it two steps, Frank had her by the shoulder and gently but firmly rotated her back to face him.

"What happened, Kerrie?"

"Don't look at me!" she wailed.

Frank took her wrists and pulled her hands away from her dirty, tear-streaked face. He had learned the hard way that some situations called for firmness, and he instinctively knew this was one of them.

"I'm going to do more than look at you, young lady; I'm going to talk to you, and you're going to talk to me. I want to help you! Now tell me what happened."

Her green eyes were tormented when they met his.

"It was the story…"

Kerrie O'Brien, along with her fellow high school journalism club members – Jared Robinson, Cynthia Davis and Chucky Donahue – had been the ones to present the Confederate Army Provisional's side of the story to the people of Columbia, firing a literary shot heard 'round the world in the process.

As Kerrie now related, they had paid a terrible price for doing so.

All of them were brought in and questioned extensively by the FBI. They had expected that, and had simply told the truth. They had broken no laws and that should have been it, but it was only the beginning.

They were all expelled from their high school at the end of their senior year, for 'abusing membership in a school club' and 'bringing discredit on the school.'

Then Kerrie had been thrown out of her house. She wept as she described how her own father and mother had beaten her bloody, calling her a "traitor" and an "un-American slut" before literally tossing her into the street and telling her never to darken their door again. She had been sleeping in alleys, doorways, and sometimes dumpsters ever since. With no money and not streetwise, she was desperate.

"I had no place to go, and I was hungry!" she wept bitterly. "There're no jobs! I held out as long as I could! I tried begging and eating garbage at first, but there wasn't enough! I didn't want to do it, but I had to eat! *God*, I'm so hungry!" Her voice broke off in loud sobs as the tears washed white streaks through the dirt on her cheeks. "I'm so ashamed!"

"Oh good Lord," Sam murmured around the lump that suddenly came up in his throat.

Ignoring her filthy clothes and the sour smell of her unwashed body, Frank pulled her to him and held her tightly against his broad chest while she shook with emotion. Sam laid a hand on her shoulder.

"It'll be alright, honey," he told her.

"It won't be alright! I'm a whore, don't you get it? I'm nothing but a dirty little whore!"

Frank put a hand under her chin and raised her head, forcing her to look into his eyes.

"No, Kerrie, you're not a whore. A whore does it for the money. You're just a girl who did what you had to in order to survive." He thought of the killing he had done himself. "Some of us have done worse – a whole lot worse."

"But –"

"No buts. You did what you had to do, and what's done is done. The past is over; it's time we look toward your future."

"What kind of a future am I going to have? I don't have a home! I don't even have a family anymore!"

Frank and Sam looked at one another, and the understanding silently passed between them. It was Frank who spoke.

"Kerrie, you have a home and a family…if you want it. You can join us. It's not much and it's definitely not very safe, but it's *got* to be better than this."

Her mouth hung open in shock.

"You…you mean you'd take me in, after…"

"Consider yourself took, little lady," the older man broke in. "Now let go and quit hogging her, Frank. Let ol' Uncle Sam hug his newest niece.

It was a long time before her tears stopped, but now they were for a different reason.

29

CHAPTER 2

Samantha couldn't wait for Frank to get back. The first time in their short marriage he had been away, Federal units had launched a raid, and she had been captured and tortured mercilessly. Even though she had more or less recovered physically from the ordeal, except for the constant lingering pain, she knew her mental state was another matter. She had "anger issues" as Tommy had once delicately put it. She also had paranoia, nightmares, irrational fears, childish tantrums and crying jags: all the classic symptoms of PTSD – Post Traumatic Stress Disorder. It affected her every day to some extent, but her husband's brief absences required by CAP missions inevitably brought on bouts of separation anxiety that were very close to panic attacks. She couldn't concentrate on her work as Communications Officer, and she jumped at every sound. This time, to make matters worse, the other residents of their headquarters – Lieutenants Rob Johnson and Tommy Richardson, along with Private Donna Waddell – were out as well. Tommy and Donna were organizing some of the more recent Columbia volunteers into a guerrilla cell, and Rob, who came and went as unpredictably as a silent gust of wind and never seemed to sleep, was meeting with what he would only refer to as "some old friends," trying to bring them on board. The only one in the house with her was the paraplegic Intelligence Officer Mike Dayton, and he was locked into something highly technical and very illegal on the computer in the basement, and wouldn't be much company. For all practical purposes, she was completely alone for the first time since her rescue, and it was a strange and scary feeling.

Angry with herself, she swore under her breath. Until a few months ago, she had lived alone for much of her life. There was no logical reason for her to feel this way.

I still feel it, though.

When the phone finally rang to tell her they were on their way, she could barely bring herself to answer it, for fear something had happened to Frank. She knew she was being totally irrational, but that didn't make the feelings go away or make them any less real. She would continue to fight it and she would beat this thing before she was through; she promised herself that, and she was a woman who kept her promises. In the meantime though, it was so damned *hard*.

Going to the mirror, she looked at herself critically. She had been almost achingly beautiful before, back when she hosted South Carolina's most popular mid-day news program. The faint scars that still marked her lips were concealed easily enough with a little lipstick, but the slight alteration to the formerly perfect lines of her nose from the fractured cartilage couldn't really be hidden. Frank insisted no one could tell the difference unless they knew exactly what to look for, but she could see it as plain as day, and she was convinced Frank's opinion was more of a case of love being blind.

Blinded by love or not, she was going to look her best for her husband when he got home. She retouched her makeup (*I don't remember that line being there!*) and hair that she had taken back to its original shade of blonde from the chestnut color she used for a disguise when they first went on the run. Giving her fingers a quick glance, she was satisfied to see the polish still concealed the last remnants of the purple deposits of blood that had pooled under her nails after they had been crushed.

She had just finished a careful inspection of her jeans (*loose enough to be comfortable, but still tight enough to be interesting*) and adjusted her blouse when she heard a vehicle pull into the drive.

She looked her reflection in the eye one more time, and it looked accusingly back at her.

So, when are you going to tell him?

When I know for sure, she lied, and ran to meet her husband.

The door opened and she threw herself into Frank's arms before he even cleared the threshold, and clung tightly to him. He bent his neck and kissed her.

"Doggone; I'm glad I was the first one in! Miss me?" he teased.

"You know I did! Did the meeting go well?"

He sighed heavily and looked away. "Ultimately, yes it did."

"Did something happen?"

"Yes, but we'll talk about it later, okay?"

Samantha nodded. She understood that concept if anybody did.

"Look," he said, changing the subject and even managing a smile, "I brought you something."

He gestured behind him where Sam, an arm around the small of her back to keep her going, was ushering a blindfolded Kerrie inside.

"She followed us home, Sammie; can we keep her?"

As Sam pulled the bandanna from the girl's eyes, Samantha barely recognized her, and was shocked at her condition.

"Kerrie! What happened to you?"

The teenager flushed.

"I...I..."

"She got thrown out of her house," Frank interrupted before she could finish. "She had no place to stay and was having to panhandle for food." He unobtrusively prompted Sam by elbowing him sharply in the ribs.

"Huh? Oh yeah," the older man added hastily, "she didn't recognize us at first and hit us up for some spare change to get something to eat."

The girl flashed the two men a look of unspeakable gratitude, and her lips quivered with emotion.

Samantha, meanwhile, instinctively knew there was something more that they were not telling her. *They might be top of the line fighters and two of the best men I've ever known, but neither one of them can lie worth a damn.*

Still, she'd worry about that later. Right now, there were more pressing issues, like this frightened, pitiful, ragamuffin of a girl. The grim story her appearance told brought the moisture to her eyes.

She instinctively hugged the filthy, smelly teenager tightly to her and Kerrie began bawling again as she clung to the woman she had once described her personal hero. Samantha somehow managed to keep a straight face, despite the nauseating odor.

"Come on honey." She disentangled herself and took the girl by the hand. "We'll go get you cleaned up, fed, and into some decent clothes."

33

Looking back, she raised one eyebrow toward Frank, giving him a highly skeptical look.

As they left the room, Sam spoke to his second in command out of the side of his mouth. "Do you think she bought it?"

Frank shook his head glumly.

"Not a chance."

This had to be a dream.

Kerrie snuggled deeper between the clean sheets, a borrowed flannel gown over her emaciated body. She was clean, her belly was full, and she felt safe and comfortable for the first time in more than a month. Beside her, sensing her need as only animals can, the giant bulldog named Thumper had wandered in and now took his ease on the mattress, his pumpkin-sized head lying across her thigh where he could watch over her and be petted at the same time.

She had bathed in hot water for the first time in what seemed like forever, and Samantha had scrubbed, brushed, combed, and occasionally sworn under her breath until she got the grease and tangles out of her hair. Once she finished and Kerrie was dressed in her nightclothes and fed, the CAP communications officer led her down the hall and literally tucked her in bed, pulling the sheet and blanket up around her. For the third time that night, overcome by the simple fact of someone actually caring, the girl broke down, and this time it was the woman who sat beside her on the bed and held her as she let everything out, including the reason the two men had lied for her.

"Please don't be mad at Frank! He only did it for me!"

"Hush," Samantha said soothingly, kissing her on the forehead in a sudden fit of maternal instinct that surprised both of them. "You just go to sleep and let me deal with Frank Gore."

Within a minute after she left, there was a quiet knock on Kerrie's door.

"Come in."

It opened and there stood Colonel Samuel Wirtz, Commander of the South Carolina Theater, former militiaman, and current CAP

34

guerrilla chieftain, with a pistol in his belt and a teddy bear in his hand.

"Thumper!" he snapped, seeing the big white dog. "Get off there and leave her alone!"

"It's alright," Kerrie told him, putting a restraining arm around the dog's neck. "I like having him here."

Thumper's enormous mouth split in a toothy grin and his tongue lolled at Sam as if to say, *up yours, partner; I'm not going anywhere.*

"Well, whatever," he grumbled. "If you like having that flea-bitten monster in your bed, I reckon he can stay.

"Anyway, I used to keep my Goddaughters at my farm a lot during the summers," he explained gruffly, "and it was hard for them to sleep in a strange place. Sometimes a little stuffed animal helped. I found this one in the closet; here." He pulled back the covers far enough to slide the little gray bear in beside her, patted her on the shoulder and turned to go.

She remembered how he had referred to himself earlier, when they had found her. "Thank you, Uncle Sam."

Gathering moisture was plain in his eyes when he turned back to her.

"You're welcome, honey. You sleep tight now, you hear?" He sniffed and rubbed at his eyes. "Damned allergies!"

Softly, he closed the door behind him.

"...we cannot harbor any illusions, and we have no right to do so, that freedom can be obtained without fighting. And these battles shall not be mere street fights with stones against tear-gas bombs, or of pacific general strikes; neither shall it be a battle of a furious people destroying in two or three days the repressive scaffolds of the ruling oligarchies; the struggle shall be long, harsh, and its front shall be the guerrilla's refuge, in the cities, in the homes of the fighters..."

"Frank?"

He lowered the guerrilla warfare manual he was studying. Most of his almost non-existent free time had been taken up that way lately, soaking up knowledge like a sponge. Always a prolific reader, since the war began he had amassed quite a collection, from Napoleon's Maxims to Sun Tzu's millennia-old works. His companion this evening was a treatise by Che Guevara. Marking his place, he laid the volume aside, setting it on top of a U.S. Government-issue infantry manual and almost knocking over the too-high stack in the process. He barely caught a technical study of General Forrest's campaigns before the Wizard of the Saddle could hit the floor.

At least his wife couldn't complain about the books; she had an equally large and precarious stack on her own side, works on public relations and propaganda. She was a professional who took her job just as seriously as he did his own.

Still, Samantha had been unusually moody of late, but he supposed that was to be expected. Most of the PTSD effects would wear off with time and the understanding and patience of those around her...at least, he desperately hoped so because the alternative was too awful to contemplate.

He sighed in resignation. *I know that tone. Here it comes.*

"Yeah Sammie?"

"Are you still sticking to your story about Kerrie being a beggar?"

He nodded, not trusting himself to speak.

"Kerrie told me what she was really doing when you found her, and why you and Sam lied for her."

Frank regarded her silently, unsure where this discussion was going to go, and decided to play it safe. *You have the right to remain silent...*

"Besides lying to me by covering up for her, you do know that you two broke every rule in the book and jeopardized the security of our entire operation just by bringing her here? You put *everything* and *everyone* at risk for one poor, lost little girl and her hurt feelings."

He was busted, guilty as charged and there was nothing he could say. If he said he was sorry, that would have been another lie, because he didn't regret it one bit. He just nodded again and calmly said, "Yeah, I reckon we did."

It was her turn to nod as she reached out and traced a finger across his chest, brushing against the old brass locket he always wore.

"I thought I knew what kind of man you were, Franklin Gore, but I was wrong. You're actually more wonderful than I ever imagined. You ornery, rotten, *wonderful* man; I love you so very much."

She kissed him then and he pulled her close, and one thing led to another.

Frank drifted off to sleep soon afterwards, but Samantha lay awake in the darkness, one hand on his arm. Since her rescue, she found it impossible to sleep unless she was physically touching him. Even on sweltering nights during the rolling blackouts that had become the norm, when the summer temperature climbed so high even a sheet was intolerable, let alone closely cuddling with another warm body, she always made certain at least the tips of her fingers rested on the man she loved. It was more than she could deal with to do otherwise.

Samantha, you're a mental basket case.

God knew she was trying; she had good days and bad, but lately the good were starting to predominate a bit more – at least she thought so, or maybe hoped so. If it weren't for Frank, though, she knew she couldn't make it.

Reaching out, she brushed away an errant strand of her long hair that had fallen across his face and he mumbled in his sleep.

He looks so innocent and peaceful.

Looks, however, were deceiving; she wasn't the only one scarred by the violence around them. This same man lying beside her, who had cared for her so patiently and gently while she was recovering from her captivity, had also personally killed three Federal agents and one of his own men turned traitor in order to achieve her liberation. These same arms that cuddled her when she went on one of her crying jags were now waging a total and seemingly hopeless revolutionary war against the single most powerful country in the world. This same man carried both a Bible and a gun, and knew both with equal intimacy. And this very same man blew another man's brains out to make a point and brought home a poor starving kid all in the same night. He was able to do both without any apparent conflict. Outwardly, he was calm and rock solid, and never seemed to have a problem with any of it.

She knew better; after all, she slept with him.

Frank had his demons, and he fought them in his dreams. More nights than not, as the parade of dead friends and foes passed by in the darkness, he relived his struggles, thrashing, grinding his teeth, and growling terrible curses, even though he almost never used profanity beyond the occasional 'damn' or 'hell' during his waking hours. Once he had even shot all the way to his feet straight out of a deep sleep, standing naked and raging on the mattress, his fists clenched and raised in a fighting stance as he shouted an incoherent battle cry that woke up the whole house. She would never forget that moment as long as she lived. He was a terrifying image in the near darkness, like some ancient god of war suddenly gone mad.

He couldn't – or more likely *wouldn't* – tell her what that particular dream was about, and she didn't press him, since she wasn't at all sure she really wanted to know.

Worst of all were the nights when he dreamed of her ordeal. When he cried out her name, she would pull him to her and whisper to him that she was all right. Those particular dreams were the only time she had ever seen him show any weakness, but they left him helpless and clinging to her desperately.

More than once she had thought of him as a modern version of a knight in armor, pure of heart and strong of arm, living by the Code of Chivalry. She still thought so, only now she realized the part the legends never spoke of: the terrible price paid by the paladin and by the woman who loved him. Even while he was relaxed in sleep, she could make out the deep lines and tiny flecks of gray that hadn't been there even a month ago.

This was no storybook war, of white chargers and single combat, or even of depersonalized thousands of men maneuvering like chess pieces while immaculate officers crisply shouted orders and cannons blazed. This was guerrilla war: conflict at its filthiest and cruelest, where guns and knives flashed in the shadows, bombs tore apart the innocent and the guilty equal indifference, and to be the victor was to be the survivor. There was no glory here. She doubted there ever was.

'Into the valley of death, into the mouth of Hell...' the poet's words went, and it was the best description she had ever heard.

Frank had walked that valley, and looked into that grim portal every day since this war had started. It would take a fool to think it would have no effect on him. Another quote immediately came to mind:

'Look not too long into the abyss, lest the abyss also look into you.'

Frank had looked into it deep and long, and in return the abyss had looked back.

Blinking away the tears that welled up along with that thought, Samantha didn't wait for his nightmares she knew would come. She snuggled against him and enfolded him in her arms, pulling his head against the softness of her breast. In the darkness of the night, she lay there awake and prayed for her warrior.

CHAPTER 3

Nights are black in the wooded mountains of southern West Virginia, where you have to look straight up to see the sky even in the daytime. The darkness of the hardwood and hemlock forest was broken only by the pinpoint of a kerosene lamp shining through the window of a rough tarpaper shack that had served as a deer camp in happier times. Now it was home to a different kind of hunter

"So, what can I do for you?"

Jonathon Edge returned Jack Boggess' stare levelly. Inside, he marveled at how much this sandy-haired, jug-eared firebrand looked like his late brother Wayne, who had been one of the CAP leader's two real friends before his murder, and that of his family, in a raid by Federal agents. *I hope you've got the same fire, boy. I'm counting on it.*

"To put the whole thing in a nutshell, we want you to join us. We're both fighting the same enemy – the Federal Government – and the more of us there are, the better our chances of success."

Boggess studied him carefully, and the third man at the gathering, sitting on an upturned five-gallon bucket at the large cable spool that served as a table, spoke up. "The question is, are we fighting for the same thing?"

"You tell me. Jack's fighting to avenge his brother, so it's personal with him; it's a feud. You're one of the leaders of this mine strike, though. You all went out when Wayne was killed; you've shut down the entire Appalachian coalfields, and defied the Federal court orders to go back. They tried to make you, and now you're fighting them too. Why don't you tell me what you're fighting for?"

The man – Darrel Putney – raised the Styrofoam cup to his darkly bearded face and spat a stream of tobacco juice into it before answering. "Do you know the history of the West Virginia Coal Mine Wars, Mr. Edge?"

"Very little," the Virginian admitted.

"I ain't surprised; most people don't, even here where it all took place. They don't teach too much about it in school; they're afraid it might give people ideas.

"Back in the nineteen twenties, when our people were still working themselves to death for the company store under the guns of the hired mine thugs, a town constable named Sid Hatfield in a little burg called Matewan down in Mingo County stood up to them. Some Baldwin-Felts 'detectives' were evicting a fired miner's sick wife from a company house at gunpoint; took her on her bed and set her right out in the road in the pouring rain. They had no legal authority, so Sid Hatfield and Mayor Testerman went to place them under arrest, and they shot the mayor down right there in the street. Well sir, Sid started shooting and miners came a' running with their rifles, and by the time the smoke had cleared, there stood Sid with a pistol in each hand and a string of seven dead company thugs laid out along the railroad track.

"They tried him, but they found out that there were people on the jury that all the mine owners' money couldn't buy. Sid walked out of there a free man.

"That didn't sit well with the politicians in the pockets of the coal companies, so they summoned him back to court. The whole thing was a setup, and the Baldwin-Felts men ambushed him and shot him down on the courthouse steps in broad daylight. One of 'em even stepped up and put a slug in his head while he lay there bleeding, right in front of his wife. They never even had a damned trial over that one.

"An army of miners came down out of these hills then, ten thousand strong. *This* was our symbol." He pulled the red bandanna hanging around his neck out of the collar of his civilian camouflage shirt. "This rag was our uniform. It's we used to identify ourselves and that's where the term *'redneck'* came from. Our great grandfathers came down from the hollers, and they kicked ass and took names. We fought the sheriff's deputies and the companies' hired guns to a standstill at Blair Mountain, and didn't give up until they sent the army against us, complete with a chemical warfare unit and mustard gas.

"This is a lot like that. When they killed Wayne and his family; they killed a union man's union man, and there ain't gonna be no coal brought out of these mountains until his killers are brought to justice!"

Edge pursed his lips and drew an invisible design on the rough wooden surface of the makeshift table with his finger. He was silent for so long they thought he wasn't going to respond. Finally he said, "I hope you've got more guts than your grandpas."

Both Mountaineers' eyes narrowed.

"I think you'd better explain that remark," Putney told him in a dangerously quiet tone.

Edge looked first at one and then the other, as calmly as if his hand were resting on the Para Ordinance P13 .45 on his hip, instead of on his stomach. Of course, they didn't know it was only an inch away from the big pistol's more compact but equally powerful little brother, a P10, tucked out of sight into an inside the pants holster.

"What I mean is this; are you going to stay the course, or our you going to throw up your hands and quit the first time somebody waves the Stars and Stripes in your face?

"In what little I do know about the Mine Wars, I know the miners backed down less because they were out-gunned than because they weren't willing to shoot at United States soldiers. If you feel that way, we might as well end this conversation and your strike right here and now as a waste of time, because United States soldiers are *exactly* what you're going to be shooting before you're through, whether you decide to join us or not."

Putney's face reddened, and Jack attempted to diffuse the situation before it got out of hand. His friend was fearless and dangerous as well as powerful, but something in the Virginian's cold blue eyes told him Edge was a killer.

"Look, you need to understand that a lot of us have kin in the military – more so here than in any other state – and most of us have fought for our country ourselves. That means something."

"Really? When did you fight for your country? I was career military, Navy SEAL Teams. I've gone into places and done things you've never heard of. I went through war after war, campaign after campaign, and I never once fought for my country. Seems to me the only ones fighting for their country were the ones we were busy killing to take their own countries away from them. You can hide behind all the rationalizing and slogans and sound bites you want to, but it all boils down to this: we didn't fight for our country, or for freedom for that matter. We fought because we were soldiers, and going where he's told to go and fighting who he's told to fight is a soldier's job. Once we got there, we fought to stay alive and keep our buddies alive. That's all there was to it, no matter how much we lie to ourselves that it's otherwise.

"Besides, exactly what is your country? The United States? I've got some late-breaking news for you boys: the Republic of Washington and Jefferson died way back in 1865, when they sacrificed the American Republic to preserve the Union; Lincoln said so himself. What it's been ever since is an empire, and a poorly-run one at that."

"So what do you suggest?"

"You both knew Wayne and what he stood for, so you know what I'm suggesting. We are resurrecting the Confederate States of America and, like the first Confederacy, we intend to reclaim the legacy of liberty and the States' rights Republic bequeathed to us by men like Washington and Jefferson during the first Revolution. What we have now is not our country; our country is what we're trying to build. Do you want to be part of it, or do you want lick the boots of a government that murdered a good man like Wayne Boggess and his entire family in their own home, then dishonored his memory by claiming it was a domestic murder-suicide? If that's the America you want, then have at it; you're welcome to it."

The two men looked at each other. They already knew the score; they had been discussing it for weeks, before ever agreeing to meet with the CAP Commander.

"Let's just say," Jack finally said, "just for the sake of argument mind you, that we're willing to get onboard this revolution of yours. What's in it for us; I mean right now?"

"What do you want? Men? Training?"

44

"We've got men, most of them with military experience. We need real arms: military grade hardware."

Edge considered that for a moment, then the light of an idea flickered and a plan began to take shape that just might solve a couple of his problems: one if it worked, the other if it didn't: a win-win situation. He was unable to suppress a smile at the thought.

"I believe I can arrange that."

Putney, still smarting from the CAP leader's earlier comments, spoke up. "That's fine and dandy, but if we join this thing, that means we're under you, right? I mean you're the one in charge from what I hear." Edge nodded once, without expression and the miner continued. "Alright then, how do we know *you're* for real? For all we know, you could be a stinking undercover Fed, trying to set us up. All I've seen are your videotapes and propaganda; I ain't seen any proof."

Edge's voice was cold and flat.

"Who do you want me to kill?"

He locked eyes with Putney, and the big man was the first to look away.

A few hundred miles to the South, another strategy session was in full swing in the Palmetto State, but this one involved only one man. The newest Confederate Councilman, Neil Larson, was on his fifth cup of coffee and the ashtray on the corner of his desk was overflowing. His keen eyes red from lack of sleep and his belly protesting the abusive affects of the caffeine, he kept going, not trusting the security of his computer's hard drive this time, but scribbling on a pad, taking notes, drawing outlines and graphs, anything that would keep his mind on track.

Neil was a risk-taker, but one given to meticulous planning. Even before he had agreed to trade his men for a Council seat, the seed of this particular idea had begun to germinate inside of him, and he had been worrying it like a dog on a bone ever since. Tonight – or rather this morning – the pieces were finally beginning to fit together.

Although without a lot of formal education, the former militia leader was highly intelligent as well as a great student of human nature, and he had made it a point to study the natures of the people around him until he felt certain he knew how they would react in any given situation. All he had to do was create that situation, give things a little nudge, and it would be like the old *Mousetrap* game that had been his favorite toy as a child; the action would continue on its own. Balls would begin to roll, wheels would turn, levers would flip, and the trap would come rattling right on down.

DAY 72

CHAPTER 4

"Sammie, I want to thank you." Frank smiled at her over his cup of morning coffee, then sipped another mouthful of the increasingly expensive black brew, cut with chicory and roasted dandelion root from the backyard to make it stretch. They were both early risers, and made a habit of savoring this pre-breakfast ritual together. It was nothing elaborate; they just sat and drank coffee, enjoying each other's company in an all-too-rare moment of privacy before the others arose. Both of their sanities demanded every moment of domestic normality they could snatch, however brief, even in the middle of a war. Maybe especially then.

"What for?"

"Well, if I started making a list, it would take all day. Mainly I wanted to thank you for what you've done with your voice."

"What are you talking about?" She knew of course, but with everything else he had on his mind, she was surprised he had noticed. *I can't put much over on him.* Then she thought about the other thing and her heart sank. *He'll find out eventually, if I don't tell him first, and then what will he do?* She realized he was speaking again.

"You know good and well what I'm talking about. When we met, you'd lost your native Southern accent – had it scrubbed out of you in one of those schools so you could find work in your chosen career field. Here lately, you've been picking it up again, until you use it about half the time, too often for it to be accidental. I can tell you've been trying hard to change it back, and even though I never asked you to, I know you're doing it for me. I just wanted you to know that I *have* noticed. I loved you so much without an accent, I don't know how I could love you anymore than that with it, but I do appreciate it. Your voice is absolutely beautiful, just like you."

Abruptly she stood, came to him, and sat on his lap facing him, straddling his legs and slipping her arms around his neck.

"Have I told you how much I love you?"

"Not since last night," he said with a grin and a wink, "but we've got a few minutes yet, so you just help yourself."

She did, and sat there for a little while, snuggling and kissing, making the most of it. There was something else though – *besides that other thing* – that kept intruding into her thoughts, and she finally decided it wouldn't do to let it wait any longer.

She turned her eyes down and pursed her lips for a moment. She hated to upset her husband, especially during this special time, but there were some things he had to know. Maybe it would be easier just to show him, since she would need to anyway. He had to see this with his own eyes, or he would be hard-pressed to believe it.

"When you and Sam brought Kerrie in, did you happen to strip her and scan her like you were supposed to?"

He looked at her sheepishly. "We scanned her, but we didn't strip her. I *know* that's standard procedure, but after all she'd been through, neither one of us had the heart. We ran the wand over her on top of her clothes and stuck it up under her shirt, but that was a close as we came." He hesitated a moment before continuing. "If you wouldn't mind, we thought it would be best if you did that, being a woman and all. It would be easier on her."

She looked down, unable to contain a smile. *That was just like those two. Hard core guerrillas, ferocious warriors, and they couldn't bring themselves to cause more pain to a girl who had already had so much in her short life.*

Such things were her constant reassurance that she was on the right side.

"Would you come with me and talk to Kerrie, please?"

Frank gave her a puzzled look. "Sure; why wouldn't I? Is something wrong?"

"Yes, something *is* wrong." She extended her hand as she rose and he took it. Together they walked down the hall to the girl's door.

"Wait out here for just a minute," Samantha told him as she tapped the wooden panel. There was a sleepy reply from inside, and she opened the door and slipped in, closing it behind her and leaving an increasingly curious Frank standing outside. He heard a briefly whispered conversation, then the door opened and Samantha beckoned him.

Kerrie was standing beside the bed, hair tousled and her eyes red from sleep, chewing on a corner of her lower lip and nervously wringing her hands in front of her.

"There's something you need to see. Turn around Kerrie." She blushed as she obeyed and turned away stiffly. To his astonishment, Samantha lifted the back of the teenager's nightgown until its hem was around her neck, revealing that she wore nothing but her skin beneath. "I saw this when she was getting cleaned up last night. I didn't tell you then because I knew you'd get so worked up over it you wouldn't be able to sleep."

Frank had difficulty believing what he was seeing, which was far more than simply the results of malnutrition. The girl's skinny body, from her thighs to her upper back, was covered with a maze of scars crisscrossing her flesh. There were dozens of them. The greatest concentration could be seen on her buttocks; at some point in the fairly recent past, the white flesh had been nearly shredded, cut clear down through the skin and into the meat.

The worst ones were still dark and fairly recent, but not all.

Samantha knew what was coming, but she watched the change with fascination nonetheless. As if he had looked upon the Medusa, Frank's face began to harden, like a statue carved from mountain granite. The lines became sharper and his nostrils flared ever so slightly. His narrowed eyes were 'hard and hot as the hubs of Hell' as she heard someone say once. She could barely hear a growling in his chest, augmented by the sound of his teeth grinding together. Frank seldom became angry, but when he did, he was extremely dangerous: never to those he cared about of course, but often fatally so to anyone who had hurt them.

He stepped forward and studied Kerrie's back, as if to absorb every bit of the damage, wishing he could take her pain upon himself. Reaching out his right hand, he softly traced the raised scar tissue of one of the more prominent stripes under her shoulder blade with his fingertips, and the girl shivered under his touch.

Frank nodded silently at Samantha, and she lowered the gown. Taking the girl by the shoulders, he turned her with remarkable gentleness to face him. She looked into his eyes and paled at what she saw there. It took him a moment before he could even speak.

"Kerrie," Frank asked softly and deliberately, although he was pretty sure he already knew the answer, "who did this to you?"

"M-my parents. The night they threw me out…"

He closed his eyes and took a deep breath. *Lord Jesus, give me strength!*

"You're telling me these scars are more than a month old and they still look like this?" She nodded. "What did they use to make those marks?"

"A piece of wire cable-like thing; Dad keeps a roll of it around to hang pictures and I guess…I guess it was handy."

"I saw older scars too; this isn't the first time this has happened, is it?"

She shook her head. "No, but never this bad. They had been drinking pretty heavy, and it was like they just went nuts. The whole time they were yelling about how I'd ruined Dad's career in the legislature, what a disgrace I was, and what people would think of them for bringing up an un-American terrorist whore…like me…" She began softly crying again.

Frank knew what discipline was, and heartily approved of it in general. He was brought up to the tune of Granny Gore's willow switch himself and he knew the South would be a better place if more parents were willing to apply a little more of the same, but he also knew the difference between being disciplined and being abused. As a long-time cop, Frank had seen abuse before, but seldom this bad or this…*deliberate*. He reacted to the savagery against a child – against a young woman in particular – with the deadly fury only a Southern man can muster.

I was part of the cause, so taking care of it is my responsibility

"Sammie," Frank said, turning to his wife, all business now, his voice that of her Captain rather than her husband. "Please get the camera. I want this documented, and then I want every piece of information you can lay your hands on concerning the O'Brien's: names, address, jobs, the works. And I want it *yesterday*."

She nodded curtly, her own eyes hard, and Kerrie spoke up in a voice tiny and hesitant. "What are you going to do?"

There was as every bit as much mercy in his eyes as there was ice water in Hell, and his answer was a single word of fatal implications. "Justice."

"Please don't kill them!" she cried, shaking with emotion. "They did awful things to me, but they're still my parents and I-I still love them. At least I think so – I don't *know*! I just don't want them dead! Please!"

A battle raged within him for a few seconds, and finally he closed his eyes for a moment and swallowed hard.

"Alright," he sighed. "Understand me, I won't let this go – *I can't!* Even if I didn't know you, even if you were a grown man, as a Confederate officer I can't stand by and let retaliation against *any* of our supporters go unanswered; no guerrilla movement can survive that! And as a man, I'll be damned if I'll let somebody abuse a little girl like this – not on *my* watch! There will still be justice and they will be punished *severely*…but I won't kill them. Not for their sakes, but for yours and yours alone. I won't kill them." He repeated this last as much to convince himself as her.

"Promise?"

He raised his right hand and used his thumb to rub away one of the tears from her cheek.

"I promise, Kerrie. I give you my word."

She nodded, satisfied, and hugged him tightly. That was good enough.

Kerrie and Sam joined them for breakfast, along with Rob who had appeared just as they were setting the table. Breakfast – and every other meal – had been pretty basic lately as they tried to scrimp on every penny they could, but today they had gone all out for their newest member. They tried not to stare as the starving girl ravenously devoured enough for three grown men. Eggs, grits, sausage, and buttered biscuits went down her throat at an unbelievable rate. The others had to choke down the lumps in their own throats that the thought of what she must have gone through. Finally full, she sipped at a cup of coffee heavily laced with cream and sugar.

Sam, who had been briefed on her condition, was as furious over what had been done to her as Frank was, and feeling just as guilty, even though none of them could have foreseen the results of their actions in allowing her to become involved. Notoriously softhearted towards young people in general and the female sex in particular, he was the one who finally asked what they were all wondering.

"Kerrie, I know you had a hard way to go because of the story, but tell me something; are the others alright? You know, Jared, Cynthia and Chucky?"

"Oh, Jared's fine," she told them coldly, looking intently into her coffee cup. "I heard some things through the grapevine early on. He publicly apologized and repudiated his involvement in the story as a 'mistake', and said that he had been *misled and manipulated*," both by you all and by the rest of us. His parents pulled him out of school and sent him to a private academy somewhere. That lying little *bastard*!" The last word came out as a hiss, before she hung her head.

"Sorry, I –"

"You of all people don't have one damned thing to be sorry about," Sam told her, laying his hand reassuringly on her shoulder, and trying not to shudder as he felt the prominent bones through her skin. "I reckon after all you've been though, if *bastard* is as strong a language as you can muster, your moral fiber is one hell of a lot stronger than mine." Although he didn't like to cuss in front of ladies, he couldn't help muttering, partly for Kerrie's sake, "I never did like that snotty little son of a bitch anyway," under his breath.

She tried to smile her appreciation for his gesture, but it wouldn't quite come.

"Cynthia's uncle is a lawyer, and he filed a court order to get us back in class pending a hearing. I didn't know anything about it at

52

the time, since I was already out on the street, but I guess that's what 'saved' me if you want to call it that.

"On her first day back at school, Cynthia was dragged into a bathroom and gang raped in retaliation by a bunch of niggers. Poor Chucky died trying to save her."

"What?" Rob's eyes were wide with disbelief. Strangely, the nerdy, bespectacled cameraman had been his favorite ever since he had caught him surreptitiously trying to record the guerrillas. As far as the former Spec-ops soldier was concerned, the little son of a gun had an admirable dose of guts. "How?"

"He saw them grab her and pull her into the boys' room and he went in after her. There were half a dozen of them in there, all bigger than him and he knew it, but he went anyway, and th-they...they beat him to death. I heard he was unrecognizable by the time they were through with him. Somebody said they finished him off by drowning him in a toilet. Then they...raped Cynthia – all of them."

"By God! By *God!*"

Rob, so notoriously unemotional and uncommunicative about anything that Tommy had once colorfully described him as someone who 'wouldn't say *'shit'* if he had a mouthful of it', was overflowing with a rage that surpassed even that of Frank and Sam. Neither he nor the others would have expected the boy's death to hit him that hard.

"Wait a minute," Samantha said, "I stay on top of the news; it's part of my job. Why haven't I heard anything about this?"

"Because the school and the prosecutor's office covered it up. They claimed Chucky 'fell down and hit his head' and that the sex with Cynthia was consensual, like she was a whore..." At that last word Kerrie's face fell and she looked down, lower lip quivering.

Samantha slipped an arm around her and pulled the girl's head to her shoulder.

"You go ahead, Kerrie. It'll be alright."

I'm probably lying. Sometimes I wonder if anything will ever be all right again, for any of us.

Rob's thin leathery lips twisted and squirmed with emotion and he abruptly got to his feet without a word and went to the window, turning his back on the others. He had been career Special Forces, a government trained stone killer and was notoriously unflappable, even amongst the guerrillas, so what they thought was his shoulders shaking must have been just a trick of the light. The others, torn with rage and grief themselves, understood his need and left him alone. After a few minutes he returned to the table with his already hard face much, much harder. His slitted eyes held all the mercy of a shark's and his voice was icy and clipped.

"I want names – the killers, the prosecutor and the school officials involved in the cover-up – all of them."

"I don't know for sure; you'll have to ask Cynthia."

He nodded once, crisply spun on his heel and left the room. Frank and Sam rose immediately and followed, catching up with him in the hall.

"Rob…" Sam began, but was immediately cut off.

"It's never wise to give an order you know will not be obeyed."

Sam started to reply, but Frank beat him to it. "What makes you think we intend to give that kind of an order?" Rob stared back at him silently. "Tell me this; what do you intend to do?"

"I intend to kill them all." If the reaper himself had spoken, it couldn't have sounded more final.

"Agreed."

Both men looked at him in astonishment. It was hard to tell which was more surprised.

"You're not going to interfere?"

"Only this far: I want you to do it my way.

"Here's the deal. Gather all the information you can; after you talk to Cynthia, go see Mike – that's his forte – and be ready to act on it, but don't do it just *yet*. I know from that look in your eye, no matter what we say, you're going to execute them, so that's a given and there's no point in arguing about it further. Before you do, however, we need time to brainstorm this thing and see how to make sure your actions are to our best advantage and, more importantly, don't hurt us. We need to decide if we want a public or a covert hit, or if we just want them to disappear. Since it's going to happen anyway, we might as well make the most out of it. Agreed?"

"Will you let me lead the team?"

"Would I have any choice in the matter? Now go on and start gathering your intelligence – just make damned sure it's accurate." Frank looked him straight in the eyes. "No innocent people are to be killed in the process, and I mean that. And watch your butt."

Rob treated them to another nod before walking out the front door.

The words had come naturally to Frank, but once he had voiced them, he realized there was another ramification he hadn't considered. He sighed and turned towards Sam.

"I owe you an apology; that happened instinctively. I know I should have let you handle this, but I didn't want us to lose control of Rob…"

"After that little performance of yours, you don't owe me anything. I was right last night. I've never seen anyone handle men like you do. How did you read the situation that well?"

Frank hesitated before answering. "Well, I know of a similar situation that caused a big argument between two friends awhile back, over burning out an informer."

Sam's mouth opened in surprise as the answer dawned on him. "Your bedroom window back at the farm was right above the porch when John and I had our little *discussion* over that woman who was responsible for getting Mary killed."

"Yep. I wasn't trying to eavesdrop but the window was open and…well, face it; your voices tend to carry when you two get testy."

"I reckon so, but that's neither here nor there. You heard it and filed it away upstairs, not just the specific situation, but also the principles behind it, then you pulled it back out and put those principles into practice in a similar scenario; if something is inevitable, make it work for you. You understood that and used it one hell of a lot better than Jonathon Edge ever has. I was right about you; you've got what it takes to command."

Frank waved away the compliment. "Well, it wasn't exactly the same thing the General was faced with."

"Oh yeah? In what way is it different then?"

"Edge didn't know Mary, so what happened to her wasn't personal, at least as far as he was concerned," he said, in a voice every bit as grim as Rob's had been. Sam noticed his eyes, and shivered inwardly at the cold hardness there. Frank had a lot more anger built up inside than he had realized. "As far as I know, he'd never even met the lady. In this case, what happened to those kids is a direct result of something I was part of; therefore I have a certain amount of responsibility in the matter. That makes it personal. This wasn't a hard decision for me, because if Rob wasn't so dead set on killing them, I was going to. I don't reckon I would've given any more of a damn about what anyone else thought of it than he did, either."

He left Sam staring at his back as he turned and walked back towards the kitchen.

Samantha handed Kerrie a napkin and the girl wiped her eyes with it.

"I'm sorry; it just seems like I want to cry all the time."

Samantha took her hand. "Then cry honey. Whenever you need to, just let it out. You'll find no shortage of shoulders around here to do it on; I can guarantee you that."

"I know," she said, the frustration evident in her voice, "but I feel like such a baby!"

"Kerrie, you're not the only one; welcome to '*Trauma City*.' In times of stress like these, emotions run high for everybody, not just you. When they first rescued me and brought me back to the safe house, I cried constantly. It seems like it must have been a dozen times as day I'd just start bawling for no reason and couldn't stop, sometimes for hours at a time. I've seen Frank's shirts with salt stains on the shoulders from my tears. Every now and then I still let loose; it's all part of the healing process, I suppose. Frank told me once that tears are the best medicine to wash out a wound on the inside."

Kerrie looked at her with both gratitude and something close to worship, sniffing slightly.

"I...thank you, Samantha. I've never had friends like you and Frank and Sam before; not even my own family."

Samantha looked away in embarrassment over the praise, and an idea struck her. "Look, I still need to scan you properly, since the two '*Rambos*' who picked you up couldn't bring themselves to do it, so let's go to your bedroom and get that out of the way. It's not that we don't trust you, just standard operating procedure. Everybody gets it when they first come in.

"Afterwards, if you don't mind, would you please do me a favor? Can you fix a plate and take Mike's breakfast down to him? He seems to have neglected to come upstairs for it *again*."

In fact, Mike Dayton almost never came upstairs anymore. It was as if their chief of cyber-warfare had become a prisoner in the basement of his own home. Despite Tommy's reassurances to the contrary, he seemed to be withdrawing, and she was becoming concerned about his mental health.

Talk about the pot calling the kettle black, her conscience chimed in annoyingly.

"Sure, but who's Mike?"

"Mike is...well, Mike. He owns this house and runs our computer systems. He's a genius, but he gets so wrapped up in his work, I swear he'd stay down there in that basement and starve to death if we didn't keep after him."

Mike Dayton was entering a final line of code when he heard the tiny personal elevator door open behind him. He smiled without turning; it must be breakfast time, and Samantha or one of the others was coming to pester him about getting lost in his work again. He knew they meant well, and were probably right for that matter, but still...

When no one spoke or approached, he swiveled his wheelchair around, and nearly fell out of it in shock at the sight of the pretty redheaded girl standing there with a tray of food.

I knew they brought her in last night, but I was so busy I didn't realize...

57

For her part, Kerrie had stopped and was gazing around the room in fascination. With the walls lined with worktables, shelves and stack after stack of electronics, the place looked more like the bridge of a science fiction star ship than a South Carolina basement. She had never seen so much hardware at one time, even in a computer store. The colored LED's looked like starry constellations in the low light.

The man looking at her was equally strange; he had the pale, untanned face of a serious computer geek, with short, tousled brown hair and a shorter, somewhat scraggly beard. His upper body, sealed in the tight black T-shirt, rippled with muscles (Probably due to the weight machine sitting incongruously in one corner, she reflected.), while his legs were atrophied from his long confinement in the wheelchair.

"Hi. Are you Mike? I've brought your breakfast."

"Thanks, uhh…"

"Kerrie," she told him, blushing slightly for some reason. "Kerrie O'Brien."

"Right; you're one of the high school reporters who got our story out."

She nodded, blushing still more deeply.

"Good job." He swept some papers aside on the desktop. "Umm, you can set the tray right here if you want."

"Oh, I'm sorry! Here."

After putting down the food, she turned back towards the elevator. "I guess I'll let you get back to work…"

Overcome by a feeling of minor desperation he couldn't quite place, Mike hastily spoke up.

"You can stay awhile if you want." He gestured at the tray. "As usual, there's way more than I can eat here anyway; join me?"

She smiled back at him. "I'm already stuffed, but I'll stay and keep you company while you eat…if you want."

Mike definitely wanted, and he nodded his thanks as she pulled up a chair. He knew he didn't interact enough with people, especially girls, and most especially pretty redheads like this one (*even if she was a little skinny* he amended), and he wasn't going to miss out on the chance.

CHAPTER 5

Lieutenant Tommy Richardson woke up on the floor in the midst of an intensely erotic dream. That he had dreamed about sex wasn't overly surprising, as his social life had been reduced to zero since the war began a few months ago. No, the surprising part was *who* the dream was about: Donna Waddell, Samuel Wirtz's Goddaughter.

Damn, that was so real!

Looking at it logically, he guessed that, despite having considered her to be something almost like a mascot and kid sister rolled into one for years, she was the one he would be dreaming about. After all, besides being almost nineteen and a young woman now, she and Tommy had been posing as a couple for more than a month. Their role as the cohabiting tenants of Mike Dayton's upstairs was the perfect to camouflage the comings and goings there, but it had required the two to be in almost constant close contact and to be convincing about it. Unknown to the authorities, they were a vital element in the Confederate Army Provisional's Columbia Command. It was up to them to run most of the errands for the guerrilla headquarters, do the shopping, and take care of else that came up, and they almost always went together. On the occasions when they spoke to the neighbors, they made it a point to enforce their cover story by holding hands or one casually slipping an arm around the other. At first, they both thought it was funny as hell, but now that he thought about it, he realized that lately neither one of them had been laughing.

He suddenly realized something else too; the reason the dream was so real was probably because Donna *was* sleeping beside him right now, nestled in the crook of his arm with her head on his shoulder, one arm across his chest, and a long bare leg thrown over both of his, putting pressure on his groin.

Uh-oh!

It took him a moment of frantic thinking to get his wits together enough to realize that both of them were fully clothed in tee shirts and jeans – cut-off shorts in her case – and six other snoring men

61

were asleep on the floor around them. They had missed the citywide curfew, working well into the night on the building one of the members of his new squad had provided for their use; in fact he could still smell the sawdust and drying paint. They finished the evening with some delivery pizza (The city, fearing a general open rebellion, not to mention even more business closings and a resulting loss of taxes, had exempted licensed food deliveries from the curfew, along with commercial traffic.) and a fairly substantial quantity of home-brewed beer. With no furniture, all of them had simply bedded down on floor of the large, central room. Donna had naturally bunked beside him, the one she knew best, and had evidently rolled over in her sleep and cuddled up to him. Finally, seeing that nothing had actually *happened* between his friend and commander's Goddaughter and himself, he breathed a sigh of relief and mentally wiped a bead of sweat from his brow.

Still, he couldn't deny his faint disappointment that it *hadn't* happened either, any more than he could deny the fact that it felt good having her there in his arms: a little *too* good considering what her thigh was resting on. Studying her face as she slept, he consciously noticed for the first just how pretty she really was, with her full lips slightly parted and her long brown hair spread out in a morning-after mess –"

Watch yourself, partner! Don't go there...

He sighed and, even as he roundly cursed his intruding good sense, slowly and carefully began scooting just a bit to move that tempting leg off his crotch. Gingerly he put his hand on her thigh to push it down a few inches, and her arm instinctively tightened around him. She opened her sleepy green eyes to look into his.

He had no idea as to how she was going to react when she discovered the compromising position they were in. Abruptly he realized his hand was still lying on her smooth skin, but somehow he couldn't seem to muster the will power to pull it away.

For Donna's part, if she was surprised, it didn't register on her face. Taking in the biker's familiar features, long dark hair and short beard, she impulsively did something she had never done with him before, something that shocked him to the core. Leaning forward, she put her fingertips against his cheek and, softly and unhurriedly, pressed her lips against his. He responded instinctively, feeling the moist warmth of her breath and tasting the sweetness of her mouth, all too aware of that long, slender leg under his hand – his caressing hand now – still pressing against him. The kiss only lasted for a few seconds before she gently broke contact, resting her chin on his chest and looking at him with an enigmatic smile through her tangled locks.

"Good morning," she said, her voice still husky from sleep.

"Good morning," he returned, completely at a loss. He was saved from having to decide exactly what to say next by a voice from several feet away on his other side.

"I don't know what the hell's so good about it! Oh my aching back!"

Joel Harrison's moaning woke up the others in a chorus of grunts, groans, along with "I'm getting too old for this crap," and "Somebody start some damned coffee before I freaking *die*!"

The mood broken, Tommy and Donna moved apart, but continued staring into each other's eyes for a long time, both wondering what they were seeing there.

The three men moved slowly and carefully though the dense second-growth forest, weaving themselves around the hang-on-a-minute thorns of blackberry and woodbine that would dig into clothes, make noise, and shake whatever brush they were attached to. Boots were set down with infinite care, feeling through the soles for that dry stick hiding under the leaves, ready to snap when stepped on. The leaves themselves made enough unavoidable noise without a loud *crack* to give them away.

Watching him move, Putney was developing a grudging respect for Edge, even though the Virginian still rubbed him the wrong way just to look at him. Obviously Edge's earlier life had taught him many things, including how to operate quietly in the woods.

In the meantime, the CAP leader was observing his companions just as critically, and was satisfied with what he had seen so far. Both Putney and Boggess had been in the military (Marines and

Army respectively), but much more to the point, they were experienced deer hunters, used to stalking wary white tails with rifles and bows. The sport had taught them to move like ghosts, moving and halting, waiting for that gust of wind to cover the noise from their next few steps.

Of course, each side was also trying to impress the other, and it was an unspoken fact that a noisy wilderness *faux pas* would put a quick cap on the offender's status.

All three of them were wearing face paint and off-the-shelf hunting camouflage, topped with gillie suits homemade from netting and multi-colored burlap strips. The suits exacerbated the already-stifling heat and humidity, but it beat the hell out of being spotted and shot.

There were a pair of snipers on this team: Edge and Boggess. Putney, armed with a spotting scope and a Chinese-made, semiautomatic version of the AK47 that looked like a toy in his big hands, would act as spotter. Jack had his pet deer rifle, a Remington Model 700BDL in .300 Winchester Magnum with a long 4-12X Redfield scope to take advantage of the rifle's flat-shooting capability. Edge, never one to do anything halfway, was packing his favorite heavy artillery: thirty-seven pounds of .50 BMG Barrett with three pounds of Springfield Armory 3rd generation military 4-14X 50mm scope on top. Edge didn't travel with the monster, of course, but he liked the weapon so well he had half a dozen identical models stashed in various places throughout the South, and one had been close enough to send one of Boggess' men after it the night before.

Putney tried to convince himself that that Edge was compensating for something, but he had to admit that nothing about either the man or the way he handled his big gun said 'poser'.

Near the top of a ridge, Jack held up his hand. The three huddled together, and the Mountaineer's voice was little more than a breath.

"We're almost there. The spot is at the edge of a power line cut just over this crest. We'll have a clear field of fire at about three hundred feet of road at a distance of four-hundred-fifty yards."

The plan was simple. Vehicles – usually Humvee's or other heavy SUV's – full of Federal paramilitaries attached to the Kentucky/West Virginia FEMA district patrolled the mountain roads frequently in hopes of suppressing guerrilla actions both by the striking miners and by the Boggess clan. The miners' idea was for another of their men, hidden a mile or two down the road, to call them up on the cell phone – muted, set on vibrate and stashed in Jack Boggess' breast pocket – and let them know when one was coming. Then they would proceed to shoot it up along with its occupants from a fairly safe distance before getting the hell out of Dodge, in this case via an escape through a warren of old mine shafts that went all the way through the mountain. Nothing could be simpler.

Regardless, some sixth sense crawled like a centipede up the Virginian's spine on cold, pointy feet. It was a feeling he couldn't explain, but one that had kept him alive more than once, and he wasn't about to ignore it.

"You said you've done this several times. Have you ever shot from anywhere near this particular position before?" he whispered.

"No, we're not that crazy. It's just one of a double handful or so we've scouted out."

"So there're not many ideal spots?"

"Not a lot. Why?"

He glanced at the ridge's crest a few feet away.

"Mr. Putney, please loan me your spotting scope."

The big miner's face took on a puzzled expression.

"You can't see the road from here; you have to go all the way to the cut to get a sight through where the trees open up."

"The road isn't what I'm looking for."

"What the hell *is* he looking for?"

Jack shook his head. Edge had taken the 30X scope and crawled forward almost half an hour ago. He had lain still since then, other than tiny, incremental movements of the powerful optics.

"He's stalling – he's scared!" Putney hissed, before spitting a stream of brown juice on the leaves.

Boggess didn't know what to think, but Mr. Edge's credibility was definitely taking a nosedive in his estimation.

Suddenly the CAP General's right index finger crooked, gesturing for them to come forward. They started to rise, but he made a quick hand motion for them to move up low and slow. Carefully they complied, stopping when no more than their eyes showed over the ridge.

"What is it?" Putney demanded in a whisper.

Edge slowly slid from behind the eyepiece so he could have a look.

"Opposite hillside, across the road: see that big beech tree about halfway down the hill?"

"Yeah." The miner placed his eye to the scope.

"Okay. Look down at the base of it: to the left, in that mess of fallen branches. Look for something black."

Putney squinted, peering at the tangled mess for two minutes before suddenly going pale. He had found the black spot – a small circle with a hole in its center. Following it back, he soon made out a shape that didn't belong, then another and another, culminating with the toe of a boot. A gust of wind came down the mountain, and a pair of bulky shapes were delineated by the different fluttering action of their burlap gillie suits against the surrounding leaves.

"What is it?" Jack asked impatiently.

"Unless you've got some other men over there you haven't told me about, it's a Federal sniper team – a shooter and a spotter. From the way they're pointing, I'd have to say they're watching your chosen shooting position," Edge whispered without inflection, carefully watching Boggess' face while his hand casually moved to the hilt of the Gerber Mark II combat knife hanging from his web gear. If he saw anything in either their words or mannerisms that didn't seem right, anything at all, he would presume that the trap was meant for him in particular. In which case he intended to quickly and hopefully quietly kill both men before they realized he was onto them.

Fortunately Boggess looked totally surprised, so Edge relaxed slightly.

"B-but…how could they know? We never told anyone!"

"You didn't have to. Even though you made it a point to change positions, you developed a habit of doing things a particular way. The Feds aren't stupid. Once they figured out how you operated, all they had to do was scout around and find the ideal spots for the kind of long-range sniper attacks you all favor and stake out as many of them as they could. Eventually, they were going to get you."

Putney blew his breath out. "Damn, that was close. Look, I think I owe you an apology…"

"Save it for later. Right now, the question is, what do you want to do?"

"What do you mean?"

"Do you want to take them?" There was a clear hint of challenge in his voice.

Jack considered. The distance was well over six hundred yards. Still, he felt capable of handling it, and he wasn't about to back down in front of Edge; he'd already lost enough face as it was.

"Alright, we'll do it. Same get-away plan as before, only we're a few hundred yards further away from the mine. We should still have time to make it before the choppers come, if the Lord's willing and we don't let grass grow under our feet. How about it?"

Putney responded with, "I'm game," and Edge nodded. While the big man peered through the scope, the others locked down their bipods.

Settling into position, Edge whispered out of the side of his mouth. "Let me take the shooter and you the spotter; the triggerman is the immediate danger to us, and the .50 caliber is more efficient at this range."

"Done. You fire first, and I'll be right behind you."

Edge motioned towards his right.

"Move a few yards that way before you set up; this thing going off throws out a serious blast wave."

Boggess silently nodded his thanks for the warning and complied.

They seated their stocks into their shoulders with their left hands, supporting them there as they welded themselves to their stocks, until man and rifle were virtually a single cybernetic organism: a lethal hybrid of flesh and steel. Edge breathed deeply twice to saturate his tissues with oxygen as he settled the crosshairs on the Federal sniper. At the end of his exhalation, his index finger squeezed the familiar surface of the trigger. Burning gasses vented from the recoil compensator, blowing aside the leaves and brush to either side of the muzzle in a miniature hurricane, and the heavy rifle rocked with brutal force against his shoulder.

On the opposite hill, the Federal sniper's head literally exploded like it had been hit by a supersonic axe, painting the ground for several yards behind him with a spray of blood, brains, and bone fragments.

His spotter didn't even have time to realize exactly what had happened when Jack took his turn. The Fed had instinctively started to rise when the soft-nosed 180 grain boat tailed hunting bullet shattered his sternum and tore his heart apart before the expanded projectile exited, leaving a fist-sized hole in his back where a section of his spine used to be.

By the time his legs made a final, spasmodic kick, the three men on the opposite hill were up and running for their lives.

Half a mile isn't very far, but through thickets of laurel and rhododendron clinging to a steep West Virginia mountainside, it can be one hell of a long way.

All three men were in good shape, but every one of their chests was heaving as they charged through the thick brush, plunging along a deer trail. Putney was falling behind and looking more and more like a potential cardiac case by the minute, and they could all hear the blood pounding in their ears.

Even over that noise, they could make out the thumping of the incoming choppers.

"There it is!" Boggess yelled, ripping his way through a stand of blackberry briars and making a beeline towards what looked like a rockslide. Coming closer, Edge could see that someone in years past – probably the mining company in an effort to lessen their liability – had sealed off an old shaft by the simple expedient of bulldozing rocks in front of it. One or two of the smaller boulders at the top had been pulled away, leaving a space just large enough to accommodate a man's body. Jack scrambled over the rocks and dove headfirst into the hole like a groundhog, rapidly disappearing with a wiggling motion.

Edge spared a glance to the rear and immediately saw two things: one was the pair of choppers close above the trees, and two, Putney wasn't going to make it. He was a good fifty yards from the hole, and the helicopters, nose down like monstrous black dragonflies, were in firing range. Catching more detailed glimpses through the leaves and branches, the CAP leader blinked once in surprise; they weren't fooling around this time. They had brought in fully equipped military Blackhawks, flat black in color with 'chain guns' – electrically driven Gatling guns, capable of blasting out over seven thousand rounds of huge, banana-sized 20mm cartridges every sixty seconds – jutting from under their blunt noses.

Edge did a quick and cold analysis even as the first burst of automatic fire began chewing up the woods. The visibility through summer's leafy canopy was almost nil, but it improved rapidly as entire treetops began coming apart when the big bullets cut through them, sending a blizzard of leaves and limbs crashing to the ground. Behind the running miner, the litter on the forest floor began to dance as the rounds ripped into it, burying deep in the earth. Edge didn't like Putney, and frankly didn't give a damn if he got killed; however, he knew it would be both to his advantage and that of the movement if the man lived and owed him big time. Besides, Edge hated the Feds and he had a reputation to maintain.

He shouldered the huge weapon, which was so heavy it was nearly impossible to hold steady offhand, but then helicopters are big targets, and these were alarmingly close. As quickly as the lead craft passed in front of his crosshairs, he squeezed the trigger, racked the bolt, and repeated the action. The Blackhawk may have been armored, but armored or not, few windshields can stand the impact of a .50 caliber full metal jacketed slug. The first round blew through the thick panel and ripped right between the startled pilot and copilot before slamming into the cockpit roof, and the second knocked out a corner of the glass where it attached to the starboard window frame.

Not expecting anything that powerful and suddenly face-to-face with his own mortality, the pilot jerked the stick, whipping the machine to port. Seeing the sudden evasive action of the first helicopter, the second took it as well, turning hard to starboard, trying the figure out what was happening over the shouting of the other pilot into the radio.

Enough was enough. Edge turned and slithered through the hole just as Putney reached it. The big man was still crawling through when Boggess shouted to them. "Let's go! If they decide to cut loose with rockets, we're gonna be in deep shit if we hang around here!"

The warning seemed to lend wings to their feet, and they sped down the tunnel through the bedrock of the mountain as fast as they could go. Behind them they could hear the roar of the 20mm as it chewed up the rocks piled at the mine's mouth in frustration, and sent splinters of stone and metal pinging off the rock walls and ceiling. Finally recovering his composure, the pilot dropped as low as he could to the shattered treetops, and pored a steady stream of fire at the small hole the men had just past through With that many rounds being expended, quite a few found their way inside, slamming into the bedrock walls, ricocheting around, and encouraging maximum speed from the fleeing trio until they were out of range of the stray projectiles

Knowing their escape route in advance, all three men had brought flashlights. That was a good thing, since it wasn't just dark inside the abandoned mine; it was black: black as Hell, and almost as uncomfortable.

"Dark as a dungeon, damp as the dew," the old song went.

It was more than damp. By the time they got a more than a few yards from the entrance, they hit mud. The floor was covered with it, ranging from boot sole to knee deep, and interspersed with stretches of bitterly cold stagnant water that almost took their breath away when they first stepped in it. The only place they were dry was when they had to scramble over rock falls, unnerving evidence of the old tunnel's instability. Finally Jack Boggess held up his hand, motioning them to stop at a section that looked particularly unstable.

"This one suit you, Darrel?"

The big man shone his light on the broken ceiling with a critical eye. "Looks as good as any," he said, reaching into his pack and pulling out a small bundle of dynamite.

As the two former miners began capping and placing the explosive, Edge was concerned that they had lost their minds.

"What exactly are you planning to do?"

Jack grinned without humor.

"It's a little surprise for the Feds. They'll have a team in this tunnel, probably within the hour, and I want to have a little more breathing space between us and them."

"So you're going to blow the tunnel behind us?"

"Nope – they are, right on top of 'em. Otherwise it'd be a waste of good dynamite." He held up a wooden pincher clothespin with a bare wire wrapped several times around each jaw, held apart by a wafer of plastic cut from an old bleach jug. "Booby trap. Probably not as fancy as what you're used to, but it works just the same. Just hook one of the battery terminals up to the wires and the trip wire to that little piece of plastic. They pull that out, the spring snaps the clothespin together, the wires make the connection, and *Boom*! It'll at least get the one who tripped it, but I'm hoping to collapse this whole section and take out half a dozen or more of the sons of bitches."

Edge gazed uneasily at the obviously less than stable walls and roof.

"Isn't there a danger of this blast bringing down the whole mine?"

"Naw," Putney told him as he strung the trip wire just under the surface of the muddy patch right before the rock-fall and smoothed the mud back over it. Securing the trigger in a crack in the dry rock fall and suppressing a grin, he added, "at least I don't think so."

Forty-two minutes later they had left the main corridor behind and made their way into a labyrinth of side tunnels and older shafts, when a distant roar sounded from back the way they had come. They froze, all of them instinctively looking toward the ceiling. There was a faint vibration under their feet, a puff of air moved past, pebbles and grit fell, and bats swirled around their heads screeching in startled protest. The noise, along with lesser tremors, continued for several seconds. Edge, always slightly claustrophobic, was more than happy to see that was the extent of the disturbance. He twisted his wrist to shine his light on his watch.

"It looks like they were a little quicker that you thought. They shaded your ETA by about seventeen minutes."

The miners grinned evilly through faces covered with filth that had adhered to their greasepaint.

"I reckon they must have had a team ready and waiting to be flown in once their snipers took care of us," Jack speculated as they resumed their travels. "They probably had some more backup close by that heard the shots and called out the cavalry. That'll teach 'em to be so damned efficient. From the sound of it, the whole section came down right on their heads, and maybe then some. I hate to admit it, but I was beginning to worry that explosion might have given us a little more than we bargained for, if you know what I mean."

"Yeah," Putney muttered as he took a final look at the rock only inches above their heads and wiped a bead of sweat from his brow, making a dirty smear, "me too."

The Virginian shone his light on their footprints in the mud. "That ought to slow down their ability to follow our trail, at least until we get out of here."

Jack's teeth glittered in the artificial light.

"They won't be able to track us now. As rotten as these old shafts are in the first place, anybody would have to be a damned fool to try to get past that cave-in; that whole end will be completely unstable. Unless we screw up and manage to knock the place down on our own heads, we ought to be in the clear."

"Thanks," Edge said dryly." I have to admit, you all have done well."

"We wouldn't be doin' at all," Putney remarked as they entered another tunnel, one that required them to bend almost in half at the waist in order to clear the low ceiling, "if it wasn't for you. Thanks, man; I owe you."

"Don't mention it," Edge told him.

Just remember it

DAY 73

CHAPTER 6

"Cynthia?" Rob asked quietly. "May I talk to you?"

Cynthia Davis looked up from the coke she was sipping. She had been sitting alone in the trash-littered park, watching some of the few squirrels left uneaten by hungry citizens chase one another while carefully thinking about nothing. She hadn't noticed the man's approach, any more than she had noticed him watching her house and shadowing her until he cold catch her alone. He was just suddenly *there*, and looking about as mean as they came, but somehow she didn't see him as a threat. That was odd in itself, because lately everything seemed threatening...at least when she could be bothered to care.

"Do I know you?"

"Yes ma'am. I was wearing a ski mask the last time we met."

"You're the one who caught Chucky trying to film inside the van," she said, abruptly recognizing his gravely voice. She sobbed suddenly, just once, thinking about her dead friend, and promptly choked it off.

"That was me, and I can't tell you how sorry I am about Chucky." His slitted eyes blinked rapidly for a moment. "He's what I wanted to talk to you about – him *and* you. May I sit down?"

Wordlessly she scooted away from the middle of the bench to make a place for him, and he folded himself into it, leaving a comfortable distance between them.

Rob studied her covertly from the corner of his eye. From pert and petite she had gone to sad and small. While not exactly unkept, she was definitely indifferent to her appearance. Her short blonde hair had grown some, without the benefit of contact with a stylist's scissors, and her pretty face was bare of any hint of makeup.

"So," she asked him, "do you have a name?"

"Just call me Rob."

"Okay, Rob, what do you want?"

He sighed. "First, I want to apologize to you on behalf of myself and the others. If we had any idea that any of this would happen to you, we would never have involved you kids in this – *never*!"

She looked at her feet.

"So you know, huh?"

"Yeah, we know; we just found out yesterday."

"I guess everybody knows." She gave a single snort of utterly mirthless laughter that sounded for all the world like a punch in the gut. "Just out of curiosity, who told you?"

"Kerrie O'Brien."

She sat up straight and her eyes showed the first glimmer of real interest since the conversation began.

"Kerrie? Where's Kerrie? How is she? I'd heard she was…" Her face abruptly flushed and her voice tapered off as she ran head-on into a wall of guilt, suddenly bringing home to her that she had been so wrapped up in her own problems she hadn't even thought to try to help her friend. Rob accurately guessed what she was feeling, but he affected not to notice.

"Kerrie's fine now, and she's someplace safe. I don't know what you heard, but whatever Kerrie may have done was no more than she had to do in order to survive. That's the best way to put it and the only right way to think about it."

She looked at him curiously. "You're a lot more understanding than most people."

"You can't do what we do and be most people."

"I guess not. Look, I'd really like to…well, is there anyway I can see Kerrie again and talk to her for a while?"

Rob began counting all the risks and violations of security protocols that would entail, lost track, and said to hell with it.

"I'll arrange it." He didn't know just how, but he intended to do it.

"Thanks; that would mean a lot to me. She's probably the only real friend I have left…at least I hope she still is. I'd really like to see her."

They sat in silence for a minute as a pair of joggers came bouncing down the walk. Once they passed out of sight around the bend in the path, Rob finally broached the subject.

"Cynthia, I need the names and any other information you have on the ones who attacked you and Chucky, as well as the ones who covered it up."

Her voice was weary. "What for? The police aren't going to do anything."

"We're not the police."

"That's true. Let me ask you this then; what difference will it make?"

"It makes a difference to *us*, damn it!" he told her, showing real emotion for the first time.

She sat thoughtfully for a minute before making her decision.

"Alright." She told him all she knew, and Rob carefully jotted it down in a pocket notebook. Once she finished, he stuffed it back in his shirt pocket. "I'm sorry to put you through all this. Are you going to be all right?"

She smiled with all the humor of a grinning skull.

"No, Rob, I'm not going to be all right. You see, at least one of those bastards who raped me was HIV positive. Now I am too, and word got out. It was bad enough having all those niggers grunting all over me; now it's the opposite. The few *friends* I had are afraid to even touch my hand now. Do you know how that feels, never to feel a human touch? It's almost worse than the damned rape was. This is all I've got to look forward to for the rest of my life, what little is left of it that is."

"What do you mean? They have medicine –"

"No medicine; that's rationed too. Oh, I've got the prescription for all the good it does me. The drugs to control HIV have gotten scarce with all the sanctions, the depression and all, and they're shipping them off to the big cities, mostly up North and out on the West Coast. What little gets down here is distributed by something called 'local community-based action programs,' and the designated local community agency in Columbia is the NABP. They give it all to their own people; there's nothing left for me." Her body began shaking with sobs as she finally broke down and buried her face in her hands. "Even my damned rapists get treatment, but I don't. I'm only seventeen and I'm dying, and I haven't even had a chance to really live yet! Oh God, Rob, I'm so *scared*!"

Rob reached out and laid his calloused palm on her shoulder.

"I'm not afraid to touch you, Cynthia."

She flung herself against him and held on tightly, shaking with emotion. Embarrassed, he stroked her hair as her tears flowed.

"You're going to live, Cynthia, because you're going to have your medicine. You can count on it."

She had no idea how he was going to do it, but there was something in his voice that left her no room for doubt.

Samantha, along with Frank, Sam, Rob, and Tommy, who had finally made it back, sat around the kitchen table for their evening command briefing. Mike also had the rank to attend, but he preferred to leave the decision making to others and concentrate on mining the information necessary for them to make those decisions. He lived with an almost pathological dread of compromising his objectivity. As he explained it, if he knew exactly what they wanted to hear, there was the chance of a tendency developing to ignore data that didn't support it. None of them could fault his logic, so they didn't push it. Since Samantha had appropriated Kerrie for the Confederate Army Provisional Communications Division, she sent her and Donna downstairs to provide whatever assistance they could to their computer whiz. That left the officers sipping cold beers (with the exception of Samantha, who decided to have iced tea instead) and discussing the business of the day.

"How'd it go, Tommy?"

"Pretty well, I think. I've got a six-man cell now." He passed out a list of names and pertinent information. They recognized Joel Harrison, whom they had met before, but none of the others.

Samantha shot a glance of teasing accusation at Frank and Sam before responding.

"You *did* strip and scan them, didn't you?"

"Of course; my mama didn't raise no fools!" Having heard the story of his Commanders' reluctance to do the same to Kerrie, he was unable to resist a little dig, not even trying to suppress a grin at the pair as they reddened slightly. "Mike cleared 'em all on the background check too. I think they're solid."

Frank pursed his lips in thought as he looked at the print outs, knowing they could only tell him so much.

"What's your assessment of their abilities?"

"Not bad – fair, I'd guess. Two of them have some military experience, one in a combat MOS: Airborne Infantry, the 101st. The rest vary. None of them are slobs, but only a couple of them are in tip-top physical shape. Still, they're true believers and willing to learn, so that counts for a lot."

"That counts for ninety percent of it. How are you going to do their training?"

"Steiner owns an old building, so we converted it into a dojo – a martial arts school – and are going to hang out a shingle saying 'PRIVATE INSTRUCTION BY APPOINTMENT ONLY'. Of course, our appointment book is always full if anybody calls, but we'll put them on the waiting list. We'll do the training in there, in the evenings."

Frank thought about it for a moment, and then suggested, "Let's do one better. Do any of these fellows actually know any martial arts?"

"Yeah, Joel's a brown belt in Tae Kwon Do."

"What about the guy from the 101st?"

"Steiner? Well, I he knows what hand to hand combat the army taught him, plus what he's picked up along the way."

"Are either of them working right now?"

"Just odd jobs, temporary work – whatever makes ends meet, you know."

"Good. Put those two together and help them develop a full-fledged dojo. Hang a black belt on Joel, a green belt on Steiner, and tell them to go into full-time business. As a matter of fact, I want you to be head instructor; be there occasionally as your duties allow.

Take Donna with you when you do; she's not known, and she could use the practice."

"What?"

"Hide in plain sight. You open up anything the least bit secretive and you get people's attention. On the other hand, something that's open to the public is the perfect cover. Anybody – cop, Fed, Black, White, whatever – can come in and sign up, and you take their money with a smile. When we need to have a meeting there or do some special training, you simply say you're giving some private lessons to a group that pays extra for the privilege, or maybe a belt test, and everything looks like it's on the up and up. In the meantime, they make a few dollars for themselves and the Columbia Command; Heaven knows *we* can use it. In addition, by having the chance to observe their regular students closely over time, we have a potential recruiting pool. We use those observations to get a list of names that can be approached by one of our recruiters outside of the class and with no connection to it.

"What do you think?"

Rob nodded in agreement.

"That sounds like a hell of an idea. Everybody will already be used to people coming and going, and the noise that training makes. Plus, for hand to hand, you've already got the equipment there."

Tommy looked at Frank and shook his head ruefully. "I think I see why you're the Captain and I'm just a lowly lieutenant. Consider it done.

"One other thing; these fellows *really* want to meet you – and you too, Sammie."

"What for?"

"What do you think?" Sam broke in with a big smile. "Everybody wants to meet the legendary Frank and Samantha Gore. You all are folk heroes; you're the face of the movement to most of these folks."

"I shouldn't be," he growled, exasperated. "I'm just a minor player here; I've only been involved for a couple of months."

"What difference does that make? And 'minor player' my butt, by the way – you're a living legend. These people look up to you, and getting to meet you personally would be one hell of a boost to their morale."

Frank sighed heavily and took a sip from his beer.

"Alright, if it means that much to them, we'll put in an appearance."

"It does, and thanks," Tommy told him.

"Okay." Frank looked over his hand-written list in the pocket notebook in front of him. "That's out of the way. Rob, what about those AIDS drugs for Cynthia? Do you have any progress on that?"

"Yeah. She'll have them within a week."

"What's the plan?"

The older soldier's weathered face split in a rare smile as he told them, and by the time he was through, they were all grinning.

"Hallelujah, there's justice in the world after all!" Sam bellowed, slapping his knee with a laugh.

"You, sir, are an gentleman and a scholar," Frank teased him. "One thing though; you're not going to do this alone. Take Tommy and the boys from his new cell as backup." Rob opened his mouth to protest, but Frank cut him off with "that's an order," and the older Lieutenant immediately subsided, realizing it made a lot more sense to be careful than proud. "I know you're more than capable, Rob, but you know I'm right too. Besides, it'll be good experience for the new guys to work with another professional besides Tommy for a change, in order to break them in for bigger things. Low-risk ops are perfect for that.

"Alright." Frank looked from one to another. "What's the next order of business?"

"It's Kerrie," Samantha said, "we're going to have to figure out exactly how we're going to play this O'Brien thing before we make our move."

"Can you explain, please?" Frank asked her. "It seems simple enough; we know what we intend to do to them, so we scout them out for the best opportunity, take Tommy's squad and go do it. End of story." The other men nodded their agreement, but she shook her head.

"No, honey, it's just the beginning of the story. No disrespect, but while you all might know how to fight a war, you don't really know your hind-ends from a hole in the ground about how the media works, or especially how to work the media."

All of them smiled at her frankness; it was easy, since they knew she was right. None of them had even a pretense of media knowledge.

"We have a potential powder keg in this situation that, if it's not handled properly, could blow up right in our faces and alienate the very people we need to get on board. We're talking about parental rights here."

Tommy was too infuriated to contain himself. A one-time paramedic on a rescue squad, he, like Frank in his past life as a cop, had seen too much abuse too many times. As the official medic for the group, he took care of all their ills, and one of the first things he had done on his return was to examine their newest member. What he had seen enraged him.

"I want to know just what the hell right does a *'parent'* – if I have to dignify those mother…" he paused to struggle for control due to Samantha's presence and Sam's constant harping on his to watch his language when she was there, "…by that name – have to cut a poor little girl to ribbons like that? It's a wonder she survived the beating, let alone the infections she must have had in her condition before it healed, if you want to consider all those damned scars healing! And then they threw her out, right in the middle of a depression when people are hungry all over, with no money, no food, and no way to live! I've examined her; this latest time might have been the worst, but it's not the first time she's been beaten like that either, not by a long shot. That girl's been trapped in a cycle of abuse her whole life. When people see the pictures, they'll know –"

Samantha politely raised her brows and her index finger for permission to break in, and Tommy bit off the rest of his rant and gave her the floor.

"That's just it; most people will never see those pictures."

Sam was clearly puzzled. "But the media is always hot after child abuse cases."

82

She shook her head sadly.

"Only when it suits them. Broadcasting the news was my career before I had my eyes opened rather…abruptly, shall we say. The media has a definite agenda, and it chooses what, how, when, and even *if* to depict events based on what advances that agenda.

"Think about it; do you remember those four people out in Kansas City who were kidnapped, raped – men and women both – and then murdered by two brothers?"

They all looked blankly at her.

"No, I don't remember hearing about that," Frank ventured.

"Or how about up in Tennessee, where a gang of four men and a woman kidnapped a couple, then raped, castrated, burned, and shot the man while making his girlfriend watch? Then they raped her for days, cut off her breasts, and poured cleaning fluid into her mouth before leaving her dead, stuffed into a garbage bag. Do you remember that?"

Their eyes spoke their ignorance, and Sam looked nauseated.

"There's a reason why you never heard of incidents like that; *it's because they weren't widely reported.* Those were Black on White crimes, so they didn't fit the damned agenda; I know they were officially blacklisted at our station. On the other hand, let some Black ex-con get dragged behind a truck, and it stays in the media for years. It's like right across the border in North Carolina, when that colored stripper hollered rape after a White party, the media was all over it, but when, the very next year, a White college girl at the very same school reported a rape by a Black athlete, guess what? That was only local news, and very lightly covered even there. *That's* the way the media works, and that's why they'll steadfastly ignore what happened to Kerrie, but will have a field day over what we do to the O'Brien's."

Samantha stopped, and swallowed hard. She had built herself up into what was almost a rage, and it took her a minute to get it under control.

"So you're saying that there really is the kind of mass nation- or world-wide conspiracy that people like Neil Larson are always talking about?" Frank asked.

"Oh yes, and you should know; you were the one who first introduced the concept to me and got me thinking about it under that blanket in the backseat of Mary's car."

Sam's mouth opened slightly in shock and Tommy, sotto voice, said "*Ooh-la-la!*"

It was Samantha's turn to redden when she realized how what she said must have sounded, but Frank came to her rescue before she totally embarrassed herself.

"It's a long story; don't get excited, there were no juicy parts," which was true, "and the whole thing was purely Platonic," which was not quite as accurate.

Tommy replied with a broad, knowing wink, and Sam cleared his throat to get his attention. Samantha gave him a smile of thanks as she recovered.

"Samantha?" It was Rob, this time, abnormally talkative. "I don't doubt your word, but how does the media fall into lockstep like that? Who could possibly control it? I mean, it's so diverse."

"First, I'm not at all certain it *is* a conspiracy in the conventional, carefully planned, tightly coordinated sense. It could just as easily be a natural tendency of similar people with similar agendas pulling in the same direction. Either way, though, it doesn't really matter, because the end result is still the same.

"It's not an individual person but a group – three groups, actually, and not particularly diverse at all. You mentioned Neil Larson; he's the one who put me onto it. To be honest, I thought he was full of BS when he told me, so I decided to use Mike's expertise to prove him wrong, only to end up proving him right."

"That's a scary thought," Sam muttered, to no one in particular. Sam and Neil went way back, and their relationship hadn't always been a smooth one.

"You know the media is controlled to a great degree by the government under the new regulations and the fact that they decide who gets the broadcast licenses, as well as who gets White House press passes, gets to embed reporters in military units, things of that nature. As I'm sure you can also imagine, the corporations who spend the big advertising dollars also have a strong say in what is

84

published or broadcasted, but that's not all. You see, very little of today's media is locally owned; the vast bulk of it is controlled by syndicates and conglomerates: newspapers, radio, TV, and even the big Internet news sites. These companies are so big that, in reality, only seven men control over 90% of the US media, and they all have one thing in common."

Frank chuckled. "You got this from Larson? Then I'd wager a guess most of them are Jews." Neil Larson's dislike of that particular race was so consuming it was notable, even within a movement full of racially conscious individuals.

"You'd lose that bet, honey. Most of them are not Jews; *all* of them are Jews. Not only that, but right or left, if terms like that still mean anything, doesn't matter. They all support the same core causes. All of them support Israel and everything it does *unconditionally*; all are major donors and toadies to our avowed enemies, the NABP, the PJP and their allied leftist and neo-con causes, and all of them, without exception, hate us and everything we stand for with a passion. It like they're at war against us, against Whites in general and the Southern people in particular. You can tell it in their reporting and the fact that you see the exact same take on every really important issue, regardless of the station or paper."

"What about the other 10%?" Tommy asked, all seriousness now. "What's to stop them from reporting the truth instead of propaganda?"

"Those seven big boys can shut them down in a heart-beat. They simply flood the papers and airwaves with reported accusations of 'racism,' 'anti-Semitism,' or 'sympathy with terrorists,' and it's all over but the shouting. Their customer base is so large and they have so much economic influence that, immediately upon even a hint of that type of scandal, the smaller station's sponsors will pull all their advertising, shutting the offenders down. Even their viewers or readers who would support them are afraid to complain because anybody who does stands to be accused of the same thing. If that happens, 'you'll never work in this town again'."

She let them digest that for a minute before continuing. "So you see our problem: to the media, this has nothing to do with the issue

85

of child abuse versus parental rights, and everything to do with what they perceive as good for their 'progressive agenda' as my old boss used to refer to it."

"I have a suggestion," Frank told her, as the others leaned forward with interest, "a two-pronged attack. Sammie, it's your professional opinion that the media – right and left – will take the same line and smoothly switch from opposing to supporting parental rights in this case, right?"

Frank's habit of asking questions whose answers seemed obvious irritated many people not used to him, who tended to put it down to posturing or even mental slowness. Those close to him, however, knew nothing could be further from the truth. Frank was who he was, and wouldn't know how to posture if his life depended on it. As for slowness, it was just the opposite; Frank was an instinctive tactical genius who had often, since he threw in his lot with the Confederates, been compared to General Nathan Bedford Forrest. He was unusually quick to grasp patterns in most situations and rapidly put them together in the most logical order to solve them. The repetition he wanted was simply to get things set in his mind, look at it from the angle of the other person, and give him time to snap the pieces into place.

"Alright; I presume we'll have to use generally the same sort of media release we did when we first got our story out – minus the kids, of course. Foreign news, radical internet, short wave radio, pirate radio stations, etcetera." Samantha nodded her agreement. "In addition, since this is a primarily a local matter, I suggest we saturate the White neighborhoods of Columbia with a few thousand flyers immediately afterwards, complete with an explanation of why we did what we are going to do, spun in such a way that it clearly shows that it's the Confederate Army Provisional who are upholding family values and Southern traditions. We need not only to play to people's positive emotions – empathy for the girl, the need for justice – but also their negative ones, namely fear. Everyone out there needs to understand in no uncertain terms that there will be a price extracted from *anyone* who harms one of our supporters. That will make things much easier for us in the long run.

"In order to make them understand both these things, we've got to get their sympathy, which in this case, shouldn't be too hard. I hate to do this to poor Kerrie, but we're going to need to include photographs of the scarring." He sighed at the thought of further exposing the girl who had gone through so much already, but there was no help for it. "I won't have her pictured naked though; put her in something like a very brief bikini or a thong. No," he amended suddenly and so decisively it brooked no argument, "a bikini at least to give her that much privacy. I'm not going to make her look like a whore." He hung his head for a few seconds, ashamed at the necessity and furious at that it was, in fact, a necessity in the first place. He was also more than a little surprised at the intensity of his own feelings. A thought seemed to pass between him and Samantha.

Have we just given birth to a seventeen year-old daughter?

The men, understanding his feelings because they were also their own, nodded in silent sympathy. Samantha reached out and put her hand on his, giving it a reassuring squeeze.

"It's alright, Frank. Kerrie's a tough girl; she'll understand and do what needs to be done."

Which won't keep me from feeling just as lousy as you do for asking her, though.

Frank smiled in thanks.

"The second prong of the attack is to hit the press itself for their coverage of it *before* they actually cover it. You told me once that most people tend to believe the first thing they hear so we'll take a page right out of the enemy's rulebook and level the accusations *before* they act, since we already know what their reaction will be. We can nail them on the fact they're switching sides, so to speak, and in such a heinous case, and then tie it all together with a sympathy angle; you know how to do that better than I do."

"I suggest a third prong," Samantha offered. "We also attack the O'Brien's themselves. I've seen the press do hatchet jobs on people they don't like – I've been involved in one or two of them, as I'm certain Chief Perkins would attest." That was certainly an understatement; her skewering interview with Big Jim Perkins that exposed the official lies of the Columbia Capital Riot had become an international legend, and was, much more than the riot itself, the spark that had actually, if inadvertently, started the conflagration of Southern rebellion. "I'll get Mike on an investigation right away. The father is prominent in the Republican Party and a long-time South Carolina House member; in fact, I seem to recall him voting to remove the Confederate Battle Flag from the Capital dome in the first place."

"You got that right," Sam told her angrily, pointing his finger like a gun. "He was also one of the driving forces in the fight to remove it from the State House grounds entirely. Damned *scalawag!*" He said the last word with all the disgust he would have used to describe a piece of rotten meat that had somehow landed on his upper lip.

"Good, that's just the kind of thing we need to reach our own target audience.

"Using our alternative media sources, we will use the enemy's own tactics against him, and, at least amongst our own potential sympathizers, blacken his name until a fly wouldn't light on him.

"One thing, though," she told them, her voice all seriousness, "I'll use only the truth, and nothing else. I'll dig though his dirtiest laundry and spin it to our best advantage. I'll fold it, twist it, staple it, and mutilate it, but I *will not* lie about them, no matter how much they deserve it. There are some things I can't sink to and maintain my self-respect as a journalist, not to mention the reputation of our movement. I know there's a place in war for purely fictional propaganda, but you'll have to get somebody else for that; I just won't do it." She said this last defiantly, and unconsciously crossed her arms over her breasts, halfway expecting resistance.

Frank looked at the others with an easy-going smile.

"You see why I love this woman?"

God, I don't know what I ever did to be blessed with her, but thanks again.

"Yeah; yeah, I do," Sam told him, clapping him on the shoulder. "You're a lucky man."

Samantha blushed slightly. She needn't have worried about their reactions; after all, she was on the right side. That feeling was slightly clouded by what Sam said next.

"There's only one problem; Jonathon Edge. I don't know how he's going to take it when we notify him of what we plan to do."

Tommy sneered at the mention of the Field Marshal, the expression exacerbated by the facial scar he had picked up in the Charleston raid, which gave him a piratical air. Frank's voice was cold.

"I'm not going to be micromanaged, Sam, especially not from halfway across the country. I have no intention of notifying him until after the fact, when we put it in the regular report. This act is a result of decisions we all made; it's purely a local matter, and as long as nobody dies, it's a relatively minor one in the grand scheme of things. It's none of his business, or anyone else's on the Council, the way I see it."

"You know *he* won't see it that way, and there'll be hell to pay if I don't let him know."

Frank slid his thumb up the condensation on the amber glass of his bottle in a motion as graceful and telling as a knife slicing flesh.

"He'll take it a whole lot worse if he orders me not to and I do it anyway. After what happened when you paid back that informer who got Mary killed, I'd think you'd know that."

Sam nodded glumly, unable to argue without being a hypocrite. With Frank and Edge on either side, he was caught between a rock and a hard place, and that already-limited space was getting tighter by the day.

DAY 74

CHAPTER 7

"Thanks Donna."

"Don't mention it," she said as she squeezed out another finger-full of ointment to rub into the scars on the Kerrie's upper back, between her shoulders where the slightly younger girl couldn't easily reach by herself. "I just hope this stuff works; the TV commercials say it's supposed to reduce scarring and make it fade out some."

She rubbed on a little more as Kerrie sat facing backwards in the bedroom chair.

"There; that's got it all, I think."

Kerrie refastened her bra strap and let the back of her tee shirt fall, hiding the marks while Donna wiped her hands on a towel.

"Everybody's just so nice here, it's like…like…"

"Home?" Donna offered without thinking, and then wished she had bitten her tongue off instead of saying something that stupid. "Hey, I'm sorry! I didn't mean –"

"It's all right," Kerrie told her, turning around to face her. "I know you didn't, but in a way, you're right. The only thing is, here it's like a home should be, not like mine was."

"I'm sorry."

"It's not your fault; lots of people had it worse I guess. It wasn't so bad, really, unless mom and dad were drinking or all stressed out over the latest political fight, and then I learned to stay out of their way. Still, they bought me stuff, you know; I never wanted for anything."

Donna felt slightly sick just thinking about that, and suspecting things that Kerrie was not saying. She had noticed the older scars too, although at least she had managed to keep her mouth shut about that and not to ask about what else they may have done.

She *had* asked Tommy after he examined their newest member, and he had pointed his finger at the end of her nose and told her

91

bluntly and very sternly that it was none of her business, and had absolutely *forbidden* her to *ever* bring it up again to anyone, particularly in front of Kerrie and *most particularly* to Frank.

I guess I have my answer; if Frank even suspected something like that, no power on Earth would keep the O'Brien's alive.

"They're probably there now, aren't they?" Kerrie asked in a very small voice.

"Yeah, I expect they are."

"Will Frank…"

Donna sat down on the edge of the bed, took both of Kerrie's hands in hers, and looked directly into her eyes.

"Frank made you a promise, and when he does that, you can bank on the fact he'll keep it, come hell or high water."

It's a good thing too, for Kerrie's sake. I'm glad it's not me because I wouldn't. I'd kill both of those monsters.

"Is this your daughter – Kerrie O'Brien?" the masked figure asked, holding the photograph before the couple.

"Not any more," Bob O'Brien snarled, having recovered somewhat from his earlier shock. He and his wife Rhonda had returned home following a Republican fundraiser that had hosted no less a personage than the U.S. Secretary of State only to find his large, expensive home full of masked men and one woman, all with pointed guns. Both he and his wife were loud and aggressive by nature, and they had imbibed heavily at the function, making them even bolder than usual. "I threw the treacherous little slut out of my house and wrote her out of my will! As far as I'm concerned, she's disowned!"

"And did you put these scars on her?" The man went on in an un-modulating tone as if he hadn't heard, and held up another picture: this one a back-view of Kerrie wearing a small bikini with a high-cut bottom that clearly showed the marks crisscrossing her flesh.

"So what if we did?" Rhonda O'Brien snapped, despite the growing fear that was beginning to creep over her. "We've got the right to discipline our daughter as we see fit. After turning her back on her country, she had it coming, and she got it! End of story!"

"No," the man told them, pulling off his mask, "that's only the beginning." The couple paled with horror as the danger of their situation suddenly became all too real, slicing through their alcohol-fueled courage like a white-hot knife through butter. Even with the beard he had grown, anyone who watched the news or read the papers could recognize the iron-hard face of Frank Gore. Their terror compounded when a second mask was pulled off and they looked into the burning blue eyes of Samantha Norris. If anything, she was the more frightening of the two; those twin orbs looked like acetylene flames.

Frank was against her coming, but she had insisted on it.

I can't hide in this house forever she told had him, *and you're not the only one with responsibilities in this matter! It's my fault too!*

He had simply nodded and said nothing more. Responsibility was one concept Frank Gore understood full well. What might be the ultimate consequences of allowing her to fulfill that responsibility, though, he wasn't so sure.

I guess we'll find out.

"Besides your long record of treasonous actions in actively supporting and voting for the destruction of our heritage and the subjugation of our people, you have also abused your daughter and, by your own admission, you have retaliated against, not even a supporter, but simply a *reporter* who dared to tell the simple truth about the Confederate Army Provisional. In doing so, you made us your enemy.

"Even then, even though you were in the wrong, she's your daughter, and you could have taken a belt or a switch to her and no one would have said a word; *that* was within your rights, but *this...*" His voice rose as he shoved the photo at their faces. "In the name of *God*, what kind of human being does *this* to their own child?"

He raised the photo and held it up before Sam, Rob, and Tommy, along with his squad members from the dojo, gathered for the occasion.

"These scars on this girl were over a month old when this picture was taken. She was whipped with a piece of wire that cut all the way through her skin, clear down into her flesh. She will carry these scars for the rest of her life. Then she was thrown out hurt and bleeding into the street to starve. This had nothing to do with discipline; this was an act of pure, selfish sadistic cruelty! I ask you, gentlemen – does this qualify as child abuse? You!" He pointed to Sam, anonymous behind his mask. "Is this abuse or is it not?"

"You're damned right it is!" he shouted, glaring at the O'Brien's.

"Yeah," Rob said in a clipped voice as cold as ice, not waiting to be asked.

"Thank you. You!" He pointed to Harrison.

By the time he had circulated, every man in the room – Tommy's entire squad except for two who were on lookout duty outside – had been shown the picture and asked the question. All answered in the affirmative, Tommy strongly suggesting that they should go ahead and "gut-shoot both of 'em!"

"Robert and Rhonda O'Brien, you have confessed to the crime of criminally abusing your daughter and of gross neglect and abandonment by throwing her out in the middle of a depression with no way to survive. In doing so, you have also admitted your guilt in performing an act of violent retaliation against an asset of the cause of Southern freedom, which is treason, punishable by death. You have been found guilty as charged by a jury of your peers. Your punishment will be carried out immediately."

The couple began stammering a series of "you can't's" and "my rights," but Frank ignored them except to order them gagged.

"As much as it would please me to execute you both, I will not do so, for one reason and one reason only: the request of a little girl. The request of *this* little girl!" He held the picture of Kerrie's scarred back up again, shoving it towards the O'Brien's faces before turning so the others could see it once more. "This gift and sacred charge from God Almighty that you abused, scarred for life, and threw out to die like a piece of garbage, has asked me –" he choked in his fury "– *begged* me to spare your *damned miserable lives* because you were still her parents and she still loved you despite what you did to her. It's for her sake and for hers alone that we won't kill you both right here and now just like you so richly deserve."

94

Even Samantha, angry as she was herself, was surprised by the ferocity in his voice. Frank was a man given to cold rage, not hot-blooded savagery. She realized how hard it was for him to keep his fury in check in order to keep his promise to Kerrie and let these two live. She knew him well enough to be confident he would, but she also knew what it was costing him emotionally.

I know what it's costing me! I could kill them both right now and go out for dinner.

"However," he went on, "you will not get off Scot free. This is no longer the United States, where your drinking buddy the judge will let you walk because of who you are. This is the Confederate States of America, and neither treason nor violent crime will be tolerated here, particularly not crimes against children! I won't kill you; instead, I'm going to make an example of you. Since Dixie is a Christian nation, I'll refer back to the Good Book to find your punishment: an eye for an eye, tooth for tooth…and *stroke for stroke!*" One of the men produced a pair of *sjamboks*: mass-produced whips, originally used by the South African police for riot control duty. The tapered, flexible rods of extruded plastic were over a yard long and as black as a nightmare. Frank took one and Samantha, at her previous insistence, the other. He tested his, and it hissed like a snake as he swished it through the air.

"Strip them."

"Are you alright, Sammie?"

She slipped beneath the covers before answering. "I'm fine."

Frank looked at her thoughtfully, but said nothing, and for some inexplicable reason, that irritated her.

"You're wondering how I held up flogging the O'Brien woman?"

"Not exactly; from where I was standing, you held up while you were flogging her just fine." She had been more than fine; she had been downright vicious. To Frank, the beating of Robert O'Brien had been an unpleasant duty that he was surprised to find had been much more pleasurable to contemplate than to actually carry out, although he did it as he did every duty: thoroughly and to the very best of his ability. Samantha had administered her first stroke to the woman that same way, with her brow furrowed and her full lips tight, but by the time she finished, her teeth were bared in a snarl and her eyes were wide and bright as she plied the *sjambok* with an almost out of control rage and all the force she could muster. He supposed if he hadn't been counting the strokes – forty minus one, like in the Bible – she would have continued lashing Rhonda O'Brien until her arm dropped off. As it was, while he didn't have to actually have to forcibly restrain her, he did have to gently but firmly pry the whip out of her reluctant fist when it was time to stop. At first he thought she was going to resist letting go, but she had suddenly blinked, and then assumed a carefully blank, neutral look as she allowed him to take the bloody rod.

Looking around, she had seen the others' eyes on her, staring through the holes in their masks that couldn't hide their shock. After that, she hadn't spoken beyond monosyllables until now.

"Just remind me not to keep *sjamboks* in the house in case you get angry," he continued. "No, I'm concerned about how you're holding up after the fact."

"So I'm a nut-case now? You think I can't handle it?" she snapped, then quickly turned to him and put her arms around him. "I'm sorry, Frank! I didn't mean to take that tone with you." She mentally swore at herself.

You're acting like one now! What the hell is he supposed to think?

For that matter, what the hell do you think?

He hugged her, a little stung but not letting it show. So far, outwardly at least, he had managed to weather the unpredictable emotional storms she was prone to since her capture and mistreatment with equanimity, although it was not always easy.

What really worries me is that she seemed to be getting better for a while, but over the past few weeks, her mood swings seem to be getting worse and more frequent. And that look in her eyes tonight...maybe she actually is going crazy.

He would have died before he would have let that particular thought show on his face.

"I know you didn't mean it, and you know that's not what I meant. Post-traumatic stress is *real*, Sammie. I've seen it break the strongest men. I love you, and I worry about you."

"I know, and I love you too," she said, and hid her face against his chest.

"Do you want to talk about it?" he asked, obligated even though he already knew the answer.

He felt her head shaking negatively.

"Not now; not yet," she whispered.

I don't even want to think about it!

Samantha wouldn't tell Frank, but she had seen something inside herself tonight that was as unfamiliar to her as it was to him, and it frightened her.

Tommy looked up at the sound of a faint tapping on his door. His room was in darkness, illuminated only faintly by a nearby streetlight filtering through the window screen. He had been lying flat on his back, hands clasped behind his head while he stared at the ceiling, his mind unable to let go of the way Kerrie had been brutalized. Even though he had observed the O'Brien's punishment with satisfaction and a certain sense of closure, it still didn't seem to have been the full measure of justice they deserved. It couldn't take away a single disfiguring scar from the young girl's back, let alone the much worse ones cut into her soul over the years. That bothered him not a little.

With a grunt he sat up with the sheet to his waist and called for who ever it was to come in.

Donna opened the door and stood there, silhouetted by the hallway light.

"I-I didn't wake you did I?" she asked softly in a voice just above a whisper.

"No, I was just lying here unwinding, getting the adrenaline out of my system so I can sleep." As he answered, he saw that she seemed nervous, her hands balled in the hem of the greatly oversized man's tee shirt she was wearing for a night gown, twisting it unconsciously and showing a fair amount of slender, well-tanned thigh in the process. A late bloomer at eighteen, he noticed once more that she had finally begun filling out, leaving a little of her teenaged coltishness behind and taking on curves in interesting places: places that were amply highlighted by the light behind her shining through the thin cloth and making it obvious she wore nothing beneath.

He guessed that's what it was, anyway. Perhaps it was what he thought before: where the two were almost constantly together, posing as a couple, maybe he had just gotten to know her better until she ceased to be Donna, Sam's Goddaughter, and become Donna, the young woman.

"Is everything okay?"

"I-I..." she began stammering again, totally out of character. Her hands twisted harder, and she was visibly shaking, even in the poor light.

Wordlessly, Tommy pulled back the sheets beside him and Donna shyly stepped inside and closed the door behind her.

DAY 75

CHAPTER 8

Mildred Bass was still in her housecoat as she walked her toy poodle around her front yard in the first light of dawn. Unusually short, and nearly as big around as she was tall, the elderly widow's gray hair was still frizzed out from her bed.

"Come on, Mitzy," she urged as the dew began soaking through her cloth slippers, "Mommy needs to get back inside."

If the little dog understood her, it paid no attention; instead it trotted over to sniff at something in the hedge. The ball of fur on the end of its tail bobbed back and forth.

"What have you got there, baby?" She squatted laboriously beside the animal, and was infuriated to see the plastic bag containing a piece of paper caught under the carefully trimmed boxwood. "Gracious! Some people just have no respect for other folks' property." Grunting as she reached for it, she stood and opened it, and was suddenly confronted by the image of a familiar face.

Why, it's the little O'Brien girl! A vague wave of guilt swept over her as she recalled the commotion the night Kerrie's parents – Mildred's next-door neighbors – had thrown her out. Mildred had heard the curses followed by the screams and the blows, and seen the sobbing child, her blouse spotted with blood, shoved through the front gate. She knew then that she should have said something or done something, like call the police maybe, or even let the girl stay with her. She should have, but she didn't. She hadn't wanted to stick into other people's business, and she had wanted to keep as good of relations with the O'Brien's as she could, even though she secretly found both of them obnoxious and detestable. She had often wondered what happened to the girl.

When she dropped her eyes to the second picture on the page and saw the scars, she suddenly knew.

She clamped her hand over her mouth. *Oh my Lord!* She was even more shocked when she read the text.

"ATTENTION CITIZENS OF SOUTH CAROLINA AND THE CONFEDERATE STATES OF AMERICA:

Our people and our country are the last bastions of Godly and civilized behavior in the world today. It is this fact that makes the C.S.A. special, and it is also this fact that makes crimes that violate our ways be that much more heinous. Treason and child abuse are the most heinous crimes of all."

She read on as the paper described the O'Brien's acts much as Frank had described them to the O'Brien's themselves earlier, and ended with a final warning.

"Taking retaliatory action or informing against any supporter of Southern independence for their efforts to forward that independence is treason, a capital crime, and will be dealt with accordingly. All citizens are hereby notified that any further acts of this nature by anyone in South Carolina will result in a sentence of death upon conviction.

"The Confederate Army Provisional recognizes that discipline is a necessary and far too often overlooked part of bringing up children. Parents should take it seriously and apply it as needed; however, there is a very clear difference between discipline and abuse. Child abuse is a crime against the most helpless members of our society, a crime against God and nature, and will not be tolerated in the Confederate States of America, and particularly not in the Great State of South Carolina.

"Look to the example of the O'Brien's to see the consequences of treason and abuse."

It was signed *By Order of Colonel Samuel Wirtz, South Carolina Command, and Captain Franklin Gore, Columbia Command, Confederate Army Provisional.*

Mildred's eyes rose to look into her neighbors' yard and her multiple chins fell. Both of the O'Brien's were bound standing, face-first, against the red maple in their front yard, strips of duct tape covering their mouths. Both were stark naked, and the closely-spaced pattern of bloody welts showed clearly in the fat, white flesh

100

of their backs, buttocks, and thighs. She also saw similar papers to the one she held scattered in yards all along the street.

She gasped again, wondering what she should do, and then suddenly tittered. Snatching up a startled Mitzi, she waddled as quickly as she could toward her front door. Once inside, she grabbed the phone and began mashing buttons.

There were two rings, then a sleepy feminine voice: *"Hello?"*

Mildred hadn't called the police; after all, she didn't believe in messing in her neighbors' business. Of course, that didn't mean she couldn't notice it.

"Vera?" she said excitedly to her friend across the street. "Take a look out your front window at the O'Brien house!"

Newscast, Columbia

A Columbia couple was brutalized last night in an attack by neo-Confederate terrorists. South Carolina State Representative Robert O'Brien and his wife Rhonda were taken from their suburban home and sadistically flogged in a style reminiscent of the Ku Klux Klan or of radical Taliban Islamic regime. Law enforcement believes the family was targeted both for Representative O'Brien's extensive record of supporting civil rights for minorities, and because they both objected to their daughter's association with the domestic terrorist organization, the Confederate Army Provisional. The daughter, who, as a juvenile, cannot be named, is reportedly a known prostitute and suspected drug dealer, and is currently being sought by the FBI as a person of interest in several terrorist acts in and around Columbia. It is believed that she has had a longtime association with the wanted Confederate terrorists, Franklin Gore and Samantha Norris, and it has been speculated by FBI profilers that she may be the third part of a twisted sexual relationship involving the infamous fugitive couple. They also say that the pair had encouraged her into prostitution and other crimes in order to fund their terrorist activities.

The doctors at Columbia General Hospital have confirmed that both Mr. and Mrs. O'Brien are in critical condition. They have declined to state the extent of their injuries, but have confirmed they will be permanently disfigured.

The FBI, along with officers from the South Carolina Law Enforcement Division and the Columbia Police Department, are currently investigating. They have confirmed that a small group of neo-Confederate terrorists was involved, and that the terrorist leaders, Gore and Norris, personally administered the beatings ...

British Press Service Online editorial excerpt:

...Was the flogging of the O'Brien's by Confederate Army Provisional guerrillas a despicable act of terrorism or a justified comeuppance? That is the real question. As a civilized people, we must of course oppose all private violence and vigilante-ism as something abhorrent. And yet, when you see the photographs of this lovely young girl, whose back was literally torn to shreds, I'm afraid many of us may find our sympathies lie, at least secretly, with the actions of the guerrillas...

French Press Organization editorial excerpt:

Far be it from France to criticize the punishment of collaborators, when we ourselves have a strong history of doing much the same thing. In fact, compared to some of our own ways of dealing with those who aided the Nazis during World War II, the actions of the Southern guerrillas seem fairly restrained...

Conservative Internet forum exchange

Message 20691
Posted by Fireball

Justice returned to South Carolina with a vengeance last night as two child abusers felt the wrath of the Confederate Army Provisional (See links to the story and to a .pdf file of the CAP pamphlet below). What the controlled, Jewish-run media did not tell you, however, *was that the battered little girl was not a criminal; she was a hero. The reason the media hates her is because she committed the ultimate crime of reporting what they would not, because it didn't fit their agenda. Their lies and mischaracterization of her are nothing more than the usual smear campaign we have come to expect.*

You may recognize the name of the girl; she was one of the four young high school journalists who exposed the Federal conspiracy in Columbia, whose agents, under the auspices of the current neo-conservative Republican administration, slaughtered citizens and framed Frank Gore and Samantha Norris for daring to tell the truth about what happened. Truth is a dangerous thing to the ZOG; so dangerous it caused a helpless child to be savaged by her own parents and caused a good cop and a great reporter to be at the top of the FBI's most wanted list.

As far as I'm concerned, the guerrillas showed remarkable restraint in their treatment of these two child-abusers…

Message 20692
Posted by Moderator

The previous post is in violation of a number of rules of this forum, and has been removed. Fireball has also been blocked from any further postings on The New Conservatives. Free speech does not include to right to criticize America, engage in racist conspiracy fantasies or support terrorists.

Message 20693
Posted by Giblet

In other words, free speech doesn't include the right to disagree with you or you Zionist-Republicrat masters, or to support anything you and they oppose?

Message 20694
Posted by moderator

The previous post is in violation of a number of rules of this forum, and has been removed. Giblet has been blocked…

Kerrie sat beside Mike, staring at the scarred image of herself on the computer screen. About her parents, she was now emotionally dead with no feelings left at all; all she knew was she was glad Frank had kept his word and let them live. Still, even though she understood the necessity of her own exposure and had agreed to it, she blushed and hung her head at the thought of millions of people seeing the pictures, now all over the internet, even though most of her classmates worn as little at the beach last summer as she did in the photo. Somehow it especially bothered her that the man sitting beside her at the desk saw it as well.

Mike noticed her expression, and closed the screen.

"It's alright," he told her. "They're just scars, and we've all got 'em, inside or out." He gestured at his dead legs. "Believe me, I can understand that."

"I just feel like a freak, like I'm on display for everybody to gawk at! I know it has to be this way, but it's so *hard!* It's almost as bad as…" Her voice trailed off and she blushed even deeper, thoroughly humiliated, and unsure how to finish, since Mike didn't know her secret.

"Kerrie, I don't usually eavesdrop on my friends," he told her quietly, even though, as a matter of personal survival in a notably factious movement, that was not at all true, "but sometimes voices come through the floor in certain spots, and I can't help but hear." She looked at him and he nodded. "Yeah, I know about it."

Her lip quivered, and it was obvious she was about to cry again.

"You might as well know; after that news report, the whole world knows I'm a whore."

"Damn it, don't say that! You're not a whore!" he shouted, slamming his fist down on the desk with a force that made the keyboard jump and the monitor screen flicker.

"I've known whores," he continued, his voice intense yet calmer, "and I know you, Kerrie; you're not a whore. You're one of the sweetest people I've ever met.

104

"I know a couple of other things too," he went on, looking at her tenderly as she stared at him, wide-eyed like a deer in the headlights. "You're strong; strong enough to live, whatever it took. I admire that. I also know Samantha told you there'd be no shortage of shoulders to cry on, and she was right. There's one right here in this basement if you ever need it." Surprised at his own boldness, he reached out to her and took her hand.

She slowly shook her head, a deep sadness in her eyes.

"Please, Mike. I'm not ready for this."

"Ready for what?" he asked, puzzled.

"You know – for sex. I just...well I like you – I really do..." she swallowed hard, "but after what happened to me, what I had to do, I don't know if I'll ever want it again. I'm sorry..."

Mike's chin fell to his chest in shock, and it took him a moment to recover.

"What are you talking about?"

"You know; I thought that was what you wanted."

"What the hell do you think I am?" he exploded, dropping her hand as if it had suddenly turned red hot as she shrank back from him. "I was trying to be your friend, damn it!"

Abruptly he swiveled his chair away from her and turned back to his computer.

Kerrie was beginning to cry.

"But...I thought –"

"I know what you thought! You thought I was some kind of sick-minded pervert ready to take advantage of you now, when you're at your weakest and most vulnerable. Thanks a lot, Kerrie, but flattery will get you nowhere!"

"I'm *sorry*! Please, I thought you were like other men!"

He snorted. "The compliments just keep coming, don't they? No, I'm not *like other men*; I'm a freaking geek stuck in this damned wheelchair with two paralyzed legs and a nerve-damaged pecker that doesn't work so well anymore, if you must know! So don't worry, Kerrie; sex wasn't what I was looking for, and even if it was, it probably wouldn't do me a whole hell of a lot of good. I was looking for...ah hell, never mind. It doesn't matter anyway."

105

He tried to ignore her, only to hear her voice from behind. "I'm sorry," she whispered. "Oh God, I'm so sorry! I didn't know."

He blew out his breath. "No reason why you should know; no one else does except Tommy. Anyway, I'm the one that's sorry. I shouldn't have jumped on you like that, after all you've been through. It's not your fault, but it's just that it gets so frustrating sometimes, and so damned *lonely*."

Suddenly he felt her hands on his chair, rolling him back. Once she had room, Kerrie moved in front of him, between his chair and the desk, and knelt down on the carpet. She put her hands on his knees as the tears poured down her face.

"Forgive me?" she sobbed in a tiny voice. "Please?"

He sighed and patted her hand.

"You know I do. Now get up off the floor; you're getting your jeans dirty. Friends don't have to beg each other."

She made no effort to rise.

"Are we still friends?"

"I hope so."

"You know," she said after a moment, still looking into his eyes, "I don't think that chair is what makes you different from other men. I think it's your heart."

Embarrassed, he didn't know what to say.

"Can I still use your shoulder?"

"You know you can."

She took advantage of his offer, ending up climbing onto his lap like a child and crying the way she needed to. Mike hugged her to him, stroked her back and whispered clumsy, inexperienced words of comfort. They sat there for a long time, two scarred, battered people holding onto one another as they finally began healing.

106

DAY 78

CHAPTER 9

The roar of, "*You son of a bitch!*" rang through the house, followed first by the sound of a blow and then by grunts and furniture breaking. The hallway wall outside Tommy's room shook as a body collided violently with the other side, sending a framed picture crashing to the floor.

Frank and Samantha were on their feet in an instant, Frank dropping his coffee in his hurry to draw his .45. As they rushed down the hall, they recognized the voices of Sam and Tommy yelling and cursing, and that of Donna screaming and pleading for them to stop.

Frank yanked Tommy's bedroom door open; unfortunately he did it precisely at the time the two fighting men drove toward the portal. He managed to move his gun muzzle aside a split-second before they slammed into him and carried him with them, barely missing Samantha. All three men crashed against the opposite hallway wall hard enough for Frank's back to break the plaster.

Dropping his pistol to keep from accidentally shooting someone in the melee, Frank desperately tried to separate the two, but to no avail, getting an elbow to the ribs, a head butt to the chin, and a foot stamped down hard on his toes for his pains. Angry now himself, he finally settled things by the expedient of first sweeping Sam's feet out from under him, then grabbing Tommy's forehead and throwing him backwards over an extended leg. Both men hit the floor hard, and Sam was the first to recover. His attempt to scramble to his feet failed due to Samantha, who jumped on his back before he could get his legs under him.

"Stop it Sam!" she yelled with one arm around his neck and her lips an inch from his ear. "Stop it *now!*"

Sam was unwilling to fight a woman, especially one with a pistol butt raised above his head, to all appearances fully ready to club him into compliance, and he subsided into mumbled curses.

Meanwhile Frank threw himself astraddle of the biker's chest, and Tommy responded instinctively with a right fist aimed upward at his face. Frank parried it to the outside and his left arm wrapped over and around Tommy's right like a snake, pinning the biker's wrist in his armpit and locking the elbow. Simultaneously Frank buried the fingers of his right hand in the tender area behind Tommy's collarbone, while his thumb dug into the pressure point in his armpit. His grip began to close as he grabbed his right wrist with his left hand and started straightening his arms, hyper-extending the smaller man's elbow and using that leverage to force his fingers still deeper into the nerve centers. Tommy gasped, astonished at the pain.

"Be *still!*"

Tommy wasn't one to give up easily, but something in Frank's face made him hesitate. Despite the agonizing pressure on his elbow joint and the equally painful nerve pinch, he didn't think his friend would actually go so far as to intentionally break his arm...he hoped. Still, he knew if Frank applied just a little more pressure, he would probably embarrass himself by involuntarily screaming, so he decided to surrender to the inevitable.

"Alright, man, I give. Let me up."

Frank nodded and began releasing his grip when he heard his wife chortle behind him. It took him a moment to figure out what she found so funny, and an instant later, he realized he was sitting atop a buck-naked Tommy. He leaped to his feet with a grimace of disgust.

What a pretty picture that must have been: like amateur night at the gay bar!

Using his right foot, he kicked a small throw rug at the biker to cover up with.

Mike Dayton's voice echoed from the basement, full of concern. "What the hell's going on up there?"

"Just a little accident," Frank called back. "Everything's okay."

"Yeah, right," the faint grumble came in answer. "I'm a paraplegic, not a dumb-ass!"

Frank glared at the two men. "That's what I'd like to know too; just what the hell *is* going on in here?"

His question was answered when Donna tried to slip past them in nothing but her socks and the long T-shirt that was her nightgown of choice. It was obvious from her appearance she had just woken up. The problem was it was Tommy's room she was coming from.

Frank and Samantha's faces fell, any humor in what would ordinarily have been a ridiculous and even flat-out hilarious situation gone as they grasped the very real implications for their group's unity. Disgusted since their very first association with the infighting rampant in the movement and its negative impact not only on their prospects for victory, but on their own personal chances for survival, they knew the last thing they needed was yet another crack wedged open. The moral aspect was not their business, but then again, considering who was involved, it was not a moral question; it was a pragmatic one.

Frank's face began to redden with frustration, and Samantha spoke up in a voice colder and harder than any of them had ever heard her use.

"Sirs." She used Sam's and her husband's formal military titles, indicating the official nature of her communication. "I am *Private* Waddell's direct superior officer, since she is attached to my office, is that not correct?" Frank nodded. "Very well, then as my subordinate, she is *my* responsibility and I'll handle her. If you'll excuse us, I'd like to discuss this matter with her privately." She turned to face Donna, fury in her eyes and ice in her voice, and pointed down the hall. "In the kitchen please."

Uncharacteristically, Donna refused. Bluntly.

Samantha's eyes narrowed and her breathing quickened slightly. "I said I wanted to speak to you, *Private*. I gave you an *order*, and you will either walk to that kitchen on your own, or *I* will physically take you there. Make your choice and make it up now."

Sam's mouth began to open, but wisely snapped shut when Samantha flicked her eyes towards him like an opening switchblade. She looked positively dangerous.

The girl crossed her arms over her breasts and defiantly tucked her chin. "I don't want to talk about it right now!"

It was the wrong answer. Samantha's hand moved like a striking snake. Before her younger subordinate realized what was happening, the Communications Officer's right hand had plunged through her long brown hair and snagged her left ear in an iron grip. Samantha twisted and lifted sharply, causing Donna to come up on her toes.

"Oww! Stop it! Don't you dare! Don't you dare!"

Ignoring her demands, Samantha began striding toward the kitchen, dragging a yelling and thoroughly mortified Donna along with her. The girl was on tiptoe with her head cocked sideways, pawing ineffectually at her superior's imprisoning hand.

All three men stared in open-mouthed wonder. Samantha was generally the mild-mannered one who calmed everybody else down, and this was completely out of character, even considering her erratic behavior of late.

"Damn!" Tommy softly exclaimed. "What got into her?"

Frank shook his head and then returned to the subject at hand. "Never mind her. Get your pants on, Tommy, and meet us in the living room; we've got some things to talk about. We're all men here, so hopefully we can work this out a little easier than those two."

The ex-cop took another look towards the kitchen.

I'm really beginning to worry about her.

Mike had suggested to Kerrie that she go upstairs, ostensibly to get something to eat, but actually so she could find out just what was going on. She was at the table, stirring up a glass of instant chocolate milk when the kitchen door flew open and Samantha escorted Donna inside, still with a firm grip on her ear. The girl was red faced with humiliation and not a little pain, and was still howling protests.

"Kerrie, please give us this room!" Samantha ordered, raising her voice, so she told herself, in order to make herself heard over Donna's yells. Kerrie analyzed the situation and Samantha's tone within a second, and did the only reasonable thing. She promptly fled back to the basement, leaving the half-stirred glass on the table.

In the meantime, the CAP communications officer seated her captive by the simple expedient of positioning her slender rear end next to a chair and twisting her ear downwards until she sat in it.

Samantha gritted her teeth and tried to control her breathing, doing her best to gulp back the anger that threatened to totally overwhelm her. She tried being reasonable

"Donna…"

"You had no right to treat me like a child!" The girl was furiously rubbing her sore ear and blubbering from embarrassment. "You had no right to do that, especially in front of Frank and Tommy! You're not my mother!"

"No, I'm not you mother, a fact for which you should thank your God right now!" *So much for reasonable* an unheeded voice inside her quipped. "I am your commanding officer, and as such, I have every right. You were given a choice and you made the wrong one, not only a moment ago, but last night as well, from the looks of it!"

"I'm eighteen! Who I sleep with is *my* own business!"

Samantha leaned down until their faces were close, still fighting to regain her composure. "Yes, that's your business. As your friend, I care, but as your commanding officer, it's not my concern if you spread your legs for everybody who walks by this house. This is not a personal issue and it's not a moral issue; it's an issue of action and reaction, cause and effect. When who you *sleep with*, as you like to euphemistically put it, affects this unit's morale by putting its members at each other's throats, then it becomes *my* business! Do you understand that? The cohesiveness of this unit has to come first."

"What I did with Tommy has no effect on this unit!"

Samantha straightened up, cocked her fists on her hips, and looked at Donna as if she were a moron.

"Then, if it has no effect, why were two of our officers trying their best to kill each other over it? Answer me that!"

"It was Uncle Sam's fault! He had no right!"

"He is your Godfather; how did you expect him to act? Damn it, Donna, it's not just what you did! He had no warning, no idea of what was going on until it slapped him right in the face first thing in the morning! We all live in the same house, and you had to know you couldn't keep that kind of a secret. What did you think Sam was going to do when he finally found out: pat him on the back and say, 'Congratulations on screwing my Goddaughter, Tommy! Was she any good?' If we hadn't broken that fight up, one of them, or maybe both, would either be crippled or more likely dead right there in the hallway! They weren't playing, young lady, and thank God neither of them had strapped on their pistols yet. I don't know if you noticed, but Tommy's thumb was reaching for Sam's eye, and Sam was doing his best to get his knife out of his pocket when Frank finally broke them apart. What do you think would have happened if either of them had succeeded?"

"Look, I didn't think –"

"That's just it: you didn't *think*, and that set off a chain reaction where *they* didn't think, which nearly got somebody badly hurt or killed. Let me tell you something else. It doesn't *matter* who has the right to do what. Right now, we are in a war, in case you haven't noticed, and what you have the right to do doesn't matter nearly as much as the results of what you do. Can't you understand that?"

"What do *you* know about this war?" Donna leapt to her feet, shouting. "You only came into it a few months ago and got captured early on, so you don't have nearly the experience I have! I grew up with this Movement! You're just some jumped-up Johnny-come-lately who doesn't know a damned thing about this war!"

Much to her surprise, Donna suddenly found both of Samantha's fists buried in the front of her shirt, and the older woman actually heaved her off the floor in her rage, before slamming her down on her back on the kitchen table, knocking the breath out of her, bowing the metal legs, and sending Kerrie's milk spilling unheeded onto the floor. Stunned and pinned, Donna's eyes widened in fear as Samantha bent over her until they were almost nose-to-nose. Samantha began to lecture her in an almost incoherent fury, her face contorted, spitting her words between clenched teeth and punctuating her sentences with hard shakes that bounced the girl against the table's surface again and again.

112

"I don't know anything about this war? Damn you, you spoiled little brat, have *you* ever been held down and cavity searched by a pair of bull-dyke guards? Do *you* know what that's like, having their filthy hands pushed up inside you while they stand there and laugh? Did *you* ever piss blood for two weeks straight because your kidneys were pounded halfway into jelly? Did *you* have your fingers stomped on with combat boots until they broke and the blood squirted from under your nails like ketchup? Did *you* have the wonderful experience of having a stun gun forced into your vagina and up your ass until you smelled your own flesh burning from the electrodes?" Tears of anger and memory poured unheeded down her face. "Do you know what it's like to have parts of your body hurt every hour of every damned, stinking day and night because of what was done to you, and to wake up in cold sweat screaming your lungs out because you dreamed about it *again for the hundredth time*? Do you know how it feels to live with that? Until you've experienced that, don't you *ever* tell me I don't know anything about this war! *Don't you ever!*"

Samantha gulped hard, struggling with emotion and desperately trying to get a grip on herself. Slowly, she forced her hands to release their hold on Donna's tee shirt, noticing the white-hot agony in her still-healing fingers for the first time as her rage diminished. Still, she maintained her position above the girl, trying to control her breath that was coming in hitching sobs. "What I know about this war," she said, somewhat more calmly, "is its consequences. I know those all too well to be willing to allow you, or me, or my husband or any of those men out there to suffer what I did, and if morale collapses and this unit fractures, that's exactly what will eventually happen. I won't allow it. You might not think of me as your friend anymore – I can't help that – but understand this from me, both as your friend *and* as your commanding officer. No matter what you do or how you feel about me, I'll love you, Donna, like the sister I never had, but I *will* make any sacrifice necessary to preserve this unit so what happened to me never happens to anyone else in it – *any* sacrifice. That includes me, and that includes you. You may not like me anymore, but I hope you at least understand me, because I mean it."

Samantha suddenly clamped an aching hand to her mouth. Turning away, she rushed to the sink, barely making it before she threw up. She swore at her body's own weakness and wondered how much longer she could keep it hidden as she turned on the cold water and rinsed her face and mouth. It was only after she finished that she realized Donna was sitting there on the edge of the table, looking very young in her big tee shirt and crying for all she was worth.

"I'm sorry, Sammie! I shouldn't have said that! I'm so sorry!"

Samantha crossed to Donna and stood in front of her for a moment, then sighed. She reached out tentatively and took the girl into her arms, and Donna buried her face in her shoulder, still crying. While she patted her back in reassurance, the Communications Officer mentally shook her head.

I seem to be doing a lot of this lately; are we all going insane, or is it the whole world?

Or is it just me?

"I know, honey; I know. I'm sorry too; I shouldn't have been so rough on you. This war has been hard on us all; let's just not make it any harder, okay?"

"I love him!" Donna whispered desperately as she clung to her. "I love him!"

Samantha nodded understandingly as she took Donna's face in her hands, lifting her head until their eyes met.

"I know you do. After all, you're not the kind of girl who would have made love to him otherwise." Both of them managed a smile. "Don't worry, we'll work it out someway, alright? I promise, we'll work it out."

Tommy and Sam looked like the walking wounded, glaring at one another from across the room with bloody noses and split and swollen lips. Tommy had a big knot on his jaw, while Sam had a mouse under his right eye that was growing larger and darker by the minute. Each one of them also had a major attitude, one not improved by the pain that was beginning to set in, and Frank was getting nowhere fast. It didn't help matters that Tommy was also frustrated that he hadn't been able to take the older man before Frank interfered, but Sam had got in the first lick and partly stunned him, as well as having the psychological advantage of a clothed man over a naked one.

"Look," Frank finally said in exasperation, "let's do it this way. Since you can't talk to each other without yelling, then why don't you both just sit there, be quiet, and listen to what I've got to say, all right? Then whichever one I'm talking to, answer me.

"Tommy, I know Donna's an easy little piece of tail…"

Sam nearly exploded in a rage at his cavalier description, but Frank ignored him, concentrating on the biker.

"How can you say something like that?" Tommy shouted indignantly, jumping from his seat with his fists clenched. "I don't give a damn if you do outrank me, I'll kick your ass if you ever say something like that about her again!"

"Oh will you? And why, pray tell, would you do that?"

"Because she's special, man!"

"She's *special*," Frank said, sarcastically rolling the word around on his tongue like a piece of overly sweet candy. "Hear that, Sam? How about you? Do you think she's *special* too?"

Sam was already on his feet, balling his own fists.

"You know I do, and you ought to be ashamed of yourself, talking about her like that! I never thought you, of all people…"

"All right then," Frank interrupted, smiling up at the men who were glaring down at him, both on the very edge of taking a swing, "we've found common ground that you can both agree on — something I agree with too, by the way — so let's proceed from there. Donna is indeed a *very* special girl, and she means a lot to everybody here, right?"

They nodded their assent grudgingly, irritated by how handily Frank had turned their irritation from each other to an alliance against him, only to diffuse it.

"Okay, now: is this movement and this war more important than anything that took place here today?"

They both spoke up at once.

"Yes, but..."

"No buts; we've established our priorities and have a base to work off of now. Let me ask you this: since both the Cause and Donna herself are more important than either what happened last night or your little Donnybrook this morning, won't you two killing each other be detrimental to both? If one of you buys it or even gets hurt badly, aren't we not only a man short, but also an officer – a *leader* – short too? Further, what's it going to do to Donna if she loses either a Godfather or a boyfriend, or maybe both, knowing you two, because of something *she* did? I'm not just talking about either of your relationships with her; I'm talking about her mental state. If that screws up now, during this war, because of her misplaced guilt over *your* actions, what do either of you think is likely to happen to her?" Neither would answer, so he went on, intentionally brutal. "I can tell you; if she's lucky, she'll *die*, and if not...well, just ask my wife what the Feds do to women who weren't that lucky."

Both men paled at the thought. They had been with Samantha in the back of the truck following her rescue, and had seen the Federal torturers' work first hand.

"Tommy, you say what you have with Donna is not casual, and frankly I never assumed it was; I know you both too well for that. Would you please tell us how it came to this? Maybe it will help."

For the first time since Frank had known him, the normally loquacious biker was embarrassed to the point that it was hard for him to speak. "It just, like, *grew* on us, man." He looked at Sam. "I don't care what you think, I never *meant* for this to happen! I never wanted it to happen! It just *did*! We've been posing as a couple for so long, I guess we actually became one before either one of us realized it. I'd like to tell you I'm sorry, Sam, but I'd be lying. I'm not the least damned bit sorry; I'm in love with her."

Sam snorted in derision, but without as much feeling behind it as before. Frank turned to him.

"Sam, Donna may not look like it – hell, she doesn't always act like it – but she's an adult now, or at least as adult as an eighteen year-old can be. More than that, she's a veteran; she's been there. She's got to make her own choices now, and she *will* make them,

116

whether you or I or anyone else likes it or not. You know her, so you know I'm telling the truth."

Sadly and reluctantly, Sam nodded agreement.

"I also think you know, when people are thrown together, especially under stress, things like this are going to happen; right or wrong, it's inevitable. There's one thing I want you to know, though, and remember. Donna is not easy; she's just in love. If she wasn't, I think we both know her well enough to know she wouldn't be in this situation. I don't know about you, but I was young once, and I don't think I'm qualified to be the one to cast the first stone over something like this."

Sam blew out his breath and nodded again, and Frank turned his attention back to the biker.

"Tommy, I'm not going into the morality of all this; you're a preacher's son, so I'm sure you're already well aware of those ramifications. Regardless of the fact that you and Donna had the right to do what you did, you showed a great deal of disrespect for your friend and commander by doing it, especially right under his nose and most especially with no warning – you know that. We all live here in the same house, so you had to know Sam would eventually find out, and you know Sam. How did you think he was going to react when he finally discovered your all's secret, especially since he never had an inkling it was happening? As her Godfather he has a certain responsibility for her, making what you did a direct insult to his honor, one he had no other choice *but* to react to."

"I-I just never thought about it, not really *thought*, you know?"

"Yeah, I know; I've done enough thoughtless things in my life, and I'm sure Sam has too." The farmer sighed his agreement. "The thing is, we can't afford not to think – and I mean really *think* – about anything anymore, or it's going to bite us in the butt one day and someone will die. Do you know what I'm saying?"

There was a knock at the door, and Samantha's voice sounded from outside."

"May we come in?"

117

"Send Donna in; I'm just leaving." Turning back to the others, he left them some final advice as the red-eyed, contrite, and somewhat bruised girl entered the room.

"We're going to leave you all to work this out amongst yourselves because you're the only ones who *can* work it out, but remember this. We've been though the fire together, people. There's not one of us who wouldn't be dead right now except for the actions of someone else in this room, and there isn't one of us who wouldn't literally go to the wall for *any* of the others. We may be few, but like Shakespeare said, *'we few, we happy few, we band of brothers, for he who sheds his blood with me today shall be my brother.'* All of us have shed our blood beside each other, and that has to count for something. Damn it, it has to, or we've already lost, and furthermore, we *deserve* to lose!"

Frank stepped into the hall and shut the door behind him. Slipping his arm around his wife, he began walking her back to the kitchen.

"I wish it wasn't so early; after all that, I could use a beer right about now." Frank usually limited himself to no more than a single beer each day, but savored that one to the fullest.

"Not me," she told him absently, "I'm going to lay off for a while."

"I noticed you haven't been drinking lately. What's the matter?" he teased, exaggerating the expression as he ran his eyes up and down her gorgeous figure that left nothing to be desired. "Going on a low-carb diet?"

She stopped suddenly and snapped her head in his direction.

"Why? Do I look like I'm gaining weight?" Her voice was sharp, in a tone she almost never used with her husband, and it startled her almost as much as it did him.

"Sammie, you know that's not what I meant." His voice was calm – infuriatingly calm as far as she was concerned, almost like he was talking to a child.

It's because that's what I'm acting like, a child or an idiot.

Samantha gulped down her irrationally angry reply before it reached her lips. She felt guilty enough already, and she crossed her

118

arms and looked the other way to keep from seeing the hurt she knew would be in his eyes.

"I'm sorry Frank. I just don't feel well, and I need a little space, alright?" She abruptly realized she sounded just like Donna had a few minutes ago, and suddenly found hypocrisy added to the growing list of sins weighing on her conscience. *It would serve me right if someone just shook the hell out of me too, I guess.* She never had to worry about Frank doing that – he loved her too much – but the look in his eyes that he couldn't conceal made her feel much worse than if he had.

"Sure honey. I'll be in the basement with Mike if you need anything." He started to turn, then hesitated a moment. "I love you, by the way," he said over his shoulder, and then was gone without waiting for her to answer.

She went into the bathroom, sat down on the closed toilet, and cried miserably, cursing herself for a fool.

Mike and Kerrie didn't hear him on the stairs, and they were huddled much more closely together than necessary over a computer screen when Frank entered. They both started and quickly moved apart, a little guiltily unless Frank missed his guess.

Good grief, love must be in the air. I guess you can't expect any different, a bunch of people under stress crowded together in the same house.

"I'm not interrupting anything, am I?"

"No, not at all," Mike assured him, just a shade too hastily. He knew he had been caught, and knew Frank knew it too, but went on anyway as if nothing had happened. "I was just showing Kerrie how to take a footprint."

"Come again?"

"A footprint: it's the first step in hacking. Pull up a chair and I'll show you too, so you'll have an idea of what it is I do."

Frank picked up one of the mismatched wooden kitchen chairs and placed it on Mike's right, opposite of Kerrie. The intelligence officer didn't look up from the screen as he spoke.

119

"Footprinting is gathering all the available information about a potential target, particularly things that might be useful in breaking into his system from my point of view as a hacker. First, I lay the groundwork. Using multiple search engines, as well as individualized advanced searches, I to try to ascertain the general condition of the individual, business or organization."

"You mean like security issues," Frank ventured.

"Yeah, but it's much more than that. Sorting through the facts and putting them together in a logical order is simple analytical reasoning. I like to get a real feel for the target too, and that's where hacking ceases to become computer science and becomes computer art. You not only have to psychoanalyze him, but you almost have to become his intimate acquaintance. If you really get to know your target and get a real feeling for who he is and what makes him tick, sometimes abstract reasoning – intuition, if you will – will carry you inside farther and faster than logic alone."

Frank thoughtfully stroked his bearded chin. "That makes sense; I relied on that quite a bit when I was a cop, only then it was person to person."

"So is cyberspace, when you really think about it. Information and communication – that's what it's all about, whether it's face to face or half way around the world.

"Kerrie is learning to do the data collection right now; pretty soon I'll start her on sorting it out…that is, if you're not putting her in another position anytime soon."

"No, this is fine," he said, raising a hand to his mouth to hide a grin at the slightly pleading tone in Mike's voice, "that is, if Kerrie enjoys it and has an aptitude for it. Kerrie?"

The girl gave him a rare smile that he swore held more than just a touch of relief.

"I do like it, but I'm not very good at it."

"Give it time," Mike told her. "You'll make a first class hacker yet."

"So," Frank asked him, "you get all your information online?"

Mike snorted. "I wish. Well, sometimes it's all I've got, but there's nothing like on-site access."

120

"That would be kind of tough for you wouldn't it? I mean with the chair and all?"

"Oh, I'm like a troll; I almost never leave my 'cave.' I have my own little network of people who do that for me. Some of them are volunteers and others are cyber-mercenaries or even physical B&E artists I slip a few bucks to or do a favor for in exchange for their efforts.

"Don't worry, it's not much of a security risk; none of them have ever actually met me. All my internet activity and contacts are either done online through various cut-outs or hijacked computers, or physically through some of Tommy's intermediaries."

Frank whistled. "That's some system; so what exactly do these people do?"

"That depends. The ones who have regular access – disgruntled employees and the like – collect the system information and passwords I need to gain access, download files, and install some of my own spyware and back doors. The others do what ever they can, either by hacking into the network or gaining limited physical access to the target premises under some pretence. Both groups act as social engineers and even dumpster divers too; anything that gets thrown away, like floppy disks or hard copies, are all potential gold, either to me or to those analyzing it for me."

"How extensive is this network of yours?"

Instead of answering immediately, Mike turned to the girl. "Kerrie, would you mind getting us all a coke? There should be some in the fridge upstairs, and I think the ice maker still works."

She took the obvious hint with a smile.

After she departed, he spoke quietly to Frank. "I trust her, but we're getting to the point of need-to-know, if you get my drift." Frank nodded his agreement, and Mike abruptly changed the subject.

"Look," he whispered, "the real reason I sent her out is that I caught the gist of what was happening upstairs a little while ago. If it's our turn, *please* leave Kerrie out of it. I'm begging you, Frank, don't say anything to her about it. The fault is mine, and she's been hurt enough. We haven't really…done anything, you know, but if we're in trouble, I'll take the ass-chewing myself…"

121

Frank waved him to silence.

"Settle down, Mike. Yours is an entirely different situation; Kerrie isn't kin to anybody here. Just remember she's only seventeen and she's…well, kind of *delicate* right now, if you get *my* drift. Please keep that in mind, also that she's my responsibility since I brought her in, and I don't want her to be hurt any more." Mike opened his mouth but Frank cut him off. "From watching the two of you, however, I don't think I have to worry about that. I think she needs somebody right now, almost as much as you do. Just take good care of each other."

A look of gratitude passed over the programmer's face and Frank thought for a minute Mike was going to burst into tears. He really hoped not, because he wasn't sure what the hell he would do if that happened.

"Thanks, man. I owe you."

"You don't owe me anything, but if you do, then spend it treating her right and I'll consider it paid in full."

Mike shook his head. "Doesn't hardly seem fair, does it, the difference between the two situations?"

"Name one thing in this life that's fair. I reckon you know that better than any of us.

"Now, about that network?"

"It's big. I handle the tactical intelligence gathering for South Carolina, or course, but since I'm close to Edge's friend Sam, I'm also in sort of defacto charge of strategic intelligence for the entire Confederate Army Provisional. I'm like spy command-central: our intelligence clearing house so to speak. Even though most of them don't know exactly who I am, those in charge of intelligence operations in the other States report to me, and most of what they know, I know."

Frank whistled. To him, Mike had been just Mike: a friend, a genius, and an invaluable cog in the machinery of the movement, but he had so much going on himself, he never realized just how important the man was.

"Maybe I ought to salute you when I come down here."

"Ha! You start that crap and I'll start locking the damned door. Rank doesn't matter to me, just ability. *I'm* a coordinator and *you're* a commander; there's a big difference. My job is to make your job – and the jobs of a lot of other people like you – doable.

"Anyway, back to the network. Bear in mind that what I'm describing is primarily but not entirely the in the Palmetto State; I keep other resources of my own scattered all over, and I suspect all the other State Intelligence Coordinators do too, at least if they're smart. Most of their intelligence networks are probably set up about like mine, at least internally.

"First and foremost, I have the watchers."

"Watchers?"

"Yeah; that's all they do, watch and report. There are dozens of them, some of them individuals and some of them set up in their own cells. They're our bread and butter."

Frank scratched his head.

"I must be missing something here. Exactly what are they watching?"

"*Everything!*" Mike exclaimed, beaming. "They keep a cyber diary of things in their area; how many military vehicles or aircraft pass, or cars with Federal plates, along with their license numbers when possible; when the cops patrol, and what time it all happens. They watch for strangers and listen for rumors. I've got people who live or work near military bases and National Guard units who keep track of everything coming and going. They keep track of businesses opening or closing, or construction projects – anything at all that could potentially be useful. It all ends up here where I search for common threads, trends and patterns that might indicate something going on, or tell us what areas are safe and when."

"How do you keep track of it all? I'm not a computer whiz like you, but I've used them quite a bit, and that's a lot of info to sort through."

Mike tapped a button and a screen popped up showing a several groups of small, labeled circles, each connected by dozens of lines of different shades, obviously color coded.

"It looks almost like a spider web."

123

"It is; that's what we call this particular piece of software. With the help of some other geeks, I hacked and modified an existing program used, among other things, to track terrorists. What this does is show how everything connects together. For instance, see this circle here?"

"Yeah."

"Okay, that's your old buddy, Ronald Peters. These other circles in the same orbit are his close associates. The lines running between the different groups of circles, from an individual in one orbit to another, indicate known or probable relationships, and what type: business, personal, etc. You can tell at a glance when somebody's a person is of interest by how many lines run to and from him; then, if I want to know more about him personally, I simply click his icon..." He proceeded to do exactly that, and an outline in the form of a table of contents popped up. "...and I can access all known information about him. I can use this program with either people or places; it doesn't matter, but I can tell you it's handy."

Frank whistled.

"You must have hundreds of people and locations stored in there..."

"Try tens of thousands, with more being added every day."

"How in the world can your computer keep up? That must require an enormous amount of storage and processing power."

The intelligence officer nodded at an object in the far corner of the basement before answering. "Go over there and open the lid on that deep freezer."

Puzzled at the strange request, Frank complied. The chest freezer was a big one, more than long enough to hold a body, and he wasn't at all sure that wasn't what he was going to find. Instead, when he clicked the latch and raised the lid, he was even more surprised.

"Is this what I think it is?"

"If you think it's a super computer, then yep, it is: poor man's version. Tommy and Billy supplied the parts – don't ask – and I built it by hooking up the guts of fifty top-of-the-line PC's worth of processing power in a cluster. The thermostat on the functional freezer unit keeps everything running at a cool sixty degrees. It's not a Cray, but it does the job."

As he scanned the interior, Frank could see dozens of hard drives and motherboards…and a series of largish cylindrical containers scattered throughout, primarily over the hard drive sections. He turned to Mike and cocked an eyebrow in question.

"I'm glad to see you noticed the final security system. In the event of a raid, I only have to tap in a six digit code here, hit 'enter', and those thermite charges will burn everything in there beyond recovery, and probably take the freezer shell with it."

Frank nodded his approval and closed the lid.

"It's a pleasure to work with a professional, Mike, and I mean that."

Mike blushed at the compliment.

"Well, besides the watchers, I have at least partial access, undetected as far as I know, to hundreds of businesses, organizations, and even some local, State, and Federal offices. I'm careful; I don't touch anything obvious or make my presence known unless I have to take action against them, like causing their system to crash or launching a raid on their bank accounts and credit card numbers. Then I only do it through a series of cutouts."

"Do you do that a lot?"

Mike grinned. "How do you think we've been funding this little revolution of yours? Cracking enemy accounts, our little counterfeiting operation, some organized theft, a bit black marketing, and even a handful of charitable pot growers and moonshiners account for better than ninety percent of our funds." The grin disappeared. "The economy is so bad, even crime doesn't pay like it used to; we can barely keep up.

"Don't look so shocked, Frank," he said when he saw the ex-cop's expression. "We only steal from the enemies of our people. Like you're big on saying, we do what we have to do. Besides, there's a certain satisfaction in making the oppressor and his quislings pay for their own destruction."

The Captain chuckled. "I just thought of something. Did you ever hear of the *Cruise of the Raider Wolf?*" Mike shook his head.

125

"My grandfather had that book; I read it when I was just a kid. The *Wolf* was a German ship during the First World War: a commerce raider. It literally circled the globe and never made port. The ship and its crew lived and fought entirely on the spoils of their prey. The ships they took provided food, fuel and parts for the entire expedition.

"That's basically what you're doing here."

"*Wolf*," Mike mused. "I like the sound of that."

"We're not just wolves," Frank amended, referring to the traditional color of Confederate military uniforms. "We're *gray* wolves."

Samantha stepped out of the bathroom when she heard someone knock on the door, only to find Donna standing outside.

"I'm sorry. I didn't know you were waiting."

"I was waiting for you. I wanted to apologize again for what I said. I had no right."

"No," she said, shaking her head, "I had no right to go off on you like that, especially when I threw you on the table. I'm so sorry, Donna; I just lost my temper. I know that's no excuse, but I am sorry."

"You had every right to do that after what I said; you were right about the whole thing."

"I'm not going to try to stop you from being in love; that's too precious to waste. I know."

"I'm not wasting it. Uncle Sam came around; he still doesn't like it, but I think when Tommy offered to marry me he finally saw the light."

"Did you say yes?"

She shook her head with a smile. "No…not yet anyway. I want to wait a while, just to be sure, but it was nice to hear anyway." She stopped abruptly and stared. "Sammie, what's wrong?"

"It's Frank; I-I was mean to him again, and I'm so afraid…"

She began crying once more, and this time it was Donna's turn to offer comfort.

"Tell me."

126

She told her, along with the other thing she had been keeping hidden from them all. Donna clamped her hand over her mouth, grasping the implications as well as Samantha did.

"You have to tell him!" she exclaimed as soon as she recovered her voice.

"I can't! Not now!"

"Then you at least need to see Tommy."

"N-not yet –"

"Yes you *will!* You need medical care and you're not going to wait! Remember what you said to me; it's not what we have the right to do, it's the consequences of what we do that matters? Well, does that apply to you too, or only to the rest of us?"

Samantha wiped at her eyes. "You're right."

"You're damned right I'm right. I'll talk to Tommy and he'll set up a time where he can see you privately. In the meantime, you need to talk to Frank."

"I can't tell him yet! He's got too much on his mind; I can't distract him now."

"You *are* distracting him with the way you treat him." A faint trace of anger was beginning to show in her voice, and she paused to draw a deep, slow breath in order to garner time to think, as well as to get her own emotions in check before she said something irrecoverably stupid. "Then don't tell him yet; instead go find him, apologize to him, tell him you love him, and then *show* him. Don't let him hurt, Sammie." Her voice took on an even more serious note. "He, of all people, doesn't deserve that!"

"I know," she said, continuing to cry. Donna hugged her just as Tommy stepped into the hallway. Samantha's back was to him, and Donna caught his eye and silently mouthed over her shoulder, "Get Frank now!"

Donna was still holding her when Frank came up the stairs, taking them two at a time.

"Sammie, are you alright?"

She turned to her husband and held her arms out like a child wanting to be comforted.

"I'm sorry, Frank! I'm so sorry!"

127

"Shh," he told her, and surprised her by slipping one arm around her shoulders and the other behind her knees, picking her up in his arms, heedless of the girl looking on. "I know, honey; I know. Let's go talk awhile, alright?" He nodded his sincere thanks to Donna before carrying his still sobbing wife to their room, barely pausing as he kicked the door shut behind them.

Donna stared at the closed door for a second, the mixed emotions running through her head like water spilling down a rapid. She loved both those people, loved them dearly, and it hurt her to see them suffer...especially Frank. She would never admit it – *could* never admit it to anyone, but there was one man she was in love with besides Tommy. She loved him even more, and had loved him since the first time she saw him: the instant hero, the avenger of her sister, the strong, handsome man that had beaten all the odds. Then, now, and she supposed forever, he was one man she could never have, no matter how much she wanted him. She couldn't do that to Samantha, even if Frank was willing, which was an impossibility in itself. The fleeting thought crossed her mind that anything could happen in a war, that there was always the chance that...

No! I will not even think that! Oh God, I feel so awful! What the hell am I becoming?

She wiped furiously at her watering eyes, and then started guiltily when she saw Tommy unobtrusively watching from the top of the steps.

"What's wrong?"

For one horrified second she thought she had spoken aloud or he had somehow read her mind; then she realized with some relief what he was asking about.

"We've got a *really big* problem. You need to see Sammie as soon as you can get her alone."

"Okay, but why?"

She told him, and he stood there with his mouth hanging open in shock.

"Sam?"

"Hey, John. I'm glad you called; I just finished the report. You ready for it?"

Edge's voice was cold. "I think I've already got your report; it's all over the news. I had a little trouble explaining it to these boys up here, particularly since I didn't know anything about it in the first place!"

Sam's face hurt, his knuckles hurt, and his ribs hurt from the fight. He still had a headache from a hard punch to the jaw, his Goddaughter was sleeping with one of his own men, he couldn't do a damned thing about any of it, and his stock of patience was rapidly running out.

"There's no reason you should have to explain it. It's a minor local matter for South Carolina, not West Virginia. To be honest, it's none of their damned business."

Or yours either, for that matter.

"You still don't get it, do you? Everything anyone in this organization does reflects on the organization as a whole, and it reflects even worse on me when I don't have a clue about what's going on."

"Fine; I'll be sure and let you know every time I wipe my ass! Look, John, I can't go running to you to get approval beforehand for every little thing we do, and then wait around for you to give me a yea or nay. We can't work like that down here, and we won't; it's just not going to happen that way."

"That's the way it *has* to happen, at least at this early stage of the game. We only have a few hundred men scattered across Dixie; we can't throw them willy-nilly against a government that can field millions and expect to win. Right now, everything we do has to be planned for to the nth degree, less because of its immediate results than for the long term consequences. As long as we can control the action, we can win, because by doing so, we can predict the reaction. But I can't plan for that if I don't know about the action in the first place." He paused a moment, abruptly realizing the meaning of Sam's use of the word, *'we.'* "It's not you at all, is it? It's Gore again, him and that biker you're so fond of."

Sam took a deep breath and counted silently to three, trying hard to maintain his temper.

"It was a joint decision, discussed and unanimously agreed upon by every officer in the South Carolina Theater, including me.

"But he was behind it, wasn't he? This has his style written all over it!"

"Damn it, John, will you just *get over it?*" Sam exploded. "Yes, Frank defied you once and even threatened to shoot you if you got in his way; I was there, remember? You seem to forget, all the man wanted was to save his wife, and it turned out to be the right decision! If he hadn't forced us to make that raid, we wouldn't even have a movement right now! We'd be *nothing!* Frank Gore was the one who put us on the map." He paused at the revelation that suddenly came to him. "That's it, isn't it? You're *jealous!*"

Edge was taken aback at his friend's vehemence, particularly since everything he had just said hit a lot closer to home than the General would admit, even to himself. He had worked and sacrificed for years for this, and suddenly along came Frank blazing across the movement like a comet. That he was widely regarded by those outside as well as not a few inside as the defacto leader grated on Edge's very soul. The fact that Frank had never wanted it didn't enter into the equation, except maybe to make the irritation even worse.

"Look," he said, trying to get control of his anger before it took control of him, "everything any of us do has a ripple effect throughout the whole movement. If that ripple is big enough or hits in the right place, it can move things or even sink them. I'm responsible for the big picture. I need to know about things before they happen, so I can evaluate whether their ripple effect is going to be worth the direct results they're intended to accomplish, and so I can predict the likely possibilities. I need officers I can trust to let me know what's happening *before* it happens, not sometime afterwards, whenever they get around to it."

"You're never going to predict everything, and I'm never going to be able to guarantee that I can tell you in advance about every little move we make. I'll do what I can, but –"

130

"That's not good enough."

"It'll have to be. At any rate, it's over and done with, and there's nothing anyone can do to change it now, so let's move on. Since you're bound and determined to know everything we do, we've got another little project going down here too."

He proceeded to tell Edge about Rob's plan to get Cynthia the AIDS drugs. Sam desperately hoped Edge didn't say no to that, because it would lead to another, even bigger fight when they did it anyway, but, aggravated as he was, their leader could find no fault in what they were doing.

"That's a good plan for a change. We can be seen as charitable and at the same time demonstrate, at least in people's minds, that we are more powerful than the NABP. It'll work if you handle the PR right."

"It'll be handled right; Sammie's already on it."

Edge didn't let it show as the conversation continued, but the warning radar went up inside his head. The fact that his best friend – his only friend – was close enough to Frank to be referring to Samantha by her husband's pet name for her, made him wonder just how close they were becoming. This was something he was going to have to think hard about.

DAY 79

CHAPTER 10

Davy Holden climbed back into the driver's his delivery van with some relief. He had only one more stop in this neighborhood, and then he could relax for a while as he drove cross-town. Double-checking his list, he verified the next drop as the regular delivery from the pharmaceutical company to the local NABP headquarters, and he'd be damned glad to get it over with. They weren't the easiest customers to deal with.

Bunch of assholes, really.

He started when someone unexpectedly tapped him on the shoulder from behind. Turning, he found himself first looking down the barrel of a 9mm Glock, then into a pair of cold blue slits behind a black ski mask. The man had somehow slipped into the back of his truck while he was making his previous drop.

"Hello," Rob said pleasantly.

Newscast, Columbia

...And in further news today, a delivery van was robbed at gunpoint in Columbia. The driver, David Holden, was not injured, but was left bound and gagged in the back of his truck while the unidentified suspect made off with a single package; a package that could have tragic consequences for many in our community, as explained by the South Carolina representative for the National Association of Black Persons, Reverend Bessant.

"This stolen package contained the monthly supply of HIV drugs distributed by our community action group to those who are suffering from that terrible disease. If they are not recovered soon, many of our people may develop full-blown AIDS."

133

"Some of the calls and emails to our studio have made the claim that you only distribute those drugs to Black victims of that disease, not to all. How do you respond to that?"

"I won't dignify the accusations of racists with an answer! You don't debate the hate!"

"Reverend Bessant, do you believe this theft could have been a mistaken attempt to gain access to street narcotics or to sell the rationed HIV drugs on the black market, as the Columbia Police Department has suggested?"

"No, it was not! That robber was White! This is all part and parcel of the ongoing war of genocide against people of color since the days of slavery, and the Black man ain't gonna take it any more! We demand that the perpetrator of this heinous crime be brought to justice and the drugs my people need recovered within 24 hours, or I assure you there will be consequences. The Black community will take it to the streets; where there is no justice, there will be no peace!"

Southern Internet forum

"…The funny part is what Bessant didn't say, and the reporter didn't dare mention. My brother is a SLED officer, and he told me, after that guy stole the drugs, the local niggers cleaned out the whole van while the driver was still tied up in the back – even took his wallet and his cell phone! He laid there for over an hour before anybody bothered to call the police…

Russian Press Agency Online: English Edition

…a message purportedly from the Confederate Army Provisional of the American Southern States was delivered to our offices, and is reprinted below.

Confederate Army Provisional of the Confederate States of America Columbia, South Carolina Command Official Press Release

134

"...Due to the racially discriminatory practices of the National Association of Black Persons in denying the HIV/AIDS drugs they are given to distribute to the White people of Columbia, our people who have the misfortune to be infected with this terrible disease are dying, including children who have it through no fault of their own. Therefore, in the name of common humanity, the forces of the Confederate Army Provisional have liberated the latest shipment intended for the NABP's racist misuse, and have distributed it to children who are HIV victims, and who otherwise would have no access to the urgently needed medicine and are in danger of developing full-blown AIDS..."

In related news, this latest American Civil War has given birth to a controversial and stubborn fashion fad throughout Europe; the wearing of tee shirts with images of Southern guerrilla leaders Frank Gore and Samantha Norris superimposed over a Confederate flag, along with gray military fatigue pants and combat boots. The clothing has sparked protests and some violence from immigrant groups in Europe, particularly in France and Great Britain, but its popularity still seems to be growing both east and west; almost a million have been sold in Russia alone.

If you live in the United States, though, you're out of luck. The American government has banned the shirt's importation. Some Americans have been making their own, blowing up the pictures of the originals from the internet, but the Attorney General has ordered the arrest of anyone caught wearing them, citing international laws against the piracy of intellectual property, which, in the US, carries a sentence of up to ten years in prison. One has to wonder, though, if that's the real reason..."

"Cynthia," her mother called from the foyer, "are you expecting a package? Some guy just dropped this off."

Cynthia Dover got up from the couch where she had been disinterestedly watching a distinctly un-funny TV sitcom and went to the front door. Her mother held a large box she had just signed for, and it was obvious from the woman's expression that it was fairly heavy. Cynthia helped her set it on the coffee table.

"Do you know someone named Rob?" her mother asked, looking at the label. "That's all it says on the return address."

Cynthia ignored her after hearing the name of the sender; she ignored everything but the box. At first she was almost too afraid of disappointment to touch it, but once she began, she tore at it so desperately and with such single-minded determination that Mrs. Dover became concerned. Opening the cardboard flaps, she saw bottle after labeled bottle of multi-colored pills, like miniature Christmas decorations. Her mother put on her glasses and began reading the names of the drugs aloud: "Sustiva, Viracept, Crixivan," and on and on, until both of them gasped as they realized just what they were looking at.

"I'm going to live, Mom," she said, her voice deceptively flat despite the tears of joy running down her face. "I'm really going to live."

Her mother was sobbing with relief too, as Cynthia pulled a card from the package. It had a cartoon on it, of a little yellow kitten with big eyes and a bandage on its paw, along with the words, "GET WELL SOON." She unfolded it to find it signed with the first name of her benefactor, along with "Frank", "Samantha" and "Kerrie."

"That's *them*, isn't it?" Her mother asked, looking at the names.

"Yeah Mom, that's them."

Her mother hugged her.

"Bless their hearts!"

"Damn it, Governor, you have to call out the National Guard!" Columbia Mayor Bill Sidler demanded, shouting into the phone. He was part of a four-way conference call between the mayor, Governor Jeffery Simms, Lieutenant Governor Barry Bender, and FEMA head Ronald Peters. "This thing is going to blow up, and we need to be ready when that happens."

"The Governor is not going to call up the National Guard, Mayor; I can't permit that."

136

Bender was almost begging, "Mr. Peters, at least let the Governor put them on alert in case we need them."

"It doesn't matter whether you need them or not; you're not calling them out. Period."

"Governor, talk to him!"

"I have," Simms said tiredly, defeat plain in his voice. He had obviously tried to deal with Peters before "It doesn't do any good."

The Lieutenant Governor was getting so frustrated that he was very close to losing control and throwing a genuine hissy-fit.

"By God, if you won't protect the people of Columbia, I will! I'll —"

"You'll do absolutely nothing!" Peters snapped suddenly, in a loss of temper that was completely out of character. "If you make an attempt to call out the National Guard, I'll Federalize them, countermand your order, and stick your ass so far back in a Federal prison they'll have to pump sunlight in to you! If you think I'm bullshitting you, then try me."

Bender was silent for a moment, struck by the normally laconic Peters' outburst. He knew the FEMA head's ruthless reputation well enough, however, to have no doubt he would carry out his threat.

"I guess my police will have to handle it," Sidler said with no hope in his voice. "I'll call SLED in and get every SWAT unit we can lay our hands on in position; maybe we can blunt it."

"There will be no shooting of African-Americans by the police, Mayor; save that for the terrorists."

"My men aren't savages, Mr. Peters. The won't fire unless fired upon.

"I don't give a damn if they're fired upon; there will be no shooting! If they're shot at, they can fall back and let the riot run its course."

"Why? Will you at least do me the courtesy of telling me why you are willing to sacrifice the lives of police officers and possibly even the Capital City like this?"

Peters regained control over himself, and his voice was back to its usual flat calm monotone.

137

"Because it's what the terrorists want. The concerns of Bessant and his African-Americans are a factor, sure. It will stir them up even more if you even put the Guard on alert, let alone bring them in or allow the police to shoot, but that's not the main reason.

"Like I've told the Governor before, sending uniformed troops against civilians at this time plays right into these neo-Confederates' paranoid fantasies. They'll immediately start shouting, 'See! See! We told you so!' and it will bring more credibility to their cause. That's not going to happen, not on my watch, whatever the cost."

"What if the cost is the City of Columbia?" Sidler asked quietly.

"As long as it's not at the hands of the terrorists, it's a price I'm willing to pay."

Besides, unless I miss my guess, it will finally draw them out where I can reach them! This will be too big for them to ignore.

Sam was on the speakerphone on so Frank could participate in the call with Jonathon Edge. Edge wasn't overly fond of the idea, but the Colonel had insisted that Frank was need to hear whatever the General had to say from his own lips as to the situation with the NABP in order to avoid any more 'misunderstandings'. Samantha was also there, waiting in silence and ready in case she was needed in her official capacity.

"I just heard from my contacts in the Columbia PD," Sam was saying. "They've got Federal paramilitaries from the FBI, BATF, Marshal's Service, and every other agency pouring in here."

Edge's voice was grim. "I'm betting it's not to deal with the riots either, is it?"

"No. It's to deal with us when we react to it. They know we won't sit by and let those NABP thugs destroy this city, and God knows how many of our people. The whole thing is a trap set just for us and they're using this riot as bait to draw us out."

Edge remained deep in thoughtful silence for so long, his friend finally asked him, "What are we going to do?"

"Nothing."

Frank's face showed no expression, but Sam was aghast.

"John, they're bussing niggers in for this thing from as far away as DC, including a whole bunch of Black Warrior Society radicals! The cops are estimating there may be as many as ten thousand converging on Columbia!"

"There aren't enough cops to deal with them, General," Frank broke in. "They'll destroy a substantial portion of this city. We haven't been able to come up with anything even resembling a workable plan, and we had hoped, with your greater experience, you might have an idea we can use to address this."

Frank and Sam had had a long conversation on the subject of Edge's suspicions earlier, and the Captain made the suggestion both as a genuine if somewhat forlorn hope, and also as a peace offering. He couldn't see any way they could confront the rioters with a bunch of Feds hoping they would do just that so they could swoop down on them. It was his last hope that the General might have an idea, and that, by deferring to him in that way, whether he could come up with something or not, he would see that Frank recognized both his capability and his authority.

Unfortunately, Edge didn't see it that way, and took umbrage at the situation. Phone lines can't equal face-to-face meetings, where you can watch and analyze the other person's expressions and body language. Without that, and only a disembodied voice distorted by the encryption and speaker phone to go on, he began to suspect that Frank knew as well as he did that nothing could be done, but had decided to make him look bad by asking for something he knew the General couldn't give. It took him a minute to get his anger under control, and a trace of it still showed in his voice.

"Captain Gore, how many men do you have? Maybe fifty tops? That's assuming you can get everybody there on such short notice, and we both know that's not going to happen. If it were just the NABP, I'd send you against them anyway, but I won't allow you to waste lives and other resources by throwing them into a no-win battle against hundreds of well-equipped Feds who are laying in wait expecting us to do exactly that."

Frank, sensing the cause of Edge's irritation, tried to mitigate things, opening his mouth to agree with him, telling him that those

139

were his thoughts exactly, but Sam interrupted and the opportunity passed.

"People are going to blame us! We brought this on them, and they'll expect us to fight!" Sam exclaimed.

"People in our position don't last long doing what anyone expects. You both know that."

"What about Columbia?"

Instead of answering, Edge asked a question. "Is anyone else there besides you two and the Communications Officer?"

All of them looked at each other, the surprise written large on their faces, and it was Sam that finally spoke. "Except for the Intelligence Officer who's filtering and disguising the call, that's it. How did you know she was here?"

"Because you wouldn't have allowed anyone else to be present, and if she wasn't there, you'd have been cussing by now.

"Lieutenant, in your professional judgment, what will be the public opinion towards the NABP if they severely damage Columbia? Locally in particular."

Samantha thought about it for a moment before answering, also taking the time in the process to insure she had control over her own voice. She loved her husband, and Edge's treatment of him rankled her to say the least. "They'll hate them, and it will increase the racial tensions already present, but –"

"I was thinking the same thing. Now if they were to do this and someone were to punish them for it later – do something major to them that could be seen or propagandized as punishment for those actions – how would the public respond?"

"Our constituency – the White Southern public – would be generally supportive, provided we play it right and they get the opportunity to hear our side."

"Thank you. That is the plan: do nothing. Keep your men clear of the whole thing."

"But –" Sam began.

"No buts; even if I was willing, there's no way we can stop this, so the best we can do is avenge it. This is for your ears only, but I already have a plan to do just that. When we do, it will dwarf

140

anything we could accomplish tomorrow by orders of magnitude. Lieutenant, I suggest you begin a propaganda campaign playing up the criminal actions of the NABP, to be released immediately after the riot is over, building up to the ultimate goal of justification of our future actions."

She agreed, and the three looked at one another, unsatisfied, but also having no logical argument to make against it.

"I'm sure that'll be a comfort to the people of Columbia," Sam observed quietly.

"Maybe it will make them get off their butts and fight for a change. It's their city too; let them stand up and do something for themselves."

There was still heat in Edge's voice, and Samantha decided to cut off that line of discussion before things could get out of hand.

"Sir, I have a suggestion. The domestic media is such that there will be little of propaganda value coming from them. If we want something we can use, we'll have to collect it ourselves. I propose we put as many of our people out there as possible with video cameras. They can capture the violence on film, and the odds are we can get enough to do more damage to them with the information than we could physically on such short notice."

"Excellent idea; get your people on it. One thing though: *none of you* – nor Lieutenants Richardson, Johnson, Dayton, Privates Waddell or O'Brien, nor anyone else who has been to your headquarters – is to be outside it during this riot. That's a direct order; it's too big of a risk if one of you should happen to be captured. Is that clear?"

He waited until he heard all of them assent verbally before he went any further.

"I know you all want to do something, but rest assured you are. By allowing this to happen, you are letting them weave the rope we will hang them with. Much of guerrilla warfare, particularly in the earliest stages, is theater. It's perception rather than power, and symbolism over substance. It is our skill at manipulating that perception that will eventually give us the power we need."

Sam hung up the phone.

141

"Shit! Sorry, Sammie, but just...shit!"

"Yeah," she said, thinking about the impending damage and deaths, "I know what you mean."

"Well," Frank told them, resignation heavy in his voice, "we have at least one consolation: he's right."

"What?" both of them exclaimed together.

"Does anybody have a better idea? Look, I'm willing to do whatever I can to help these people, but there is literally nothing we can do without destroying everything we've built here. We'd be accomplishing absolutely nothing besides dealing a heavy blow to the Confederate Cause ourselves by the resulting destruction of our resources. That's bigger than Columbia, or even South Carolina. It looks like this city's going to have to take one for the team.

"This time it's going to be up to the people to stand up on their hind legs and defend themselves. We'll do everything we can to alert them, and make sure they know what's coming. We'll try to stir them up, but in the end it's up to them. Maybe they *do* need to get bloodied a little in order to get them fired up enough to get behind us."

He looked to Sammie. "Either way, like both you and the General pointed out, the result will be the NABP alienating the people of Columbia; they'll even tick off at least some of the local colored population as well, because their homes and businesses will be damaged too. Even more importantly, they'll alienate every White law enforcement officer in South Carolina, giving us a wedge into their ranks, and giving us a leg up for recruitment of the most valuable members we could possibly get. Sam, you know yourself how valuable the ones are we already have inside the Columbia PD – even that degenerate Willie Duckett." Frank's voice was getting faster and becoming more excited as the plan continued forming even as he spoke; they could almost hear the pieces snapping together inside his head, *click, click, click,* one after another just like clockwork. "Now picture a sprinkling of *our* people, or at least our sympathizers, in SLED and in police departments and sheriffs' offices – and municipal and other political offices – all over this state, and think of the implications. Just as soon as this is over, if we

142

immediately begin recruiting efforts targeted in their direction while their dander is still up, well…"

Sam thoughtfully watched him from the corner of his eye. Frank had not only just taken their highest-ranking commander's plan – all they'd been given to work with – and made it better. He'd also extended it, beginning the process of extending the Confederate Army Provisional's presence into every corner of the Palmetto State, and taking the first step toward really consolidating their power here, a necessary step in winning this war. That was pretty impressive.

Considering the way Jonathon Edge viewed the ex-cop, it was also pretty scary, although when he really thought about it, Sam still wasn't sure to which one.

DAY 80

CHAPTER 11

"Gentlemen," Frank told the half-dozen men assembled in the martial arts studio. "I trust we're all wide awake now. It's my pleasure to be here. I wish it was under better circumstances, but then it's up to us to better our circumstances; they're not going to improve by themselves."

The men from Tommy's cell – Joel Harrison, Ralph Steiner, John Sergeant, Archie Baker, Tim Handley, and Randy Collins – sat in rapt attention. It spoke for their dedication that all of them braved the curfew to meet there within minutes of getting the middle of the night call. None of them, with the single exception of Harrison, had met him or Samantha more than once before, briefly during the O'Brien incident, and they were still a little star-struck, much to Frank's embarrassment. Even Harrison was somewhat awed by him, despite his sincere attempts to discourage such feelings.

Instead of using the handful of guest chairs, Frank gave his speech from the floor, kneeling on the mat in the traditional *seiza* posture common to most martial arts. In fact, he had already briefly worked out with them as the best way to get to know them, taking them through some calisthenics in order to get them awake and warmed up for the action to come. Contrary to his hopes of relaxing them by making them see he put his pants on the same way they did, it seemed to make them worship him even more.

If anything, Samantha, now kneeling beside her husband, was more taken aback by their adoration than Frank. Even though she had taken rape defense courses and Frank had been taking her through some very basic workouts the past few weeks to help her healing process along, she couldn't pretend, even to herself, to be anything more than the rankest amateur. It was uncomfortable for her to be put on a pedestal and treated like some sort of goddess by men much stronger and more skilled than she was likely to ever be.

145

Still, since it was really her first time 'out' of a safe house or transportation to or from one since her rescue, she made the most of it. She had swallowed the lingering pain of her injuries, sucked it up, and worked out with them, barely managing to keep up. She thought that would make them know she was only human, but they only idolized her all the more for it.

They're also a little afraid of you after your performance at the O'Brien house. They think you're crazy.

Maybe they're right.

"I hate to put you to work again this soon, before you've really gotten yourselves solidified as a unit," Frank continued, "but needs must when the devil drives.

"You all know what happened concerning the confiscation of the AIDS drugs from the NABP yesterday. You should, since you helped Lieutenant Johnson take them. This was a necessity to keep a Southern child alive, and I make no apologies for it.

"No apologies needed, sir," Harrison remarked. "That was a proud moment."

"Yes it was; however, that proud moment may have some serious consequences.

"As you know, James Bessant, the head of the South Carolina NABP, has threatened to 'take it to the streets' if the case was not solved by the Columbia PD within twenty four hours.

"That twenty-four hours is tomorrow – now today, only a few hours from now, and the NABP is going to make a move. They're going to have to, after they got their butts soundly kicked during the Capital Riot a couple of months back." The men grinned; all of them had been involved in the protest and subsequent violence. "If they don't make a push to reestablish themselves as a power now, after Bessant made his threat, they will lose all credibility.

"They're going to march in Columbia today, which might be no big deal except for the information that came in last night. Even as we speak, the NABP is bringing in several busloads of inner-city Negroes from as far away as DC, bringing the official expectation of their numbers up to between five and ten thousand strong. Further, at least fifty radical Black Warrior Society soldiers have already moved

146

into Columbia in anticipation of the event. Surprisingly, SLED showed some guts, put their foot down and has refused to let them openly carry their guns like they normally do at every protest, but these are still some bad boys. It's my opinion they intend to take Columbia apart.

"If they have their way this town is going to burn; it's going to be like the LA Riot back in the nineties. It will be fire and looting, rapes, beatings, and murders. Their marching route is going to take them right along the outskirts of some of the predominately White neighborhoods, and when they get there, if my guess is right, all hell is going to break loose. The police won't be able to even begin to handle it.

"Unless the Columbia PD picks up somebody at random and charges him with the theft in order to buy enough time for things to calm down it's going to hit the fan and hit it hard."

"Why haven't they done that – arrested some warm body to blunt their complaints?" Steiner asked. "They could always drop the charges and turn them loose later after things cooled down."

"They haven't done it for the same reason the Governor hasn't called out the National Guard. The local authorities are not in control; the Feds are. This riot is being allowed to go on because it's the bait in a trap that's set for us. Peters has moved hundreds of heavily armed Federal paramilitaries into Columbia, not to confront the rioters, but to take us down the instant we respond."

The men looked at one another, puzzled.

"Sir," Harrison was the one who finally asked, "how can we stop them then?"

Frank felt like hell about what he had to say, but he never let it show in his voice as he told them, "We can't. Not only do we not have the manpower, but we've received direct orders from General Edge to stay out of it and let it run its course." Seeing them all staring in shocked disbelief, he added, "Believe me, I don't like this anymore than you do. It was my job once to protect these people once, but we still have our orders."

"Sir, I can't believe we're expected to just sit here and do nothing."

147

"You won't be doing nothing. You've been assigned a vital mission." He glanced at his wife. "Samantha?"

Her own eyes were hard and more than a little angry, although it was less for the holocaust that might be coming to Columbia than towards their General for his attitude towards her husband and the position his orders had put Frank in, in spite of his agreeing with them. Every time she thought about Edge, it rankled her even more.

"We can't prevent this tragedy, so we might as well use it. I'm asking you to do something, rather than ordering it, because it will be extremely dangerous."

As hungry for action as they were, this got their undivided attention. Besides, whatever they thought of her mental state, all of them were a little bit in awe-struck love with her, and would have probably walked barefoot over hot coals if she were to ask.

"We are going to give the NABP a chance to exhaust any and all credit they may still have in the eyes of our people. In order to do that, we need to document their violence. I need volunteers to videotape the march and subsequent riot from various vantage points. I'm too well known or I'd go; besides, everyone from headquarters has been explicitly ordered not to take a physical role in this particular mission. General Edge thinks it's too big a risk if we're captured."

"What good will it do to take pictures of niggers chimping out?" one of them asked.

"The primary purpose is to use the images as propaganda, to drum up support amongst Southerners. Many will respond positively due to their anger and fear that it can happen to them, and some of them will make the emotional or intellectual leap that lets them finally choose our side."

"The people of Columbia are going to have to stand up and fight this time if they want to save their homes and businesses," Frank broke in. "In order to help them do that, hours ago our non-combat resources began quietly spreading the word amongst the ordinary citizenry in the path of the potential destruction. We're leafleting and we've got a sort of call chain going, alerting people to either prepare to fight or get out of the way.

148

"There is something else I need to tell you as well. This is classified and I won't go into details, but you have my word on this. Just because we have no choice but to let them run amuck for now due to the Federal presence, it doesn't mean that we will be letting them get by with it. This information you help gather will be useful once again when we justify our vengeance to the people. And as God is my witness, they will be avenged and the people will applaud us when we do it!"

The men looked into his cold gray eyes and nodded, content if not entirely satisfied.

Harrison suddenly began reciting a quote from Kipling.

"'They were not easily moved,

"They were icy – willing to wait,

"Till every count should be proved –"

"'Ere the Saxon began to hate.'" Frank finished for him. "Bingo."

"How's it look?" Harrison asked into the cell phone.

"Fine so far," Steiner's voice returned through the tiny speaker, "but the way they're hooting and hollering, they're working themselves up to it. I don't expect it to be long, either."

The two men, each with the two others they were in command of from Tommy's squad, were paralleling the NABP march a block away on either side of the route. Armed with video cameras – plus as few other things – they watched and waited, staying in communication with each other. As they proceeded along their respective areas, they noticed several people watching fearfully from their windows, and several more on their porches and out in their yards. The men noted with approval that most of those outside were men of varying ages, heavily armed with rifles and shotguns, as well as tools, lengths of chain, pickaxe handles, baseball bats, and at least one compound hunting bow. Others weren't staying at home, but were moving in the same direction as the squad, forming a loose, parallel counter parade on either side of the NABP along the still quiet back streets. These were mostly young men in their teens and twenties, primarily a mixture of local toughs, bikers, and skinheads,

149

along with a heavy sprinkling of country boys who had come to
town to do their part, or maybe just relieve their frustrations by
getting a chance to kick some ass. Still, for many of the crowd, even
though they had no homes in the potential path of destruction –
several were out on the street with no homes at all – they felt a duty
to protect those who did. They were operating out of a sense of
righteous anger, and that made them the most dangerous of all.
Having no reason to, they paid little attention to the slowly circling
helicopters overhead, watching and waiting.

The Dojo squad knew very well what the choppers were waiting
for however, and made it a point to shoot some footage of them.

"Here it comes!" Steiner suddenly shouted into the phone. "Gotta
go! Good luck!"

The breakout of the NABP march was sudden. No one ever
established the exact source of the spark that set it off, but, as if a
keg of powder had exploded, the noisy march broke instantly into a
full-scale riot. Led by the Black Warriors, the mob threw themselves
against the police line, several of them opening fire from concealed
weapons in the process. Despite FEMA's expressed desires to the
contrary, the cops, as frustrated as everyone else – maybe even more
so – immediately pulled their own side arms and returned fire, and
the air was filled with the popping of pistols and the scattered crack
of sniper rifles from the SWAT teams stationed on the rooftops.
Still, even though they got the worst of it, dozens of rioters broke
through the lines on either side. Glancing up the side street, Harrison
saw the mass moving their way, heading right towards them. Flames
shot up from the closest house to Main Street as a Molotov cocktail
shattered on its front porch.

The rising volume of shouting and gunfire echoed plainly as
Harrison raised both hands to his mouth in a makeshift megaphone
and addressed the loose crowd of Whites. "Get ready, boys!" he
shouted loudly enough that the other people on the street could hear
him. "They're coming!"

"So are we!" came a cry, followed by the roar of an engine and a
massed rebel yell. Harrison turned to look and saw a Battle Flag
flying from the antenna of bright red Dodge step-side pickup rolling

up the street, and picking up speed as it went. That wasn't all it was picking up; armed men threw themselves into the moving truck bed as it passed, while others jumped onto the bumpers and running boards. Within seconds it was full but more still scrambled aboard, climbing out onto the cab roof or precariously hanging onto each other. The driver kept the horn button mashed, and the tones of *Dixie* filled the air in a continuous rallying cry as the truck rumbled like a juggernaut towards the advancing rioters.

"I hope you got a shot of that license plate," Harrison told Tom Sergeant and Archie Baker, each of whom had their cameras glued to their eyes.

"Yeah, I think so," Sergeant replied. "Why?"

"Because I want to know who he is. After this is over, I want to recruit that son of a bitch! Let's go!"

He and the others quickly hurried after the truck, running along with the rest because there was no room on board.

Report by Sergeant Joel Harrison to Headquarters, Columbia Command, Confederate Army Provisional
Subject: Summary of squad accounts and video evidence

The NABP march remained relatively peaceful until they actually reached the capital grounds. As far as could be ascertained, following a speech by Bessant, he led the crowd in a series of chants that culminated with an attempt by the crowd to break the police lines along Main and Gervais Street. The police held for a few seconds, using clubs, teargas, and small arms, but their line quickly collapsed. Some of the Negroes stayed, battling with the police, but the rest of the rioters spilled out into surrounding neighborhoods (It was sometime during this process that Bessant and his entourage slipped away unseen.). The police eventually arrested or drove away the ones attacking them, shooting several (film #1), and clubbing many others so severely they had to be taken away by ambulance. (Films #1, 2, 5)

151

The rioters who escaped the area began overturning and burning cars, throwing rocks through windows, and setting fire to buildings. At this point the residents – mostly White – began responding with gunfire, and with direct hand-to-hand attacks with makeshift weapons. The gunfire was more or less continuous, and eventually the Negroes were forced to retreat, either scattering or moving back through the police lines. On a few occasions, the beleaguered police formed defacto temporary alliances with White civilian forces to drive the rioters from the streets (film #1). At least one rioter was captured and hanged from a streetlight by residents (films #3, 4).

At each outbreak of fighting, Federal paramilitaries immediately arrived on the scene and began arresting any armed Whites in the area (films #1, 2, 4); however, in at least one case the Whites resisted with force, and were shot (film #5, shot from concealment beneath a residential front porch). All bodies and prisoners were taken away immediately in unmarked vans (films #2, 4, 5). The Federal forces finally pulled back, however, because the NABP rioters targeted them too, and there was considerable fighting between to two groups, with the Federal forces firing on the Negroes and killing and wounding several. Those casualties were also taken away (film #4).

Although we attempted to avoid conflict as ordered, each of our sections was forced to defend themselves on multiple occasions, but the entire squad escaped arrest and serious injury and reported in a timely manner to the rendezvous point.

Network News Broadcast
USA

An NABP civil rights march in Columbia, South Carolina turned violent today, leaving over forty people dead and two hundred-fifty wounded, mostly African Americans.

Angered by the theft of HIV drugs needed to treat their people, the Reverend James Bessant led almost ten thousand of his organization up Columbia's Main Street today in a march to the Capital. That march was interrupted by White extremists, and when

152

the two sides collided, the civil rights marchers were met with knives, baseball bats, gunfire and even reported lynchings...

Russian Press Report, English Edition

The American city of Columbia, South Carolina, was rocked by heavy rioting today. A demonstration by several thousand American Negroes quickly turned violent when they began vandalizing, looting, and burning a large portion of the business district near the Capital. Riot police were unable to contain the situation with clubs and tear gas, and pitched battles erupted all along the line of march that included scattered gunfire.

In the surrounding neighborhoods, however, it was a different story. Our sources tell us that last night, Confederate Army Provisional guerrillas quietly passed the word to the local people to either evacuate or be ready to fight, and many of them chose the latter. There are a large number of registered firearms in the city, and many more illegal ones, and it was with these and other makeshift weapons the citizens confronted the rioters. The South Carolina law enforcement sources tell us that there are fifty-three confirmed dead and over two hundred fifty wounded, the majority by gunshots. The police officially deny that they fired any live rounds, but witnesses report that several police officers, sometimes in an alliance with White vigilantes, did exactly that. Black uniformed Federal paramilitary forces also entered the melee, rappelling from helicopters and firing on Blacks and Whites alike, then taking away the bodies. Our reporter on the scene, Sasha Hyrchenko, was given this exclusive footage taken by civilians in the area...

"Damn you, Perkins, what the hell were you trying to do? I gave specific orders that there was to be *no* gunfire from the police; now look at this mess!"

Chief Perkins cringed back in his seat before the seething FEMA head, who had lost all of his usual calm demeanor. Peters was so angry he hadn't even summoned the Columbia Police Chief as he usually did; instead, he had barged into Perkins' office and confronted him there, leaning his fists on his desk and screaming in his face, spraying him with a faint mist of saliva in the process.

"Sir, I'm only in charge of the Columbia PD; I have no control over the actions of either the Sheriff's Department, the State Police, or SLED, and especially not over the Federal forces you brought in. You'll have to talk to them."

"Don't you tell me what I have to do, you fat, stupid son of a bitch! *You* were in overall command of the scene, and that makes it your responsibility! Now why the hell did they fire?"

"Because they were being shot at, sir."

"They had their orders !"

"Sir," Perkins began, doing his best to control his voice, "you didn't give me any orders. You never even spoke to me at all on the subject; instead, I received my instructions from Mayor Sidler telling us specifically not to fire unless fired upon. Those are the orders I relayed, and the orders my officers acted under. Besides, when someone is shooting at you, you don't care who ordered what; you shoot back to stay alive and keep your buddies alive. It wouldn't matter if the President of the United States came down here and personally ordered it himself; it's too much to expect people to die for an order."

Ronald Peters rocked back, momentarily stunned that the Mayor would change his orders, but even more so that the Chief would dare bring up the President, which he took to be a not-too-thinly-veiled dig to remind the FEMA boss that he had someone over him too, someone who would not be at all pleased with today's actions.

"Damn you, you piece of shit!" he hissed. "I know what you're thinking! You think I'm on my way out! Well, you get this and get it good; if I go, I'll take you down with me! Do you understand me? Nothing and nobody will protect you, and you'll be a dead man before I leave Columbia!"

Big Jim Perkins simply nodded, his shoulders slumped. He had understood that for a long time.

DAY 82

CHAPTER 12

"What are you trying to tell me, Jerry?"

Jerry Garvey's bland Midwestern voice on the other end of the
phone line was tense and a little higher pitched than usual; nobody
liked being the one to give the boss bad news, even a former boss
like Ronald Peters...*especially* like Ronald Peters. Garvey had
worked in for FEMA for years, even before it had been transferred to
the auspices of Homeland Security. Although they were not exactly
friends, he had associated with Peters off and on in their professional
capacities long enough for the two to have repeatedly played the
'you scratch my back and I'll scratch yours' game. He was talking to
him now from the Charleston Naval Base where they had taken the
suspected CAP members captured during the NABP riot. He knew
the writing was already on the wall as far as Peters was concerned,
and, barring a miracle, there was better than a ninety percent chance
that the South Carolina FEMA head was done for. Still, it cost him
nothing to deliver a warning, and if Peters somehow managed to
survive, he would owe Garvey a favor. Peters had been known to
pull some slick rabbits out of his hat before, so maybe he would this
time. At least, Garvey's current position as HS liaison to the military
interrogators involved in this job gave him the opportunity to take a
low risk gamble at potentially profitable long-shot odds.

"First, our Federal assets screwed up royally when they got
themselves in the position where they had to fire on the rioters.
CAP's propaganda people have had a field day with it. They added
that footage to that of the South Carolina law enforcement elements
doing the same thing, spliced it all together to make it look like we
were fighting the Blacks instead of the rebels, and gave it through
cutouts to a bunch of African American activist websites. There are
sympathy protests going on in half a dozen cities already, and they
broken into minor riots in Los Angeles and Cincinnati. We're trying

to keep it quiet, but the press – especially on the Internet – is blasting the stuff all over."

"Still," Peters ventured hopefully, "if we can get some good information from the suspects we captured, it'll be worth it."

"I was coming to that. I've just spoken to a friend in the Department of Defense. Basically, it's the opinion of the interrogators that all we currently have in custody is nothing more than a bunch of violent rednecks. We've questioned them and checked the records; none of them have ever been more than peripherally involved in the Southern Nationalist Movement if at all, and those only in very minor roles. None of them are known CAP associates. In addition to background checks, we've used both intensive interrogation techniques and chemical persuasion, and there have been no results: zip, zero, nada. They simply don't know anything."

Peters pushed his glasses up and pinched the bridge of his nose with his thumb and forefinger. He felt a headache coming on as Garvey continued.

"Also, I think you ought to be aware that news of their imprisonment has already become public. Several writs have been filed with the Federal Courts, as the families have been ignoring Homeland Security gag orders, and have spread the word too far for there to be any hope of containing it now. It seems that one of those arrested was the son of the Democratic Senator Ed Newman of North Carolina, and he publicly brought the matter to the Senate floor live on C-Span before anyone realized just what he was doing. Reporters and protestors are camped out around the Justice Department. The Secretary of Homeland Defense and the Attorney General are both in a meeting in the Oval Office at this time, and it is believed that the riot and subsequent imprisonments are the subject. I just thought you should know."

"Thank you," Peters said quietly, trying to figure out how to pick up the pieces that were rapidly falling apart around him. He instinctively knew things were going to get worse, although at the moment he couldn't see just how that could happen. There was only one thing that could save him now, and that would be to take down

Frank Gore and the rest of CAP in the Palmetto State. If he could manage that, all sins would be forgiven and he'd come out smelling like a rose. He had another plan already in the works to do just that, which meant he still had a chance.

Frank looked the man over carefully as the stranger sat on the motel bed. His guest didn't look back; he was blindfolded and shaking with overwrought nerves from the process of being stripped, scanned, and generally manhandled, as well as from fear of the man he had been brought to see. Nodding at Harrison and his men, their Captain told them to leave the room.

"You can take off the blindfold now, Mayor."

Bill Sidler's hands shook as he fumbled with the gauze pads taped over his eyes, and he ended up dropping the wraparound sunglasses that had concealed them in the floor. Flinching, he looked up at Frank as if he feared the CAP leader might hit him.

"Relax; I'm not going to hurt you. Remember, you came to me."

Sidler nodded jerkily. He had indeed come to Frank, and expended a lot of effort in the process. It had taken trusting his 'crazy' uncle – the family conspiracy theorist – with the information that he wanted a one-on-one with the infamous Frank Gore. He had guessed right; the relative had passed the information along, and the CAP elements who contacted him had played a game of phone tag, running him all over Columbia for most of the day before finally picking him up in the men's room of a strip club just outside of town. They taped the pads over his eyes then and concealed them with the sunglasses as they led him out through the back exit. Once inside a vehicle – it had to have been a van or an RV as it was too roomy for anything else – he had been stripped naked, scanned, and redressed in a second set of clothes before being transferred to yet another vehicle. This one drove him around for what seemed like hours before taking him to a motel. Now, in the room with the curtains pulled, he had no idea where he was except in way over his head.

"Would you like a cup of coffee?"

Sidler, thinking he was nervous enough already, started to refuse but then thought better of it, out of fear of offending Gore. Frank poured the cups and handed him one with no expression.

"So, what's on your mind?"

"I need your help."

Frank had been hoping for something like this – praying for it even, but he still approached the situation cautiously. Besides, considering some of the things his administration had been involved in, the mayor of Columbia wasn't exactly his favorite politician.

"Why me? I'm a '*terrorist*', remember?" he pointed out, raising his hands to either temple and crooking his index fingers like devil horns.

"I'm sorry I said that in my speech! Please! I-I didn't know then."

Frank picked up his cup and took a sip of coffee.

"So what's changed your mind?"

"I don't know that my mind has changed," he said tentatively, looking at the impassive guerrilla leader with dread in his eyes, "but the situation has changed. You're the only one who can help me, and I don't care what you are anymore."

"Fair enough; what do you want?"

Sidler swallowed hard, absolutely terrified at the offer he was about to make, and even more terrified if he didn't make it.

"I want you to take my family – my wife and two children."

"What do you mean, *take them*? Take them where?"

"Hide them, shelter them, please! Look, I know you've got an underground – you'd have to have. Put them there."

Frank was more than a little surprised, and it showed in his voice.

"Why do you want to give your family to me?"

"Because it's the only way I can keep them safe!" he said with a loud sob before putting his head in his hands, his shoulders shaking.

"Safe from who? We're not the type to go after families; if we don't like you, we'll come see *you*, not your wife and kids. You'd don't have to worry about that."

"I-I know that. The thing is, Peters *is* the type!"

158

"Peters?"

Sidler nodded before raising his tear-filled eyes. "He threatened my family, Captain Gore. Because I went against him and gave orders that my officers could return fire if fired upon during the NABP riot, he threatened my wife and children. He swore, if I ever bucked him again, he would make all of us disappear, secretly arresting us as terrorists. He promised he'd make me watch while the-the soldiers tortured and raped my wife and children, just like they did to those poor people in Iraq!

"He's got the power of the Federal Government behind him, and there's no place I can hide them where he can't reach them! He's already told me he put us all on the no-fly list, so I can't even get them out of the country." Sidler was crying out loud now.

"You're the only one I've got left to turn to. I either sacrifice the people and this city to his whims, or else I sacrifice my family. I know I took an oath to this city, but I can't do that to my wife and children, Captain! I can't!"

Frank handed him the box of tissues from the dresser before speaking again. If it were possible, the mayor's revelations made him hate Ronald Peters even more, but he couldn't deny that the Fed's actions had just inadvertently given him the greatest opportunity to fall in his lap since the hostilities began. He also knew the need for secrecy, and silently thanked God he had made the squad leave the room.

"You may not have to. We can do this, Mayor; We have more than sufficient infrastructure get your family to a safe place and see to it that they're well taken care of."

"Thank you, Captain Gore!" Sidler exclaimed, grasping his hand in desperate gratitude. "Thank you!"

Frank pulled his hand away. Although he wanted the advantage Sidler's defection would give, and felt for the man's family, his desperate enemy needed to understand a few things. First among them was not to take the Confederate Army Provisional – or Frank Gore – for granted. As someone under duress, not a true volunteer, and not dedicated to the dream of Southern independence, he had to be taught there would be a stick to go with this carrot.

159

"Before you thank me, there're a few things you need to know. I said we could; I didn't say we would. Your administration has caused more than a little damage to the people of this city as well as to us. As the one in charge, even if you weren't directly involved, you also bear a part of the responsibility for helping to railroad both my wife and myself for crimes we never committed. I'm certain you know what the end result of that was for her." Sidler began to open his mouth, but Frank kept going, cutting him off. "Don't worry; the Cause means more than my personal feelings, and I'm willing to do this for that Cause, not for you. Of course, that means there are some things you *will* give me in return."

"Of course...anything! What do you want?"

"First, the secrecy of this agreement has to be absolute – no exceptions – and once your family goes into our underground, they won't be coming back until *I* decide it's safe to let them go. You want them to live as normal lives as possible, not to be locked up like prisoners with masked jailers. In order to do that, I'll have to place them with a supporting family in a safe house, probably in another state. To let them go back before time would be to compromise the security of the host family, something I wouldn't do anymore than I'd compromise the security of yours. I'll see to it you all can get some communications back and forth, but it may be a while before you physically see them again. Do you understand?"

"Yes sir, I understand. I'll miss them, but I want them safe."

Frank nodded. "The second thing is this; I know politicians tend to change with the wind, but there will be no change in this case. Merely by approaching me today, let alone having my people shelter your family, you became part of *us*, of the Southern Independence Movement. You betrayed the Feds just by coming here and conspiring with me, and if you think Peters was upset with you before, think what he would do if he found out about our little meeting right now." The mayor paled. "Just so you know, I've been recording this conversation. If you decide to betray us or change your mind and refuse to cooperate, we won't have to kill you. We will we simply cease to shelter your family, and then I will see to it Peters or whatever Fed is in charge gets a personal copy of this tape, along with a breakdown of everything you've done for us up to that point. I don't think I need to elaborate on what will happen after that. Understand this: from the time you walked in that door, there was no going back – *ever*! Do I make myself clear?"

"Yes sir," he gulped.

"I know you don't believe in what we stand for, but you no longer have any choice. That means, while you return to your office and carry on your work as Mayor, you'll obey my instructions to the letter when you get them. I think you'll find me much easier to get along with than FEMA."

"What do you want me to do?"

"For one thing, I want to know everything you know about what law enforcement is up to, and especially what Ronald Peters is up to. I want to know when he comes and goes and where. Secondly, I want to know the names of anyone you know, in office, or out of it, who even remotely shows any sympathy for us. Thirdly, I want continuously updated information on anything else that might be of interest, along with the passwords that will allow us access into your computer system. You are now our agent on the inside. Occasionally we'll ask you to do something for us – and you *will* do it – but for the most part, other than relaying information, your participation will be passive. Just keep on doing what you've been doing: fulfill the office of mayor, see to the needs of the people of Columbia, and do what FEMA tells you. Say and do the same things you always do unless *we* tell you differently.

"Do we have a deal?"

"Deal," the Mayor said, "and thank you!"

"You're welcome," Frank told him, and it was the absolute truth.

You're very welcome indeed, because the consolidation of Confederate power in South Carolina has now begun!

DAY 83

CHAPTER 13

"So, Frank, how are you doing?" Neil Larson asked, setting down the bottle of Tennessee whiskey and handing his guest one of the two glasses he had just poured. The newest Councilman had abruptly appeared at one of their safe houses on the outskirts of Columbia and had requested that Captain Gore meet with him. Frank complied, using Tommy's squad for backup. Even as he spoke with the Councilman, Harrison and the rest were scattered around the immediate vicinity, armed to the teeth and ready to respond, in case of Federal attack…or anything else. As a matter of survival, Frank, like most in the movement, had developed a healthy sense of caution, and he took measures to help insure his safety in any unexpected situation, especially those where the enemy might be on either side.

Frank took a sip of the golden liquor.

"I'm fine, sir; and yourself?"

"Great. Sit down; take a load off. How's Samantha getting along? I hope she's recovering."

"She's better," Frank told him as they eased into the upholstered chairs. "She's still got a ways to go yet though."

"Is there anything I can do to help? Does she need medicine, a regular doctor, psychologist, whatever? I don't have to tell you that lady has been through a lot on our behalf, and I speak for the entire Council when I say we'll see to it she gets whatever she may need. All you've got to do is ask and it's yours."

Frank thanked him, but told him, for the moment, it might be best to let her work it out.

She's already sure I think she's crazy. If I bring in a shrink it'll confirm her suspicions, and I don't think that would be a good idea just now.

If things got much worse he wouldn't rule it out either.

Neil had his own sources of information and accurately guessed at Frank's train of thought. He nodded understandingly and took a sip from his glass.

"Ahh! Nothing like good sour mash, is there?"

"No sir. Thank you; I know this stuff doesn't come cheap anymore, when you can find it at all."

"You're welcome. Don't worry, I've got my sources."

I'll bet you do. I'd also bet you didn't call me in here just to say 'hi,' ask about Sammie, and drink whiskey.

Frank had never imagined the games involved in the struggles for power *within* a revolutionary movement, but out of necessity he became a fast learner. He knew Jonathon Edge wasn't the only one who wanted to lead the movement; Larson, MacFie, and Herdman all looked wistfully – and enviously – at the commander's chair. The latter two weren't the type to do anything too overt, but Neil Larson was a different animal all together: a man prone to action, as dedicated, ruthless and scheming as Edge, and every bit as ambitious. Frank had sensed almost as much as heard the faint rumors and rumblings of conspiracies afoot, and such things didn't bode well either for the Cause or for those beneath who might be caught between the ones struggling for power. It didn't surprise him. From what he had learned since he joined, the standard operating procedure within the Southern Movement for decades, long before the first shot was fired at Columbia, included shifting alliances, backroom deals, backstabbing, and egos run amok. The whole situation angered and disgusted him, but he kept a polite façade, never letting his true feelings show on his face. He also kept one hand near his pager button that would instantly summon Tommy and the others, and they would come in rolling hot and shoot the hell out of anything that might conceivably be a threat. If they didn't arrive in time, well, his pager was clipped to his belt next to the snub-nosed Smith & Wesson .38 he had borrowed from Tommy, and now carried tucked inside his shirt and loaded with Black Talon hollow points.

Neil Larson studied him just as carefully, in the process making the same mistake a lot of people made about Frank Gore. He knew

Frank was highly intelligent, but took his quiet, unassuming politeness as an indication of naivety and a lack of cunning. Nothing could have been further from the truth.

Unbeknownst to anyone else, Frank had quietly but very determinedly made it his business to find out everything he could about everyone around him, both up and down the chain of command, along with their mercurial relationships with each other, and filed it away in his head for future reference. He figured that, just like Edge, Larson was up to something because that was his nature.

Now if I can just figure out what...

"I suppose you're wondering why I wanted to meet with you."

"Yes, sir, that did cross my mind."

"Frank, you're the single most valuable asset this movement has right now – no exceptions."

"Mr. Larson, you're exaggerating. I'm only one soldier in one state, just doing my job."

"Hah! I'm not exaggerating one bit, and you're way more than just another soldier. In the eyes of the people, you and Samantha – but you in particular – *are* the face of the movement. You're the first one they think of whenever CAP is mentioned.

"No, don't deny it. I know it may not be entirely true, but that's the way it's perceived, and in politics, perception is everything. My point is that you're indispensable. We need you, Frank, and what's more I like you. I don't want to see anything happen to you."

Frank pursed his lips. *Now that's interesting.*

"Sir, do you know something I don't?"

Larson heaved a sigh. "I don't know for sure, but I'm afraid you may be being set up for the kill. How well do you know Jonathon Edge?"

"I've worked with him a few times in the past couple of months," he answered, keeping his voice carefully neutral.

"Very diplomatically put, son; however this is no time for diplomacy. Correct me if I'm wrong, but Edge is egotistical and extremely ambitious. Am I lying?"

"No sir, I can't say you're lying."

165

"Good – that shows you've got some sense about you at least. Now like I said, Edge is egotistical and ambitious, so much so that he already sees himself as the President of the Confederacy, and he'll walk over top of anyone he needs to in order to get there. He'll also destroy anyone he perceives as a threat." He pointed a finger at the younger man. "That's you, Frank, you're the threat: you, Richardson…and Samantha. You're all in danger of taking a bad fall."

Frank was shocked – shocked and furious, particularly since his wife had been mentioned in that regard, yet despite his anger and sense of betrayal, something deep inside nagged at him. Was it that the dramatic pause in the Councilman's voice before mentioning Sammie's name was a split second too drawn out, or was it something in his eyes or the way he held his head? His cop's instinct insisted Larson wasn't telling him the whole truth, but despite that, something else – his common sense – also told him not to discount the information out of hand. Besides, with their lives at stake – Sammie's in particular – he couldn't afford to.

Just make sure before you act!

"How and when is this going to happen?"

Larson smiled inwardly at the dark, grim expression on Frank's face and the cold tone in his voice. "I don't know yet, but I do believe it's coming. Edge isn't the only one who has spies; the Council has our own, and some of those are very close to him. They don't have the proof – not yet – but they estimate an 80-90% probability that he's going to make a move soon, within the next few weeks, or months at the outside."

"Why?"

"Because you're a threat to his authority and ambitions. You and Richardson defied him; the way I heard the story, you even threatened to shoot him. Is that right?"

"Yes, but we had to rescue Sammie, Billy and the others. We weren't going to let him or anything else stop us. Besides, it was that operation that finally put him exactly where he wanted to be – in charge."

166

"That doesn't matter to a man like that; all that matters is you mutinied. You refused to obey his orders and not only got by with it, but came out smelling like a rose and displacing him in most people's eyes as the real power in the movement. Whenever CAP in mentioned, you're the one they talk about. He'll never forget that, and he'll never forgive it. You'd have been better off to have gone ahead and shot him then and there, because now he's looking for a chance to nail you."

"Okay, I can understand that, but for God's sake, why Sammie?"

"I know a little bit about your wife too, Frank. I've seen her look at you and heard her talk about you; it's like her face lights up whenever she says your name. She loves you, son. Ask yourself this: do you think she would just shrug it off and go on working for Edge if she ever found out he had arranged for you to have a little 'accident,' let alone if he does something overt?"

Frank shook his head. He knew Sammie; she would kill Edge, or at least try too.

"I think you're beginning to understand. She becomes a potential threat if you're eliminated, and Edge won't tolerate that, particularly since he won't have to, because *you* won't be there to protect her. You'll already be dead."

Keeping his own face carefully sympathetic, Larson gleefully laughed on the inside as he watched his guest's features writhe with emotion. This was going just like he'd planned.

Finally, Frank spoke "So, what do you suggest?"

He'd have to move carefully here. Just enough bait, but not too much…

Neil Larson spread his hands, palms up. "First watch your back, and when you can't do it, make sure your men do it for you. I recruited every last one of them myself, and they're damned good men. Get their loyalty, Frank, and they'll protect you if they can. We in the Council will do whatever we can do from here, and as soon as we get any relevant information, you'll have it. Talk to Samantha, and to the biker – Lieutenant Richardson – because his ass is on the line too. Just watch yourself, and be prepared for anything at anytime.

167

"As to what else you can do, I don't know; that's an judgment *you're* going to have to make. I've quietly spoken to the rest of the Council about this situation. We can't overtly take a side because we don't have the power to take a solo or even a unified stand against Jonathon Edge at this time; he holds the cards *and* the guns. However, if there's a problem, we'll back you in any conflict between you two that comes before us, or in any...*decision* you feel compelled to make. If we're ever going to have the independence we need, we need to move the control of this organization out of the hands of one man and back into those of the Council. Do you understand what I'm saying?"

Frank nodded, and finished the whiskey at a gulp. Leaning forward, he set the empty glass on the table as he locked eyes with his host.

"Let me ask you this; where does Sam Wirtz's loyalty lie: with the movement or with Edge?"

"I wish I could tell you," Larson said carefully. This was another pivotal point, and too much pushing would raise Frank's suspicions and upset the whole apple cart. "I really wish I could, but I'm just not sure. I do know this; he's been Edge's best friend for years, but..." He shrugged. "I don't know. You just think carefully about what I told you, and you be damned sure you keep an eye on your wife so nothing happens to her."

After closing the door behind him, Frank leaned against it for a moment with his eyes closed, sorting his thoughts. Abruptly he straightened and walked out with a deliberate step.

Alone again, Neil Larson smiled broadly; he had just taken the first step towards implementing his plan of securing control of the movement. It had to be done if they were going to get anywhere. Besides simply wanting the leadership for himself, he honestly believed he could do a better job. He felt that Edge was too cautious, too slow in escalating the conflict, too unwilling to gamble on an all or nothing roll of the dice: problems Neil Larson had never had.

The best part of the whole thing was that he had subtly spun the truth rather than lied, because he was reasonably sure everything he told Frank would, in fact, come to pass. He was so certain because, if it wasn't actually in the works already, he intended to make it happen. He had given the first nudge to set the ball rolling. He'd planted a seed in Frank, and Edge's paranoia would water it for him. Larson knew Edge because, despite their differing command styles, they were of a type, and he knew that the 'Field Marshal' would have people keeping a close eye on the newest Councilman, because that's what he would do the same in that position. It wouldn't be long before Edge got wind that he and Frank Gore had a little one-on-one meeting, especially since Larson had intentionally chosen a safe house owned by a man he suspected to be one of Edge's spies. He would put what would appear to be two and two together, and then the feces would impact the rotary oscillator with substantial force. For all he knew Edge might actually try to terminate Frank, or might already be tentatively planning it anyway; he knew he would have, if he was in the Virginian's boat. Only now, Frank would be ready and on guard, and if Edge tried anything – or if the ex-cop even *thought* he was getting ready to – well, Neil had made it a point of be familiar with both men's reputations, and, while the General was good, he gave Frank a definite edge in any contest between him and his commander.

Of course, he had given the ex-cop another edge too, although Captain Gore didn't know it. He had already spoken to some of the members of his former militia and briefed them on what he wanted them to know about the situation. He knew they would still have some loyalty to him, even if they were under Frank's command. They would be watching, and they would immediately kill Edge to protect their new commander during any confrontation, and swear the General was getting ready to fire on Gore. They'd be convincing about it too, because they'd believe it themselves, since Neil had warned them Edge was planning to do exactly that.

He really hoped Frank won. Not only because he genuinely liked the movement's reluctant 'superstar' – although Larson wasn't one to let his personal feelings interfere with his plans – but because he was a combination of ideal factors necessary to further both the Cause and the Councilman's agenda; he was a necessary element towards winning this war. Frank was skilled, dedicated and famous

169

enough to do Edge's job satisfactorily if not quite as well, but most importantly he lacked the consuming ambition that made Edge so dangerous. He also lacked Edge's political experience and savvy, and would thus be a much more malleable element to deal with.

Besides, if things went like he planned, Frank Gore would owe *him* big time, and Larson knew the Captain was a man who took his debts seriously.

Even if Edge did manage to kill Frank, Larson intended to simply kill him in turn without the slightest warning. Executing the assassin of Frank Gore would make him a hero in the eyes of the movement, and would put Frank's equally famous wife definitively in his corner, perfect for a figurehead, and one still leaving him in control.

It could still fail, of course; Edge might manage to get the drop on him or even send an assassin after him. Larson shrugged; that would be inconvenient certainly, but he'd be almost sure to get word of such a plan on Edge's part first, and, after warning the rest of the Council that Edge had gone nuts and was purging his enemies, Larson would ambush him and terminate him. With Edge's reputation and pain-in-the-ass attitude, the rest of the Council would thank him for it, and be psychologically in his debt. It looked like a win-win situation.

Best of all, if he had it figured right, the only man who might be able to stop it would be cut right out of the loop.

"Dr. MacFie, Mr. Herdman, thank you for coming." Larson gestured towards a pair of chairs on the opposite side of the table. "Please make yourselves at home."

The two Council members sat down in the same safe house dining room Frank had occupied only hours earlier, eying their host warily. The three made a study in contrasts: Larson was of medium height, dark and wiry, MacFie short, gray-bearded and pot-bellied, and Herdman, tall, blonde and soft, with a typical businessman's middle age spread. Both the newcomers had been enemies of Larson's in the early days of the Southern Nationalist Movement

170

long before the current military conflict began, and none of them was about the trust the other.

"Where's Nash?" the always irritable MacFie grumbled, inquiring about the Council Chairman.

"Mr. Nash was not invited to this session. Before I talk to him, I wanted to have a little get-together with you two to discuss our mutual problem child."

Herdman looked at him innocently. "Exactly who do you mean, Mr. Larson?"

"Don't be coy. You know damned well who I mean – Jonathon Edge." The personality the former militia commander showed to these two was entirely different from the one he had unveiled for Frank. Neil was a big believer in adaptation.

Dr. MacFie snorted in disgust. He despised Larson, but he hated the General even more, not least because he saw him as the only real obstacle to his own total leadership over the movement, and because Edge had forced his compliance with direct threats.

"What's to discuss? That bastard has us over a barrel. He's the one in charge of the people with the guns, which means, even if we didn't owe him for saving us, he has the real power. Every one of us is facing a death sentence if this thing fails and we're caught by the Feds, so we don't even dare divide the movement by opposing him, because such a division would insure exactly that end result. Right now, he holds all the cards."

Without asking, Larson reached behind him to a sideboard and set three shot glasses on the table, filling them from the same bottle of expensive whiskey he had drank from with Frank.

"Gentlemen, lets not play games. The fact that you owe him doesn't mean jack shit to either one of you. You know it and I know it, so lets not waste time pretending otherwise." He ignored their shocked, guilty looks and went on. "All that matters is the meat of this situation. Edge is a tyrant, and even if we win, he'll still be in charge, this time as President of the Confederacy. And if he achieves *that* position, I doubt he'll ever surrender it during his lifetime. Do either of you disagree with that analysis?"

171

He waited until they shook their heads before he continued. "What if I told you the Field Marshal can be seamlessly replaced by someone who would, in my estimation, prove much more tractable and accommodating, and every bit as capable?"

Herdman leaned forward, a hopeful gleam in his eye, and even the professor dropped his normal sarcasm to stare in interest. "Who do you have in mind?"

"The one man who would not only make a much better *figurehead,*" he said, and they didn't fail to catch the deliberate inflection of the word, "but the one who has already displaced Edge in the affection and loyalty both of the men and of the supporting public. I'm talking about Frank Gore."

"Gore!" they both said at once, their mixed emotions evident in their voices. Both of them recognized the ex-cop's value and competence, and both liked him well enough on a personal level, but they also had more than a twinge of jealously regarding his fame, and that of his wife Samantha. MacFie and Herdman had labored, fought, maneuvered, and schemed for years chasing after dominance in the Southern Movement, and now when the movement was mentioned, the first name on everyone's lips was that of the newcomer, Frank Gore. Not only was his the top name, but he and Samantha had become virtual folk heroes to millions of the dissatisfied both North and South, while the other members of the Southern Council were regulated to the "Oh yeah, them too" category. It didn't set too well.

Larson spread his hands. "Look at it this way: you know both of them; which one would you rather deal with?"

The two looked at each other. The answer was so obvious it didn't need to be said aloud.

It was MacFie who broke the silence, after first lubricating his throat with another sip of the fiery liquid. "What makes you think he can be manipulated?"

"He's an idealist for one thing, and he's loyal to a fault for another. We play on those two things, and as long as we don't make it obvious, he'll dance to our tune like a monkey on a stick.

"Even more importantly, he's not ambitious. He doesn't even want the position he's in, meaning not only do we not have to worry about him grabbing power or taking over, but he's respectful of our authority. As long as we approach him right, he'll do what we tell him, which is a damned sight more than what we have with Edge."

Herdman looked thoughtfully at the tabletop.

"You know," he said, hope rising in his voice, "it just might work. But what do we do with Edge? I mean, he's not the type to just go away quietly, and we can't afford a public spectacle."

"I already have the answer," Larson told them, smiling for the first time since the conversation began, "one of the oldest principles in the world: divide and conquer. My sources tell me there is already considerable tension between Edge and Gore. He stood up to Edge and forced him to rescue you when our General would have left you both to rot," he said, reinforcing their opinion of both men while leaving out the fact that the only people Frank was really interested in rescuing was his wife and Tommy's biker buddy, Billy Sprouse, "and besides which, Edge is as jealous over his fame as any one of us. We just do what we can to help those feelings along and exacerbate them, and nature will take its course. I began that process earlier today."

He filled them in on the gist of his meeting with Frank.

"Knowing Edge, I suspect he will try to kill Gore; however, Frank is an extremely capable man, and is now forewarned, plus he is in extreme fear for his wife's life. If he's as good a man as I think he is, Edge will cease to be a problem if he even hints at making a move. If that happens, I believe that Frank Gore will deserve the gratitude of every man in this room: a gratitude best expressed by appointing him to Edge's position."

MacFie shifted his weight uncomfortably. An inveterate schemer himself, he was surprised by Neil Larson's subtly. He also saw other possibilities that were less pleasant.

"What if he fails, and it turns out the other way, with Edge coming out on top?"

Larson deliberately leaned forward and tented his fingers. "Julius Caesar was killed on the Senate floor by the Senators themselves,

173

and I've found that history can repeat itself quite handily. Besides, if he murders the man who has become the very symbol of the movement, he'll be a pariah, and every other Southerner out there will support our actions when we kill him. Especially," he said with a cold smile, "since, as his avengers, we'll have the full backing of the movement's official voice and co-symbol, namely the newly-widowed Samantha Gore. When she gets up there on tape all teary eyed and thanks us, we'll be golden as far as the people are concerned."

Dr. MacFie was becoming more and more uneasy, both about the plan and the planner. "Let me ask you this, then; what's in it for *you*?"

"You can relax, Doctor. I'm not after the job both of you want, namely the leadership of the movement; I've got too many enemies in it to ever hope for that. Frank can be the glorious figurehead while you two hold the reins of power. I want to see this movement united for once, because I want it to *win*. I've dreamed of Southern independence all my life. For that, we need unity, and if the cost is the life of a trouble maker and divisive element like Jonathon Edge, it's a small price to pay." Seeing MacFie looking at him skeptically, he added, "Of course, even though Frank will take Edge's place in command of the military if he lives, he still has to answer to some position equivalent to that of Secretary of War, and with Edge out of the picture, that position will also be vacant. As the only one on the Council with military experience, I'd be the natural choice to fill it."

MacFie was not at all comfortable with the thought of Larson having the armed forces of the Confederate Army Provisional behind him, but Herdman spoke up before he could voice any objections. "It's a good plan, Neil, but I only see one potential fly in the ointment. What if they don't 'come to blows' so to speak? The whole thing will be even more fractious and divided before. Have you got a back-up plan?"

He nodded affirmatively. "I may be over-estimating the depth of Edge's megalomania and paranoia. It's possible that even Edge may know enough to realize that he can't just kill Gore outright and expect the movement to survive; or himself for that matter, since the

174

men idolize Frank, even the ones in other states who know him only by reputation. In that case, eventually, one or the other of them, and I'm betting on Edge, will have to at least go through the motions of bringing the matter before the Council."

"And once he does that," Larson added, his cold smile and colder eyes glittering as he laid a 9mm pistol on the table, "we'll see to it that Frank Gore walks out large and with *us* in charge, and Jonathon Edge doesn't walk out at all.

"All three of us are going to have to stand together on this, both in the killing and the aftermath, and get our stories straight beforehand so they'll be believable both to Nash and the men. We have to be able to convince them that the *late* Field Marshal was planning to assassinate Franklin and Samantha Gore, and quite possibly the entire Council, starting with the three of us." He smiled like a shark. "That shouldn't be too hard, because after the process I started today, followed immediately by this little meeting with you two which I'm equally sure he'll find out about, it's my bet he'll be intending to do exactly that."

Herdman and MacFie's eyes widened as they looked at each other. This was going farther than either had thought, but there was no backing out now, even if they wanted to. Looking at the cold blue automatic on the table, there was no need to ask what would happen if they tried.

Neil Larson carefully contained his glee. They could have the throne as far as he was concerned; all he wanted was the power behind it.

Sam detected something wrong in Edge's voice the minute he answered the phone.

"Hey, John! What's going on?"

"Why don't you tell me?"

Sam looked curiously at the receiver. *I wonder what's up his ass this time?*

"What exactly do you mean?"

"Are you aware that Frank Gore paid a visit to *your* old buddy Neil today?"

175

"I'm aware he got word that some of the members of the Council wanted to speak to him and he went to meet them at one of the safe houses here in Columbia. I figured they wanted a briefing or needed a little reassurance or something; another dog and pony show probably, you know how it goes. Besides, Frank's been wanting to get up with Neil when he got the chance anyway. He wanted more detailed information on the unit he inherited from him. I figured it was no big deal."

"No big deal?" Edge hissed, his voice simmering with anger. "He didn't meet with the Council; he met one-on-one with Neil Larson, and not three hours later, Larson was closeted up with Herdman and MacFie. Gore met with him and I want to know why!"

"Well why don't you ask him then?" Sam growled, beginning to heat up himself. "I didn't take him to raise."

"Why didn't *you* ask him?"

"Because if it was any of my business, he'd tell me. *Some of us* still respect the authority of the Council, such as it is, and if they call we come; it's as simple as that."

"So in other words, the Council – Larson, MacFie and Herdman – come first in your loyalties now, is that it?"

Sam gritted his teeth and counted to three before answering. *Friend or not, he's really starting to piss me off!*

"My loyalty," he said, struggling for control, "is not to the Council and not to you; it's to the movement – *period!"*

"So you agree with the rest of them and think I ought to be replaced for the 'good of the movement,' is that what you're saying?"

"Damn your hard headedness! You know good and well that's not what I said! What the hell is wrong with you?"

"What's wrong with me is this," he replied in a voice pregnant with warning, "I know Larson – along with MacFie and Herdman – are plotting with your precious Frank to replace me with one of them. You'd better start making a decision as to which side you're on!"

"That's bull shit and you know it! Frank isn't plotting with anybody! He's *never* been against you!"

176

"I'm only going to tell you this once. You either get a handle on this thing or I'm going to come down there and deal with it my way, and when I get done, there won't be a problem!"

"You'll play hell!" Sam exploded. "You let me tell you something; I don't know who in the hell you think you are, but I'll be damned if I'm going to sit by and let you come down here to South Carolina and start shooting Council members, let alone Frank Gore! It's not going to happen!"

"So you're in with them too?"

"Damn you, you hard headed son of a-"

There was a sharp *click* as Sam was cut off in mid-curse and left listening to a dial tone.

Tommy blew out his breath in a disgusted rush and had no trouble at all finishing the very same epithet.

"...bitch!" he muttered fiercely, and then repeated himself. "That dirty, low-down son of a *bitch!*"

Samantha sat there stunned, unable to speak. After all she had been through, now *this*, just when her life finally seemed to be getting back to what passed for normal in a war zone. The best man at her wedding was now apparently intending to murder both the bride and groom.

"The thing is," Frank told him, "we don't know for sure yet. At the moment, it's still a matter of probabilities rather than facts."

"That's crap and you know it as well as I do. You know how Edge is, man, and you can't deny he's capable of it."

"Look, Tommy, there's a difference between being capable of something and intending to do it."

"You're too damned trusting."

Frank's eyes were cold and hard, and his smile was anything but humorous. "No, that's where you're mistaken. There are very few people I completely trust, and most of them are right here in this room. I don't trust Edge, but I don't trust Larson either; I don't know what his game is. Does he really care, or does he want a rival out of the picture? We all know there've been power struggles going on behind the scenes in the Council since before the war even began

177

and the newest Councilman showed up, and one side or another is constantly trying to suck us into it. I *hope* that's all it is and that this information is wrong, but I don't trust in that hope enough to put our lives on the line for it. Besides, one scenario doesn't necessarily cancel out the other; it could well be both. Considering what's at stake here, we have to assume it's true, make some plans to deal with it, and secure ourselves in case it comes to that."

The biker thought about it for a moment, then spoke carefully. "We could just take him out."

Frank pursed his lips in thought; thoughts he never would have entertained a few months ago in another life that now seemed no more than a hazy memory.

"That would do it, but it could have unfortunate consequences. If this is nothing but a power play by Larson and maybe some of the others, then we'll simply exchange one danger for another. They'll definitely have the motivation of get rid of us then, because word getting out that they had a hand in Edge's death could very well destroy the movement or queer their chances for leadership if we win. Besides all that, if Larson knows anything at all about me, he has to know I'd kill him if we ever found out he'd used me in that way and turned me into a murderer.

"Then there is the fact that Edge is the most competent man to run the military arm of CAP. I've been studying those people, and nobody else could do the job half as well, for all his faults. Larson was so paranoid he wouldn't even set up a chain of command within his own unit. He's good at small unit tactics, but he lacks Edge's competence when it comes to bigger military matters, particularly the broad vision needed for an actual war as opposed to a raid. If we lose Edge, we could very well lose this war, and if that happens, we *all* die. There's nobody else in our ranks I'm aware of qualified to take his place, and frankly I wouldn't trust the rest of the Council to lead a college fraternity on a panty raid. They're statesmen, but just to be honest, I don't think they have any military abilities whatsoever.

"All that aside, I need to be certain before I kill a man...or two, for that matter. After all, Larson keeps claiming Edge sees me as a threat, but I know Larson wants the Field Marshal's position, so wouldn't that make me a threat to him as well? As Byzantine as the internal politics are here, I wouldn't put it past Edge and Larson to be conspiring together in an alliance of convenience to eliminate someone they think of as a threat to both of them, namely us! Me moving against Edge would be the perfect excuse for that."

Tommy bared his teeth without humor. "Congratulations; you just got a crash course on the Southern Movement. Of course, it wasn't quite this bad before the shooting started; then they'd just blacken your name instead of trying to kill you."

Samantha shook her head.

What a mess!

"So what do you suggest?" the biker continued.

"The Irregulars are under my command; on the surface at least, they seem to have little residual feelings for Larson, and they've never had any contact with Edge. As far as I can tell from some of the remarks they made, their former commander didn't keep them informed of very much and kept his distance from fear of being displaced. If I can win their loyalty, we'll have a personal guard of sorts, who will obey my orders – at least against Edge – in the event push comes to shove."

"Harrison's squad will do the same," Tommy assured them, "with Edge or Larson; they don't give a damn about either one, but they worship the ground *you* walk on. You can count on them!"

"Good. The only thing is, we'll be on missions and such, which leaves one thing still unsecured." He nodded meaningfully towards Samantha, who finally spoke for the first time.

"Then maybe I need a guard of my own. Kerrie would fight for me, but she's not trained. Donna's fairly competent, but not mature enough to be dependable in that regard. I can only think of one other man I trust fully."

Simultaneously realizing who she was referring to, both men smiled broadly. Samantha, meanwhile, wisely said nothing about her other developing plan this would fit nicely into.

They all hushed abruptly and looked up when the door opened.

"I hope I'm not interrupting."

179

"No, Sam," Frank told him, "just hashing some things out."

The older man grunted noncommittally and poured himself a cup of coffee before sitting down to join them.

"Anything I can help with?"

The three looked at one another before Frank answered. "No, I think this is something we're going to have to work out for ourselves."

Sam kept his face blank, but he was hurting inside. He knew what that 'something' related to, and was well aware that neither side trusted him now. He also knew, before it was over, someone was going to die; even worse, he had a horrible premonition that he was going to eventually have to be the one to decide just which one of his friends it would be.

"Just don't believe everything Larson tells you, alright?" he said quietly. "He's a patriot, but he's as ambitious as Edge and all the rest. I've known him for a long time, and he's not someone you particularly want to trust."

The others exchanged cold looks, their suspicions that Edge had them under surveillance confirmed by Sam's statement.

"Okay, Sam," Frank asked carefully, without inflection, "just who can we trust?"

With a sad look in his eyes, he quietly admitted, "I don't know. I'm sorry, but I just don't know."

Down below them in the basement, Mike Dayton stared at the ceiling above him, with an electronic sound amplifier hooked to his ear that had delivered every word of their conversation to him.

He didn't know who to trust either, but he was damned sure going to find out.

DAY 84

CHAPTER 14

Tommy opened the back door to find one of his best friends standing there.

"Hey, bro'!" he yelled and threw his arms around Billy Sprouse, presenting a hilarious picture since he didn't even come up to the other man's chin.

Tommy's breath whooshed out as the big man returned the bear hug, crushing him and almost making him disappear in the folds of his tattooed, tree trunk-sized arms.

"You missed me, Tommy! I should've known you'd always love me!"

The smaller biker's voice was an almost inaudible squeak. "Let me go, you big dumb-ass!"

"Yeah," Donna called out, "I'm getting jealous!"

"Of him or me?" Billy roared, dropping the gasping Tommy and reaching for the girl. Donna squealed like a little kid as he grabbed her around the waist with both hands and lifted her over his head, pressing her back against the ceiling while her legs kicked in empty air. "Look at you; all grown up and living with this loser; what the hell am I gonna to do with you? Give Uncle Billy some Eskimo sugar!" He lowered her down and she laughed as she rubbed noses with him just as she had when she was a child.

As soon as he set her down, Sam was next in line for the good-natured mauling, finishing with Billy planting a big sloppy kiss on the end of his nose as the older man struggled and blushed redder than any of them had ever seen him.

"Now don't play hard to get, *Uncle Sam*!" he said, falsetto voice. "You know you like it!"

"And looky here! It's my favorite couple!" he declared, looking at Frank questioningly.

The ex-cop grinned even as he shrugged in resignation. "Oh, what the hell? Go ahead; you're dying to anyway!"

An instant later, he and Sammie both fell victim at once to the huge arms as Billy mashed them together in a breath-taking group hug.

"Ossifer Gore, my hero! And Shotgun Sammie, the prettiest girl to ever shoot a Fed out my truck window! Umm-um!"

He let them go, grabbed Samantha's face in his hands and kissed her on the forehead before slapping Frank on the back with a blow that almost sent him careening into the wall.

"You lucky son of a gun, you!" His big shaggy head began swiveling, scanning the hall. "Where's Mikey?"

"Downstairs," Tommy told him, having recovered his wind, "but go easy; Kerrie's down there and –"

"What?" the giant shouted and headed toward the steps chanting, "Mikey's got a girl friend! Mikey's got a girl friend!" at the top of his lungs.

As the thunder of his size fourteen boots receded, they shook their heads in wonder, the shocked and battered survivors of a one-man tidal wave.

"If you think this is bad, you should have been living with him the past few months."

They turned to see Jim Reynolds standing there on the stoop, overlooked in all the excitement that followed Billy everywhere he went.

He shook hands all around.

"How you doing, Jim?" Sam asked. "You're looking good."

It was a lie and everyone knew it. His recovery from the trio of bullet wounds in his back, one of which had pierced his right lung, was going unnaturally slow. His breathing was labored, his skin pale and sickly looking, and his eyes hollow. Still, he smiled.

"Oh, could be worse I reckon."

"Surely that big ox didn't wool you around like that!"

"Nah. Just the opposite, really: he treated me with kid gloves and tried to wait on me hand and foot once he was able to get around again. It was like living with my grandma."

182

Frank looked in the direction that the subject of their discussion had disappeared. "We are talking about the same Billy, aren't we?"

"Oh yeah. He just relieved right now; he was going stir crazy back in Georgetown. I guess I was the lucky one. See, the Feds don't know me, but they sure know who he is, and Billy kind of stands out, if you know what I mean. He couldn't leave the house and it was driving him nuts."

"He always was into something," Tommy commented, "always keeping busy – he never could sit still for very long."

"I'll say! Do you know what he did? While he was laid up, he got to watching some of those home improvement shows and got all inspired. As quick as he got on his feet, he completely remodeled the inside of the Ford's house; painted, hung paneling and sheet rock, even rewired the place, all by himself. If that wasn't enough, he rebuilt the motor on their car." He chuckled. "Old man Ford didn't know what to say – hell, he couldn't begin to keep up with what all Billy was doing – but he was Mrs. Ford's little darling. She must have baked a hundred pies and a gunny sack full of cookies and brownies this past month; said she loved to see a man eat."

Sam laughed out loud at that one.

"If that's the case, she must have thought she had died and gone to Heaven!" Billy's appetite was legendary, and fully matched his enormous size.

"I'll tell you what though," Jim continued, wincing as he eased himself into a chair, "it's a good thing you called when you did. He was beginning to get depressed."

"Billy?" several voices gasped incredulously, and Jim nodded.

"Yep. He'd started turning real serious and hardly ever laughed, and that just ain't like him.

"Thing is, when we got word you wanted us here, it was like somebody threw a switch and he was instantly a changed man, back to his old self, and then some. I figure he'll be back to normal – as normal as he gets anyway – in a day or two. He's just making up for lost time."

Tommy dried his hands on a towel in the tiny half-bath off the bedroom that, at the moment, had been pressed into service as a temporary medical clinic. He had a very worried look on his face.

"What are you going to do, Sammie?"

She sighed in resignation from her seat on the bed. "I don't suppose there's much I can do except to keep going as long as I possibly can."

"I'm worried about you, and I'm also worried about how Frank's going to take it when he finds out."

"Don't worry about that, because I don't intend to tell him; not yet, anyway."

"Damn it, Sammie, he's got the right to know! He's your husband!"

"I know, but not yet. Think about it, Tommy; he's got the training with his new unit coming up, he's having to watch his back from his own leaders every step of the way, and he's got whatever this secret mission of Edge's is to plan. He doesn't need the extra stress. I'm worried about his health already; he doesn't sleep well as it is, and if he thinks he's going to have to start taking care of me again –"

The medic cut her off. "*Your* health is what I'm concerned about. I don't have to remind you that you've been through a lot of physical and mental trauma recently, not to mention the everyday stress – now this! Frank needs to know!"

"I'll tell him, Tommy, just as soon as this immediate mess is over. I promise."

He looked her dead in the eyes, all seriousness.

"I'll hold you to that. Frank is my friend; more than that, he's the best man I've ever served under in any capacity – hell, maybe the best man I've ever known. I think the world and all of you, but if you don't tell him as soon as this mission's over, I will."

"Fair enough then," she agreed as she patted him on the forearm. "Thanks."

DAY 85

CHAPTER 15

Sam looked warily at the three women seated at the table with him. *A woman and two girls,* he amended. The guerrilla chief had been married for several years before becoming a widower, and he knew enough about the opposite sex to know when they were up to something. That was especially obvious this time, since they had waited for Frank to be closeted in the basement with Mike before approaching him. He had the feeling that, whatever it was, it was going to be major and he wasn't going to like it one little bit. Still, he refused to give them the satisfaction of showing it in his face.

They had carefully planned out their attack in advance. Donna and Kerrie glanced at Samantha waiting for her lead, and Frank's wife began speaking, her voice carefully modulated. "Sam, we need to talk to you."

He took a sip of coffee. *Like a damned poker game!*

"Alright; what's on your mind?"

He nearly fell out of his chair when she told him.

"No! Absolutely not!"

She explained. He refused.

"Those men are killers!"

Then she explained again with the help of Donna and Kerrie. Sam felt himself weakening, being worn down by their combined attack.

"No!"

Smelling blood, they went in for the kill. They began explaining all over again, this time with a pretty reporter's most persuasive smile and two girls' insistent "I want" looks. He cursed under his breath as he threw up his hands in surrender.

"Alright, *fine*! Since you won't listen to reason, you just go right on ahead, but you remember one thing. Frank is literally going to sh–

" He caught himself, but barely. "I mean he is going to flat out go ballistic!"

Samantha assured him she could handle Frank with much more confidence than she actually felt. For the first time, she was about to do something that she knew her husband would be opposed to in the extreme, and she wasn't at all certain how he would react when he found out.

Especially when he learns about the other thing!

"What's up, Mike?" Frank asked, straddling the chair backwards as he sat, leaning his muscular forearms on the backrest. "Kerrie said you wanted to see me privately."

The programmer was clearly troubled as he turned his chair to face his commander. In fact, Frank had never seen him so serious.

"We've got big trouble; there's a Federal spy in the unit you inherited from Larson."

Frank remained quiet as he digested the information, his face hardening.

"Are you certain?"

"Positive." Mike watched the scarred knuckles whiten as they gripped the chair back. "You remember that surveillance equipment you all had that cop install – you know, what's his name, the pervert."

"Duckett." Frank answered coldly before Mike could turn back to the keyboard to look it up.

"Yeah, him. Well, it paid off again. You know the Feds are still using part of the Columbia PD facilities instead of the Federal Building. I guess it's neutral ground for the different bunches to meet. With all the inter-agency rivalry, no one from the FBI, for instance, wants to lose face by meeting in the BATF office. Well, by pure, dumb luck, a bunch of them decided to have a conference in one of the rooms Duckett bugged for us.

"Frank, they know about Blair; they mentioned him by name. They've also got names and dossiers on better than half your men, and descriptions of the rest. They know the exact location where the meeting took place, and I gather from what they said that they dusted

186

for prints and confirmed that both you and Sam were there. Someone must have given them book, chapter and verse."

"Do they know about this house?" Frank's voice was dead calm, but his mind was racing, sifting though his options. Unconsciously, his right hand dropped to rest on the comfortably familiar butt of his .45.

"No, not yet, but they damned sure want to bad enough. That's why they didn't raid you at the meeting – well that and where they didn't know *you* were going to be there until after the fact. They want to take the leadership down instead of simply the followers. They want to make sure their targets are there this time, both for practicality and because Peters' ass is literally on the line if there's another screw-up like the one that happened when they took down Sam's farm."

"So we have a short breathing space then –"

"Not really. Like I said, Peters is being pressured all the way from the White House on down to do something, and do it *now*. Whether they can net us all or not, they plan on making their move very soon. They left quite a few of their resources here that came in for the riot, and they're quietly moving reinforcements into this part of the country to have them ready: Federal paramilitaries from the FBI, Secret Service, BATF, Marshals, private mercenary contractors, any warm trigger finger they can lay their hands on. This has been confirmed by my watchers, who notice strangers and can usually spot a Fed real quick. From what they said, they'll be tracking your unit by transmitter, and they plan to wait until you get settled into your training area; that will give them enough time to scramble all the forces necessary to completely seal you in."

Frank sat silently, looking for a way out of this trap that was already all but sprung. Quickly patterns formed in his mind, were rejected and rearranged, possibilities weighed and probabilities sifted. Mike was wise enough not to break his train of thought, and after several minutes the Captain lifted his head.

The Intelligence Coordinator shivered despite himself. Looking into Frank's eyes was like gazing into the implacable orbs of the Death himself, and his voice sounded just as cold. "I need a copy of everything to do with that meeting – *everything*. I also want the location of all known Federal resources in our area: where they're staying and everything you know about them."

"Then I have your authorization to pay for a private detective? We might need one to get this stuff quick."

"Yes, get whatever you need to do the job ASAP, whatever the cost. Too much is on the line right now to worry about pinching pennies; we'll make it up somehow. Contact Sam, Tommy and Rob, and get them here *now*." His nostrils were flaring with anger. "And most of all, I want the name of that traitor."

He didn't like what Mike told him.

Day 86

CHAPTER 16

"Are you sure you're going to be okay?"

Samantha looked up at her husband and smiled. "I'll be fine, Frank, except for missing you already. Just don't worry; Billy and Jim will take care of things here, and Tommy's squad will be on call. If Mike or I don't hear from you for more than twenty-four hours, I'll brief them on what we talked about and go to ground."

He kissed her, enjoying the taste of her mouth, but remaining genuinely puzzled. Only days ago, she was on the verge of going out of her mind every time he left the house for a few hours; now today, when he was expecting to leave in less than an hour and be gone for the best part of a month, she seemed to take it in stride.

To be honest, she's taking it a hell of a lot better than I am. I feel like my heart's being torn out.

Something else nagged him in the back of his mind. Something was not at all right here. He sensed his wife was hiding something, but for the life of him he couldn't figure out what.

The James Furniture Company warehouse, across the South Carolina border not far below Charlotte, was just one more victim of hard times. A silent blue metal building behind a chain-link fence a couple of miles from the interstate, its faded sign and weed-grown gravel lot told its sad story. Any passerby who might have cared to glance at the big Peterbuilt that entered late Tuesday morning and backed into a loading dock would have assumed the warehouse had finally been sold or leased to someone else. It had been, very temporarily, to a company that didn't exist except on a letterhead.

Of course, since the truck was backed into the loading bay flush against the roll-up door, they wouldn't have seen the live cargo of twenty-nine men leave the trailer and enter the building. Inside, Frank was waiting for them.

"Gentlemen," he addressed them, loud enough that the ones in the back could hear, "we're going to have to do a little reorganizing. First, I need to brief Sergeant Caffary, then the squad leaders, then the rest of you. Please be patient. Smoke 'em if you got 'em.

"Sergeant Caffary?" Frank walked fifty feet to a plywood room setting in the middle of the open space that had once served as an office and opened the door. The sergeant followed him in and the door closed behind him.

Inside, Caffary found himself looking down the fat, silenced barrels of a pair of MP5's held by Rob Johnson and Tommy Richardson. Samuel Wirtz sat behind the room's desk, his hand resting on his old .357 magnum that lay on the dusty, coffee-stained blotter. Startled and angry, the retired Marine's head swiveled toward Frank.

"What the hell is this?"

"What this is Sergeant, is a precaution. Putting it bluntly, we have a traitor in our midst. We know it's one of you men, but we don't know which one, so we're going to have to check all of you. At least one of you is carrying a transmitter, and I intend to find out who."

He produced a portable scanning wand. "This is how it's going to work. Notice that device on the desk?" He gestured at a box that resembled a small amplifier. One line trailed from it to the plug-in, and two more went to the wall and circled the room, held up by bits of duct tape. "That produces severe interference across most channels, rendering this room a virtual electronic dead-zone. Nothing we say right now can be transmitted, including our location.

"The thing is, our scanner won't work while that's on either. What you are going to do is strip. Once your skivvies hit the floor, I am going to turn off the box and scan you. Of course, if you are the culprit, your transmitter will probably pick up and broadcast anything we say. If you open your mouth or make any sound at all until we clear you, these men *will* kill you immediately and with no further warning. Do you understand?"

190

Caffary nodded.

"Good. Take 'em off."

Frank didn't speak again until they were done. "I hope there're no hard feelings, Gunny."

Caffary grinned back at him as he buttoned his shirt over his grizzled chest hair.

"Not a one, sir. Shit, I'd have been disappointed if you hadn't checked me as well. That was pretty slick; you never cease to amaze me, Captain."

"Thanks. Would you bring in the next man, please?"

They checked them all, beginning with the squad leaders, and found what they were looking for with the tenth man.

Marvin Connolly was a thirty-year old former member of both the militia and the Klan, originally from up near Cheraw. There was nothing outstanding about his appearance, medium height and build, brown, slightly receding hair, a prominent nose and unusually big pores. He had been one of the most active agitators in both the militia and Larson's crew, always urging violence.

As soon as they explained things to him, just as they had to Caffary, he began to complain, and then to balk until the red flags went up with the First Sergeant. Caffary pulled a well-worn Marine Corps K-Bar knife from a sheath at his waist.

"Connolly, you take those damned clothes off right now or I'll cut 'em off you!"

As soon as he was standing naked, Caffary grabbed his subordinate's hair, pulled his head back, and placed the blade against his throat.

"You even cough, boy, and I'll open you up like a can of sardines!"

The voice transmitter was a flat, fingernail-sized device in his belt, where the leather had been split, and then glued and sewn back together. None of the men had seen anything like it before, so it must have been something new from the government labs. A second device – a "Legionnaire" as they called the personal identification chips that were becoming more and more popular – was under the skin on the back of his neck, the bottom fringe of Connolly's hair

191

partially hiding the scar. Whoever was in charge of the informer knew exactly where he was, and evidently had a real-time ear on what was happening around him.

His face grim, Frank dropped the transmitter into a small electrified multi-layer metal box that would prevent any signal from going in or out.

As a precaution, they flipped the scrambler back on, and Frank nodded curtly at the First Sergeant. "We can talk now."

Caffary wasn't in a talking mood. He kicked the traitor's feet out from under him and slammed him face-first into the concrete floor. Connolly smashed down on his nose, crushing the cartilage and splitting his lips.

"It was you! You damned son of a bitch, it was *you!*" Straddling the bleeding man, he caught his hair once more, jerked back, and slid the K-Bar's razor edge back under his chin.

"Sergeant, *halt!*" Frank shouted, punctuating his order by drawing his .45 and pointing it at Caffary's head. The top sergeant looked up at the muzzle, eyes wide and furious, and for moment Frank thought he was going to kill Connolly anyway. The former Marine was so angry he was visibly shaking.

"Sergeant Caffary, I understand you're upset..."

"Upset? *Upset!* Do you know who this bastard is and what he did?" Frank shook his head without letting the pistol waver in the slightest, and the sergeant continued, "When the Feds broke up the Klavern I was in, this son of a bitch was in it too. We knew someone had informed; we just didn't know who! As a result, the best friend I had in this world went to the Federal pen! He lasted less than a year till the damned niggers in there murdered him. The militia down in Conway too – he was a member when the Feds took 'em down and Josh Michaels went up for life. You're the common thread, aren't you Connolly? *Answer me, you asshole!*"

He pressed the knife tighter and Connolly began to scream as a thin trickle of blood began to pool around the blade.

"Yes! Yes! Please! Don't kill me! Please!"

"First Sergeant Caffary!" Frank barked, "I am giving you a direct order; you will bind and gag the prisoner and put him in that corner.

We have more men to check, because where there's one spy, there may be more. We might as well deal with all of them at once. Do it *now*!"

Cursing under his breath, Caffary finally relinquished his position atop the prisoner, and within a minute, Connolly's hands, feet and mouth were brutally and efficiently wrapped with duct tape and he was unceremoniously dumped in the corner. Frank turned away the First Sergeant's offer to cut the chip out with his K-bar, less from concern for Connolley's welfare and more from not knowing if the tiny device would send out some special signal if it were removed. The prisoner secured and out of the way, Frank ordered Caffary to summon Connolly's squad leader, who had already been cleared.

"Buchanan!"

"Yes sir?" the man called out as he hurried into the room. Bravo Squad's Sergeant Andy Buchanan was a tall, lanky product of a Piedmont farm. Twenty-seven with an over abundance of freckles and an unruly mop of carrot-red hair, he had a strange, almost lurching gate, as if his long arms and legs would entangle one another given half a chance. He gave every appearance of being an uncoordinated goofball.

Looks, however, were deceiving. A former Army Ranger and decorated combat veteran, Andy Buchanan was an extremely competent and dangerous individual.

Buchanan looked at the bound, bloody Connolly, and his brown eyes narrowed in disgust. "I reckon you found what you were looking for." He spat on the floor in the general direction of the prisoner and repeated Caffary's earlier words in an angry hiss. "You damned son of a *bitch*!"

Frank nodded and handed him the shielding box.

"I've got a mission for you. Inside this box is a Federal transmitter and possibly a tracking device, so don't talk to yourself while you're carrying it. Take it to the truck outside; there's a boom box with a few CD's of Confederate music in there." He glanced at Tommy, who nodded, verifying that everything was as he said. "I want you to open the box, give a little speech like you're talking to a group, and tell them we're getting ready to head out to our main headquarters, where they'll get the chance to meet General Jonathon Edge himself in the next day or two, and in the meantime, we're going to play some inspirational music. Then turn it on shuffle play and crank up the sound to give who's ever on the other end something to listen to. As soon as you're done, come straight back here."

If Buchanan had any questions, he kept them to himself. "Yes sir." With that, he shot Connolly another glare, and headed out at a brisk walk.

Frank turned back to the others.

"Now, while the Feds are expanding their cultural horizons by listening to some good music for a change, we'll have time to finish our business here before they decide to come looking for him. I think we've bought ourselves a safety margin; they won't raid to take me down alone, not when they think they can just follow the transmitter and let it lead them to General Edge too. Just in case I'm wrong, however, issue weapons to every one of those men we've already cleared and put them on watch. Lock and load, safeties on. Instruct them, if anyone other than one of our people tries to enter, or anyone inside tries to leave without one of the officers saying it's all right, shoot them. Then send in the next man."

Frank was thankful that Connolly appeared to be the only traitor in their midst. Not only could he not afford to lose the men, but what was going to have to be done was not something that neither he nor any other sane man enjoyed.

He looked around. After loosing Connolly's legs and putting his pants back on, he had two of the men drag the prisoner out into the open warehouse area, where nothing but a sea of grim and angry faces awaited him. They released their grip on his bound arms, and he collapsed to his knees on the concrete floor. Frank nodded at Tommy, who reached down and ripped away the tape gag, taking most of Connolly's moustache with it, before rising and backing away. The prisoner gasped at the pain as tiny drops of blood began welling up where the tape had torn out his facial hair, and immediately began begging again.

"Shut up!" Frank ordered sharply. "You know what the charge is; do you have any thing to say in your defense?"

"Please!" He was crying openly now, the tears flowing down his face. "It wasn't my fault! They made me do it!"

Frank heard several muffled obscenities from the troops, just low enough that he could pretend he hadn't.

"How did they *make* you do it, Connolly?"

"They caught me with a pipe bomb. They were ready to send me to prison! I didn't have any choice!"

Frank found it difficult to keep the disgust out of his voice. "So in order to save your own skin, you betrayed your friends and comrades then and now, along with this entire movement. Even worse, the same intelligence that clued me in to you also informed me you gave the names of everyone you knew in this company to the Feds. Now they not only know who the men in this room are, they know who their families are too, isn't that right? If they don't get these men, they'll do just like they did in Iraq and take their families hostage; you knew that too, didn't you?"

Everyone in the room knew; the practice of the United States military during the occupation of Iraq of taking the relatives of the resistance fighters to the infamous Abu Ghraib prison and other locations, and torturing, raping, sodomizing, and sometimes killing them was common knowledge. Connolly's voice could barely be heard over the outraged expressions of the men, who suddenly understood the full depth of his betrayal and just what it meant. There was a strong undercurrent of fear running through the profanity and anger; fear not for themselves, but for their wives and children. A couple of them staggered under the implications, and Wayland Fowler of Bravo Squad, who had four daughters at home, actually collapsed to his knees, crying out, "Oh my God!"

"No! It's not like that!" Connolly yelled, desperately trying to be heard. "I didn't have any choice! Don't you understand? Nobody would go to prison if there was a way out!"

195

"Gentlemen," Frank said, turning back to the assembled men. "There's no sense in drawing this thing out any further. Mr. Connolly is charged with treason and espionage. We found the transmitters on him, and he has confessed. Because of him, none of you can go home again until this damned war is over. His traitorous and deliberate actions have put not only this movement, and not only you and I in grave danger, but your wives, children and parents as well. He's your comrade, so you make the call. What's your verdict?"

The roars of "Guilty" were earsplitting.

"Very well. Marvin Connolly, you have been found guilty of capital crimes by a jury of your peers, the sentence for which is death. The sentence will be carried out immediately. May God have mercy on your soul."

Over Connolly's protests, First Sergeant Caffary's trained voice rang out loud and clear. "Captain Gore; I request permission to speak!" Frank nodded for him to go ahead, particularly since it was obvious from the old Marine's beet-red face that he was either going to speak or bust wide open. "Sir, this man was one of us. It was our unit he dishonored and our people he hurt. I request that we be allowed to carry out the death sentence ourselves, in our own way."

Connolly blanched as the rest of the company murmured their agreement. Frank had a general idea of what that would entail and was about to dismiss the request out of hand, even though to do so would drive a wedge between himself and his men. Beyond despising wanton cruelty, however justified, he knew if he ever allowed the men of his company to act on their own in such a manner, all sense of discipline would be destroyed. Contemplating the best way to handle the situation, he was struck by a sudden inspiration.

"That's up to Mr. Connolly, Sergeant. How about it, Connolly? I suspect if I turn you over to your comrades, your death would be a long, painful, drawn out process. However, I'm prepared to offer you a way out of that. You have information concerning your Federal contacts that might be valuable to us. I will give you ten minutes to tell us everything about your handlers you think may be of even the

196

slightest interest. At the end of those ten minutes, rest assured you *will* die. If the information you have given us is sufficient in my judgment, your death will be a quick and simple execution by firing squad, over and done with in seconds. If it is not, I will give you to these men to do with as they will, and I'll give them all the time they need to do it; I've got all day. Understand that I am a former police officer, and trained in spotting a liar. If I even *suspect* you are telling me anything less than the full truth, you will get no second chance. Instead, I'll give you to Sergeant Caffary and the men of this company to play with. Is that clear?"

A resigned Connolly nodded solemnly, head hanging.

Twelve minutes later, Frank led Connolly, his hands still bound behind him, to a battered folding chair at one end of the room. The prisoner's legs were wobbly and without his commander's support he would have fallen. Frank assisted him to his seat.

"Dante said that the lowest, most miserable pit of Hell is reserved for betrayers. If you want to pray, now would be a really good time."

"Yes…uh, Sir. I-I don't really know how."

Frank sighed inwardly. He hated this man – literally despised him – but he also understood his duty, and the full spiritual implications if he failed in it. He thought he had a pretty good idea what Hell was like; he had seen it in his own wife's eyes when they took her back from her torturers. He couldn't bring himself to wish to see anyone – even this traitor – with that look on his face for all eternity.

I do wish I were Catholic though, because a few thousand years in Purgatory wouldn't do the son of a bitch any harm either!

"Would you like me to pray with you?"

"Would you, sir? Please?"

In answer, Frank knelt beside him. Both men bowed their heads. At first there was some muttering among the rest of the men, but it soon silenced in the gravity of the moment.

After several minutes, Frank and Connolly raised their heads and looked at one another.

197

"It's good that you got things straightened out with God."

The bound man nodded. "Yeah, I reckon so. I guess we might as well go ahead and get it over with – I'm ready to go." He swallowed hard. "Ready as I can be, anyway."

Frank nodded and reached for a bandanna in his pocket.

"Would you like a blindfold?"

"No, I reckon not." He gulped audibly. "I'd like to know when it's coming."

Frank nodded his approval. "Sit up straight then. This is the last thing you'll ever do in this world, so do it like a man."

"Yes sir…and thank you, sir."

Frank nodded and walked back to the squad.

"Bring the men to attention, Sergeant Caffary."

"Yes sir. *Attention!*" Every man snapped into position, the building echoing with the stamp of their boots.

"Bring the squad forward."

The six men, selected by lot, stepped into line ten yards in front of Connolly, all of them armed with M16's. The light 5.56mm rounds may not have been the ideal choice for the purpose, but it was what they had and it would serve.

Outside, in the delivery bay, Tommy revved the engine of the semi to cover the noise.

Frank gave the order himself, yelling over the motor's roar.

"Ready. Aim. *Fire!*"

He dropped his hand, and the roar of six simultaneous rifle shots echoed deafeningly in the confines of the sheet metal walls. All of the Irregulars knew how to shoot, and at that close of a range, the pattern of holes that suddenly appeared in the center of the prisoner's chest could have been covered by a man's palm. Connolly, along with the chair, upset and fell backwards on the floor, his body splashed with blood. His right leg curling upward and then straightening as it relaxed was the only movement he made. Frank drew his .45 and crisply marched forward. Reaching the fallen man, he fired the *coup de grace*: the traditional, merciful, finishing shot to the head. It wasn't really needed.

198

Turning back to the others, he kept his face carefully blank. "Lieutenant Johnson, get the men aboard the truck ASAP. I don't know if there's anything in that legionnaire that was hooked to his vital signs, or if it can even transmit at all, but if there was and it can, then somebody on the other end of that transmission is probably filling his pants right now. Sergeant Caffary, police up that brass so we don't leave them any more evidence than we have to, and let's get a move on. While they're doing that, I want the squad leaders to check every man's weapon and ammunition. This time I want full clips in place but no rounds chambered yet; we can't afford the attention of an accidental discharge. Anyone who disobeys and fires off a round will answer to me. As soon as that's done, we're moving out. We'll be heading for our real destination now."

"Sir, this isn't our training area?" Caffary asked.

"No," Frank told him, jerking his head in the direction of Connolly's earthly remains. "This is our killing ground."

There had been a single brief stop; Tommy pulled the rig into a roadside rest a few miles down the road, and had put the transmitter into the unlocked cab of an unoccupied Freightliner while its driver was in the john, sticking it beneath the seat with a wad of gum. Since they presumed it was sending signals that were being picked up by a tracking satellite, it was much safer this way; as far as the satellite was concerned, a truck broadcasting the signal pulled in and a truck doing the same thing pulled out, leaving an entirely false trail behind it.

As they rumbled along in the heat and dark of the trailer, the men had been murmuring for some time before the First Sergeant, backed by the squad leaders, approached, feeling his way to Frank, who was no more that a shadow in the darkness.

"Sir?"

"Yes, Sergeant Caffary?"

Frank's voice sounded slightly tired, wrung out. Seeing treason in their own ranks up close and personal had taken an emotional toll on him, much greater than the one of actually executing the traitor, although that had been bad enough.

"Sir, the men are worried about their families…"

"I've already taken care of that," he told them, and even though he couldn't make out the other troops in the confined space, he could almost hear them listening. "Believe me, I understand what you're going through right now."

There were scattered grunts of assent. All of them – along with most of the world – knew the now almost legendary story of Frank Gore and his wife.

"I had a plan already in place. It'll take some time – I'd estimate a window of twenty four to seventy two hours – for the Feds to get to wondering about their boy, and even longer for them to make a decision on what to do. That gives us a little breathing space, hopefully enough to do what I've got in mind. Colonel Wirtz, are you listening?"

"I'm all ears."

"Do you feel comfortable if I give them the general details?" At his superior's assent, Frank continued. "We have a fairly substantial number of peripherally involved non-combat personnel, sympathizers and the like. They're totally dedicated, but unfortunately a lot of them are too young or too old or too crippled up to make effective troops. But most are still willing to do something potentially dangerous if need be."

"As soon as I got the intel that there was a traitor in our ranks, I had our people get in communication with these folks, and got some safe houses lined up ASAP. Every one of them has a short list of the names and addresses of your loved ones, and they were on the ground in their vicinity just waiting for the word. You noticed me on the cell phone earlier? As soon as I knew who the traitor was, I immediately made the call that sent these people out to quietly bring in your families. We'll put them in our underground; they may not be too comfortable, but they should be relatively safe. We'll let each and every one of you know when your family is safely accounted for, and I'll try to get all of you a chance to visit as soon as we can, or at least talk with them on the phone. That might be a while, but I give you my word I'll do my best."

Excited voices filled the space, their tone best summed up by a hand from one of the Irregulars, unseen and anonymous in the darkness, dropping on Frank's shoulder.

"Thank you, Captain. We won't forget this."

The sound of the voice and the others that followed made it very clear they meant it. Even though that wasn't the reason he did it, for saving their lives and those of their families, the Irregulars now owed Frank far more than they could ever have owed Neil Larson. The men were no longer their former leader's or anyone else's; now they were his.

"Don't worry about it. I'll make a call to our blocker and have him double-check to make sure it's set it up and the girls have got them rolling on it."

At the mention of "the girls," Sam squirmed. He had the feeling, when Frank found out just what the girls had done, there was going to be hell to pay.

Once we arrive, I think I'll take a quick trip to the bathroom and stay there until everything blows over.

CHAPTER 17

A couple of hours later, Tommy stopped the truck again; this time at a closed farmer's market along route 74 just across the border in North Carolina, and the sweating men exited the trailer via a loading dock again, this time into an even larger building that would be their home for the next few weeks. Rob, not currently known to the Feds, traveled a few miles ahead in radio contact as point man in the luxury of the Ford, while Frank and Sam, both with prices on their heads, perspired with the Irregulars.

Exhausted and somewhat dehydrated from the heat, clothes plastered to their bodies, they gathered in the comparative comfort of the un-air conditioned loading dock. Rob, already arrived, had a large, orange barrel-type cooler full of ice water waiting for them.

Screw up number one, Frank thought, mentally kicking himself. *Next time put the water in the back of the truck where we need it!*

He was raising his second cup of the cooling liquid to his lips when he noticed something out of place in his peripheral vision. Turning, he was more than a little surprised to see Samantha, along with Donna and Kerrie, standing several yards away, dressed in jeans and T-shirts and watching him nervously.

What in the hell?

Suddenly he knew what she had been up to, and Samantha's eyes widened at the stormy expression on his face.

As calmly as he could, Frank set his cup down, walked over to his wife and took her gently but firmly by the arm. He escorted her off to one side, out of earshot of the rest, and spoke to her more forcefully than he ever had. "Sammie, what are you doing here?"

"Jim brought us up, with Tommy's squad acting as security. We're here for training."

"Training?" Frank exclaimed, his face darkening with rare anger: rare at least as far as his wife was concerned. Seeing Tommy staring at Donna open-mouthed and looking just as surprised as he was, the

Captain's head swiveled as he looked for the obvious culprit, who had already made himself scarce. "Sam's behind this, isn't he? I'll -"

She cut him off by gently laying her fingertips across his lips, and began her carefully rehearsed speech.

"Please, Frank, hear me out. It's not Sam's fault; we ganged up on him. We – the women – need at least some basic training. I can't go through another capture; I mean it, I just can't, and I can't stand feeling helpless because I don't have the skills I need. We not only have to have the ability to defend ourselves when you're off on a mission, but you know as well as I do that some of the things we'll have to do will need women as part of them for cover. Besides, this way you won't have to worry; Billy and Jim will be able to help Mike, Tommy's squad will be there for backup, and I'll be where you can keep an eye on me."

"You planned this all along, didn't you?"

She lowered her eyes at the accusation in his voice, unable to deny it.

"Yes."

He gestured with both hands in frustration.

"Why didn't you just *ask* me?"

Unused to his harsh tone, her lip quivered slightly, and moisture rose up in her eyes.

"Because you would have said no."

Frank, never able to stay upset with her for long, particularly when whatever irritated him was already a *fate accompli*, and most particularly when she was making a certain amount of sense (*At least on the surface!*), was still so irritated in being out-maneuvered – especially in such an unacceptably risky way – that he couldn't suppress a remark on the obvious.

"And I suppose wanting to be with your husband didn't enter into your calculations?"

Stung a little by the truth of his allegation, a hint of her own fire flashed to the surface. "So what if it did? Is it a *breach of military discipline* to finagle a way to be with the man I love?"

"A very serious breach," he told her in a cold official voice, "and as your commander, it is my duty to carry out your punishment." He paused for dramatic affect, deliberately putting the gravest look possible on his face. "I sentence you to a good, old fashioned spanking – see me in my quarters tonight after training." He waited until her eyes began to widen in shock before suddenly dropping the strict facade and grinning lecherously, accompanying his leer with a broad wink.

Her lips parted in a relieved and thoroughly disarmed smile. *I was so afraid!* Happy he had taken her action well enough to joke about it, she winked back and had just given him an exaggerated *'purr'* and a little wiggle in return when she heard the giggling behind her. Donna and Kerrie, unseen, had edged close enough to catch Frank's last words and her response.

"See!" Donna exclaimed louder than she probably meant to, causing a couple of the nearer men, including Tommy, to glance their way. "I knew they were kinky!"

Tommy pursed his lips and turned his eyes upward with pointed nonchalance, suddenly finding something interesting to look at in the steel ceiling beams overhead, Kerrie clamped her hand over her mouth to stifle a rare laugh, and Samantha blushed to the roots of her hair.

Good enough for you was Frank's unspoken thought as he shook his head at his thoroughly mortified wife's expression.

"We'll talk about this later," he said in a low voice meant only for her before addressing all three of them.

"Enjoy yourselves while you can, ladies, because in the next few minutes, I will cease to be Sammie's husband and your friend. During the training periods, I will be your commander, and you will be subject to *real* military discipline, the same as everyone else here. You'll be given orders and you *will* obey them, or I promise you'll be given cause to wish you had. Do you understand?" He looked at each of them in turn, straight in the eyes, and didn't look away until he got individual nods of assent. "There will be no favorites and no exceptions. You wanted to train with these men; well, now you will. You'll do everything they do, and you'll be expected to keep up; there will be no special consideration because of your sex.

"You all wanted training, and you're going to get it. By the time this is over, you may wish you'd stayed at home."

Over the next few days, they had cause to remember that final sentence, and to reflect more than once that he may have been right.

The first day had been a nightmare for the women. Frank put Hodges in charge of the senior non-com's duties of helping to get the company's equipment issued, barracks and training areas laid out, duties assigned, and every man generally squared away. Meanwhile, he had turned the three feminine latecomers over to the tender mercies of First Sergeant Caffary to be taught the basics of firearms handling. Under the old-school Marine's somewhat less-than-genteel guidance, they learned every part of their three basic weapons – the M16, 9mm Glock semi-automatic pistol, and MP5 submachine gun – intimately, inside and out. They stripped and reassembled them over and over again until their hands were raw, none of them had a fingernail left to their names, and Samantha's damaged fingers were in absolute agony. Donna had just enough knowledge about the guns to be cocky, but Caffary quickly and brutally put her in her place, his profane sarcasm leaving her in barely-suppressed tears.

It was fully dark outside when the First Sergeant finally dismissed them.

"Good job, ladies. You've surprised the hell out of me; it looks like you just *might* possibly be able to learn something useful after all. I'll see you bright and early in the morning, and we'll start all over again!"

Staring daggers at the departing Caffary's back, Samantha grimly reflected that she understood now why they hadn't issued them any ammunition to go with the weapons.

"Have a seat, Sergeant," Frank said, gesturing at the chair in front of the desk covered by a pair of laptops and a lot of paperwork. The others had fallen out for the evening, and Frank, Sam, Rob, and Tommy had been going over the events of the day, and their plans for the ones to come.

"Thank you, sir." Caffary eased himself down into the questionable comfort of the metal folding chair, which was the only kind they had.

"How'd they do?"

Caffary looked at Frank and nodded a little uneasily. "Pretty well, sir, all in all. Donna Waddell is skilled with weapons already, but I wish she had half as good as she thinks she is." Frank, Sam and Tommy all grinned at his observation; that was Donna all right. "The O'Brien girl's never had a firearm in her hand in her life and it sure as hell shows, but she's trying hard, and I think she'll do okay."

"I notice you left one out."

"Well, sir, I don't know exactly how to put this..."

"Let's put it this way, Sergeant: there are no favorites here. She may be my wife after lights out, but in training she's just another recruit, to be treated no differently from anyone else. If she's got a problem, spit it out."

"Yes sir. She tries harder than either one of the others and she's learned a lot, but she's not doing too well. She seems to have trouble with hand strength and fine manual dexterity."

"I'm not surprised; she had her fingers crushed only a couple of months ago, when she was a prisoner. Three of them were broken."

"Why the hell didn't she tell me that?" Caffary exploded, then suddenly remembered who he was talking to, and belatedly added, "sir."

"She's too proud."

"If we Southerners have a national vice, it's just that: pride." He paused, shaking his head. "You've never taught women to shoot, have you Captain?" After Frank shook his head, Caffary continued, "I didn't think so. Well I have, and I'm going to tell you something; most women aren't worth a damn with a semi-automatic pistol to start with. They tend to have weaker grips, and thus a lot of trouble racking the slide all the way back for one thing. That seems to be her main problem, and considering what happened to her, it's not surprising now. It would have saved me and her both a lot of aggravation if I'd known that before, sir."

207

"Or if you'd come to me when you first noticed the problem," Frank observed dryly.

"I suppose so, sir. I just wish she would have told me, but you're right; she was too proud for that, I reckon."

"I reckon so too. So, what do you recommend?"

"Revolvers, sir, for her and the O'Brien girl both. Private Waddell has been handling weapons long enough to be used to semi-autos, so she won't have any problems once I knock that damned cockiness out of her, but in the interests of time, we might as well give the other two something they can reliably use now, not somewhere down the road. The less time we spend on that, the more we can spend on the other stuff."

"I knew there was a reason I picked you to be First Sergeant," Frank told him, then gestured towards Tommy. "Talk to Lieutenant Richardson; he's our ordinance man."

It was late when Frank finally came to bed, but Samantha was still awake, waiting for him in the darkness. Thinking she was long asleep, he quietly stripped off his shirt in the converted office that now served as the commander's quarters. It had a pullout sofa bed that was not overly comfortable, but was better than the folding cots along the edge of the training area the men were using, or the behind the makeshift cardboard partition reserved for Donna and Kerrie.

Even in the dark, he looked nearly spent. She had never seen him this way, and she abruptly realized the reason was probably because he wouldn't allow himself to show it if he knew she could see, because he wouldn't want her to worry.

He looks so tired!

Surprisingly he didn't finish undressing and come to bed. Instead, shoulders slumped with the weight of fatigue and responsibility, he lowered himself to his knees on the hard cement floor. His back was to her, and it took her a moment to realize her husband was praying.

She knew he prayed, of course – she had done a lot of it herself in the past month or so – but other than grace over a meal or joining in a group prayer with her or some of the others, he kept his personal talks with the Lord private. Samantha had never actually *seen* him like this. She couldn't hear his words, only the intensity of his whispering as his bowed back shook with feeling. She felt a little guilty, almost like a voyeur, but she was comforted at the same time.

Finally, after several minutes, he finished with a quiet *amen*. Turning, he caught the glint of her open eyes and smiled tiredly.

"What are you still doing up? You'd better get what sleep you can; it's a long day tomorrow."

"If this is any indication, yours is going to be a lot longer."

He sat down on the edge of their bed, wearily pulling off his boots. Samantha rose up on her knees and began massaging his thickly muscled neck and upper back, digging her long, slender fingers deep and kneading the flesh to loosen the tension. With her fingers not fully healed and further aggravated by the day's activity, it hurt like hell to do it, but she kept going anyway. It was worth the pain to her to be able take some little bit of his away.

"Umm," he groaned with pleasure. "Command responsibility – it goes with the territory."

"That can't be good for you."

"Neither is war," he told her as he finished undressing and slipped between the sheets beside her.

They lay silently for a few minutes.

"I heard you had to execute a man today – a traitor."

"Yeah. If Mike hadn't been on the ball, we'd be up to our eyeballs in Fed troops right now, and I doubt any of us would have come out alive – *any of us*."

She couldn't mistake the emphasis he put on those last three words.

"It was that close?"

"Oh yeah. He was wearing a transmitter, and his job was to be the beacon to lead them right to our final destination. Peters practically had an army on standby, ready to swoop in and take us down." He bared his teeth without any trace of humor. "It would have been one a hell of a fight, but bottled up like that, the end result would have been a foregone conclusion."

She could feel the remnants of the fear of what could have happened in his voice.

"I...I think I understand now why you were so upset with me earlier. I thought it would just be training; I didn't realize the situation was that dangerous."

"It's always that dangerous, Sammie; today it was just a little more immediate than usual."

"Frank, even with all that, I'd be lying if I said I'm sorry I'm here with you, but I am sorry I went behind your back to do it. Are you still angry with me?"

He reached out his arm and she came to him, laying her head on his chest, just as she had on their first night together.

"No, I'm not mad at you. Your reasoning is sound for wanting to be here, and to be honest, I like having you around, especially with this thing with Edge and Larson going on." He gave her a little squeeze. "It's not really fair to the men, but it's done now, so there's no point in worrying about it. The bad part is just that it really brings home the danger you're in – from all sides. I trust in God, but I'm still scared, Sammie. I'm so *damned scared*, especially for you."

"I know what you mean."

"Yeah, I reckon you do at that." He paused for a moment before continuing. "One more thing though. I love you; I want you know that so you'll understand where I'm coming from. I want your promise right here and now that you'll never pull another stunt like this again – *ever!*"

"But Frank, I – "

"No buts." His voice was tender but hard, like a velvet glove with an iron hand inside it. "You took a terrible risk coming up here the way you did: an unacceptable risk for an insufficient reason, and that's *not* going to happen again. I'm your husband *and* your commanding officer; if you want to go on a mission with me, you ask me first. Promise me, Sammie."

She swallowed hard; she knew herself too well. "I don't know if I can promise that, honey."

He stared at her, and even in the dark, she saw the hurt in his eyes at what he was about to say.

"This would be easier if you were simply my subordinate instead of also being my wife. You're more than my wife; you're my life, and I don't want to hurt you. Please don't put me in the position where I have to begin ordering the others to see to it you don't leave the safe house unless authorized. You're risking your life every day as it is, and I'm not going to allow you to add any more risk to it without a damned good reason."

She flushed and was furious for a moment, but quickly swallowed her anger down like a bitter draught of medicine. She couldn't deny, as her commander, he had every right to do this, and as her husband, he was doing it because he loved her. She also had no doubt he meant every last word of it. Even though he knew it would humiliate her beyond imagining if he told the others to baby-sit her, he would give that order if he thought it necessary to protect her. Because he was who he was, she also had no doubt that, love and respect her as they might, anyone at headquarters would – reluctantly and apologetically no doubt, but they still *would* – do exactly what he told them, even if it meant handcuffing her to a toilet. Even so, to meekly submit to his order rankled her, and went against everything she had ever imagined herself doing as an independent woman.

You couldn't imagine this situation you've been in the past few months either, or what was done to you. You also couldn't imagine you'd ever find a man like this one, or be in love as much as you are…even if you do act like you're going crazy. Maybe he's right to worry, and with all he's got on his mind, that's one thing he doesn't need more of.

"That…won't be necessary, Frank. I promise; I give you my word."

"Thank you," he said as he kissed her. "That's good enough for me."

Still smarting a little, but satisfied that her presence at the training camp had brought about no undue tension in their relationship, she changed the subject, hoping the talk would help him wind down.

"How is the unit coming?"

"Well, I think. Unfortunately, I have very little to base my evaluation on; I've never really commanded anything to amount to much since I was in the Reserves. It's a new experience for me, and one I'm not sure I'm up to."

"I'm sure you're up to it if anyone is. I know you, Franklin Gore, and I've never known you to give less than your very best to anything you do, and that goes double for something this important."

He lay there so long before answering she thought he had gone to sleep.

"I appreciate the vote of confidence," he finally told her, "and I *am* giving it my best. The thing is, there's so much riding on what I do; not just you and me, but the lives of twenty-eight men, and possibly the fate of this whole revolution and all the people involved. What frightens me the most is the thought of what will happen if my best isn't good enough."

He shuddered at the only logical answer to that thought.

Then we'll all die...if we're lucky.

Frank soon drifted off, but Samantha lay there awake beside him, cuddled in the crook of his arm, just as she had on so many nights. Nearly asleep, she brushed her hand across his chest and touched the locket he never took off. Softly, half-consciously, she laid her hand across the ancient brass. In his sleep, his right hand rose and closed on hers, trapping the locket in her palm just as her smaller fist was trapped in the comfort of his larger one. Her eyes blinked and slowly closed –

Suddenly she sat up straight, gasping and fighting for breath with tears pouring from her eyes, and jerked her hand away as if it had been burned.

It must have been a dream! It had to be!

For an eternal instant, she had been swept up into a brutal kaleidoscope of the past. She had not only seen, but heard, smelled and felt –

Bagpipes howled like damned souls as the bright plaid of her kilt swirled against her bare legs and men shouted ancient Gaelic war cries in her ears as muskets roared and claymores flashed like lightening bolts across the sky –

212

Fifes and drums now, and she felt the jarring of the horse under her as the cavalry thundered down on that cursedly precise red-coated line, headlong into a living wall of fire as regular as a heartbeat that rumbled like rolling thunder and stank of brimstone –

The ear-splitting Rebel yell filled the air and tore her own throat raw as she charged a blue enemy this time, straight into the guns belching a hail of grape and canister, and she screamed as the flying blood of her comrades ahead filled her open mouth and stung her face like hot sleet –

She stuffed most of her fist in her mouth and bit down hard on her knuckles to keep from crying aloud, desperately trying to clear the chaotic vision from her head as her breath came in racking sobs. In that one horrible second she had fought a thousand battles in a hundred wars, smelled the stench of torn guts and felt the numbing shock up her arm of a sword cleaving flesh and biting bone. Worse yet, she had screamed the wavering, mourning cry of the broken women who crouched in the ruins of smoldering cabins that reeked of burned wood and charred flesh, having just lost *everything*.

Eyes wide and wild, she stared at her husband. A dream brought on by what Frank had told her about the locket's history or a genuine vision, this was his past before he *was*, burned into his being, into his very genes just as certainly as his eye color. The words of a long-ago preacher came back to her:

Flesh of one flesh…

She knew then; she had joined with him, and it was her past now too. Worse, it was her future. It was the *price* of a dream.

She looked at Frank, his eyes moving rapidly beneath the lids in REM sleep, lost in dreams of his own, and she finally understood the warrior's path her husband walked, why he was so afraid for her, and why he prayed so hard.

So be it! I am where I belong, and some things are worth fighting for.

Suddenly she remembered something Frank had told her their first night together, hiding, frightened and on the run.

"*Love alters not with his brief hours and weeks, but bears it out even to the edge of doom*" the Shakespearean quote went.

To the edge or over it, where he goes, I will follow.

Samantha softly kissed her husband's bearded cheek and lay back down beside him. Gritting her teeth, she deliberately reached out and placed her hand within his again, taking the locket in her palm once more, this time in acceptance. In moments, she drifted into a peaceful, dreamless sleep.

"So, what do you think?" Sam inquired into the phone, his own voice heavy with fatigue.

"That was some useful information: very useful," Edge grudgingly replied. Earlier in the day, before the call, Edge had received a color JPEG file of a landscape painting in his email. Using a prearranged rotating pixel count from various established points, each color value in the selected individual pixel matched a number that, in turn, matched a particular letter of the alphabet; an order that also rotated periodically. In a short time the message had been deciphered to reveal the names, addresses, and other information concerning the late Marvin Connolly's Federal handlers.

"So," Sam continued, carefully using euphemisms to avoid any 'code words' that would alert any monitoring Federal computers that might be listening it. Despite the fact they were on scrambled lines, unless someone like Mike was managing it directly, one couldn't be too careful. "Do we terminate them or bring them home?" He was asking if the CAP commander wanted the Federal agents dead or captured.

"We've already got them, alive and talking; I have no doubt we can get some useful data from them. As far as we've been able to tell, the action was just in time; we don't believe that they'd put their partners on alert, or even put two and two together yet themselves."

Sam was surprised at the swiftness of the action and puzzled by the identity of those carrying it out.

"So, which of our people did it then?"

"None of the ones in South Carolina. In order to keep peace in the family, I had some elements sent over the border from North Carolina; those boys are so jealous of their '*rights*' they throw a hissy-fit if they even think somebody else is infringing on their

214

territory. Suggs and Tarbox were about to lose their minds when they found out we're using the farmers' market up there. I gave them the targets in your neck of the woods in an operation to demonstrate to those yahoos that their precious pride in state sovereignty is secondary to working together and winning this war."

"I wish you had informed me of that beforehand," Sam said, somewhat rankled.

"Why? Don't tell me you're going to start that crap too!"

"That *crap* has less to do with it than the fact that I need to know when outsiders – even allies – are operating here. There could be collisions with my own elements mistaking them for someone else. We don't need any friendly fire incidents."

"You know, Stonewall Jackson once said that mystery was the key to success."

"Yeah, and Stonewall Jackson ended up getting mistakenly shot by his own men because he was somewhere they didn't expect him to be."

There was a pause as Edge attempted to regroup after Sam's own telling point. "Well, at any rate, you'll have plenty to keep you occupied. You all will have to deal with any subjects we learn about once our sources really start talking. I'll relay the information, and you have your 'golden boy' plan those operations against them on his own, and have his people carry it out – keeping me informed *beforehand* – while you continue to act strictly as an observer. I want to see if he's as good as you let on before we go to the next step, and if he fails, I don't want you tainted with it."

Sam frowned at both the words and their tone. "You still can't just accept him, can you, even after he dropped this intelligence coup right in your lap?"

"Let's just say if he steps in it, I'll be disappointed, but I won't be heartbroken. The same with his personnel; being as how their primary loyalty was to Larson, I consider them potentially untrustworthy until I know different. Both he and they are more expendable than certain other proven assets with a demonstrated loyalty."

215

Sam exploded on his friend. "After all you've been through together, how the hell can you feel that way? I know; it's because he told you 'no' isn't it? He defied you and even threatened you; that's what's got your panties in a knot! Larson's people were also brought in over your objections too, and you can't deal with that either, can you? And now this deal with Larson himself; somebody farts without consulting you first, and you think it's a conspiracy. This – *organization* – has been torn apart by personal bullshit since its inception; why the hell are you still doing it?"

"Look," Edge told him smoothly, carefully although with some difficulty hiding his anger from the only friend he had left: one whom he no longer fully trusted, "let's just call it a gut feeling and leave it at that. He's already one loose cannon; you're not going to start rolling around the deck too, are you? Just get him on the stick and let him prove himself to me."

"He'll do his job, don't you worry about that, but I don't think proving himself to you is very high on his list of priorities. Look, I'm friends with both of you, and I'll tell you something: he's a damned capable man, and totally dedicated. You may not know it, but he supported you when some of the others had doubts, for one reason, and one reason only: he thinks you're the only one able to hold this conglomeration together until we win this thing. Don't screw with him, John; I mean it. He's the kind of man who can only be pushed so far until he pushes back."

"That sounds like a threat." The growing heat was becoming more evident in the General's voice.

"It's not a threat; it's a fact. I'll tell you something else; you'd best not let that ego of yours do your thinking for you. We can't afford to lose either one of you, let alone both, and I'm getting tired of putting out all these brushfires you keep starting."

Edge struggled to rein in his temper. He wasn't a man who brooked opposition easily. When he finally got hold of himself, his voice was cold and deadpan.

"Whatever; you just be sure he does his job. I want those people trained and ready in three weeks time. I'll use my own resources to investigate the information in-depth, and have the expanded intelligence ready for his use; put it together with whatever your people come up with. In the meantime, I'll make arrangements to have the information from the 'data package' that was just delivered to my headquarters sorted and evaluated."

Long after he hung up the phone, Sam lay awake in his bunk despite his exhaustion. He had a very bad feeling that he was about to lose a friend very literally: maybe even two. He'd do what he could to prevent it, but he could see an inevitable collision coming: a head-on, hundred mile an hour smash-up that would probably derail the revolution. It was also likely to cause him to make the hard choice he feared most. Their movement might – *might* – possibly survive the demise of one or the other, the leader or the rallying point; it would not survive the loss of both, whether that came in the form of two deaths or one, with the other's loss of credibility by being known as an assassin. Sam's loyalty was to that movement first and foremost, and he was not going to see it tear itself apart, even if he ultimately had to choose himself as to which one of his friends and comrades survived the looming clash.

Silently but fervently, he prayed that God would let that cup pass from him.

DAY 87

CHAPTER 18

"Captain Gore, I don't mean any disrespect to the Cause, but I don't understand how we can hope to stand against an army as technologically superior as the United States military forces. Could you please explain that, because I just can't see it?"

Standing before them, Frank briefly swept his eyes over the company, and saw the same question silently repeated in the faces of most of the men. Not all; a few of the younger ones were so gung-ho and convinced of their own immortality they never gave it a thought, and Caffary and one or two of the others already knew. Most however, did not. It spoke volumes for their character and their dedication to the Cause by the fact that they were there anyway.

"I won't tell you technology doesn't matter; it does, particularly in a conventional conflict. However, it is not the be-all and end-all of guerrilla war. The Palestinians, the Irish, the Iraqis, the Viet Cong, and others like them kept going against vastly technologically superior armies. Technology is simply a tool that enables an army to work more efficiently, but it has less to do with the overall strategy and situation than you might think, as tactics can be changed to fit its presence. Rather than simply being a matter of having better 'toys', it is the universal principles of timing, strategy, courage, endurance, the ability to think outside the box, and the capacity for utter ruthlessness when necessary that has everything to do with victory.

"The odds are against the revolutionary right from the start. Historically speaking, the normal end for a rebel – any rebel – is against a wall or at the end of a rope, unless he is smarter, tougher, meaner, and, most of all, has a stronger faith in their cause than those he is trying to overthrow. If he can do all those things, he stands a reasonable chance for success."

Frank's wife raised her hand.

"Yes, Sammie?"

"Frank-er, Captain," she corrected herself amid the snickering and one whisper of, "Oh hell, call him Frank!"

"Can you explain just exactly how guerrilla warfare works? Some of us aren't as well versed in it as others."

"Guerrilla warfare is not an end in itself, but a step by step accelerating process that gradually wears down and weakens the enemy. At the same time, it strengthens the rebel forces in terms of domestic tolerance and foreign assistance: foreign assistance, because he has proven himself to be a viable force, and domestic tolerance because the government will inevitably alienate the populace by crackdowns and reprisals as they desperately search for the elusive rebel. This is despite the fact that, as a weak force, the guerrilla is a violent nuisance rather than an actual danger to the government. In perception, however, the need for his elimination becomes an all-consuming obsession, because his very presence demonstrates to all and sundry that the government is *not* all-powerful. Indeed, such a crackdown is part and parcel of successful guerrilla strategy; often he intentionally works to bring about the temporary suffering of his own people at the hands of the existing government.

"Guerrilla warfare is about action and reaction; for any given action, there are only a certain number of logical reactions, which can thus be predicted to some degree. As long as the guerrilla controls the action, he also controls the reaction, and eventually the increasingly desperate regime in charge will take it out on the uninvolved populace for *'supporting'* him, which will have the reverse effect of driving their support to him. Sometimes, if he is successful, more and more will flock to his standard, and the guerrilla army may become so large it morphs into a conventional force itself.

"No revolutionary movement, other than military coups, *ever* began with superior forces – or even nearly equal forces – and very few began with majority popularity, even in countries where you think they would have had it, like 1916 Ireland. Most never really achieved genuine popularity until after the fact of victory, and some not even then, but it doesn't matter. Those within revolutionized countries inclined to actively oppose the victorious forces are usually either imprisoned, in exile or dead, and the remaining unmotivated majority simply sigh and adjust to their new 'masters' just as they always do.

"Make no mistake; one had better want their liberty very badly before they consider guerrilla action. Guerrilla warfare is Iraq, the West Bank, or Belfast a generation ago. It is nothing even remotely like most Americans think of war. A revolutionary guerrilla conflict is war at its worst: a war without mercy and with only one moral code: win at any cost, because if you lose you *will die*. Unlike conventional warfare, there are no rules or restrictions other than those the guerrillas choose to place for temporary advantage or propaganda purposes. It's never pretty, but it's the only way for the less powerful to force their will on the strong, and if they do it at a time when the enemy is at his weakest – as the U.S. is now – they stand a fair chance of bringing it off, historically speaking."

They had all expected tough training, but Frank Gore's *'First Columbia Irregulars Special Warfare School'* more than exceeded their expectations.

First, he divided the company into three rotating groups of two, two, and one squad each, so that they could keep smaller, continuous classes going all day long while maintaining squad integrity. He also split up Sammie, Donna and Kerrie, sending one to each group. Sam gave the daily political lecture and instructed them in the basics of intelligence, while Rob taught small unit tactics, including room and building entry and clearing. Tommy worked them on demolitions and first aid, and Frank instructed them in combat shooting and hand to hand fighting, as well as leading a grueling morning PT workout that left them all in puddles of sweat. Everyone was constantly busy, sometimes for fourteen hours a day or more, stopping only for eating or the call of nature. Any of the officers not teaching at any given time were assisting in the other classes or, in Rob and Tommy's case, occasionally making a supply run.

221

On their first full day, Frank stood facing one of the groups, his hands clamped behind his back.

"Gentlemen," Frank hesitated before adding, "and lady; welcome to the first installment of the close combat section of your course.

"First, I know most of you know how to fight. That doesn't matter; you can forget about fighting because you're not here to learn how to fight. You're here to learn how to kill, in the quickest, most efficient way possible. This war isn't a contest, and there are no rules except win or die.

"There are places where it is next to impossible to get a weapon into, and your targets may be in some of those places. Further, in a covert situation, you may be attacked when you're unarmed. In either event, you're not going to fight your enemy; you're going to kill him."

His was physically the toughest of all their classes. They sweated, grunted, and sweated some more as Frank put them through the paces. He pushed them farther than many of them thought possible, and then he pushed them some more. He was infuriatingly cold and exacting; it would be done until it was right, and then it would be done that way over and over until it was second nature.

They learned a distillation of military hand to hand combat, street fighting, and traditional martial arts that Frank had developed; a stripped-down style that was no frills and all death. He hadn't lied; they learned to kill with improvised weapons and with no weapons at all; short, quick, and brutal, overwhelming the enemy with raw aggression and a few basic techniques learned until they were reflex. He used his experience to build their counters, not so much to street attacks, but primarily to police and military close combat tactics.

The most unnerving, particularly for the women, were the assassination techniques. Everyone learned to use a garrote, a knife, a club, or their bare hands to take the life of the enemy before he knew they were there. It was almost surreal to Samantha, the otherwise gentle Frank coldly explaining the art of death.

...Stick the blade in, twist it, and cut your way out; leave the biggest wound you can...strike here to sever the medulla from the

spinal column for an instant kill...jam your thumb under the eyeball
and scoop it out like a spoon...Try it again...Again...Again...

She learned, though; by the time he finished with them, every last one was a walking weapon, waiting to be pointed at a target.

Surprising herself, Samantha managed to at least hold her own in all the classes; however, she and everyone else were shocked when she discovered a hitherto unknown talent for instinctive point shooting with a handgun. The afternoon of the second day, the trio of Frank, Tommy, and Caffary had taken away her Berretta and given a stainless steel Smith and Wesson 686 .357 magnum revolver they had taken from the body of one of Peters' death squad members in Charleston. Tommy had been pretty impressed with the skill of whoever had done the gunsmithing on it before, but now that it was going to Samantha, he installed a lighter spring and slicked up the action a little bit more. Loading it with lighter recoiling .38 special ammunition in deference to her injured hands, they had her try it out, and everyone – especially her – was astonished at the results. Over the next few days, she fired dozens of rounds, getting used to the process, and somewhere along the line, something clicked inside her. Even though she had never used a pistol in her life, the technique seemed natural to her, and before long she could draw, fire, and hit a close-range target better than ninety percent of the men. Even though she remained little more than acceptable in aimed fire, the close-up ability was still a source of pride for her – as well as to Sergeant Caffary, who happily took the credit for it – and a relief to Frank, who wouldn't have quite as much reason to worry about her...although he still would.

The feminine presence among the men during training wasn't the distraction Frank had feared it would be; in fact, it was of some benefit because the men subconsciously tried harder under the influence of the male instinct to impress the opposite sex. Samantha was his wife, and though half of the Irregulars fell in love with her immediately, they left her strictly alone other than professionally and the occasional lustful stare when they thought no one was looking. Some of them, particularly the younger ones, tried to approach Kerrie in what little spare time they had. She was friendly enough in

223

a quiet way, even though clearly out of her depth, but she remained slightly withdrawn and distant to their advances. Donna, on the other hand, became something of a flirt. Her wild attitude was a mystery that more than one of them were determined to get to the bottom of, but as far as Frank, and the ever-watchful alliance of necessity made up of Sam and Tommy could tell, she gently fended them off before it went too far.

DAY 89

CHAPTER 19

"You wanted to see me?"

"Yes I did, Tommy." Frank had just finished taking a class through the close combat course, and was wiping the sweat from his face with a towel. Dropping it around his neck, he told his friend and subordinate, "Let's take a walk."

Only when they had reached the far end of the building, out of earshot of the rest, did Frank speak again. "You know it wasn't my idea to have my wife here in the first place."

"Hey, that was Sam; I had nothing to do with it. I wasn't exactly thrilled when Donna showed up either, you know?"

Frank waved off his denial. "I know that. The thing is, she *is* here, and that puts me in a quandary. As much as it hurts me, for the sake of morale, I can't play favorites, not even with her. I also can't allow the rest of you to do it."

"I…don't know what you mean," the biker said uneasily, in a tone of voice that actually said *I know exactly what you mean* pretty plainly.

"Don't play games with me, partner. I've noticed the men cutting her a whole bunch of slack in the hand-to-hand combat workout whenever they think I'm not looking, and sometimes even when they know I am. Sammie's too proud to complain if they broke half the bones in her body, so I know she didn't ask them to take it easy."

"You know how it is. Men automatically give special consideration to women in marital arts classes; it's instinct."

"It's an instinct she can't afford. God forbid she ever has to use this for real, but if she does, do you think some gung-ho enemy soldier is going to show her any consideration because of her sex? No, he's going to ram a bayonet in her guts if she can't stop him from doing it. As much as my heart jumps up in my throat and I feel like crying myself every time she slams down on the floor, I don't intend to let that happen. She has to learn the real thing; I love her too much for anything less."

He eyed Tommy with a raised brow. "Besides, I caught one of the Worley twins doing it a little while ago, and took him aside and asked him about it, only to be told that Lieutenant Richardson had ordered him to do so. I want to know why."

Tommy grimaced inwardly. *How in seven kinds of blue hell do I get myself into these messes?*

Not wanting to lie to Frank or break his promise to Samantha, the medic decided to split the difference.

At least it's close to the truth. I suppose a little is better than none at all.

"I ordered it for health reasons. She hasn't fully recovered from her ordeal."

Frank's hand clamped down on his shoulder like a vice.

"What's wrong with Sammie?" His eyes were wide and his voice was almost panicked.

"Frank, we've got kind of a doctor-patient confidentiality thing here; she asked me not to tell you –"

His commander's tone abruptly changed and became cold and dangerous, more so than Tommy had ever heard directed at him; in fact, it was downright scary. "I'm her husband, Tommy. I want to know what's wrong with my wife and I want to know *now*."

Tommy had been in more hairy situations than he could remember, and he knew another one when he saw it coming. Not even considering the size difference, he had practiced with Frank on a regular basis, and despite his own high level of skill, he knew he wasn't even in the same league with his commander, especially when the Captain was righteously – and rightfully – pissed. Frank might be his friend, but the medic had no doubt, regardless of that, he might very well beat the hell out of him and quite possibly hurt him badly in his concern for Sammie. The worst part of it was that Tommy couldn't really blame him. His mind raced and he quickly came up with an answer.

"Her uterus; I don't think it's fully healed after all the times she was punched and kicked by the Feds, as well as – well, the other things they did. She's been having some feminine irregularities, and I don't want to risk any permanent damage."

Frank was aghast.

"Why didn't she tell me?" he shouted.

"Shh! Keep your voice down, damn it! She didn't want to distract you. You've got enough on your mind without that."

"But – is she going to be alright?" Inside, he was suddenly horribly afraid, as his mind started chanting, *what if – what if – what if…*

Abruptly he went white.

"What if *I've* hurt her? I mean we've been together – you know, we're husband and wife!"

"Frank, you don't have to explain the birds and the bees to me! I know what you two have been doing, and it's all right. As long as she's not complaining of any pain during intercourse, it'll be fine. For that matter, I think she'll be fine; it'll just take time, that's all. In the meantime, though, I don't want to risk too much shock to her system."

"Damn it!" He slapped himself on the forehead in anger. "I'll pull her out of close combat –"

It was Tommy's turn to interrupt. "You'll do no such thing. Like you just said, she needs to learn it. Besides, I've told the men in her group what to do and not to do. Everything will work out all right.

"Don't you be telling her you know either, or she'll have my ass; you know how she is when she gets mad."

"Okay," Frank finally said, after mulling it over, "I won't say anything, but in turn, I expect you to keep me informed on her progress – *fully* informed this time. Deal?"

"Deal," Tommy replied, mentally crossing his fingers and simultaneously calculating the increasingly intimidating dimensions of the hole he was digging for himself.

He's going to royally kick my ass before this is over; I just know it!

DAY 89

CHAPTER 20

"Mr. Peters, it's good to see you, sir."

Peters stepped inside the hot, palpable humidity of the James Furniture Warehouse and almost staggered from the stench.

"Let's dispense with the small talk, Agent Ralston. I don't want to spend any longer in here than I have to. What have you got?"

"It's over at the other end of the warehouse, sir. Here," the FBI agent told him, handing him a charcoal-permeated filter mask before slipping a second one over his own mouth and nose. "This'll cut down a little bit on the smell; it's pretty bad over there."

As they walked across the dirty concrete floor, the FEMA chief asked him, "Are you certain this is our man on the inside?"

"We found the transmitter in Idaho, in the cab of a long haul trucker. We're still questioning him, but it doesn't look like he knows anything. Someone probably planted it there at a truck stop or something to throw us off after they killed our man. The body in here has the implanted ID chip, but of course we won't know for sure until we compare biometric identifiers such as dental, DNA, or fingerprints."

When they reached their destination, Peters stared dispassionately at the bloated, blackened, maggot-ridden mess that had been Marvin Connolly. Three days of summer heat in the sealed metal building had sped up the decomposition process several times over, and the corpse was in bad shape, well on its way to liquefying. Nearby, a crime scene investigation team waited with a body bag while they sweated in their white protective suits.

"No one has moved anything?"

"No sir; after the body was discovered, no one touched anything. We took the photographs and began setting up to collect the remains and other evidence, of course, but we followed your instructions."

Peters nodded, and continued staring at the scene, as if to absorb every bit of it. Finally he turned back to the agent. "Any theories so far?"

"He appears to have a gunshot wound to the head and other trauma, possibly multiple gunshots, to the upper torso. His hands are behind him and presumably tied, although we haven't moved the body yet to see for sure yet. We believe he was either sitting on or fell into that chair when he died; as you can see, he's still laying across its backrest where it overturned."

As Peters digested this, he motioned to the agent to go ahead and have the technicians bag Connolly up.

"What's your hypothesis so far?"

Ralston swallowed; he was on dangerous ground now. It would not be a good career move to give Peters the wrong information. Even if he was on his way out, as the scuttlebutt indicated, he could drag others down with him or make life hard while he was still here.

"Bearing in mind that this is only speculation at this moment, pending further investigation –"

"I'm well aware of that. Get on with it; it stinks in here." The smell had increased exponentially when the CSI team began gingerly trying to move the body into a bag, doing their best to keep the grotesquely swollen mass from popping under the pressure of the gasses built up inside it.

"Yes sir. At this juncture, it appears likely Marvin Connolly's activities on our behalf were discovered, and that he was summarily executed by firing squad, probably while seated in that chair. There appear to be some blood splatters on the floor several feet behind it." He gestured towards a string of dark spots covered with still more squirming maggots. "We've also discovered dents in the metal walls in the direction of the splatters, as well as a couple of spent bullets on the floor; apparently they no longer had enough energy to penetrate the sheet metal after passing through the deceased."

"The hands are bound behind the back with what appears to be gray duct tape" came the voice from one of the techs, muffled and anonymous from inside his full protective hood. Suddenly the voice exclaimed, "Holy shit! Would you look at that chair!"

The technician eased the corner of the chair from beneath the body, and they stared grimly at the metal back, perforated with several small holes.

"It appears you were right, Agent Ralston. We also have to presume he gave up certain information before he died, information that led directly to the disappearance of his handlers."

Ralston nodded his agreement. "That's the most likely scenario, sir. God only knows what they're squeezing out of those guys right now."

Despite the heat, Peters shivered as a cold chill ran down his back, as if someone had just walked over his grave.

Angered at his own fear, he turned back to the agent. "Let these people finish up here; you're coming with me. I've got a plan –"

As the techs moved the body a little further, carefully rolling it in an attempt to ease the open body bag underneath, there was a *ping,* and a piece of metal bounced from under it and hit the chair.

"What the hell –"

"Grenade!" Ralston screamed at the top of his lungs, recognizing the metal lever more by instinct than conscious thought. He threw himself down, brutally clothes lining the startled Peters in the process and taking him to the floor with him.

Sergeant Caffary had put an old guerrilla trick to use before the Irregulars departed. He had pulled the pin from a fragmentation grenade before lifting Connolly's body and placing it underneath as an unpleasant surprise for those who would be coming to collect him. The weight of the dead man's body had held the priming lever in place until the corpse was shifted far enough to release it.

Two of the CSI techs, both military veterans, instantly threw themselves to the ground, a third turned to run, and the fourth, the one who had found the deadly object, simply stood frozen in panicked immobility. As a last act, he took the Lord's name in vain with great feeling.

The internal fuse reached its end, and the grenade went off with a roar, the fragmentation coil within it sending a storm of shrapnel in all directions.

The tech standing beside the body had no chance; his legs and lower body were torn to bloody rags and he was dying by the time he hit the floor. Several pieces of flying metal sliced into the legs, butt, and back of the man trying to run, causing him to fall against the wall and collapse, first gasping and then screaming in agony.

Other than some relatively minor cuts, the rest of the team, including Ralston and Peters, would have been unscathed except that Connolly's body, already gas-swollen to maximum capacity, exploded along with the grenade. Bits of putrefying flesh stuck to them and rotting fluids soaked them to the skin.

Shaken, the survivors cautiously sat up, and the remaining CSI members ran to help their comrades as more agents, alerted by the blast, came pouring inside, weapons drawn despite their gagging at the eye-watering smell.

Peters' ears were ringing so badly he could barely hear Ralston shouting at him.

"Are you alright, Mr. Peters? Are you alright?"

No, I'm not all right; I'm not all right at all.

As the putrid filth dripped down his face, another man might have been nauseated, or fearful at the near miss. A man like Peters would normally have been furious.

The thing was, Ronald Peters was not angry, nor was he sick or afraid. Instead, much to his own surprise, he was tired...tired and depressed. He had a very bad feeling that, for the first time in his life, he just might be in over his head after all.

Network Newscast, USA

Following the torture and execution-style murder of an undercover FBI agent and the death of another from a booby trap, Federal, state and local law enforcement agencies launched a massive series of raids in South Carolina this evening in an effort to suppress Confederate terrorism. Several suspects were rounded up during the sweep, and a female terrorist reportedly murdered her own son before dying of a self-inflicted gunshot wound rather than be taken alive.

"This only goes to show the savagery and fanaticism that drives these racists," said Homeland Security Chairman Paul Leibowitz...

Newscast, British News Service

There was panic in the American state of South Carolina last night as Federal paramilitary forces swept through the region in a series of house-to-house raids on the homes of suspected Confederate sympathizers. Witnesses reported doors smashed in and suspects brutally beaten and kicked. In one case, a mother with a young son died, according to the official reports, from "self-inflicted" gunshot wounds: a designation so increasingly common that it cannot help but strain credibility...

DAY 90

CHAPTER 21

Frank looked up at the rapping on the door.

"Come in. Have a seat."

"Thank you, sir," Arnel Scot of Alpha squad answered as he closed the door behind him. Parking himself on the chair in front of the desk, he looked curiously at Frank, as well as the three men with him: First Sergeant Caffary, his squad leader Sergeant Hodges, and Corporal Jack Lewis. Frank had discovered that Corporal Lewis was a Christian Identity pastor and, as the only ordained minister in the bunch, had appointed him as chaplain to the group whose actual denominations varied from Fundamentalist to Baptist to Catholic, and everything outside and in between.

"You wanted to see me, sir?"

Frank sighed. "No, Private Scot, I hate like hell to see you right now. I've got some bad news for you."

As Frank took a breath before continuing, Scot put it together. "It's my family, isn't it?" he asked, his voice unnaturally calm.

His commander nodded, watching the man carefully. The broad shoulders, hips and face, short reddish brown hair, and sunburned neck of the farmer all spoke of solidity, but there was no telling how a man would react at what Frank was about to lay on him.

"I'm sorry, Arnel; they're dead. Your wife and son – both of them."

"How?" The voice sounded as hollow as if it were coming out of a drainpipe.

"Feds. I sent my people after them just like I promised, only they weren't home. The man I sent waited awhile, then decided to come back later. Unfortunately, he got caught up in a roadblock with a pistol in his car. They hauled him off to jail and were holding him incommunicado as a suspected terrorist, so we never got the word. Your wife and son came home later, and the Feds stormed the house

235

late last night. I guess – at least, our sources on the inside claim – she grabbed a gun when she heard them knock the door down; she probably thought they were thieves. When they opened fire, your boy was standing right behind her. Neither one survived.

"I'm sorry," he added lamely, well aware of how little comfort were in the words even as he said them, because they brought no comfort to him either.

I failed one of my men. God help me, I don't know what I could have done differently, but I failed him!

Arnel sat there for a long time, not saying a word. Finally, when he looked up, Frank could see the barely suppressed tremors beginning.

"Sir, could…could I be alone for a while?"

"You can have this room for as long as you need it, Arnel," Frank told him, using his given name for the first time as he stood. Walking around the desk, he put his hand on the man's shoulder before leaning down to look him in the eye. "If you need me, or any of us to talk to, you just say so. I don't know what the hell we can say, but we can at least listen. Would you like Reverend Lewis to stay?"

Arnel shook his head, and Frank nodded his understanding.

"Alright. One more thing; I know you've got that pistol on your hip. I suppose, considering the circumstances, I ought to ask for it for a while, but I'm not going to. You're a good man, and I think you know that using that weapon right now won't help anything. We can't bring your family back, so you need to stay alive to help avenge them. Rest assured, there will be a payback for this. I know that's damned cold comfort, but they *will* be avenged. You have my word on that."

Scot looked straight into his eyes as he nodded assent, and Frank recognized the very same gaze that had stared back from the mirror at him when the Feds had murdered his grandmother, and when Samantha had first been taken.

The world wasn't wide enough or Hell hot enough to keep Arnel Scot from his vengeance.

DAY 100

CHAPTER 22

The nights were the best part. After a hard twelve to fourteen hours of training, once everyone had cleaned up and been fed, the barriers of rank dropped and what Frank began referring to as the social hour began. A beer apiece was rationed out to every man not on guard duty, and they broke up into groups, talking about anything and everything. A couple of times the talk became a bit too spirited and degenerated into fistfights, but they were soon broken up and forgotten. Some preferred the TV or radio, while others stuck their noses in the box of books Sam had provided, reading to relax.

Many nights, however, brought the jam session. Among the men were four guitars, a banjo, a fiddle, a couple of harmonicas, and even a set of bagpipes brought along by Casey Graham of Alpha Squad. Several more of the men, along with Donna, Kerrie, and, to Frank's surprise, Samantha, could handle the guitars with a fair amount of skill, so the instruments were regularly passed around.

Their musical tastes were broad; the White Power music fans were split into two camps, heavy metal and ballad, but the metal-heads were mostly left out due to the lack of electric instruments. More conventional rock and country each held equally strong followings, while Celtic and traditional folk and bluegrass seemed to be universal favorites. In a short time, a sort of fusion musical style seemed to evolve, much to everyone's delight.

One night in particular stuck in Frank's mind. It was during the third week, and everything just seemed to come together.

It started with Sam; while guitars, banjo, and fiddle supplied the tune, he sang a rousing version of '*Stonewall Jackson's Way*'. Not to be outdone, Tommy launched into '*Long-Haired Country Boy*'. Hodges and two of the other skinheads performed an acoustic version of the Bully Boys' White Power tune, '*Jig Run*', while Caffary managed a pretty fair imitation of Johnny Cash and '*The Orange Blossom Special*'. Frank's great weakness was in his singing ability; Tommy put it charitably when he observed that Captain Gore "couldn't carry a tune in a bucket." However, once it was found that, as a poetry fan, he knew the words, he was drafted into reciting '*Scots Wha Hae Wi' Wallace Bled*' while Private Graham howled away on his bagpipes.

Then, at their demand, the men surrendered to floor and the guitars to the women, and were instantly mesmerized. Frank in particular was surprised, because he had no idea his wife knew how to play.

"There are a lot of things you don't know about me," she told him teasingly, all the while trying desperately not to let it show in her eyes that she had one thing in particular she was hiding.

It seemed that Kerrie knew every Irish Patriot song in existence, and she crooned '*Rising of the Moon*', '*White, Orange and Green*', and '*Men Behind the Wire*' in a sad, honeyed voice that left the room utterly void of a dry eye.

It was Donna's turn then. She had a very pronounced Southern drawl, and she put it to good use as belted out half a dozen country tunes, beginning with '*Strawberry Wine*' and ending with '*Redneck Woman*'.

Finally Samantha took over. She chose a song that some of the men had introduced her to, a number made famous by a pair of twin sisters who went by the name of 'Prussian Blue.' The fingers that had been broken still moved a little stiffly and she hit the occasional sour note, but no one cared.

To every man who doesn't dream,
I am the dreamer.
To every man who doesn't believe,
I'm the believer.
To every man who doesn't receive,
I'm the receiver.
To every man who refuses to bleed,

I will bleed for you!
I will bleed for you!

After that, coming from her, they put the instruments away for the night. There was nothing else to add.

Frank looked out at the men with pride: *his* men, and *his* unit. They had come a long way in three weeks, much further than he had expected, but they still had a long way to go before they achieved the total unity he had hoped for. Still, they were damned good men, they were what he had, and looking them over, taking the time to look into each one's eyes in the process, he knew they would do.

They'll have to.

"Gentlemen as much as I'm sure you've enjoyed this little vacation," he said, promoting some laughter from the crowd, "playtime is over. I am going to have to cut our training short, because we have been ordered back to Columbia. Apparently there's some sort of problem that the First Columbia Irregulars are the only solution to."

Some of the younger and less experienced men cheered, but the others looked at him skeptically, as skeptical as Frank himself had felt ever since Sam relayed Edge's order to him. Something about the impenetrable secrecy surrounding the operation, particularly since the General was the one who conceived it, raised the hairs on the back of his neck and made him feel like he was about to put his foot smack in the middle of a bear trap.

A wolf trap, he mentally corrected himself, thinking of his earlier conversation with Mike, *and if I do, the trapper better make damned sure he's got a good hold!*

"Sir," Hodges called out. "Can you tell us what this mission is we've been selected for?"

"No, Sergeant, I can't, because I don't know yet myself." He glanced at Sam. The ex-farmer had insisted that Edge hadn't confided in him either, and Frank was willing to take him at his word, at least until proven otherwise; he owed him that much. "I don't know who, what, where or when yet, but don't worry; I

239

guarantee you won't be bored while we're waiting. You see, we have been ordered to plan an action against some of the enemy elements in our area of operations, and besides that, I have a few irons of my own in the fire, and the 1st Columbia is just the hammer I need to strike them!"

It was Sam's turn to glance sharply at Frank. This was the first he heard of whatever he had in mind.

I should have guessed he wouldn't be sitting on his hands waiting on Jonathon Edge. Lord, this is getting complicated.

He wondered if he should ask Frank as soon as they were alone, then decided against it. Frank would tell him when he was ready, and the last thing the older man wanted to do was to widen the gap between them by appearing to mistrust his increasingly nominal subordinate. Edge did enough of that for everybody it seemed.

DAY 107

CHAPTER 23

Back in Columbia once again, they had set up a temporary headquarters in the basement of an old grade school that had been closed due to consolidation. A month ago, at Sam's direction, one of their underground supporters had relayed a juicy bribe to a member of the school board, and he was allowed to temporarily lease the building for "warehouse storage." Despite the school's dilapidated condition, it was large, roomy, partly furnished, and most importantly had several windowless basement rooms and bordered in the rear on a heavily brush-lined alley that allowed for unobserved access as long as they were careful.

"Here's how it's going to work, Gentlemen," Frank said from the head of the folding table. Tommy and Rob sat to the right of him, while Basil Caffary and three of the platoon sergeants were seated around the table, beginning at his left. Sam had quietly parked himself in a corner. He was not a direct part of the operation by direct order of General Edge, but he was observing keenly.

"Squads Bravo, Charlie and Delta will each be assigned a particular target, and you will concentrate only on that target. *No one*, including the squad leaders in this room, is to know who any other squad's target is, and the men are not to know if the others even have a target at all. Secrecy is paramount; this way, God forbid something goes wrong with one squad's mission, it won't compromise the rest."

He turned to Caffary. "Sergeant."

The First Sergeant handed a sealed manila envelope to each man, with their squad's name written on the front and information on Federal personnel in the vicinity of Columbia inside. Once they had them, Frank continued. "All of the information we have been able to gather on these targets is in these envelopes in the form of data disks and hard copies. You will not open them until you're in your own squad rooms, and they will not leave those rooms without authorization. Lieutenant Johnson has the most experience in these matters, therefore he will be in overall command, with First Sergeant Caffary his acting XO. With their assistance, you will evaluate your targets and plan your missions. Lieutenant Johnson will present the finalized plans to me for review exactly two weeks from today. Bear in mind, and drill it into your squads, that these targets are to be taken prisoner if possible, and not killed except in cases of extreme necessity. We need their intelligence, and we can't get that if they're dead. Also, I don't want any collateral casualties. Are there any questions?"

There was a chorus of "No sir" all the way around. Sam had a question, and wished like hell he could ask it.

Frank, something this important, why are you delegating it instead of being directly involved?

He knew Frank, so he knew there must be a reason, and for some reason he had a growing feeling that he wasn't going to like the answer, and that Jonathon Edge was going to like it even less.

While he mulled over the possibilities, the squad leaders began filing out and Caffary barked out Hodges' name. After the big skinhead entered and the door closed, Frank motioned for him to be seated.

"Sergeant, do you like to raise hell?"

Hodges wasn't exactly sure what he was getting at, and wondered if he was in trouble for something. His mind raced, but he couldn't think of anything he'd done lately, so he decided to be truthful and let the chips land where they would.

"Sure Captain; born to it."

"Good, then you'll enjoy this mission. Lieutenant Richardson, who's another one just like you – only smaller and hairier – will be commanding, with you as his second. We're going to need more funding to finance these missions we're setting up for, so I want you two to take Alpha Squad and hijack an armored car full of money." He handed Tommy an unmarked computer disk in a plain jewel case. "Here's all the information we have on the different companies, regular routes, customers, pick-ups and drop-offs, vehicle statistics, along with summaries of both successful and failed attempts at what you are trying to do. Evaluate it, make your plan and a list of what you'll need, and have it finalized and ready for my review in one week. Since this is an operation against a neutral target, casualties are to be kept to an absolute minimum, meaning preferably none. Think you can handle it?"

Tommy and Hodges looked first at one another and then at Frank, grinning like two kids at Christmas, and answered in an enthusiastic, if somewhat profane affirmative. Sam, meanwhile, looked as if her were about to burst a blood vessel.

Edge didn't order this! He's going to crap!

The biker and the skinhead left, chattering excitedly, and at Frank's command, Sergeant Kowalski entered the room with his usual goofy, hangdog expression.

Pete Kowalski was an enigma of sorts. Larson had once described him as 'half-Yankee and looking like it'. He had huge 'Dumbo' ears that stuck out at a ninety-degree angle on a head that seemed to be neck-less, to all appearances sitting directly on his broad, sloping shoulders. His face looked stretched out, with a long, humped nose and a long chin. All of these features were a legacy of his father, a Marine from Milwaukee who had somehow convinced a pretty Charleston girl to marry him before he got himself killed in a helicopter crash. With his homely looks and slow talk, people tended to underestimate Pete. He had been a Marine himself, Recon to boot, and despite his inherent good nature and self-depreciating humor, was not someone to be trifled with. That he was the one his squad chose unanimously as their sergeant said a lot for his ability.

"Sergeant, I have a special mission for Echo Squad, and I'll be directly commanding. We're going to begin work on a little project that I've had in mind for a couple of months now. I intend to move on Ronald Peters and kill him very soon, but I need more intelligence to do it. Here's what we're going to do…"

As Sam listened, he paled.

"Damn it Frank! You can't do this!"

243

Frank, finally alone with Sam in the room, looked at his friend innocently, although both of them were well aware it was an act. "Can't do what? Our General gave me a list of targets –"

"You know good and well Edge didn't order *all* of these little 'projects' of yours; he is literally going to *shit*!"

"Then he'd better grab a roll of toilet paper. I'm not doing this for him; I'm doing it because it's necessary.

"First, I'm not going to have Feds operating in our area with impunity; those already here are a clear and present danger, and one I intend to neutralize very soon. Besides, Edge ordered that, and he'll get some prisoners and their intelligence, so he has no cause for complaint.

"Secondly, we've got to have that armored car. After providing the money for this training, our funds are almost depleted, and this is the quickest and safest was to raise them. I'll fulfill every reasonable order given by the General, but I won't be micro-managed on my own time and in my own theater. Edge is involved in the big picture – I'd guess he's not even in this state at the moment – but I'm responsible for the little picture: the right here and right now. He might make the outline of this painting, but I'll be filling in the details in my part of it, so he may as well resign himself to that fact."

"Listen," Sam said, trying to affect some sort of compromise so as not to rock the boat too badly, "you can probably get by with the armored car heist, but there's no way in hell that Edge will stand by and let you begin an operation of this magnitude – killing Peters – without his input."

"It needs to be done, and once I do it, he won't be able to say no. After all," he said with a disarming grin, "the last time I insisted on doing things my own way, the results put him in the cat bird's seat over the whole movement, so I don't think he has too much to gripe about."

The older man instinctively knew argument was useless, but he decided to try one more time. "You don't know him like I do. Listen to what I've got to say and maybe you'll understand where he's coming from. John was always a type A personality, but he wasn't always this paranoid. He got involved in this movement because he believed in it, and his competence and ambition took him all the way to the top ranks. That's when the trouble started."

"More jealousy?"

"Exactly. He and Jameson (before we found out he was a traitor and a Federal plant) were real tight at one time, but both of them wanted to be in charge. Edge came out on top, but Jameson, with behind the scenes support from our own Council members MacFie and Herdman (who hoped to take advantage of the resulting confusion and take things over themselves, under the auspices of their own organizations) started a smear campaign that utterly destroyed Edge's reputation. They accused him of everything under the sun, from falsifying his military record to rigging votes to stealing organizational funds. Jameson even accused *him* of being a government agent. They clogged up cyberspace with that crap, sending out literally thousands of email accusations, some of them with hundreds of names on each, to anybody they thought might even remotely care.

"Well, if you sling enough mud, some of it will stick, and pretty soon every pecker-head out there will start hollering, 'Where there's smoke there's fire,' and repeating it over and over again like a talking parrot. They told their lies long enough and loud enough that most of the people in the movement, even some who'd known Edge for years, turned on him. He was effectively shut out, *persona non grata.*

"That wasn't quite enough for them, and Edge was too stubborn to quit. They started a whispering campaign outside the movement then, dropping information to the Feds. I honestly don't think Herdman or MacFie wanted it to go that far, but when you're a stinking Fed like Jameson, there're no limits. Before long Edge was under government investigation and placed on the no-fly list. As a result of the continued harassment of the people around him, he lost his job and was even asked to leave his church.

"Right in the middle of all this, his wife and teenaged son died in a car crash."

Frank's antennas perked up. "They murdered them?"

245

"No," Sam said, shaking his head, "that was just some little old blue-haired lady, so old and half-blind she should never have been behind the wheel. She didn't see them and pulled right out in front of them, and when they swerved to miss her, his son lost control and went over an embankment. They were both killed instantly.

"You'd think at a time like that, even your worst enemies would cut you some slack. Do you know how many expressions of sympathy he got, a man who had once headed an organization of thousands? Exactly twelve, and one of those was mine. You know how many of them came to the funeral? One – me. Oh, Herdman and MacFie each sent him an email, but then Herdman, on that rinky-dink blog he had, turned right around and published Jameson's accusations the day after the funeral."

"What accusations are you talking about? Good Lord, they didn't keep after him did they?"

Sam nodded. "Yep, or at least Jameson did, with Herdman's help; all in the name of *'unbiased, non-partisan reporting on Southern issues'*, of course. Jameson carefully dropped the suggestion that the deaths were both suspicious and convenient, and pointed out that John was the beneficiary of the large life insurance policies, totaling well over a million dollars. He included a picture of Edge entering his house after the funeral with a young red head who remained there overnight, along with a caption about Edge's *"Mystery Date."* Herdman neglected to mention something he knew: that redheaded girl was my own Goddaughter, Linda, Donna's sister who was killed in Columbia. John had known her since she was a baby. I had asked her to stay with him for a few days, ostensibly to help him get things in order, but mainly because I was afraid he might kill himself if he was left alone. I played right into their hands and didn't even know it."

Frank stood in silent shock, his mouth hanging open. As a cop, he though he had heard it all, but apparently he was mistaken.

"And Herdman and MacFie went along with that?" he demanded with growing disgust.

"Herdman did, but so covertly that he appeared innocent to those who didn't really know him; you can sometimes do more damage with what you don't say than what you do. MacFie, on the other hand, still had enough principles to be scandalized and severed all his relations with Jameson over it. That was what caused Jameson to abandon the Cause of Southern Independence; once the Southern Majority organization pulled away from him, his power was shot with that faction, so he created his own in order to continue being a pain in our ass. But MacFie didn't issue a statement as to why, because he didn't want Edge back in the movement either.

"Edge did something then that no one, least of all those who knew him, ever expected: he stopped fighting. He was hurt, tired and burned out, and refused to even answer their allegations, to which one of Jameson's right hand men trumpeted, and I quote: *'His silence speaks volumes!'*

"What they didn't know, and couldn't know, was that Edge had something else in mind and the money in his pocket to make it happen. Everything he had was gone, and as he told me, *'Nothing left to lose means total freedom of action.'* Before they realized it, he had formed another organization: Southern Cause, which proceeded to assist in the election of half a dozen Southern Nationalists into office in four states. Suddenly, Edge's face was all over the media, and once again, he was too big to ignore. Therefore, when Roger Nash put together the Confederate Council, in an effort to put an end to all the infighting, he had no choice but to give Edge a seat on it. Despite that, he, Jameson, Herdman, and MacFie have been in a constant state of cold war with one another, in the shadows of course, with alliances shifting every day and Nash trying to hold everything together.

"That's why Edge is always convinced that everyone is out to get him; everyone always has been."

Frank took the sip from his cup and grimaced slightly at the bitter taste of the grounds. *The more I hear, the more disgusted I become.* After a long silence, he raised his eyes to Sam's.

"I think I understand Edge a little better now. I don't excuse him for his attitude, mainly because it's one we can't afford, but I do understand why he has it."

247

I also won't excuse him plotting to kill me, let alone Samantha and the men in my unit, if that's actually what he's doing. I just wish I knew for sure, one way or the other, so I'd know whether to go ahead and deal with it once and for all!

"The thing is, there's something he needs to understand too. I have this unit to run. It's a job I never asked for and never wanted, but it's mine now and I intend to do it right. Everyone's lives depend on how well I accomplish that, not just mine, but my men's and my wife's. Since you're here, your life does too, for that matter.

"Edge is responsible for the long view, and he should be. That's not my job; my job is the right here and right now, and that's all I'm immediately concerned with.

"First, we've *got* to have more funding – no question about it. Your people – Mike in particular – have done a tremendous job so far, but it's no longer enough. When I think about how many supplies we need, how much stuff we have to buy on the black market and how many bribes we have to pay out, it boggles the mind. If we are to continue to function efficiently, we can't nickel and dime it any more. We *have to have* a massive influx of cash, and an armored car is the best and most practical way to get it."

"I'm not arguing *that* point, Frank. I can smooth that over as a minor incident. It's the other I'm worried about, especially Peters. Think about it; do you really have to do this right now?"

"Yes I do. Peters is our main enemy here. That snake-eyed bastard has all the power of the Federal Government behind him; he's an immediate menace as long as he's alive, and that's something I intend to rectify as soon as possible."

"And what if this screws up something Edge is planning?"

Frank shrugged. "If he's planning it in our territory then he should have told us about it. Look, time is short; FEMA is going to have to make a move and soon, or Peters is going to be out of a job. After all the stuff we've done during his watch, his butt's already in the wringer. He'll be desperate, and desperate men tend to do desperate things. I don't know what he's up to; I just know he's fully capable of hurting us real bad. I intend to hit first – preemptive strike."

248

"Yeah. Listen, Frank, have you considered that you're acting just exactly the way – as independent as a hog on ice – you complain about us acting?"

He thought about it for a few seconds, and then shrugged again.

"Yeah, I guess I am; it must have rubbed off. Well, you know what they say: when in Rome…"

Sam blew out his breath in a very audible and exasperated whoosh.

"Damn it, do you know who you sound like?"

Frank considered a moment. "You?"

"Got it in one; give that man a cigar."

"I must have had a good teacher."

Sam looked him in the eye and laid a hand on his shoulder, all seriousness. "Answer me honestly Frank; this is one thing I've got to know for my own peace of mind. This mission, is it for the movement, or is it personal?"

Frank returned his gaze levelly.

"It's both."

"Is that a good thing?"

"No, Sam, it's a stupid, selfish thing, but it's something I have to do anyway. Everything that's happened, Peters been directly responsible for. First he framed me and destroyed my life; fine, I can live with that. But then he killed my grandmother, the one who brought me up, the last of my blood kin on this earth. After that, he murdered Mary Wheeler for no other reason than that she helped me. He burned your house, killed your sister and your men, all because of *me*! Then, what those...those *sons of bitches* did to my wife…God help me, but that's one thing I can't live with! Every damned night when she cries in her sleep or wakes up screaming, it's like somebody's pouring hot acid right into my soul! *I can't stand it!*" His last words were punctuated by slamming his calloused fist down on the nearby table, nearly cracking the heavy laminated top.

Sam watched him warily. He had only seen Frank lose his ironclad control one time, and it was more than a little frightening. Frank shivered with emotion, and a single tear was coursing down his cheek as he looked at his friend and commander and hissed through his clenched teeth.

"Can't you understand? If I don't get him now, they may replace him, and then he'll be beyond my reach. I can't deal with that, Sam. I mean it; I just can't deal with that. I've got to finish this!"

The older man bit his lip and nodded. Frank and Edge were both more alike, in some ways, than either would admit. It was comforting in a way, because it proved they were human, but it also complicated the hell out of things. Still, Samuel Wirtz was a man who understood feuds and blood debts; he had some of his own he intended to collect on. He also understood his the nature of his race, that for a Southerner, there are some things that just can't be let go.

We are who we are. God help us!

"So be it, then."

DAY 111

CHAPTER 24

"Well, how did it go?"

Tommy grinned happily.

"That truck was one tough mother, that's for sure." Always an admirer of powerful machinery, the biker-cum-medic had been so impressed with the specs he began reciting them from memory. "The damned thing was a Streit Manufacturing rebuilt Ford F-450, complete with glass/polycarbonate laminated armored windows and ballistic steel body; it would take a .50 caliber or better to punch through it. If you hadn't insisted on limiting casualties, it would have been a lot more simple; we could have just caught it in an isolated spot and busted her wide open with a LAWS rocket."

"I don't like collateral damage if it's at all avoidable," Frank told him. "Those guards aren't our enemies; they're just trying to make a living like everybody else. Besides," he said, gesturing toward the stack of bags, "at better than a half-million dollar haul, it looks like you managed alright."

"Yeah, but it wasn't nearly as much fun. Turns out we had an experienced man with us."

"Who?"

"Casey Graham. It seems that before Private Graham signed on with Neil Larson, he was involved with an Aryan splinter group somewhere out west for a while. To raise funds they had knocked over a couple of armored cars, one in Idaho and one in Washington State, both without casualties. Since he knew what he was doing, we let him have his head and pretty much run things, and we just backed him up. He likes to keep it simple."

"Good idea," Frank observed dryly, and softened the following remark with a smile. "If we could get that habit to spread to debriefings, we'd do well."

Tommy returned a grin of his own to show there were no hard feelings.

"Well, Graham puts on a business suit, takes a big handful of papers, and walks up to the guard as he was loading the last pickup of the day. Then he sticks a gun in his gut and opens his jacket to show the guy the fake plastic explosives strapped to his body in a suicide bomber vest. Both the driver and his partner got real cooperative real quick. We took them and the truck, and left the guards bound and gagged in behind a country post office after hours. I expect the post master will find them this morning, a little stiff and sore maybe, but none the worse for the wear."

"What did you do with the truck?"

"Buried it. I got the idea from an old Korean War vet I talked to once. They stole an officer's jeep, threw a tarp over it, and buried it outside of camp. Anytime they wanted to go on some R&R, they just dug it up again and fired her up. We are now the proud owners of a fine armored personnel carrier, if we customize it a little, maybe add some bench seats, a battering ram, and possibly an industrial strength flamethrower if I can make room for the tanks and the pump. We can dig it back up and work on it once the search dies down."

Frank looked at him, stunned.

"And just how, pray tell, do you bury an F-450?"

"With a bulldozer and a backhoe." He left it there and smiled innocently at Frank, forcing him to ask.

"Okay, I'll bite; where did we get a bulldozer and a backhoe?"

"Stole 'em of course – about a week ago. Once we painted over the Department of Highways colors, they were as good as new."

Thinking of his former employment as a police officer, Frank had to laugh. It certainly was a turning world.

"This is insane. You know that, don't you?"

Sam could only nod. "Yeah, I know it, but those are his orders, as of about fifteen minutes ago. He's already got the whole thing planned out; the 1st Columbia is to make the pickup in the morning."

Frank took in a deep breath and blew it out in frustration. *Just when everything seemed to be going so well.*

"If Edge plans to invade Ohio and steal arms for West Virginia, why isn't he using forces closer to the area instead of five hundred miles away?" Making a disgusted noise, he abruptly rose to his feet and turned, clasping his hands behind him and facing the wall, trying to get his normally even temper under control. "Do you realize the extra risk to my men just by traveling that far, into unfamiliar territory to boot, not even counting the mission?"

"Look at it as a vote of confidence," Sam said to his back. *Lord, I hate this!* "Yours is the best and most organized large force available right now. You should be proud to be trusted with a mission that will bring another group on board." Even as he said it, Sam knew how empty it sounded. Slowly, Frank turned to look at him.

"Are you still my friend, Sam?"

"You know damned well I am," he answered without hesitation.

"Friends don't lie to each other. No matter how hard you piss down my back, you're not going to convince me it's raining."

The former pig farmer hung his head for a second, and then sighed in resignation as he made a decision to just dump it all on the table.

"What the hell am I supposed to say, Frank? I'm just trying to put the best face I can on it, but I think we both already know the truth."

"Yeah," he said, nodding once, "we're going because in the eyes of 'Field Marshal' Edge, my men and I are expendable."

Sam didn't bother to deny it.

"You're also capable of doing the job. I do know for a fact he wants it to be a success; there's a lot riding on this."

"I'm sure that'll be a great comfort to the widows."

"Why are you so pessimistic and morbid all of a sudden?"

"Because I don't know if I'm going on a mission or walking into a set-up purposely designed to kill me and the men I'm responsible for!"

Sam desperately wanted to say that Edge wouldn't do that, but found he couldn't: at one time, maybe, but not now. Finally, he simply said, "I damn sure hope not, because I'm coming with you."

It was Frank's turn to be taken aback.

"I thought you were ordered to stay here?"

"I was."

Frank understood the ramifications of what Sam was doing, what he was risking, and why, and he extended his hand.

"Thank you."

"I'll tell you whether you're welcome or not when we get back."

If we get back.

CHAPTER 25

Frank sat in Mike's kitchen, holding Samantha's hand as she tried not to cry. There was no point in asking or scheming; she knew there would be no going with him this time. Outwardly she was holding up well at his impending departure, but he could feel the faint tremors coursing through her. Tommy was on her other side. Frank looked across the table at Billy Sprouse, Jim Reynolds, and Mike Dayton, the only other people in the room. It was time.

"What's on your mind, Frank?" Jim finally asked.

Frank looked at the table for a moment before answering. "I need your help."

"You've got it." Billy boomed.

"You don't know what it is yet."

"I don't give a damn what it is. I owe you and Tommy my life. Whatever you need, it's yours."

"Same here," Jim said. "You were crazy enough to risk your life for me, and I'm a man who pays my debts."

Frank shook his head. "You don't owe me anything. If you're going to do this, I want it to be because you want to do it."

"We're not doing whatever it is you want because we owe you; we're doing it because we like you. Now out with it; what the hell do you want us to do, shoot the Field Marshal?"

"It may come to that," he said evenly, leaving Jim and Billy in shocked silence, and Mike pretending to be; he was still frantically trying to figure out what was actually afoot. "What I'm going to tell you is not to leave this room."

Starting at the beginning, he and Tommy outlined the difficulties with Edge, both established fact and rumor. All of the men knew part of the story, but none of them knew it all until now.

"You can't go up there, Frank – or you either, Tommy." Billy was deadly serious for once, and Mike and Jim backed him up a hundred percent.

"We've got to," he sighed. "There's not enough hard evidence that he's actually targeted either me or my unit – I'm estimating 50-50 chance. Until then, there's a war on and I have a duty to obey orders. Of course, I'm not going to be stupid about it; I've made some contingency plans he knows nothing about just in case.

"I've made sure my sergeants know the score, and I've got a company full of men who don't know him, have no reason to trust him, and who I trust to take care of both themselves and yours truly. That's not the problem."

He glanced meaningfully at his wife. "Right here is the problem.

"If Edge, Larson, or anyone else in CAP actually *is* out to get me, Sammie is a loose end, and that makes her a potential target. I can't be in two places at the same time, and when I'm up there, I can't concentrate on both situations at once. I can't do my job worrying about my wife. I have to leave her with someone I can trust.

"That's why I'm asking you three to guard her for me and keep her safe – *please.*"

Billy put his big forearms on the table, making it creak under his weight as he leaned across it.

"You let me tell you somethin', partner; the next time you think you have to beg me for somethin' like this, so help me, I'll knock you right outta your chair! What the hell do you think I am?"

"A friend," Frank answered simply.

"And don't you forget it!" He looked at the other two, and they grimly but unhesitatingly nodded their agreement. "We'll guard Sammie with our lives, Frank; we'll protect her with our very last breath if we have to. You go do what you have to and don't worry about things here; we'll take care of it. If we even *think* Edge or Larson or anybody else might hurt her, we'll put his ass in the *ground*, no hesitation, no mercy, and no questions asked."

"I'll tell you something else." It was Jim this time. "God forbid, but if this is a setup, and you don't come back, we'll personally eliminate the threat to Samantha. You can count on that too."

As Frank thanked them, he thought, not for the first time in his life, that it was good to have friends.

256

DAY 112

CHAPTER 26

It was as close to midnight as it was to morning. The stars outside had not yet begun to fade, and Samantha lay beside her husband, holding him like she would never let him go. Their passions sated earlier in the evening, they reveled in the simple, pleasurable lover's comfort of skin-to-skin contact. Although neither would have voiced it to save their lives, both of them knew this might very well be their last night together.

"It's about that time," he told her.

"I know – more like past it, I think."

Be strong for him, Samantha; be strong!

"I'd best be getting up, or Tommy'll be beating on our door."

"Yeah, I guess so."

Still, neither one of them made a move.

"Have I told you lately how beautiful you are, and how much I love you?"

Despite her sadness and fear, she smiled. "Yes, but you can tell me again; I don't mind."

He opened his mouth to do just that, when the knock came.

"I'm sorry, you two," Tommy said quietly through the panel, his voice subdued, "but it's about that time."

"On my way," Frank called back, then kissed his wife again. "On my way."

As they pulled away in the darkness, Samantha watched through the window, but deliberately turned away before they got all the way out of sight.

It may be an old superstition, but I'm not going to take any chances. Just come back to me, Frank!

She had handled it well, all in all, better than she expected, at least on the outside. Inside, she felt like she was dying. Looking at Donna, standing by her side and bravely sniffling over Tommy, she decided there was no point in holding back anymore. The two held each other, weeping and praying for a very long time.

At 9:02 AM, the pair of men watched carefully as the red Peterbuilt tractor-trailer pulled off the road onto a wide gravel turn-around beside West Virginia State Route 60 along the Kanawha River. Often used for trailer drops and impromptu flea markets, the spot was currently deserted except for the big rig. The driver sat there in full view, one hand on the wheel and the other on the shift, engine idling.

The two men watched it for a moment from their hidden vantage point in the dewy weeds and brush just over the railroad embankment only yards away.

"Well?"

"Well what?" Jack Boggess replied, his voice tense. "I guess this is my ride. See you."

"You be careful, you hear?"

"Always. By the way, if anything happens to me, make sure Putney shoots Edge, will you?"

The other spat, his eyes cold. "He won't get off that easy."

As the second man stayed hidden, radio to his lips, a dozen other Mountaineers carefully watched through the crosshairs of their riflescopes from concealed vantage points in the surrounding area. Boggess stood and walked slowly and much more calmly than he felt towards the truck, changing direction when the driver jerked his thumb to the rear.

"Hey Possum?" Boggess' companion spoke into the microphone. "Everything clear?"

"Ten-four, as far as I can tell. They do have a blocking car, though: a blue Chevy. They pulled off about a half-mile ahead of your twenty, and got in the position so they can turn around and get back your way in a hurry if they need to. I make out two men."

"They've got another one behind," another voice broke in; "an old green Suburban, looks like an eighty-something model. As soon as the rig stopped, they pulled off too, 'bout a mile back. There's two in this one too."

"Do they look like 'revenuers'?" The West Virginians had adopted their old term for liquor enforcer in place of the more common 'Feds'.

He heard a chuckle over the radio before the one called 'Possum' came back on the air. "If they are, they're some damned ugly ones! I'm looking at this big son of a bitch through my scope right now, with a shaved head and his arms pert near covered up with tattoos: swastikas and the like."

"Probably legit then. Suspicious bunch, ain't they?"

Possum laughed. "Ain't we all?"

Just as Boggess reached the rear of the trailer, there was the sound of a latch popping and the door opened, courtesy of a specially modified mechanism that allowed the trailer to be opened from inside as well as out.

Frank reached down a hand and helped his passenger up into the trailer.

"Hello – Jack Boggess," he introduced himself as the door slammed and the truck lurched as it pulled out immediately. Wobbling off balance for a moment at the unexpected motion, he recovered only to pale slightly at the silenced submachine guns aimed at his chest.

"I'm Frank Gore, Mr. Boggess. Nice to meet you." He gestured towards the device on the floor. "That little box produces severe interference across most channels…"

Five minutes later, the mountaineer, having been stripped and fully scanned, was re-buttoning his flannel shirt.

"No offence, Mr. Boggess, just SOP. We can't afford to take chances."

"Just call me Jack, Mr. Gore; *Mr.* Boggess was my daddy. No offence taken, you just startled me for a minute. I'm just glad you all weren't playing *Dueling Banjoes*." Everyone in earshot chuckled at the stale old joke. "In fact, that scan was a damned good idea; wish

I'd thought of it. Could you possibly get me one of those boxes, or at least the schematics so my people can build one?"

"Call me Frank, and I reckon that can probably be arranged; I'll talk to my technical people once we get back. It's an honor to meet you; I've heard a lot about all the good work you've been doing up here in the mountains."

"Huh! The honor is mine. You're the famous one." He grinned good-naturedly. "You're not as big as I figured: I thought you'd be at least ten feet tall."

Frank laughed out loud at that. Something had clicked between the two men, and the banter came easily.

"So," the ex-cop added after a moment, "what can we do for you? General Edge wasn't too clear on your function during this mission."

"Other than liaison with our first stop, I'm here primarily as an observer. I want to see how you operate." What he didn't say was that he wasn't the type to buy a pig in a poke. Before he threw in his lot with someone, he intended to see if they were both serious and capable.

"Well, this isn't exactly a typical mission…"

The ride was a long run, particularly with the men and their small arms crammed in the back of the forty-eight foot trailer. They had strung some battery-powered lights along with a couple of fans, but the latter only seemed to move the increasingly stale around without really doing much good. The smell from the already-overloaded chemical toilet they had installed for the trip didn't help either, nor did the odor from the vomiting four of the men had done when the sway of the trailer on the curvy mountain roads had proven too much for their stomachs.

"You sure that equipment will be there at Vinton?" Jack asked as he sat on the floor, fanning himself with a piece of cardboard.

"Yeah," Frank told him, "pretty sure. General Edge set the whole thing up with a couple of sympathizers he has up in that area, watching things." He didn't say it, but he'd taken the precaution of having Mike quietly double-check it with his own watchers, who verified at least most of the information Edge had given him.

"That's one thing that puzzles me; why send you Palmetto boys all the way up here? If this organization is as big as he says it is, why aren't people doing this from right next door, in Kentucky and Virginia? Even North Carolina is closer than you all are."

Frank's eyes were hard and he was unable to keep the faintest trace of hostility out of his voice. "Let's just say the General has personal reasons for wanting us on this little safari and leave it at that."

The Mountaineer looked at the floor and pursed his lips, carefully considering his next words. "Can I ask you something – between you and me, man to man?" At Frank's affirmative nod, he went ahead. "Can Edge be trusted? I know he's competent as hell, but there's just something about him that makes me want to keep looking behind me, if you know what I mean…"

Tommy, no fan of Edge and never particularly subtle, snorted a half-audible obscenity that indicated he knew precisely what Jack Boggess meant.

"If you ask me, I think that would be a damned good idea," he added.

Frank ignored him as he mulled over an appropriate answer. He didn't trust Edge himself, of course, but it wouldn't be conducive to bringing the West Virginians on board to express those feelings to their leader. Of course, he reflected, they could trust him on at least this early part of the mission, if for no other reason than the fact that Boggess was with them. As far as Frank was concerned, the Mountaineer's presence was a load off his mind, because if Edge was setting them up, he wouldn't have sent Boggess with them. Frank considered him an insurance policy, since his death would end any chance of bringing the Mountain State on board.

At least, I hope so!

Frank sighed inwardly. He knew Edge was a vital part of the movement, and his leadership would give them their best chance of winning the war. He just wished he knew for sure what the Field

Marshal's intentions were towards him, one way or the other, but since he didn't, he chose his words carefully.

"If it's something he considers to be good for the movement, then yes, you can trust him totally, although what he thinks is good and what you think is good may be two very different things. He's also obsessive, egotistic and ambitious as hell, and he tends to take things way too personally. Still, for all that, he is very competent leader overall. His strength is that he sees the big picture, and he's hard enough to order things done that he sees as needing done, no matter what they are. I wouldn't want to spend a week on a fishing trip with him, but he knows his stuff and he's the only one I consider capable of leading this revolution."

"I reckon, when it comes right down to it, that's about all that matters."

Frank didn't answer, but inside he wondered if that were really true. Then he thought about Sammie.

No, damn it, that's not all that matters at all!

Behind the two, Caffary sat silently, not appearing to be listening, but taking it all in just the same; not only what was said, but also what was carefully left unsaid. In addition to what Larson had secretly told them, he had been briefed on the situation by Frank and then, unbeknownst to the Captain, in greater detail by Tommy. Like any good top sergeant, he made it a point not to cut his subordinate NCOs out of the loop. Glancing at the others, he nodded slightly and their eyes silently blazed their own understanding.

Not a little to Frank's surprise, the first stop – the one set up by the Mountaineers rather than Edge – went off like clockwork. They pulled into a small National Guard post where they drove the rig and blocking cars around back while the guardsman, waiting as Edge and Boggess had arranged, opened the gate for them.

That the guardsman in question, Spec-6 Fred Estep, was Jack Boggess' second cousin and the only one on duty at the time simplified matters considerably. He threw open the yellow block building with the ubiquitous deactivated rusty tank decorating the patch of grass in front and welcomed them, if not with open arms, then at least with open doors.

Less than an hour later they were rolling out again, this time packed into four canvas-topped Humvee troop carriers. Every man was in a standard set of Army issue camouflage fatigues and carrying either an M4 or vintage M16 from the now-empty arms room. They had also acquired an obsolete M60 LMG that the Guard unit still had, an M79 grenade launcher, and a dozen extra M16s. There was little else worth taking from the small post except information; at Mike Dayton's instructions, Tommy had planted some well-disguised back door software in the post's two computers and made a quick call. Back in Columbia, Mike was already downloading the entire contents of their hard drives and putting their passwords into use, secretly burrowing deeply into military cyberspace.

Holding the gate open for them again when they pulled out, Spec-6 Estep waved with a big smile and went back inside, fondling the envelope Frank had given him on Edge's orders.

Ten thousand bucks out of Columbia's coffers without even so much as a by-your-leave: I suppose that's what they call an un-funded mandate.

Frank looked at Boggess sitting beside him on the hard bench in the back of the truck.

"How's your cousin going to talk his way out of this?"

Jack shook his head with a grin that stretched from one big ear to the other.

"He ain't going to have to. He's got a plan."

"It's none of my business, but the curiosity is killing me; I've got to ask."

"Well, he's been looking for an excuse to get out of the country for a while now. His whore of a wife not only left him for another man – a nigger, no less – but she took him to the cleaners. Now she's living with this clown in Fred's house over in Falls View, driving Fred's truck, and all on Fred's money that he has to pay her every month in alimony. She even took his dog, and I think that's what pissed him off more than anything else. Fred loves his coonhounds.

"He's going back in there and draw about a pint of his own blood, soak a jacket with it, and drag it to the door and across the lot to where we were parked. You and I'll get the blame for killing him that way, but then considering what all we're wanted for already, what's the difference, right? Then he's going to have his brother drive him to the Charleston airport, where he'll use another cousin's passport to buy a one-way ticket to Belize. He won't be coming back; he's got a buddy that runs a dive shop down there, and he'll go to work for him."

"Needed the ten thousand for running money, huh?" Frank asked.

"Yeah, but when you get right down to it, I reckon he would have probably done it for free. He just wanted out, and you gave him not only the opportunity to disappear, but also the excuse."

"He was a big help to us." Reaching over to the cooler sitting in the middle of the truck bed, Frank pulled out two cans of cola and handed one to Jack. Popping the top, he raised the can.

"Here's to cousin Fred; may he drink a pina colada on his tropical veranda for me!"

Jack laughed and took a swig from his own can.

"Amen to that!"

CHAPTER 27

Corporal Andrew Gray, Ohio National Guard, stood idly, leaning against one of the three the troop carriers and casually smoking a cigarette. His M4 – loaded with blanks – leaned beside him. He had been selected to guard the vehicles while the rest of his maintenance company was on refresher maneuvers, collecting chiggers and ticks in the Southern Ohio woods not far outside of little town of Vinton. He took a deep, appreciative drag. With the summer's heat and murderous humidity, it looked like he might have lucked out. Besides, it was clouding up and the sky was looking dark to the west; it would be raining within the next hour. He thought he caught a hint of distant thunder…thunder and something else.

He turned his head at the sound of engines.

The Guard unit was parked along one of the gravel roads that crisscrossed the isolated area along Raccoon Creek. Having been logged over many times, the whole place was a choking tangle of thick brush competing with the trees, with a few patches of open fields here and there. The multiflora rose and Russian olive brush hid the oncoming vehicle from sight, if not from hearing.

Finally the source of the noise came around the curve, and Corporal Gray dropped his cigarette, grabbed his rifle, and straightened up; the Colonel's eagle on the Humvee's front license plate told him this was no casual visit. He could make out the rugged features of the officer in the passenger seat despite his mirrored sunglasses, while the second occupant, a PFC with a military police armband, sat behind the wheel. Behind the Hummer, three more troop carriers like the two he was guarding came rumbling up.

The vehicles ground to a halt in a cloud of dust, and Gray saluted.

"Good afternoon, sir –"

"I haven't got time for the bullshit, Corporal," the officer snapped as he excited the vehicle. "Where's your commanding officer?"

"Sir, Major Rodgers is taking part in the field exercise with the rest of the company –"

"Get him back here – now!"

Gray gulped once, his prominent Adam's apple bobbing, and grabbed the radio.

The rain had just begun as the company commander, bits of brush and leaves still clinging to his fatigues, looked uneasily at the abnormally large number of MP's who had dismounted from the troop carriers and were forming a perimeter. Unlike his own weapon or those of his men still in the field, their muzzles weren't covered with the flat red tip that indicated the use of blank ammunition, and every rifle had a clip locked in place.

"Sir, with all due respect, I can't believe there are terrorist sympathizers in my company –"

"Major Rogers," the colonel rasped, "I hope I don't step too hard on your tender feelings, but I really don't give a rat's ass what you believe. An investigation under the auspices of the Homeland Security Department has determined that at least three of your men are connected in some way to the Confederate Army Provisional rebels – at *least* three."

"Sir, I'd like to know what evidence –"

"The evidence is classified, Captain, and not only do you not have requisite security clearance, you also don't have the need to know."

"They're my men...*sir.*"

"They're the United States Army's men, and the United States Army wants them out here ASAP. And if the next word out of your mouth isn't into that radio accomplishing exactly that, I'm going to be taking *four* men in for suspected collaboration with terrorists instead of three. Unless you want an all expenses paid trip to '*Gitmo*', I suggest you get with the program and do it now!"

As he watched the National Guard officer frantically yelling into the radio, Rob Johnson was thinking it felt pretty good to be a colonel.

Through the Armory window, Spec 4 Slocum glanced at his watch when he spotted the headlights of the military vehicles glimmering through the driving rain as they entered the parking lot. They were about three hours ahead of schedule.

Must have got rained out. Rising from the desk and picking up the keys to the arms room, he shook his head. *That's not like the Major at all; he must be getting soft.*

As he opened the two-piece steel Dutch doors to the secure room, he could hear the vehicle doors banging and the men dismounting outside. PFC Smith assisted him in bringing the weapons cleaning equipment out into the maintenance bay; then, as per procedure, he stepped back into the smaller room and closed the bottom half of the door, waiting to check in the arms as they were cleaned and returned.

The men came in fast, and Slocum and Smith at first thought they were rushing to get out of the storm. By the time they realized none of the soldiers were familiar, it was too late. Dozens of rifle barrels were pointed at them and they were told to freeze. Smith obeyed instantly, not even daring to breathe, but Slocum tried to slam the upper half of the arms room door closed in order to lock himself in. Unfortunately for him, Basil Caffary and Frank Gore were too close.

Before the door could close, Caffary instinctively shoved the barrel of his MP5 in the crack, muzzle first. The steel door crashed against it hard enough to dent the silencer tube, but was unable to latch. Instantly grasping the situation, Frank launched a high and powerful side thrust kick inches past the First Sergeant's head and against the upper portal, slamming it back into Slocum and knocking him away. Caffary took advantage of the situation and lunged forward, throwing himself against the shelf welded to the top of the lower door, and pointing the silenced submachine gun into the room.

"Freeze!" he shouted at Slocum, but the panicked soldier ignored him and ran for the phone on the wall just to the left of the door.

There was a trio of dull pops as the sergeant's professionally controlled three-round burst punched the guardsman in the chest.

Slocum's momentum kept him going forward, but he was already dead by the time he collapsed on the concrete floor and slid against the wall.

Frank turned his head to order the building secured, but the First, Second, and Third Squads were already ahead of him under Rob's command, spreading out through the facility at the double, each squad in search of their assigned objective. He gave the thumbs up to Tommy on the other side of the room, who was supervising the binding and gagging of the remaining soldier. The biker turned and shouted the order to bring in the other prisoners, which included the entire company along with their commander, already trussed up and gagged in the backs of the trucks.

In less than five minutes the armory was secured, including a career sergeant they had found napping in a mild alcoholic stupor a back office, blissfully unaware that anything was amiss until he was rudely awakened by the CAP guerrillas and placed in the bay with the others. Like them, he was bound hand and foot with cable ties, gagged with duct tape, and left on the floor, all the places at the few tables being full.

Meanwhile, the Southerners swept through the place like a horde of locusts, carrying off radios, files, computers, uniforms – anything that might be useful. Others were busy in the motor pool, selecting, starting and fueling vehicles for the trip back.

The arms room though was the real prize. Normally, there would have been no more than a hundred M4's and a handful of Squad Automatic Weapons in a National Guard locker. However, as Edge's intelligence showed and both Frank and Boggess had hoped, there were nearly a thousand battle rifles, plus an assortment of other weaponry, being stored there for refurbishment prior to several Ohio Guard units' projected deployment to one of the overseas hotspots.

"Frank, I have to ask: are you going to obey Edge's orders on the prisoners?"

Frank looked pointedly at the helplessly bound and gagged soldiers, and then back at Sam. "What do you think?"

Sam thought he just couldn't see Captain Gore killing them all as Edge had ordered in the name of security and greater chance of success, and said as much. Then he listened as Frank proceeded to outline his plan, and nodded his approval. "It's a little more risky the way you're planning it, but I think it'll work. Does it bother you that the General's going to be pissed at you again?"

"Not really. Does it bother you?"

Sam shook his head.

"Not this time, not in the least!"

Thirty minutes after pulling out, the trucks rolled out of Ohio without incident, crossed the river at Henderson, West Virginia, and continued down Route 35 towards Interstate 64. They picked that up near Winfield, took it past Charleston, and were soon on Route 60 again. Due to the fuel shortage and the affect of the depression on the already long depressed area, there was only a scattering cars on the road. Most of those who still owned them were at work, and those who weren't couldn't afford the gas.

Despite the light traffic, the ride was tense, and the crowding and the nature of their transportation didn't help. The front seats of the trucks were little more than canvas covered pads over metal frames, and those in the rear were simple wooden benches.

Frank noticed the First Sergeant squirming, a pained look on his face.

"You okay, Gunny?" Frank had to yell to be heard over the roar of the wind through the canvas top.

Caffary squirmed again.

"Hell no, I ain't okay! My damned hemorrhoids feel like they're as big as hickory nuts!"

His caustic admission struck the other six men as hilarious, and Frank laughed along with them and shook his head.

"Thanks, but that was a little bit more information than I really wanted. You want to change places with the man up front?"

Caffary refused profanely. "I was doing this when your momma was changing your diapers...*Sir!* I get too old to sit on a bench, I'll let you know!"

"Don't mind him, Sir," George Cox chimed in from the opposite side with a big grin. "The old man gets cranky when he forgets his rubber ring."

The First Sergeant turned dark red with anger.

"Cox, I'll kick your –"

"*Heads up!*" The shout came from Sergeant Thompson in the front seat. "We've got a roadblock coming up!"

All their humor instantly forgotten, the men locked and loaded, the noise of their bolts sliding back and ramming home making a clattering racket. Boggess slipped a 40mm anti-personnel round in the M203 attached below his M4 barrel. Rather than the more usual explosive charge, this cartridge was no more than a giant shotgun shell – almost a miniature claymore – that would send a veritable wall of steel shot shredding everything in its path at the squeeze of the trigger.

As the Humvees began slowing, Frank nodded his approval at the miner's choice; anything they had to do here would be up close and personal. He bent forward, looking across the front compartment and out the windshield, only to see little more than the truck in front of them. Rob's voice crackled over the radio from the lead vehicle, and Thompson repeated the words back to them as he stretched the mike cord, passing it through into the rear for Frank.

"It looks like a standard police roadblock: West Virginia State Troopers and some sheriff's cruisers – no obvious enemy vehicles."

Frank keyed the mike and spoke, his voice grim. "They'll probably just wave us through, but be ready in case they don't. Remember the procedure we went over."

They all remembered very well; they were to pretend to be what they appeared to be unless the cops were suspicious, in which case everything would go to Hell in a flash of fire. They were now at the point that required total mission closure. There was too much at stake, so there could be no survivors now; no one could be allowed to live to reach a radio or cell phone. Everything would be brutal, fast and fatal.

They also knew not to shoot unless it was crucial; Frank had informed them in no uncertain terms that if they made it necessary for their comrades to kill innocent civilians, it would be worth their own lives. They had all seen him deal with Blair and Connolly, and wisely took him at his word on the matter.

The Troopers were true to Frank's prediction; upon seeing the Army uniforms and vehicles, they waved them through with properly patriotic smiles, never realizing how close they had come to sudden, violent death.

As they left the roadblock behind, there were sighs all around as the tension eased.

"Shall I have them clear their weapons, sir?" Caffary asked.

"How far are we from the rendezvous?"

Boggess glanced at his watch. "About forty-five minutes."

"Negative," Frank said, shaking his head. "Make sure all safeties are on and all fingers out of the trigger guards, but I want every man locked and loaded and on full alert from here on out. Be ready for anything."

Caffary nodded his agreement, and Boggess looked at the Captain thoughtfully.

"You expecting trouble?"

"Always."

I'm just not sure who it might be from!

CHAPTER 28

"Alright," the First Sergeant bawled, "un-ass these vehicles and get going! Alpha Squad, set up a perimeter, the rest of you get started unloading! Move it!" He painfully got out and rubbed his backside with both hands, swearing under his breath.

The Irregulars needed little encouragement after the cramped ride, and the Mountaineers swarming out of the brush at the back road rendezvous were already running to lend a helping hand. Their eyes lit up like children on Christmas morning at the deadly presents the men had brought them.

Edge stood with Putney and watched in satisfaction as Frank, climbed out of the back of one of the trucks followed by Boggess. Ignoring the General for the moment, he shouted at Tommy over the noise.

"Assign Delta Squad to get our share separated and loaded up, and soon as that's done, help the rest help these boys get their stuff squared away. Let's get it done and get out of here."

He turned and towards Edge, only to see his commanding officer stalking towards him, an angry look in his eye. Frank kept his own features carefully blank, but even without his suspicions concerning the General's intentions towards him, he had been a cop too long not to recognize that look. Instinctively his body began dropping into its relaxed combat mode, and he unobtrusively slid his left foot forward, moving the .45 on his right hip further out of Edge's reach during any potential altercation. His voice, crisp and business-like, showed no indication of what he was prepared to do if necessary.

"Mission accomplished, sir, with no casualties on our side. Lieutenant Johnson has a more or less itemized list of the haul for you, and we got quite a bit more than we bargained for."

"What's this about *your share*?"

Frank's own irritation, aggravated by the tension of the mission, as well as Edge's attitude despite its success, began building, but Boggess interrupted them as he walked up.

273

"I approved it. We got way yonder more than we expected, and at Frank's request, we figured about a ten percent 'finder's fee' was appropriate to thank these fellows for helping us out."

"They don't need a finder's fee for doing their job; the equipment is yours. Captain Gore, cancel that order and have your men load it in the Mountaineers' vehicles."

"No Sir."

Edge's eyes narrowed.

"Hey," Boggess broke in, trying to make peace, "It's okay –"

Both men ignored him.

"I made an agreement," Edge said dangerously.

"And I'm the one who went and got it, and spent ten grand out of *South Carolina's* budget in the process: funds that my people acquired themselves. These folks got all the expected and more, and I'll not have my men running around with worn out, second rate equipment after they took the risks."

"I gave you an order!"

"And I'm refusing to obey it. Now if you'll excuse me, I need to get my people up and moving ASAP before Echo Squad's time runs out."

"Echo Squad?" Edge demanded, his anger momentarily blunted by the unexpected statement. "What are you talking about?"

Frank glanced at his watch.

"In a few hours, I'm going to make a call, and they're going to release the prisoners before they leave."

"Prisoners? I gave you orders not to take any prisoners!"

Forgotten for the moment, Boggess and Putney looked at one another in shock at the brutal revelation of the part of the plan Edge had neglected to inform the Mountaineer guerrillas of.

He was going to slaughter that whole Guard unit!

"I'll kill anyone there's a need to, General," Frank continued, doing his best to rein in his temper, "but I'm not going to massacre a bunch of helpless weekend warriors for having the misfortune of being in the wrong place at the wrong time unless I have to." He'd had enough, and even though his voice was calm and even, almost a monotone, when he couldn't help but add, "and I don't care who orders me to do so."

It took several seconds for Edge to find his own voice. "Step over here; I think we need to talk in private."

"Excuse me," Frank told Boggess, as he moved to follow his commander into the screen of brush surrounding the drop off point. He shot a quick but meaningful glance at Tommy and gave a brief nod before he disappeared from sight.

Tommy turned to Caffary, but he had been watching and already had a hand on Hodges' shoulder, whispering and pointing. Immediately an unobtrusive but definite movement began among the Irregular non-coms.

Looking for Edge, Sam saw him and Frank disappearing into the bushes, much to his alarm as he realized what might happen, and an instant latter Caffary and Tommy faded into the brush after them, weapons un-slung and in hand.

Oh my God! Not now! I've got to stop this!

The prayer still on his lips, he had only taken a pair of steps when Hodges was suddenly in front of him. The big man's eyes were hard and his finger was in the trigger guard of his own weapon. It wasn't quite pointed at Sam, but he got the message loud and clear.

The Colonel opened his mouth to speak, to try to reason, but Hodges cut him off with a shake of his bald head.

"Please, sir." His voice was low, intended only for Sam. "Go on back now. There's nothing you can do here."

Sam stared up at him for a moment, then quickly glanced around and saw the other three sergeants steadily eying him with weapons held relaxed but ready. On the fringes, he could see still more of Frank's men had stopped loading the cargo and taken up similar postures, forming a casual-looking line between the rest and whatever was about to happen behind those bushes.

He quickly realized a few things, besides the glaring fact that the big skinhead would reluctantly but very certainly shoot him if he tried to pass. One was the loyalty Frank Gore engendered in his men; the second that Frank had been expecting this and had neatly turned the tables on Edge, and set him up for the kill. Another was the most obvious; the situation was now out of Sam Wirtz's hands, and the world seemed to be spinning out of control.

Turning, he numbly walked over and seated himself on the front bumper of one of the trucks. As he waited for the sound of gunfire he knew was coming, he desperately wanted to pray, and was consumed with guilt because he couldn't decide exactly what to pray for.

Meanwhile, Boggess reached out his hand for their own radio as it crackled on Putney's belt.

"Yeah?"

It was their own perimeter guards Putney had concealed in the woods all around the drop-off point to secure the area hours before the arms arrived.

"There's something funny going on; there's movement among our guests. It looks like they're setting up for something."

Boggess, recognizing the situation for what it was, told them to sit tight, watch what was happening and keep them posted, but otherwise to stay out of it; it wasn't their business. They had their weapons now, and they would wait and see.

Behind the bushes, Edge stood with his back to Frank.

"When you took the oath, you swore to obey orders."

"Yes, I did, and I am. I'm here, aren't I, five hundred miles away from home, spending *South Carolina's* resources on something that's not our business and doing a job we both know someone else should be doing? I did it anyway, but when your orders go completely outside the bonds of common sense and decency, or put my men at undue and unnecessary risk, my responsibilities in that regard are greater than those to blind obedience."

Edge made his decision. There was no room for a lack of discipline if they were going to have a chance of winning this war, and he was tired of watching for enemies on two sides at once. With just the two of them there alone with no one to interfere...

Now's the time.

276

Frank saw Edge's shoulders seem to relax, and knew what it meant. It was coming. The ex-cop's hand moved of its own accord and closed around the grip of the holstered pistol he knew he was going to need. Both men were expert combat shooters, but Frank was at a distinct disadvantage, and he knew it, because there was still just enough doubt about the situation that he was going to have to let Edge make the first move before he could be sure. Frank knew that might well be fatal, but he had to chance it for the sake of the movement, not to mention that of his own soul.

"I know what you're up to," the General said, slowly turning towards him left side first, which would leave both his right hand and his pistol out of sight for just an instant. That's all it would take. Frank suddenly thought about Sammie as Edge continued speaking. "You and your buddies, Larson, MacFie, and –"

"*Freeze!*" The order came in the kind of practiced command voice that only an experienced drill instructor can muster, and Edge froze despite himself, his hand only a fraction of an inch from the cocobolo grip of the customized P13 .45 he was in the process of reaching for. Sergeant Caffary stepped out of the brush to Edge's left while Tommy appeared behind Frank. Both of their silenced submachine guns were seated firmly against their shoulders and aimed directly at General Jonathon Edge. Just as bad, at the thought of his wife, Frank had finally acted as well, and Edge found himself looking down the cavernous bore of the old automatic he had already drawn. The General knew, even without the interlopers, he would have been a dead man before his pistol ever cleared his holster. He couldn't figure out why Frank hadn't gone ahead and shot him, but he reluctantly and wisely stood very still.

"Is everything alright back there?" The concerned voice was from one of the nearer Mountaineers involved in the unloading, who was alarmed by the shout.

"Fine," Frank responded casually, all the while nodding his thanks at Tommy and Caffary. He pointedly locked eyes with Edge. "I almost stepped on a snake."

"Ha!" the voice responded, its tone changing as its owner turned away, and they could almost hear him shaking his head. "City boys!"

277

It was Edge who broke the silence. "So, what happens now?"

"That depends on you. First, if I were you, I'd keep my hand well clear of that pistol."

With no other choice, Edge did so, moving his hand slowly and carefully.

Ignoring the General, Tommy spoke. "Let's get it over with, Frank. This is as good a time as any. Let's kill the son of a bitch, throw him over in the brush, and be done with it." He looked at Caffary, who curtly nodded his agreement. The grizzled first sergeant didn't know exactly what the situation was beyond what Frank, Tommy, and unbeknownst to the others, Neil Larson, had told him, but frankly he didn't much care. Frank Gore had proven himself the best leader he had ever served under, and even more importantly, he had saved both the men's and their families' lives. Shooting any threat to him was a small price to pay in the grand scheme of things, as far as Caffary was concerned.

Frank couldn't deny the good sense of their arguments, but he reluctantly shook his head. "No."

"*Come on*, Frank!" the biker hissed, his aim never wavering. "If you let him go, he'll kill you the first chance he gets!"

"Yes, and if we shoot him now, where the Mountaineers will know it, what happens to the alliance we just formed with these fellows? You think they'll really stay on board if we gun down the head of the CAP right here, no matter how much he deserves it? This whole movement will fragment once word gets out." He shook his head again, as much to convince himself as the others. "Our only chance for long-term survival is for this movement to succeed, and it needs these men to do that. As much as I hate to say it, it needs the General too, if he can ever get over his paranoia and realize that not everybody is out to get him."

Looking at Edge, Frank pointed out the obvious.

"You'd better understand something: if I was out to get you, you'd be dead right now. Even *you* have to realize that."

He never took his eyes off his commander, who was standing there seething at his disadvantageous position. "How about it? Are you willing to drop this foolishness, get over this attitude and jealously, and get with the program, or…" He let his voice trail off. He didn't bother to look at his comrades to enforce his point; he didn't need to.

"For now; but this isn't over yet!" Edge's voice cut the air like his namesake.

"Fine. Then we'll follow procedure and take it before the Council at the next session, just like we should have already done. This has gone on far too long."

"I'll do just that!"

"That better be all you do, sir." Caffary spoke up for the first time. "I've got four squads worth of rebel whup-ass over there on the other side of these trees and another one on the way, and they think the world and all of Captain Gore, even if he is to damned soft hearted to put a bullet in your skull like you deserve. They know the situation, and we'll be watching. There's no way you can avoid all of us. If anything should happen to him, we'll see you dead and in Hell before we get done." After a moment, he added, "Sir!"

The First Sergeant thought Frank was making a mistake…maybe. Of course, he might be making a mistake too, by not going ahead and killing Edge like Larson told him too, whether Frank liked it or not. Still, he had been a non-com long enough to know that the grunt never gets the whole story, but only what his officers choose to give him. He owed nothing to Jonathon Edge, but then again, when he really thought about it, he owed damned little to Neil Larson either; as far as he was concerned, you could put them both in a bag, shake them up, and you wouldn't be able to tell one from the other. Frank Gore, though, he owed something to. If it hadn't been for his good judgment and quick thinking, every one of the Irregulars' families – including Caffary's own wife, teenaged daughter and twenty-two year-old son – would be in a Federal interrogation cell right now. He had seen that situation in action firsthand, at half a dozen places throughout his career, and the thought of how close his family had come to being there still sent chills running up his back. Frank had steered them right so far, and proven himself more fit to follow than any other officer Caffary had ever served under, either in the Marines or in the CAP. He would continue to trust his judgment.

Frank and Edge walked out of the brush side by side, together with Tommy and Caffary bringing up the rear at port arms, looking as if nothing was wrong, but anything more than a casual observer would have seen the tight-set lips, furrowed brows, and squinted eyes, and sensed that something important had just happened.

Something significant had; for the first time in a long time, Jonathon Edge had found his options suddenly reduced, his parameters set by somebody else, and there wasn't a damned thing he could do about it.

Not right now, anyway, but he wouldn't forget. As far as he was concerned, all order in the movement was rapidly falling apart, and that deterioration not only had to be stopped, but it was going to be stopped, one way or another, or everything would be lost.

Sam looked up, completely surprised and totally relieved, until he saw their expressions. Still, he put on the best face he could.

Stepping up to Edge, he said, "Congratulations, John, it looks like your plan worked."

Stunned at seeing his friend here with Frank Gore, after having specifically ordered him to stay in Columbia, Edge's fury and sense of betrayal grew. He didn't respond, but simply stepped past him as if he wasn't even there.

"Sure thing, sir," Sergeant Kowalski said into the cell phone, "we'll cut 'em loose." He thumbed the disconnect button. "Okay, boys, let's get ready to move."

The homely man was relieved beyond measure; the last few hours had seemed like an eternity. To complicate matters, one of the guardsmen's wives had shown up with their three year-old son in tow and had been taken into custody as well. After searching her, calming her down, letting her see her husband was alive – *Thank God it wasn't that guy's wife from the arms room!* – and giving the little boy a ball of rubber bands from one of the desk drawers to play with, they had locked them in the lady's room. Just thinking about it, he thanked God yet again that Captain Gore had changed their original orders.

I don't think I could have done it.

He looked at the frightened eyes of the National Guardsmen –
half a dozen of whom were women – showing above their duct tape
gags. They realized it was the moment of decision and wondering
about their fates.

"Relax, boys and girls; nobody's going to get hurt. We're going
to leave you all here, and in a few more hours, once we're well out
of the area, we'll notify our people and somebody will call the Army
and let 'em know where you are."

All of them relaxed. All but one, the drunken Sergeant who had
finally sobered up, and his eyes widened with fear. Kowalski
watched with increasing curiosity as his head began jerking
frantically, motioning to him.

"What the hell's wrong with him?" Private Drucci, the lone
Yankee in the Irregulars, grumbled, his Brooklyn accent sounding
ridiculously out of place. "Is he having a seizure or something?"

"No," Corporal Knott said, attracted to the Guardsman's strange
actions. "Looks to me like the boy wants to say something awful
bad. Is that it, Mister?"

The man frantically nodded, and after a glance at Kowalski to get
his approval, Knott gingerly peeled back the tape over his mouth,
trying not to make it hurt any more than necessary. The man gasped
for air.

"What's the problem?"

"Don't call the Army!"

"Why not?"

"They'll kill us!"

The men looked at one other, completely baffled.

"Why would they do that? They'll be coming to rescue you."

"No!" The sergeant insisted, shaking his head. "Don't you get it?
I've heard of this kind of thing before; if it's found that you've let us
live, it'll produce sympathy for you, and they can't have that. If
we're all killed – massacred, on the other hand, it becomes a rallying
point. We're more useful to the Commander in Chief dead than
alive, especially in an election year! They'll kill us all and then
blame it on you!"

"You're serious," Kowalski declared in sick wonderment.

281

"You're damned right I'm serious! I'm serious as a freakin' heart attack! If they know we're here like this, they'll send in a squad of black ops or contractors and butcher every last one of us!"

The men murmured at the enormity of what they had just been told. If they had any doubts as to the righteousness of their cause, this enemy sergeant had just put them to rest.

"Alright," Kowalski finally said. "Who *do* you want us to call?"

Carol Turpac was a hardcore feminist, a former 60's radical, a college professor, and a professional pain in the ass to the Republican presidency. An extreme liberal, she stood far to the left of the run of the mill Democrats, and made it her mission in life to point out all the things the neo-conservatives were doing wrong, which was anything they did, good or bad. At sixty years old and two hundred-fifty pounds in weight, she was loud, obnoxious and abrasive. She was also very skilled at what she did, and when she called, the media tended to come running. There was never a dull moment when Carol was on the prod.

Right now, she was nearly salivating at the prospect of what she was about to do. She hated the Confederate Army Provisional of course, with a depth of ideological hatred only a liberal can muster, but she saw the Republican administration as the much greater threat, and if this was legitimate, she just might bring them down. There would be time to deal finally and decisively with those reactionary CAP racists later, once the Democrats regained power.

"Gentlemen," she called to the cameramen and reporters behind her, all foreign journalists, since the US media was more or less fully controlled. "Let's go save some soldiers."

Newscast, European Union

"This is Neil Adams, American correspondent for the British Broadcasting Service bringing you a special report.

"Armed rebels from the Confederate Army Provisional captured an entire company of United States Army National Guard troops at their base near the small town of Vinton, Ohio today, seizing and

occupying their headquarters for a short time before making off with a large supply of arms. Surprisingly, there was only a single fatality when a guardsman was shot during the initial takeover. No other injuries have been reported, although the soldiers were all bound and gagged. One of their wives and her young son who arrived on the scene were detained and locked in a bathroom, but were otherwise unharmed. When the rebels left, they contacted the noted American peace activist Carol Turpac, who came and released the men.

"Ms. Turpac, would you care to comment?

"Neil, as you know, I think the racist agenda of these neo-Confederate terrorists is despicable; however, in this case they have shown far more mercy than regular United States troops have ever shown in any recent war. You've interviewed these men and women, and none of them reported any mistreatment whatsoever, not even verbal abuse, or force beyond what was necessary to secure them. The captured civilian even reported that their captors were scrupulously polite and even considerate.

"The guerrillas have also shown ample military capability, much more so than this administration has led us to believe they had, and certainly much more than the Republican-led military has shown in trying to stop them."

"Do you know why they contacted you instead of someone else, say the Army or local law enforcement?"

"Yes I do. Their spokesman told me that it was requested by these soldiers that he do so, because they were frightened of their own military."

"Could you please explain that?"

"They told me – and it was confirmed by one of the soldiers upon my arrival – that they feared any Army rescue party might execute them in order to blame the guerrillas for it in an effort to sway public opinion."

"Did they really think that was a possibility?"

"Looking at the previous actions of this administration, I would say they definitely had cause for concern…"

Network Newscast, Washington D.C.

An unarmed National Guardsman was murdered today in Vinton, Ohio. A large force of neo-Confederate terrorists, reportedly led by the notorious terrorist leader Franklin Gore, raided the National Guard armory in an attempt to steal weapons and equipment, taking over a hundred soldiers hostage in the process. Witnesses say the soldier, whose name has not been released, was chosen at random and shot in cold blood execution-style in order to strike fear into his comrades and insure their non-resistance. Several of the other Guardsmen were brutally tortured.

One of the guardsmen's wives unfortunately wandered into the situation, and officials report that both she and her three year-old son, along with several female soldiers, were violently sexually assaulted by several of the terrorists…

United States Presidential Address, Live TV

…Tonight our nation mourns for the brave National Guardsman in Ohio who gave his life for his country, just as it unequivocally condemns the cowardly acts of the terrorists who murdered him, and who sexually assaulted not only our soldiers, but also a wife and mother, along with her three year-old son.

These people are cowards: nothing more than racist savages who hate America and hate our freedom. The only thing they understand is fear. I'm telling them right now, they have failed. America is not afraid; America is angry!

You may be sure that we shall not rest until these terrorists are hunted down and brought to justice. I have instructed the Attorney General and the Director of Homeland Security to bring to bear the full power of the United States Government in running them to the earth…

DAY 113

CHAPTER 29

"Honey, I'm home!" Kowalski bellowed down the hallway of their headquarters. The late afternoon light filtered through the painted-over windows as Echo Squad marched in to the cheers of the rest. Frank stepped out of his office, and the sergeant saluted him.

"Have a good trip?" Frank asked him.

"Petty much, sir, except for Drucci whining about getting his clothes dirty from all the crap people had spilled on the bus seats."

"Tell 'Dapper Dan' to send me the dry cleaning bill. Did everything else run smoothly?"

"Yes sir. We changed clothes, left Vinton and drove down the Ohio side before crossing back into West Virginia at Huntington; it was pretty safe there, because there aren't as many the roadblocks up North. We left the cars and took a bus on down to Charlotte. Your boys picked us up there without a hitch."

Frank nodded his satisfaction, not only with Echo Squad, but also with Joel Harrison's squad that had made the pickup.

"Congratulations; well done! Get the rest of your people down to the meeting room for debriefing, and as soon as that's over, you can have a little time for R and R. There's a case of cold ones waiting on you, courtesy of the Confederate Army Provisional."

It was almost nine pm, and she was waiting for him at Mike's when he opened the door. Since Donna wasn't known to the authorities, Samantha had let her go, and the younger woman had been at headquarters to greet her man. Reluctantly remembering her promise to her husband, Samantha didn't risk the trip; instead she waited for hours that seemed like years. Frank had called to let her know they were all right when they arrived at headquarters early that morning, but she knew better than to ask him to come home before he knew all his men were safe. Now, though, he was all hers, thanks to Billy, of all people.

The big biker, despite his crudity and outrageousness, was sensitive and romantic at heart. He knew how much she worried over Frank, and he instinctively knew what she would want but would never be so ungrateful as to ask. He sent Jim out to round up a large quantity of take out food and a large quantity of beer, and sent everyone except Sammie to the basement for a party not long before Frank was due to arrive.

"I left some of the food for you two in the oven," he told her, "and there's a bottle of decent wine in the fridge. Just so you know, I'll keep the others all down there 'til late. It'll give you a chance to spend a little quality time with your husband, you know…"

She knew, and she kissed the big man's hairy cheek in thanks. He briefly hugged her, before going downstairs himself, sniffling manfully at the beauty of it all.

When Frank opened the door, his mouth opened with it as his jaw dropped in shock.

Samantha had dressed up for the occasion, in a slinky little black dress that she'd asked Donna to pick up for her during the girl's shopping trip the day before. She had spent hours with her hair and makeup until everything was just right, and she was waiting beside the table in the light of the flickering candles.

He simply stood there, half-in and half-out of the door, and stared for so long she became uncomfortable.

"Frank, is something wrong?"

He took a thumb and forefinger and pinched himself.

"Nope. I just thought I might be dreaming. I've never seen you dressed up before; you're so beautiful."

It suddenly occurred to her that he was right; she had never dressed up for him before. All her husband had seen her in, other than her wedding dress, was ordinary clothes: fatigues, jeans, casual dresses, or business suits…or nothing at all.

"I thought maybe –" which was as far as she got. Frank pushed the door closed, crossed the room in three strides, took her by the waist with both hands, and pulled her into a soft, gentle kiss. She knew he was holding back to prevent spoiling the hair and makeup she had worked so long on, and she loved him for it.

"I missed you, Sammie."

"I missed you too, so very much."

He brushed the backs of two fingers down her cheek.

"You're so beautiful."

"You already said that."

"I know, but it's still true." He heard music and laughter from downstairs and glanced at the basement door. "Are we expected to attend?"

She shook her head, making her blonde hair bounce slightly. "Not unless you want to."

"Why would I? I've got everything I want right here."

DAY 114

CHAPTER 30

Rob was a man who kept his promises. He had told Cynthia she would get to talk to her friend Kerrie, and two days after they returned from their foray into Ohio, he finally got enough of a break in the action to allow him to arrange it. Since Kerrie was now known and on the wanted list, it made more sense to bring Cynthia to her, even if it were only for an hour or two. It would be good for both of them, he reckoned, so he dropped the anonymous message on her email.

Rob had never considered himself a man who gave a damn for very many people, but for some reason the courage and resilience of these…these *children* struck a chord deep within him. He blinked once when he thought of Chucky.

God rest your soul, you brave little man! If there's a Valhalla out there somewhere, I know you're there.

He found Cynthia exactly where he had told her to be, in the park, sitting on the same bench where he had initially met with her. Not letting his emotions cloud his judgment, he and Harrison, along with the rest of the squad, carefully scouted the area from a distance for over an hour before approaching. She was alone as agreed, except for a large backpack resting on the bench beside her. Leaving the others acting as security, he came for her.

As he approached, he hardly recognized her. She had changed radically; she looked unusually hard, like the last person you'd want to mess with. Her hair had been dyed jet, Goth black and her eyes were hidden behind a pair of dark sunglasses. Despite her petite size, in her black tee shirt and jeans, along with the heavy boots, she looked almost dangerous. Maybe it was the set of her jaw, the tilt of her head, or just possibly the handle of a large butcher knife peeking out of her pack, ready at hand.

She nodded to him as soon as he came into view, and got up, shouldering the obviously heavy pack. Like her looks, her voice was suddenly older than her years.

"Rob. I never got a chance to thank you."

"Don't worry about it. I am curious though; why the pack? We shouldn't be gone more than a couple of hours. You must have enough stuff in there to last a month."

She nodded again. "I do. I'm joining up."

"With us?"

"Who else?"

"Cynthia, that's not necessary –"

"Oh yes it is, if I want to live. I've got no place else to go."

As they walked to the van, she filled him in on the details.

In response to the missing HIV/AIDS drugs, the Federal Government had quietly dispatched the Drug Enforcement Agency to locate them, and the local FEMA head – Peters – had given them full authority under emergency powers. Accessing the computerized medical records databases of the health department and local hospitals, they obtained a list of all HIV patients in the area, cross-referenced it with the NABP's distribution list, and began a series of house-to-house searches of every name that was on the first list but not the second. Any of the AIDS drugs they found without a pharmacy receipt were promptly confiscated, including those mail ordered from foreign sources or purchased on the black market.

"I've still got mine," she told him, jerking a thumb at the heavy pack on her back, "but only just. I was a member of a local support group for people with HIV but no medicine, and one of the people who got raided was kind enough to start calling the rest of us and warn us of what was coming." She pointedly ran her fingers through her black hair. "This is my disguise. They're looking for me, so I got out of there and I've been moving from relative to relative ever since.

"Mom and I packed this bag – mostly the medicine – and she told me to keep it with me, and if anything happened, to go to you all, since they would eventually find me otherwise. She said you were the only ones doing anything right anymore. She kissed me, told me to mind and work hard and fight for freedom so we could be together again. She also said, whatever you needed for her to do, you just ask. Anything."

"She's a brave lady."

Cynthia raised her bent knuckle to her mouth and bit it, trying to get a handle on her feelings before speaking again.

"She's gone, Rob."

He almost stumbled at her words, and abruptly jerked his head in her direction.

"What do you mean, *gone*?"

"I'm not sure what happened. All I can figure is that when they raided the house, they must have found some of the drugs. Not everything in that box was on my prescription, and we were giving what I didn't need to other people in the support group who could use it. We still had some that we hadn't given out yet, and their packages must have had some identifying marks on them or something. Mom disappeared; no one's seen her since the raid." She paused and swallowed hard. "My uncle the lawyer tried to find out what happened, only to be told it was a Homeland Security matter, and any further inquiries, attempts to spread the news about her disappearance or file any motions would result in his arrest. She's just…gone, to wherever they take people like that."

Trying to collect his thoughts, Rob opened the door for her and she tossed her pack in before climbing in herself.

"Cynthia, you know, once you enlist, there's no going back?"

"There never has been any going back for me since I was raped and infected. Besides, I've got nothing left to go back to now."

The professional soldier studied her for a moment and nodded his approval, sensing something of a kindred spirit.

That which does not kill us makes us stronger.

"Put on the blackout goggles then; you know the drill. I'll take you somewhere private and scan you first, and then we'll go meet the crew."

There was no going back for anybody; there never had been.

After she was sworn in, Frank shook her hand. "Welcome to the Confederate Army Provisional, Cynthia – Private Davis."

"Thank you, sir. What's my assignment?"

He chuckled at her eager attitude.

"Hard work; you've got a lot to learn.

"To begin with, due to your journalistic skills,"– *not to mention your sex and age* – "you'll be primarily under the direct command of my wife, Lieutenant Samantha Gore, in her role as Information Officer."

"I don't usually stand on formalities, Cynthia," Samantha told her. "I prefer to work on a first name basis with the people under me."

"Okay…Samantha." None of them could have known it, but it was an almost-forgotten dream come true. Cynthia had always wanted to work in journalism, and when Samantha had been on television before the war, especially after she exposed the truth about the Capital Riot, she had become a personal hero to her, someone she wanted to be like.

Samantha continued, "Everyone in my department knows everybody else's job just in case…well, just in case." There was no need for further elaboration. "Besides assisting me and working with Donna and Kerrie while you train on the job, you will also be assisting and training with Lieutenant Mike Dayton, our chief of intelligence. We get a lot of our information from him and disseminate a lot of it through him, so the two departments mesh."

"That's not all," Frank told her, "I'm afraid you've got your work cut out for you. You haven't had combat training yet, so you've got some catching up to do. Does your condition limit you in any way?"

Cynthia was both surprised and pleased. Frank had asked about the affects of her HIV with no difference in his tone than he would have used to ask about asthma or a bad back. Most people didn't do that.

"No sir. As long as I have the medicine, I'm fine." *At least so far.*

"Good. Everyone here does daily PT, and you will too. Get with Lieutenant Richardson – he's our medic and will have to examine you anyway – and he'll tailor a program specifically for your needs. Any time you want to work out with anyone here while they're doing their own programs though, I don't figure they'll mind. Mike has a weight machine in the basement; feel free to use it.

"You're also going to begin martial arts classes; again, Lieutenant Richardson is the man to see. He'll set you up with the school he runs. Since you have some catching up to do, I want you attending *every* time they have a private class.

"Also, your duties permitting, I want you over at the 1st Columbia Headquarters on a regular basis for additional training in firearms, tactics, and demolitions. You'll be notified when we're having a pertinent class, and you'll be working with knowledgeable sergeants in between times.

"On top of all that, you'll be given some books on military and political science, propaganda techniques, and guerrilla warfare. Study them like your life depends on it, because it does: your life and the lives of everyone in this room. If you have questions about *anything*, just ask.

"Finally, do you have a personal weapon?"

"No sir, just my butcher knife."

He suppressed a grin at that admission.

"You do now." Frank reached behind him and opened a box. He drew out a web belt –an unwilling contribution of the Ohio National Guard – with a well-worn but entirely serviceable Colt .38 Combat Masterpiece and a pair of speed loaders holstered on it. Looking critically at her tiny waist, he adjusted the belt down as far as it would go before buckling it around her middle with his own hands.

"There. Immediately following this session, Lieutenant Johnson will teach you how to load it and clean it, and I'll send you over to headquarters where Sergeant Caffary will give you a chance to try it out this afternoon. From now on, every waking hour, you are to be wearing that weapon and have it ready to use unless told otherwise. Do you understand?"

"Yes sir!" The petite girl seemed to have grown a few inches.

"One last thing; welcome aboard."

She was almost crushed by the handshaking, backslapping, and hugs that seemed to come from everywhere at once.

Strangely enough, in this impossibly dangerous situation, she felt secure for the first time since her attack.

Russian News Agency, English Edition

A videotaped statement was released by the Confederate Army Provisional today accusing drug enforcement agents of the United States Government of staging house to house raids in Columbia, and confiscating what are commonly known as 'AIDS cocktail' drugs from patients infected with HIV, and our own investigation has confirmed this. Even though these people have prescriptions for the drugs and need them for their very survival, the DEA has declared them to be in illegal possession of them, whether stolen or obtained from legal sources. Several people have reportedly been arrested, but the authorities deny any knowledge of that, citing homeland security laws forbidding them to discuss the matter. They have simply disappeared...

"Thanks for waiting up for me, Kerrie. I've been wanting a chance to talk to you in private."

The redhead looked at her friend standing there in her pajamas with her hair still wet from the shower and smiled uneasily. With the addition of Billy and Jim, CAP's Columbia headquarters was rapidly running out of space, so the two younger women were assigned to bunk together in what had been Donna's room, now that she was staying with Tommy. As they had spent the night with each other during sleepovers at Cynthia's house in happier times, they readily agreed to the arrangement.

"Well?"

"I don't know where to start."

"From the beginning?" Kerrie offered.

"It's just that…I'm so sorry, Kerrie!"

"For what?"

"For being so wrapped up in my own problems that I wasn't there for you when you needed me! I should have found you and let you stay with us, but all I could think about was…me."

Kerrie's mouth opened in surprise. "Cynthia, after what happened to you, I didn't expect you to think about anything else! My God, after…what they did, and then the HIV, you thought you were dying. And you would have too, if you hadn't run into Rob. You don't have anything to be sorry about!" She sat for a moment, then quietly added, "I'm the one who owes you an apology."

"Whatever for?"

"You don't need to feel guilty. Remember, I knew where you lived, but I didn't want to come to you and ask. After what happened to you, I didn't know what to say, and after…I knew you wouldn't want me there."

The smaller girl was dumbfounded. "Why not?"

Kerrie's voice was tiny. "Because I was a whore…"

"Because…Kerrie, you're my friend, and you'd have been more than welcome to stay with me anytime. I didn't think you would've wanted to be around me, though, because I'm infected…"

The two looked at one another and shook their heads.

"We were so *stupid*!"

DAY 119

CHAPTER 31

Edge stood behind the podium in front of the Confederate Council – and Sam and Frank – with his hands clasped behind his back.

They hadn't known he was arriving until he suddenly summoned all of them to a meeting in a safe house outside of Florence, a little less than two hours from Columbia. Well before he was due to show up himself, Frank quietly ordered Alpha, Bravo and Charlie Squads, under Rob's command, to scout the surrounding area to insure there were no surprises waiting for him, Federal or otherwise. Afterwards, they surrounded the place at a distance, and set up a recently-acquired mortar tube under a tarp in the back of a pickup truck, carefully laying in the coordinates of the area around the house. Saying nothing to Sam about it, he also moved Samantha to the Irregulars' school headquarters, where her safety would be under the watchful eye of Sergeant Caffary and other two heavily-armed squads…just in case. Tommy put his own squad on full alert and, loaded up with captured weapons courtesy of the irregulars, they were ready to spill out of their dojo and commit mayhem at a moment's notice. Billy, Jim and Mike, along with the three girls, buttoned down their command headquarters, ready and waiting for whatever might happen.

Fortunately, Edge had come alone with the exception of a single driver/bodyguard, who he ordered elsewhere before actually entering the house. Frank was surprised that the subject of the Council meeting was not the problem between him and Edge; that was evidently on hold for the moment, because, he soon learned from the General's speech, more pressing issues were afoot.

"Gentlemen, we have come to a standstill. Our current tactics have involved only the law enforcement community or covert

Federal forces, not the regular military; therefore, we are regarded in the minds of much of the public as criminals rather than revolutionaries. The Federal authorities know this as well as we do, and that's the only reason they haven't used the military openly against us. I don't need to remind you that public support, or at least tolerance will decide the success or failure of this conflict. This present situation cannot be allowed to continue. We now have the capability to face them in a guerrilla conflict, and we must make the government use regular military force against us in order to do that. This will dramatically shift the long-term social and political dynamics of this struggle toward our favor. It is time to ratchet up this war; it's time for Operation Long Knives."

Frank had heard that term before; the *'night of the Long Knives'* was when the German leader Adolph Hitler had unleashed a purge against the disloyal and undesirable elements in his own government, with the main event taking place in a single night. His brow furrowed; if Edge was referring to him, then he wouldn't have called for him to be present...he didn't think. Still, not one to take chances, he unobtrusively made certain his .45 was loose in it's holster and his pager right in back of it, and he kept his hand near both.

"I've come up with a plan, which I'm submitting to this Council for approval." He could just as well have left this last unsaid, since every councilman in the room – with the exception of the recently appointed Neil Larson, who, although he despised Edge, would support nearly anything as long as it involved the type of direct action he fervently believed in – knew they were little more than a rubber stamp for the General. After all, he had masterminded their rescue from imprisonment and torture, and besides that, they were scared to death of him. His power might have slipped somewhat, but Edge knew organizing a mission of this magnitude would do much to re-secure his position. *Then I'll deal with my other problems.* "Colonel Wirtz, Captain Gore, this is the plan you've been preparing to execute by the training you have undergone during the past several weeks.

"As you well know, several individuals and groups have dedicated themselves to the destruction of the Confederate Army Provisional, of Southern culture, and, ultimately, the Southern race. Many of these are right there in Columbia. Once you finish this mission, they will no longer be there, because they'll be dead. You're going to kill them all.

"This blow will be the hardest one we've ever struck against our oppressors. We're going to use their own tactics against them, taking a page right out of their own guerrilla warfare manuals. We are going to carry out a series of simultaneous attacks and assassinations that will utterly destroy the established opposition in the city by depriving it of its leadership in one fell swoop.

"We will destroy the current local leadership. This will demoralize the enemy and throw them into total chaos until new leaders can be installed, and probably for sometime afterward. This period of confusion will create an opportunity for some of our sympathizers on the inside of certain of the public services and agencies to advance. Every time we take one of the enemy leaders out of the picture, it creates a vacuum: a vacuum which must be filled. It will draw our people into it, or at least closer to it. Either way, in their advanced positions, they'll be able to work more effectively towards advancing our cause.

"The deleterious effect of an act of this magnitude on enemy morale will be incalculable." This was not entirely true, since, like everything else he did, Edge had calculated it to the nth degree, using historical comparisons and computer models. "The knowledge that we can strike even their highest leaders with impunity will panic both the lower ranks and shake the remaining structure. Further, the fear it'll engender will discourage all but the most dedicated from any cooperation with the opposition.

"The effect on our own morale will be overwhelming, and will boost recruitment by orders of magnitude. Further, it will give those who are still sitting on the fence, as well as certain potentially sympathetic foreign governments and organizations, a reassurance of our capabilities; quite possibly enough that they begin giving us the aid we are badly in need of.

"This act will certainly cause a massive crackdown on the citizenry of this State by the utilization of regular Federal troops instead of their law enforcement agents. We're going to force the president's hand during an election year. If Operation Long Knives is a success – and it *has* to be – he'll have no other choice. United States military forces will come pouring in with their usual heavy-handed tactics that have been their trademark since 1861. They'll begin enforcing harsh new decrees against our people, enraging them even more, further alienating them from Washington, and putting a face on the enemy – the face of the United States Government, which will become too obvious for even the most dense to ignore.

"Our people will have no choice but to recognize U.S. troops as the enemy, because we are going to put them in a very bad mood before they get here. We know what routes we can expect them to take on their way in, and I intend for the forces of each and every state they pass through to make them run a gauntlet of roadside bombs, sniper fire, and general abuse. They will react to that by taking their frustration out on the only target available – Southerners – at every opportunity. The Yankees will show their true colors. Our people will suffer, yes, but that's the way it has to be, because nothing else seems to motivate them.

"The resulting backlash from the Southern people, besides netting us a huge number of new recruits, will do one of two things. It will either ensure the defeat of the President in November, leaving us with a less-experienced foe, or it will force him to suspend the election indefinitely, at least down here, because holding one in the resulting climate of violence will be impossible. If he chooses to suspend it only in Dixie while he let's the Northern states vote, the South will literally explode. On the other hand, if he suspends it nationwide, there'll be violence like he never imagined. The militias in the West and upper Midwest will go nuts, Alaska and Hawaii may very well attempt to declare their own independence, but even more importantly, it will set our enemies at each other's throats. This is a Republican president, so if he stops the election, the cities with large Negro populations will burn without question. I don't think he's stupid enough to do the latter, but either way, we win.

"Here is the death list, gentlemen. It includes the following names: FEMA Regional Director Ronald Peters; Channel 13 station manager Philip Silverstein; NABP head James Bessant; Columbia Mayor Bill Sidler, Police Chief Jim Perkins, and Deputy Chief Trigg; each of the Negroes involved in the murder of Bob Franklin at the Capital Riot and, presuming they are found not guilty, which seems likely, the judge in the case as well; and the seven police officers accused of summarily executing prisoners during the following evening's rioting."

There was a shocked silence in the room as Frank and Sam looked at one another, then back at Edge.

"You said this was to be simultaneous, General," Frank pointed out, keeping his voice cold and scrupulously business-like. He grasped the implications of this operation, and actually thought it sounded like a damned good plan. It would help no one to stoke the fires of their feud right now, but there were a couple of points that needed to be cleared up. "You do realize we only have five squads to work with, and two of them are under strength, plus we have the other targets we were previously assigned. Unless there's something you haven't told us, the numbers don't add up."

"The previously assigned targets can be put on hold for a while. As for the rest, several of these people, plus many of their followers, should be vulnerable to being eliminated in a single strike. You see, gentlemen, the plan is fluid because it's based on the timing of the trial of Bob Franklin's murderers.

"As you know, they have waved their right to a jury trial and are being tried before a judge, and considering who he is – a known liberal activist – we have good reason to believe that those men will be found not guilty. If I'm wrong and they are sentenced, then we simply strike them and the judge from the list. The law will have worked for once, and we have other fish to fry. However, if things happen as I predict, they will walk out free and clear. The NABP has backed them from the start, both financially and by way of demonstrations, and if they are acquitted, they will inevitably follow their standard practice of having a celebration that same evening. It will almost certainly be at the Multicultural Center, since it hosts all their larger gatherings. There will be several hundred of their supporters in there, including some of the people on this list. You will only need one squad for all those present at that event, because you are going to take them all out at once with a single attack involving high explosives."

"Good *Lord!*" Frank heard Sam exclaim under his breath.

"This *has* to go right, because this is about more than just South Carolina. The following is not to leave this room, and I'm only telling you in order to make you understand just how important your success is.

"You will not be the only ones making your strike that night. Confederate Army Provisional elements in *every* Southern State will be launching simultaneous guerrilla attacks against carefully selected targets within their borders – *every* state! Like your own, none of these groups are particularly large, but their cumulative effect will be overwhelming. It will conclusively demonstrate both to our people and to the enemy that this is not a criminal or terrorist action; this is a *war*! You, however, will be the linchpin of the whole operation, because they will launch their attacks only *after* they get the word from me, and I'll only give it following the destruction of the NABP. It will be the single largest strike of this operation.

"While we're setting up for that, though, we need to be prepared to receive our guests, in the form of the U.S. Military. My belief is that they will bring in federalized National Guard troops first: Northern ones, since they doubtless suspect that Guard units from the Southern States of having some of our sympathizers in the ranks. We can do pretty much as we please to them, without alienating our own people, so I want ambushes and roadside bombs set up along their projected routes of entry beforehand. Again, this is going to happen in every state; they're going to have to fight their way through Dixie, through constant sniper fire and IEDs. I don't just want them bloodied; I want them *decimated*! I want to pile up their casualties like cordwood, both to cool the enthusiasm for the war in their home states, and have them good and mad when they finally get here. They'll take it out on the civilians, and drive them straight into our camp. Even more importantly, when the Southerners who

302

make up the bulk of the regular military that they'll eventually have no choice but to send in see these Yankees abusing their own people, they'll turn towards us. We have to have that in order to win.

"The time for half-measures is over. The day after our part in Operation Long Knives, and the strikes of your comrades across South, the face of this war will change forever. It will be the beginning of a new day for Dixie."

Herdman began opening his mouth but Larson kicked him under the table to cut him off when he saw Frank getting ready to speak once more.

"General Edge?"

"Yes Captain Gore?"

Both men's voices were still cold, careful, and formal, a fact not missed by the conspirators.

"I think your plan is sound, sir and probably workable, but I do have three points I'd like to address. First, does the destruction of the NABP, particularly in this manner, have the potential to hurt, rather than help us in the public eye? Certainly we have to target their leadership, but the method you wish to use could backfire on us in the public relations department, due to the extensive loss of life of those who will, rightly or wrongly, be viewed as civilians by both the public and the media."

Edge smiled icily. "That's why I ordered you to let their riot go ahead. When we strike them now, there'll not only be no sympathy for them amongst the run of the mill Southerners, but on the contrary, many of them will applaud our actions as simple justice, particularly if we include the riot in our propaganda as our reasoning.

"Of course there is the possibility that it will be viewed negatively by some people. However, that is less important when weighed against the big picture, namely that we need to demonstrate both our strength and our will in order to change the international perception. An act of this magnitude will bring us to the attention of nations and organizations whose interests are inimical to those of the United States. With that attention will come the monetary and military hardware support this movement desperately needs. The possibility of negative perception, however small, will be minimized by the following tactic.

"We in the Confederate Army Provisional will not claim responsibility for the blast. When asked, our official line will be that we don't know who did it – apparently some more Southern people have decided to act independently – but considering what the NABP did in Columbia, neither do we condemn the action. All the thinking people will know we're behind it, of course, but the majority is incapable of thinking that logically. Immediately after the explosion, your expendable contact in the Columbia PD is to start a rumor by an email traceable back to their network's ISP. That rumor, which is being developed even as we speak, will blame the Federal Government for that particular attack, suggesting that they wanted to get rid of the NABP themselves and used the cover of our other attacks in order blame the Confederate Forces for it. Our intelligence people will then begin spreading a conspiracy theory amongst Black blogs, to the effect that this whole war is a put-up job: a cover to an effort by the White and Jewish Republicans to blunt colored power, and put the Negro back in his place.

"I predict, within forty-eight hours of the event, there will be riots by Negroes in major cities both North and South in reaction to this phase of the operation and the subsequent rumors. This will result in more economic hardship for the Feds and put them in the position of fighting two enemies instead of just one, as well as causing the further alienation of the White populace, which means the latter, again, will be forced closer to us.

"Finally, this act will make any organized group think twice about launching any further direct attacks on ourselves and our people, because they will see the consequences we are willing to inflict, leaving us only the Feds to deal with. They'll be more than enough.

Frank mulled the information over carefully, realizing that Edge had been planning the NABP's destruction all along. He nodded his approval. "Thank you for clarifying that for me, General. Second point; we can't target the mayor."

Edge's face began to redden at the word, 'can't'. "Why not?"

304

"Sir," he replied, looking pointedly around the room, I don't know if you want to discuss intelligence this sensitive in the hearing of this many people. I'd be happy to brief you privately —"

Edge smiled inside. Now he had Frank where he wanted him, as he had just alienated the Council by telling them he didn't trust them. No one in their right mind would, of course, but Frank had just rubbed their noses in the fact.

"Captain Gore, this isn't the United States; we don't keep secrets from the Confederate Council. You can say what you have to say in their presence."

Frank shrugged. *You can't say I didn't try.*

"Very well, sir, if you insist. It's because the Mayor of Columbia is covertly on our side; I recruited him a few weeks ago in our first step towards consolidating CAP influence in the civil government. Peters made a direct threat against him, along with his wife and children, and we're now sheltering his family from Homeland Security. He's already given us a tremendous amount of assistance and information, and as we have enough incriminating evidence of him colluding with us to bury him if he tries to betray us, I would say his continued cooperation can be counted upon."

Any previous irritation they might have had swept away and forgotten, every Councilman in the room stared in wonder at Frank's coup, fully understanding why he had been reluctant to discuss it. Edge felt like kicking himself in the ass for insisting on what turned out to be a public triumph for the ex-cop, but he was the first to recover, and his anger was plain in his voice.

"Why wasn't I informed?"

"I am informing you, sir. Other than our brief encounter in West Virginia, when we were involved in other issues and time was pressing, this is our first face-to-face meeting where we've really had a chance to discuss it. I didn't feel comfortable trusting something that important but not overly time-sensitive to other lines of communication."

"Those were my feelings as well," Sam added.

Edge couldn't argue the point, since Frank was obviously right, but he was even more convinced than before that the ex-cop was plotting against him, running his own agenda and developing his own personal power base. The fact that Neil Larson was the first to offer Frank his enthusiastic congratulations didn't help matters much either.

"Third point," Frank continued, once their accolades were through, "are we – the people under my command – the only organized force in South Carolina?"

Not giving Edge a chance to answer because he was not at all certain he would tell Frank the truth, Sam took the question despite Edge's glare.

"We're it. You know we've got a bunch of independents scattered around – you've met some of them – but they're untried –"

"How many?"

Sam could almost hear the wheels turning in Frank's head and decided to give up and go with the flow to see where it ended up. Once his increasingly nominal subordinate got rolling, he was like a force of nature; there was no use standing in his way.

"Off the top of my head, I'd guess maybe fifty."

Edge broke in before things went any farther. "You'll do the operation with the trained resources you've got." There was no compromise in his voice. "There's too much riding on its success to risk using untried forces on these targets."

Frank was growing increasingly aggravated at his leader's attitude, and his response held a note of triumph. "I agree; I can and I will, but that's not why I asked. This is a good operation, but not good enough; it could be bigger. I want to expand the scope and the targets, and I'll need the extra men for that. If we're going to do this, we might as well go all-out and make it a night to remember."

He had the whole room's undivided attention now.

"We already have a good start. If you hadn't ordered it, I was planning to do some hitting myself. Even before the raid into Ohio, I already had my people developing plans to address these additional targets plus the ones you ordered, so Columbia is ahead of the game on that score. I'll just transfer the existing targeting plans for the secondary objectives – the Federal resources – from the Irregulars to these auxiliary groups, freeing up the best men for the primary action.

"We can sort out the ones who know each other into small squads – hit teams – of three to six men each. None of them will to know anything about the other squads; as far as they're concerned, theirs will be the only mission. First we need to get them here to Columbia – each team in a different location, using maximum security procedures, of course."

"What are they going to do?" Sam asked him. "This mission is too important to risk any part of it by using these guys; like I've been telling you, they're untried, some of them are a little old, or a little nuts." Actually, some of them were just plain wild-eyed crazy, but he saw no need to point that out just now.

"It doesn't matter; we need every warm willing body you can lay your hands on. Why just hit the NABP and a few of the local problems when we can bust the Feds wide open and utterly destroy the bulk of their current presence in Columbia at the same time? We've already got the plans in place; it's just a matter of assigning them to be carried out.

"Aside from Peters, who is already a target, there are six teams of Federal resources scattered in and around the Columbia area right now; part of those were listed in the General's previous orders. The probability, based on the current available information, is that two of them are some sort of regular Federal agents such as FBI, BATF, etc., two are 'private contractors', one is a Delta Force squad, and the other is almost certainly a Mossad hit team."

Every man's face clearly showed their collective shock, but again, Edge recovered quickly. "How do you know that?"

Frank glanced at Sam before answering. "I've been networking with our intelligence officer. Using the your information that Colonel Wirtz passed on, our resources expanded the investigation and have informed me there were several groups of suspicious strangers in the area who fit certain profiles we were looking for. In accordance with my position, I authorized the monetary expenditures to establish it as fact. According to the intelligence they collected, there's in excess of a 95% probability that these people are, in fact,

Federally-controlled assets, and approximately 60-75% probability that they are from the groups I just mentioned."

Sam shook his head in wonderment.

"We knew there were Feds here of course, but I had no idea you were networking to that extent with Mi – *the intelligence officer,*" he told him, realizing that Edge was the only other man in the room to know just who his source was, and the others had no need to know. "You know a hell of a lot more about them than I do."

"That's my job, now, remember? You made me acting commander, and it's now my responsibility to know." *Besides, you've got other things on your mind, being caught between Edge and me.*

"Yeah, but how do you know who they are?"

"The Delta Team was easy; extremely fit, primarily young men with un-stylishly short hair and military bearing in a rented van. We ran the plates and found it belongs to a car rental agency at Fayetteville, near Fort Bragg. Since Delta is the one who handles anti-terrorism operations, that deduction was simple.

"The private contractors are a lot like them, only somewhat older. Their vehicles have Virginia plates registered to a service company, the majority of whose stock is held by Scythian Systems, who are known to supply specialized technicians to the military, and hire mainly former soldiers.

"The Feds, of course, look and act like cops. Besides, one of the people watching them spotted a gun under the jacket of one of the members on one team. The other paid with a credit card that our people were able to trace back to the Federal Government.

"What about the Mossad?" Neil Larson asked eagerly. Neil belonged to a school of thought that, with some justification, considered Jews in general and Israel in particular to be public enemy number one as far as the White race was concerned. "How sure are you?

"Very. That one was interesting: four men in one motel room who attracted attention immediately because our people first thought they were Arabs and maybe terrorists. I wondered if they were here trying to contact us, maybe to sell us weapons or something, so I

308

decided to keep an extra close eye on them and arrange a contact if the investigation confirmed that. Turns out they're driving a van registered to a Jewish moving company out of Florida. I gave orders to find out just what we had on our hands, and one of our sources moved into the unit next door and tapped the room through the wall. Lieutenant Johnson listened to the tapes and recognized the language as Hebrew, and we had it translated. Definitely the Israelis: they've brought in some pros to do us this time."

Edge stroked his chin in thought, intrigued despite himself and his irritation at being upstaged. "So what do you propose?"

"We use our extra assets to hit them – *all of them* – at the same time the other missions are going down. If we try to wait until afterwards, we'll miss the boat, because they're going to start moving when it all hits the fan, or at least go on full alert. I don't care as much about the others, but I particularly want that Mossad unit, and I want at least a couple of them alive, along with one or two of the private contractors if at all possible."

"Whew! That's going to be a tall order." Roger Nash told him. "Can you do it?"

Frank nodded curtly. "Tall or not, Mr. Nash, we've got to do it. We can't have the enemy operating with impunity within our sphere of influence."

"You're damned right, Captain Gore," Larson told him, "especially about the Zionists. I want those bastards!"

"So do I, Mr. Larson, but probably for slightly different reasons. I've been discussing the possibilities of the situation with the Communications Officer, and she assures me the propaganda value of being able parade hired mercenaries and foreign spies and assassins in front of the camera will be invaluable to the Cause. When the people see and hear the prisoners we take read the statements we're already preparing for them in advance, it will destroy the Feds' credibility – and boost our own by the way – by an almost incalculable extent. With nailing the Israelis in particular, every White separatist, supremacist and conspiracy theorist in the country – North *and* South – will rally to our side."

"Amen to that!" the newest councilman told him enthusiastically. "We take down a Mossad unit, and I guarantee you'll instantly have hundreds, if not thousands of new recruits who have been sitting on the fence so far, not to mention some damned good press. The action will also give a boost to the rising far-right parties in Russia and the EU by adding credence to their views about Israel, and you'll get some serious goodwill in the Arab countries."

"Yes sir, and that leads directly into my next point. There's something else just as important here, and maybe even more so: the direct gain of financial and physical assets."

Edge's mind was racing with the implications, and he began to catch up with Frank's line of thought. "Scythian will pay to get their people back," he said thoughtfully, "as long as it can be done quietly so Uncle Sam can pretend to be unaware. I'm certain of that; they've done it before, in Iraq and Afghanistan. Israel, though, has a policy of not negotiating with '*terrorists*.'"

"Bull shit!" Larson snorted. "I've studied them for years, and they do it all the time. How many times have they released dozens of prisoners just to get back one or two soldiers, or even their remains?"

Edge flushed slightly, but before the situation could get out of hand, Frank cut in again. "I not talking about the Jews; I'm talking about the Arabs."

A united chorus of "What?" echoed around the room.

"General Edge, please correct me if I'm wrong, but what do we need most, besides people I mean? We need money to fight a war, sure, but even more than that we need high-tech weaponry; surface to air missiles, anti-armor weapons, ship-killers, things of that nature, and the Muslims have them. What do you think four Mossad agents would be worth in trade to the Iranians, say, or maybe the Syrians or Libyans?"

Edge had to agree, although he inwardly cursed himself for not thinking of it himself almost as fervently as he did Gore for being the one to bring it up.

Nash spoke up, his voice strangely uncertain. "Are you sure you want to do this, Captain? I mean, the Arabs are terrorists."

310

Without speaking, Herdman and Dr. MacFie nodded their agreement.

Gore's exasperation at the words clearly showed in his eyes, although the tone of his voice never altered. "Gentlemen, with all due respect, so what? What are these heathen Mossad killers, coming over here to try and murder us, and kill our people, if not terrorists? What are these Feds they're working for, torturing and killing not just combatants but innocent civilians? Tell me, sirs, for that matter, considering what we're getting ready to do, what the hell are we?"

Frank stopped a moment and gathered his temper. It wouldn't do to alienate these men, not now especially, considering that they were soon going to have to make a decision between him and Edge.

"I'm sorry; I didn't mean to blow up at you like that. You've got to understand, though, we can't afford illusions any more; we just can't. I've come to realize over the past few months that war – *any* war – is terrorism. It's making people do what you want by killing them and destroying what they have, and making them afraid you'll keep doing it. It all amounts to the same thing, regardless of which side you're on and whether you carry a bomb into a building or drop it from an airplane. The dead are just as dead and the living just as terrorized. The only difference, the only thing that separates the good guys from the bad guys is their reason for doing it. We're fighting for our liberty and for our people's survival. That can't be wrong, and it's got to be better than fighting for something abstract, like some political philosophy that's subject to change by the day. That's not real. What *is* real, is you and me, and Sammie and Donna and Tommy and that little boy that walks by here on his way to school everyday, and every other Southerner. Our beliefs, our ways, our blood: those things are *real*! They're worth fighting for, and they're worth winning at *any* cost!"

Sam looked carefully into Frank's eyes and saw neither the cold, calculating stare of a meticulous planner like Edge or Larson, nor the crazed glare of the fanatic. Instead he saw the righteous, totally confident spirit of the true believer, the crusader, to whom his God, his people, and his Cause superceded all else, even life itself. They reminded him of a photo of Stonewall Jackson he had seen, and

311

there was something about that look that swept him up and carried him along with it, washing away all doubts. He could only nod in agreement.

He only wondered which one – Jonathon Edge or Franklin Gore – would be standing when it was all over. He ached inside as the conflicting loyalties tore at him.

"In order to do this," Frank continued, "we have to make maximum use of our available resources. Mr. Larson, you are the only other experienced paramilitary commander we currently have at our disposal in this state who can be spared. If General Edge is willing to give his permission, I'd like to ask you to take over the coordination and planning of this addition to his operation in South Carolina. Sam, since he's already acting as liaison, can assist and insure we don't have any conflicts with any of the General's other plans."

Frank suggested the last in hopes of allaying any suspicions Edge was certain to have over the unexpected but necessary move. Nothing, however, could have been further from the truth. Edge was now wondering, more than ever, which side Sam Wirtz was on.

"The additions to the plan are acceptable, provided they don't interfere with the primary mission." Edge told him flatly, without emotion. As much as he distrusted Gore, he couldn't fault his reasoning. What his motivations might be, however, were another matter.

"Just a minute," Sam told him. "What about these people? They're untrained and unorganized; what if they botch the job?"

Frank shrugged. "Then they botch it; things happen sometimes. We'll prioritize, put the best people on the most important targets, help them with the planning, give them what they need and hope for the best.

"Don't get me wrong; I want a 100% success rate and if I don't get it I'll want to know why, but even if we get 50% we'll still have an astonishing victory as long as that percentage includes our primary targets, particularly since these secondary actions, successful or otherwise, will draw off any response, stretching it thin enough to maximize the success potential of the first priority missions."

Sam frowned, trying to clarify his position. "I know that, but what about casualties? These people –"

"– are more expendable," Edge finished for him, although not the way Frank would have. "We have little invested in them and if they're captured they don't know anything that can hurt us."

Even though he knew it was true, Frank shook his head. "I can't argue with that, sir, but it's not the primary reason. I want them to do it because we need them. If we don't have them, it doesn't get done, and I think this is important enough to take some risks. My men take them, and every man in this room takes them. When my wife and the members of this council were captured, we mounted a successful rescue mission with no more organization than these people will have, against a lot longer odds. As long as these folks are totally dedicated to the Cause, I trust they'll be successful as well, if for no other reason than they'll have to be, just like we did."

"Here, here!" Larson said with a huge smile that he didn't have to fake. Not only was this playing right into his own plans, but he also genuinely liked the idea, knowing its success would be a tremendous blow to their enemies and a boost to their Cause. "Gentlemen I move that we not only accept General Edge's *and* Captain Gore's joint plan – pending the General's approval, of course – but that we congratulate them both on developing a piece of pure military genius."

There were more expressions of greater and lesser sincerity all around, but Edge's eyes were fixed on Frank with the intensity of a sniper. Frank returned his glare without emotion and nodded slightly in formal congratulations.

As Frank turned to accept Neil Larson's pro-offered hand, he felt the General's stare still on him like a knife point between his shoulder blades, and sighed, realizing that he was going to have to continue dividing his attention in order to watch his back, along with Samantha's and Tommy's, even more that ever. The only sign of his growing anger was the tightening around his eyes that was not

313

missed by the three conspirators any more than they missed Edge's apparent fascination for Frank Gore's center of mass.

Larson and Herdman, meanwhile, were thrilled with yet another step taken in the direction that both were convinced would put them in position to take charge of the Council.

Andrew MacFie saw the same thing, as well as his own potential opportunities, but something was troubling him about the differences in the way Frank and Edge exchanged glares. There was something about the look in Frank's eyes...

DAY 122

CHAPTER 32

Frank broke the news about the Columbia operation (leaving out the parts that didn't pertain to them) to Tommy, Rob and Sergeant Caffary. The men whistled at its scope and audacity.

"I can't impress upon you enough the necessity for secrecy. No one other than those of us in this room is to know the full scope of what is actually happening. The squads will be divided up, and will work totally independently from one another. Like before, each squad will be aware only of their part of the mission, and will not be told that any other squad even has a mission. That way, if, God forbid, something happens to one of them, only their part in the plan is lost; the rest can go ahead as before."

"You'd better keep them apart after you brief them, then," Caffary told him. "There're no secrets in the military; soldiers gossip worse than old women."

"Agreed. Rob will be in charge of obtaining all available information on the targets; go see our intelligence officer." His Lieutenant nodded. "Tommy, you're our ordinance man. We're going to need all the explosives you can lay your hands on. Sergeant Caffary will be my liaison between here and the individual squads. During the actual operation, each of us will be in charge of a squad – we'll work out which ones before then."

Tommy looked at him sharply.

"Wouldn't it make more sense for us to take the squads, and for you to be in overall command of the operation?"

"Probably," he conceded, "but I don't intend to do it that way. Once the operation begins, there'll be nothing to do but sit and worry; everyone will be largely out of communication until they finish, since we can't risk too much chatter lest we attract attention. I be doing the same thing you all are doing; I'll be with one of the squads."

Later that afternoon, Frank stared across the kitchen table at Rob, utterly aghast.

"Do you know what you're suggesting?"

"Yeah; the only practical way to get the intelligence we need to take down Peters in the short time frame we have available. I've taken part in interrogations before, and I know what I'm talking about.

"Look, Frank, we didn't choose these tactics. *They* did, and we've got to be willing to use them too if we want to beat them. We have to fight fire with fire. Besides, they've done one hell of a lot worse to our people – Sammie in particular – than what I'm planning to do here." He paused for a moment. "It might even be good for her; giving her a chance to get a little payback of her own might help a little with these psychological issues she's been having."

Frank pulled at his face, stretching his features in frustration. "I understand that, Rob, but you've got to understand, even if I would agree to it, Sammie's not ready for this. I don't know if she would ever be ready for it; I almost hope not, in fact."

"Ready for what?"

Her husband's head slumped and he sighed as he heard his wife's voice from the doorway behind him, where she had entered unnoticed.

Things have just gotten more complicated.

"A mission of sorts that Rob proposed."

"Would it hurt for me to hear the details?"

Frank knew it would hurt like hell, but reluctantly allowed Lieutenant Johnson to brief her anyway.

He finished with, "We know his habits, we've got the plan, and we're ready to move on him at any time; we can do it tonight."

She sat silently for almost a minute, deep in thought.

"Is this the best way to get the information we need to do the job? Is there any other way that would be a quick or reliable?"

The soldier shook his head.

"Then I'll do it."

There was something strange in her voice that made Frank look at her sharply. He seriously considered forbidding it – in fact his whole being screamed at him to do exactly that – but then he would be the one thing he despised most: a hypocrite. He was constantly preaching that they needed to do whatever it took to win, and now it was time to put up the stakes.

Looking at his wife, he wondered if the ultimate cost to her would be worth it.

"Okay, Private Drucci, are you ready?"

"Hell no, sir, I'm not ready! I'll never live this down!" He glared at Kowalski as he said it, and the sergeant's studied look of innocence confirmed that he was dead right. Even though the little Yankee transplant was notorious as a ladies' man, the others ragged him a pretty boy a little too often, and he knew he'd never hear the end of this.

Frank ignored his misgivings, just as he had the Italian's protests since he had been informed of the mission. He actually felt a little sorry for him, but he wasn't going to let Drucci's feelings get in the way.

It's nothing compared to what Sammie's going to have to do.

Danny Drucci was something of a novelty in the movement. Born in Brooklyn to an almost stereotypical long-time Mafia family, his mother had moved them both to Charleston when he was fourteen, following the death of his father during a turf dispute with a Jewish mobster. "I've lost my husband to this thing," she had told him when he balked at leaving the old neighborhood, "and I'm not going to lose my son to it too!" With his thick New York accent, smallish size, dark good looks, snappy dressing habits, and seriously smart-assed attitude, he had a rough way to go in the South Carolina school system until the other students learned that he was not only willing to fight, but even eager to do so, win or lose. He gained their respect the hard way, but he gained it just the same, and graduated one of the most popular boys in his school. He became a White racialist and Southern Nationalist in outlook, even though his urban Northern childhood had left an indelible mark on his speech. Still,

317

the others liked having him around, mostly because they trusted him, but partly because they thought the way he talked was funny as hell, especially when they got him stirred up.

"Have you got the grain alcohol?"

"Yeah, I know; every time he leaves the table, spike his drink."

"I want you to know the reason you were selected for this was because you stand the best chance of pulling it off. With your accent, you won't be suspected. I consulted the experts – the women – and they unanimously felt you are the most attractive man in the company, so that'll make your job easier. You're a regular Casanova from what I hear, and it takes a man pretty secure in his own masculinity to play this role. Still, for what it's worth, I hate to make you do it."

"Not nearly as much as I hate to do it, sir. I never have liked fags anyway, and I feel weird about it."

"Well, if you feel weird about playing the part, that's probably a good sign, isn't it?"

"As long as he doesn't start gettin' funny in the showers," Kowalski observed with a lopsided grin, unleashing a torrent of profanity from his subordinate.

Ronald Peters' secretary Bruce Eisner woke up hurting and still somewhat intoxicated, despite having been induced to vomit hours earlier. His mouth felt like it was full of cotton, his head was splitting, and his shoulders were cramped. He tried to move his arms, only to find the pain increased. Abruptly he realized that he was bound lying face-up to a long table with his arms somewhere above his head.

He blinked his eyes rapidly, trying the figure out where he was and how he got there.

The last thing he remembered was…*The Tapestry*! Yes, he had been having a solo dinner and drink at that upper class establishment when he met the most gorgeous man – Danny, that was his name. Like himself, the handsome, dark haired stranger was from New York. Eisner's thoughts were jumbled; he didn't know which of them had made the first move, but before he knew it, Danny was at

318

his table, laughing and drinking and flashing his dark Italian eyes. At some point, several drinks later, Eisner had cautiously, casually put his hand on his new companion's thigh and was thrilled to find he wasn't rebuffed. He still remembered the rock-hard muscle of that leg, and how excited he became imagining the body it was attached to.

After that, everything was blurry. How much had he had to drink? A lot, but surely not that much; still, he couldn't explain it otherwise. He thought he might have left with the man who called himself Danny, but he wasn't sure. Now, here he was, and –

His thoughts ground to an abrupt halt as his eyes finally focused enough to fix on the Battle Flag hanging on the wall across from the open doorway. He instantly recognized the starry blue saltire and the red background, and understood what it meant, even without the stenciled words, "CONFEDERATE ARMY PROVISIONAL" written across it.

His eyes widened even further. A two-tiered steel medical cart had been left in between him and the flag, covered with tools and surgical instruments. Needles, scalpels, hypodermics, pliers, and a soldering iron were spread out over its upper surface, while a car battery with neatly curled cables rested on the lower.

Eisner's head swiveled rapidly back and forth, seeing only tiled walls and floors. Looking up he could see a nozzle, along with an overhead pipe. He was in a shower – a large one, like in a factory or a school. There was no sound; the place was as silent as a tomb.

He attempted to scoot a little in order to take the pressure off his arms and shoulders, but could barely move. His hands had been pulled one direction and his feet another, so the relief provided was more a matter of degree rather than alleviation. His skin goose-pimpled in the cool air, and he glanced down towards his feet, and realized that he was naked between his shoulders and thighs. Someone had taken off his shirt and put a heavy fatigue jacket on him, fastened at the neck and upper chest, and had secured the sleeves with nails through the seams to the table he was lying on. They had also put on a different pair of pants but had left them

319

pulled down to just above his knees, and nailed them down as well. Other than his head, he couldn't move.

Eisner's eyes were drawn back to the instruments on the cart in front of him and he realized what was waiting for him.

Overcome with fear, he tried to scream, only to discover part of the reason his mouth felt like it was full of cotton was that it was; he was gagged. It wasn't tight, but it was more than sufficient.

In a blind panic, he jerked frantically, making guttural noises in his throat, but he was bound too securely. By the time he exhausted himself, his shoulders were only hurting more, and he was left lying limp and helpless.

Despite the noise and violence of his struggles, no one came, and with nothing else to attract them, his eyes were drawn back to the cart, and to the instruments. They held him hypnotically, like a snake holds the eye of a sparrow, and like the sparrow, he knew the subject of his attention held his own death and pain: horrible, unimaginable pain. With nothing else to do, his mind ran wild with terror as, despite himself, he pictured what each and every one of those tools would do to his flesh. The gag denied him even the luxury of screaming, so he could only moan as the tears rolled down his face. He vaguely felt the heat of his own urine running over his legs as his bladder involuntarily let go.

He had no idea how long he had been there – hours it seemed – when the figure appeared in the doorway of the shower. Arms behind the small of its back, legs spread in parade rest, it regarded him from behind the slits of a ski mask.

Eisner began struggling again, willing the figure to speak, but it simply stared at him, unmoving, for what seemed like forever. *What do you want?* he silently screamed. *Please, just tell me what you want!* All that came out around the gag was an incoherent gargling sound that moved the figure not in the least.

Abruptly his guest stepped forward, walked around the cart, and stopped, bending almost nose to nose with him. It didn't help; all he could see was that the eyes were bright blue, and very, very hard as they looked him over like a butcher examining a piece of meat hanging on a hook.

320

No! Pleasepleaseplease!

The figure reached up and pulled the mask off. Bruce Eisner had thought he could never be more afraid than he already was. As she shook out her long blonde hair and he recognized Samantha Gore, he realized he had been dead wrong.

"Hello, Mr. Eisner," she said, her voice cold as ice. "I'm glad to see you recognize me. I know we've never met, but I'm sure you've seen my picture. After all, I understand you were responsible, at least in part, for my capture and interrogation."

Despite the fact that it was true, he shook his head violently in fervent denial, and Samantha smiled back, cruel as a cat.

"Don't be so modest, Mr. Eisner – may I call you Bruce? After all, you and I are going to be very *intimate* acquaintances. Well Bruce, like I was saying when you so rudely interrupted me, I know all about the efficiency of Mr. Ronald Peters' personal secretary. I can't tell you just how badly I've wanted to get my hands on one of the people responsible for allowing me to experience the gentle hospitality of the late Colonel Sedgeway." She smiled with all the warmth of a fox bearing its fangs at a cornered rabbit. "That was an educational experience. Would you like me to show you what I learned from him?"

Eisner shook his head negatively with even more force than before, but she ignored him. Tears were flowing in rivers from his eyes as she turned towards the table. First she tied her hair back, then picked up a rubberized apron and slipped it over her head, tying the cords at her waist, and talking all the while. "I hate to get my clothes dirty; blood and bodily wastes are such a pain to get out, don't you think?" She finished and slipped on a pair of surgical gloves, pulling them over her hands before letting go, and they made an audible snap against her wrist. "Protection against blood-borne pathogens – can't be too careful."

He blanched as she began picking up and eying the various tools on the table as critically as a debutante looking over a particularly expensive display of jewelry, periodically glancing at various parts of his anatomy as if deciding where each one would fit the best.

Finally, she chose a scalpel and held it up so it glittered in the light. Franticly, he struggled to speak.

Please! I'll tell you everything! Just don't hurt me! Oh please! Please!

She paused, scalpel in hand, and looked up at him.

"Were you trying to say something, Bruce?" she asked pleasantly, and he nodded vigorously with a flicker of hope that died abruptly as she slowly stepped toward him, the razor-sharp piece of surgical steel still in her hand. Standing to his right, she slipped one hand around the back of his neck and held the scalpel before his face. He could feel her hot, moist breath as she leaned close to whisper in his ear.

"I'll bet I can guess what it is; you're going to tell me everything I want to know in order to keep me from playing my little games with you. Is that it? Just nod if that's what you're trying to say, Brucie."

He bobbed his head up and down carefully, trying not to stick the blade, only an inch away from his nose, in his face.

"There's only one problem with that, Brucie; I don't *care* what you know." To his horror, the hand with the blade started slowly sliding down his body, not cutting yet, just gliding gently along the skin. He tried to follow it with his eyes, but her other hand caught his hair and held his head in position. "You see, after what you helped do to me, I don't care about stuff like that anymore. I don't want to hear you talk; all I want to do is hear you *scream*!"

At the last moment, she rolled the scalpel between her thumb and forefinger and pressed the dull back rather than the edge of the blade against him. At the touch of the cold metal, he screamed behind the gag at the top of his lungs, fully believing he was being emasculated.

"Lieutenant!"

She angrily wheeled her head towards the man's voice coming from the entrance of the shower. Over her shoulder, Eisner recognized him, despite his gray military fatigues, as Danny.

"I left orders that I was *not* to be disturbed!"

"Sorry, Ma'am, but Captain Gore said it was urgent, and he needs you ASAP!"

Yanking off the apron and gloves with a curse, she slammed them down on the table with enough force to rattle the instruments. As she left, she paused to shoot an anything but reassuring look at Eisner.

"Don't worry, Brucie; I'll be back, and then you and I will have some *real* fun."

Danny looked at Eisner and shook his head, tsk-tsking in sympathy before starting away himself, and the man thrashed and yelled as loud as he could behind the gag to attract his attention. Danny pursed his lips in thought, then looked both ways before approaching the bound man.

"Sorry, man," Danny told him, "nothing personal, just doing my job. I didn't know *she* was going to have you though, or I'd have never brought you in. Still, after what your people did to her, she's going to have her fun."

Frantically, Eisner pleaded with his eyes, making desperate noises.

"What's that?" Danny asked him. "You want me to take off the gag, is that it?" The bound man nodded vigorously. "Shit, Bruce, I don't know." Cautiously he looked over his shoulder. "Okay, but keep your voice down and let me know if you hear her coming back, alright?"

Eisner was sobbing as the gag was removed.

"Please don't let her do it! Please don't!"

"I don't know how I can stop her; she outranks me."

"Look," Eisner gasped, "I'll tell you everything you want to know. I know stuff – lots of it! I'll give you all of it! Just don't let her hurt me!"

Danny looked at the floor, a doubtful expression on his face.

"I don't know, Bruce; you're the first one we've captured, and she wants you pretty bad. I *could* try to go over her head and talk to Captain Gore. Maybe he'd be willing to trade your life for the information, *if* it's good enough…"

"Yes! Please tell him! I'll give him anything! Just don't let her have me! Please!"

323

Once out of sight of the prisoner, Samantha had made it all of fifty feet down the hall before she found she couldn't wait any longer and grabbed a trashcan. She didn't want him to hear her throwing up at the thought of what she had done.

"Well Sammie, Rob was right; your and Danny's good cop – bad cop act worked. Eisner is in there spilling his guts right now."

She looked up at her husband standing over her chair with his reassuring hand on her shoulder and an expression of concern on his face. She figured she must look as bad as she felt. She had seen her reflection in a mirror as she passed, and knew her eyes red, and even though she had rinsed her mouth, it still felt foul.

"I guess that's what's important."

He shook his head. "That's not all that's important, honey. I didn't want you doing this in the first place, but –"

"But I insisted; I know. I've had acting experience, and after my other – *experience*, I'm the one most qualified. As Rob pointed out when he came up with the idea, I was a double threat to Eisner: First, because I was a woman, and second, because I was the one who had the most reason to want to hurt him."

"The thing is, you didn't hurt him, and you were *never going to*; you *scared* him. That's nothing compared to what they did to you. You were only acting, and you've got nothing to feel guilty about."

She gulped hard and bit her lower lip as she made her confession. "That's just it, Frank; I don't feel guilty at all, and I *wasn't* acting. That's what's so sickening. I *wanted* to cut him! I wanted to hurt him so badly, to make him scream his lungs out and reduce him to nothing but a pile of pain, just like they did to me! Do you understand? I really, *really* wanted to! I had to force myself to stop. I-I...that's not me Frank; that's not who I thought I was!" She hung her head, and her next words were in a tiny, far away voice. "I don't like what I've become."

Frank leaned down, took her chin in his hand and lifted her face so she was looking at him once more.

"Sammie, this damned war has changed everyone it's touched. Sometimes, we all *want* to do things. What's important is that you

324

didn't do it. Vengeance is a base but perfectly natural emotion, and I think it speaks well of you that you didn't actually take advantage of the opportunity when you had the chance. You were alone in the room with him; no one could have stopped you if you had decided to go ahead and start slicing, and no one would have blamed you afterwards."

"But I –"

"Do you know how we found out where you were being held? Did any of them ever tell you?"

She shook her head. She had been so thankful just to be rescued, she had never thought to ask. Frank knelt down beside her on one knee, putting himself at her eye level.

"It was after we recovered Jim and Thumper," he said, and the big dog that had accompanied them to their school headquarters this trip raised his head from the floor at the sound of his name and wagged his tail. Absently, Frank reached down to scratch him behind the ears. "We brought them back to the garage, along with that BATF prisoner – Schneider – and the body of his partner: the one I killed with Donna's hatchet.

"We made Donna leave the room, and when you took off Schneider's blindfold, we had him face to face with the other agent's dead body, his head hanging on by no more than a thread where I had almost decapitated him during the fight. That set the tone for the questioning.

"We threatened him with torture, Sammie, but unlike what you did a few minutes ago, we were ready to do more than threaten. If it had become necessary to find out what happened to you, the three of us – Edge, Sam and I – were all perfectly willing to cut Schneider up into dog meat. Fortunately for him and maybe even more so for us, it wasn't, but we were willing. I'm not proud of it, but if I'd had to, I would've literally skinned him alive an inch at a time if that's what it took to find out what had happened to you.

"We didn't ask to be involved in this war. We never wanted it and didn't even really know it existed, but the other side made that decision for us. We didn't set the rules either; the enemy did that, and we've got to play under that set of rules if we want to win. I wish we could just meet, man to man, have it out and be done with it, but this isn't a duel. Honor doesn't enter into it anymore."

She looked deep into his gray eyes, swallowed hard, and managed a tight little smile.

"You're wrong, Frank. If it weren't for honor, we wouldn't be fighting in the first place. We insisted on telling the truth and opposing a lie, and...well, here we are."

"Yeah," he said, leaning forward and slipping his comforting arms around her, gently kissing her lips. "Here we are."

"Oh, sorry! Didn't mean to interrupt, sir...uh, ma'am."

"Hello, Private Drucci." Frank disengaged himself with a rueful smile as he rose. "Impeccable timing as always."

Danny grinned, still a little bright eyed himself from his earlier indulgence in getting Eisner drunk, but after a quick glance at Samantha he wisely decided to keep any of his usual smart remarks to himself.

"Sir, we have all the useful information Lieutenant Johnson believes the prisoner can give us. Not only do we know Peters' habits and command structure, but we know who provided the information that was used to set up the raid on Commander Wirtz's farm: Hershel Zuckerman, head of the South Carolina chapter of the Defenders of the Jewish People."

Frank's face darkened at the thought of another of those responsible for brutalizing his wife still being on top of the ground. He should have guessed; the DJP were a notorious self-appointed watchdog group, anti-White in general and anti-Southern in particular.

"He goes on the list then, with the first priority targets." *If the Field Marshal doesn't like that, he can lump it!*

"Yes sir."

"Has Eisner been untied for a while? I don't want ligature marks on the body."

"Yeah, we did that as soon as we started, but according to Lieutenant Johnson, with the way he was secured, by clothing instead of standard bindings, there shouldn't be anything incriminating. There may be some bruising, but it ought to be minor and not in the usual places. Besides, you know how these fags are, always playing their kinky little games. It would be surprising if he didn't have a mark or two."

"Alright, then, go get with Sergeant Kowalski and the rest of your squad, and get rid of him like we planned. Can you handle it, or do you want me to get someone else?"

"I'm an Italian from an old mob family, Captain," Drucci told him, sounding more than a little offended. "My great-grandfather was a hit man for the Chicago mob, and once tried to strangle Al Capone with a towel in a steam room. What do you think?" With that, he saluted, turned his back, and walked out with a strut.

"Wouldn't Edge want to keep Eisner for a prisoner?" Samantha asked. "He might be able to mine him for more information, or exchange him maybe."

"Yes, but he's out of luck. The information we've got from him is only useful as long as Peters and company don't know we have it, which he would if he simply disappeared. No, what happens to Eisner must appear to have no connection to us.

"Besides, as Peter's assistant, he bears a large portion of the responsibility for what's happened so far. There's only one penalty for that."

DAY 123

CHAPTER 33

Ronald Peters, alone in his office, was more than a little put out. For the first time in the three years he had employed him, his secretary hadn't shown up for work, leaving him to field his own phone calls, along with everything else. He was concerned enough to have checked, and Eisner hadn't returned to his motel room last night. He was beginning to worry that he might be somewhere being un-gently milked for information right now.

The phone rang and he glanced at the caller ID.

Well, what do you want this early in the day?

"Good morning, Chief Perkins."

"Good morning, sir. I'm afraid I have some bad news."

"Well?"

"Yes sir. Your secretary, Bruce Eisner, was found dead in his motel parking lot this morning, the victim of an apparent mugging." The chief waited for a response, unsure of how the FEMA head was going to react.

"You said an '*apparent* mugging'; what does the medical examiner have to say?"

"I called him in as soon as we identified the body, sir. He just arrived at his office a few minutes ago, and of course we moved Mr. Eisner to the front of the line. He's being worked on right now."

Peters was mildly surprised at the chief's initiative. *Well, what do you know? He can be taught!*

Perkins continued. "The body was found behind a dumpster by a hotel employee taking out the trash this morning, and it appears he was killed at the scene. The preliminary investigation indicates that he probably died of massive skull fractures, resulting from a blow or blows to the back of the head with a blunt instrument. The investigator on the scene believes that the murder weapon was something on the order of a baseball bat or a piece of pipe. From the evidence, it looks like he was dragged out of sight after being struck. Robbery may have been the motive, as his pockets were turned out, and his watch, wallet, and any cell phones or jewelry he may have had were missing.

"We did some checking and, so far, the last time he was seen was leaving *The Tapestry* – that's a restaurant and lounge a few blocks away from where he was staying – in the company of a dark-haired male with a New York accent. That was about 10:00 pm, and the witnesses said that both men appeared to be pretty drunk at the time. The estimated time of death was around three or four o'clock in the morning."

"So, what's your working theory as of now?"

"Well sir," he said so carefully that Peters could detect the caution in his voice, and was thoroughly satisfied by it, "we believe, based on the evidence so far – and subject to change depending on the autopsy results, of course – after leaving whatever place he went with the other man from the restaurant, he returned to his motel, and was attacked from behind by a person or persons unknown. So far, we haven't found any witnesses at the crime scene itself."

Peters had to admit the chief had done his homework on this one.

"Were there any ligature marks, say, from handcuffs perhaps, or any other trauma? And what about any drugs in his system?"

"No sir. There were some faint marks here and there, but they were fully consistent with clothing cuffs and seams in the opinion of the coroner. Other than the head injury, there is no apparent trauma not consistent with falling after being struck. I don't know about drugs yet; the toxicology report won't be ready until after the autopsy. The blood alcohol test showed he was still legally drunk at the time of death, almost three times over the limit."

Peters remained silent for a moment digesting the information before making his decision.

"Good work Chief: you might just surprise me and make something of yourself after all. Keep me informed."

There was a *click* and Big Jim Perkins was abruptly left listening to the dial tone. He stared at the phone morosely.

You son of a bitch, you don't know how much I wish it was you on that slab down in the morgue instead of your faggot secretary. I'd go down there personally and watch them cut you open, just so I'd know for sure you were dead! Maybe then I could sleep nights again.

Ronald Peters didn't know the chief's thoughts, which was probably just as well for the head of Columbia's finest. Instead, he calmly reviewed the situation. Barring something unusual from the autopsy report, it looked like nothing more than a case of bad luck: being in the wrong place in the wrong time. He didn't have time to nurse suspicions unless there was evidence for them. Even if CAP guerrillas had assassinated his secretary, apparently they had simply killed him without coercing any information out of him. Besides, a gun or a bomb would be more typical of CAP, not a Louisville slugger.

He mentally shrugged as he picked up the phone once again and punched in a one, followed by a Washington, DC area code. Eisner had been useful and efficient in the extreme, but here were plenty more just as functional where he came from. With everything else looming over his head, the casual murder of his unfortunate secretary was the least of Ronald Peters' worries.

"Well?" Frank growled as Kowalski entered alone. Remembering his manners, he added, "Sorry; just a little tired. Get yourself a cup of coffee; it's fresh."

The red-eyed sergeant gratefully helped himself to a Styrofoam cup and grimaced; besides chicory, this batch had been cut with roasted dandelion root. He was definitely late. It was almost 7:30 in the morning; not wanting to take any more chances than they had to, they had gone to ground until the curfew was up before venturing back.

"I went ahead and told the rest of the squad to go rack out for awhile; hope you don't mind."

Frank smiled. "Not at all; it's been a long night for all of us."

"You've been up all night too, Captain? There was no need for that."

331

Frank shrugged. He had lain down with Sammie for a while until she drifted off, but he couldn't get to sleep himself with his men still out there. Eventually, he saw there was no use trying, so he eased out of bed and tried to catch up on some planning. He'd been at it for hours when 5th Squad returned.

"It went well, Sir," Kowalski said, "just like clockwork. We made him drink several more slugs of liquor on the way there, and he was staggering when we let him out of the car. Probably for the best that way; he never knew what hit him.

"We dragged the body behind the dumpsters, cleaned out the pockets, and got the hell out of Dodge.

"Here." He sat a plastic grocery bag on the desk. "This is all he had on him: a pretty nice watch and ring, a wallet with two-hundred forty two dollars and a couple of credit cards in it, thirty-five cents in change, and a cell phone."

"The phone's not in here is it?" Frank asked, almost panicking at the thought of a possible GPS locator being brought into headquarters.

Kowalski grinned. "Nah. We copied all the numbers and such off it and pitched it out the window in the colored part of town. Some crack-head will snatch it up and be using it, and any attention that brings will be drawn away from us and lend credence to the idea of a mugging. The list of numbers is in the bag."

"Good job. Tell you what, Sergeant; put the two hundred in the general operating fund, and throw the forty in the beer kitty. You all have earned it."

DAY 126

CHAPTER 34

Columbia SWAT Team Captain John Carter blinked as his captors allowed him to remove his blindfold. He had been wearing it for an hour, ever since he was taken.

In obedience to his doctor's orders, he had begun his long, painful daily walk in an effort to rebuild his torn flesh and shattered bones. What made it worse was the knowledge that, at forty nine years of age in particular, his days as an active cop were clearly over; it was either early retirement or a desk from now on when he went back to work.

If he went back; after being shot not by CAP guerrillas, but by Federal forces, the magic seemed to have gone out of his career, particularly when he had been threatened with a psych-ward if he even mentioned it.

Perhaps his disgust with the direction his life had taken explained why he didn't try to fight back or even raise an outcry when the two men had quietly stuffed guns in his ribs and escorted him to a waiting car. He just wasn't sure he gave a damn anymore.

As his eyes adjusted to florescent illumination in the windowless room, he immediately recognized the figure before him, despite the beard. He should have, since it was a man who had once worked under him as a SWAT sniper, and now topped the FBI's most wanted list.

Frank frowned, not at Carter, but at the ski-masked Sergeant Stock who, along with Corporal Lewis and Private Kessler. They were escorting the captive, holding his upper arms firmly.

"Is that his cane?" Frank nodded at the hooked metal and plastic stick hanging over Stock's arm.

"Yes sir."

"Then give it back to him."

333

"Sir, you know that could be used as a weapon!"

"Yes, Sergeant, I'm aware it can be used as a weapon, just as I equally aware that Captain Carter fully realizes, under the present circumstances, just what will happen if he attempts it."

Stock shrugged with a resigned look that plainly said, *you can't tell some people anything*, and handed the stick back to its owner.

Frank gestured at an old table nearby with a pair of mismatched chairs beside it. "Let's talk, John. Sergeant, men, please wait outside; I'll call you if I need you."

The trio left with obvious concerned reluctance, and Frank took one of the chairs while looking pointedly at Carter. "You might as well sit down; it'll be easier on your leg."

Torn with emotions ranging from anger to confusion to curiosity, the latter finally won out and Carter sat. To his self-disgust, he was unable to suppress a groan of relief as he took the weight off his leg. Once he was seated, he looked Frank up and down, taking in the sharply creased gray fatigues with captain's bars on the collars he had put on for the occasion.

"Looks like you've done pretty well for yourself, Frank. Got yourself a command position now?"

Frank shrugged and nodded. "It has its moments. I was sorry to hear about what happened to you. How's the leg?"

"It's getting better." He was lying, and both of them knew it. One bullet from the three round burst had been stopped by his body armor, but the other two had shattered his femur and his hip joint – both ball and socket, which had to be repaired with plastic replacements and a wide assortment of metal rods and pins. Finally, he was unable to contain himself any longer.

"You brought me here to kill me, didn't you?"

Frank was unable to suppress a chuckle. "If that was my plan, I wouldn't have gone to the trouble of dragging your butt all the way in here. Besides, why would I want to do that?"

"That is what terrorists do isn't it?"

Frank leaned forward earnestly, resting his elbows on the table. "John, you were at the Capital, and you were at the riot outside the police department." He looked meaningfully at the other man's wounded leg. "You've no doubt heard what happened to my grandmother, to Mary Wheeler, to my wife and to God knows how many other people. You also know what happened to you when you tried to tell the truth yourself, don't you?"

Carter mentally squirmed as the guerrilla chief continued remorselessly. "So you tell me, Captain; who are the terrorists? For that matter, if criminals are the people who break the law, which ones are the criminals: us, the Feds…or the Columbia PD?"

Carter blew out his breath in frustration. *Ever since I've known this guy, he's had the ability to cut right through the chase.*

"All of us, I reckon; all of us are criminals, but some of us are still trying to maintain law and order."

"How do you plan to do that with the current Federal oversight and local leadership of the caliber of Perkins and Trigg? You know what they let happen – not just during the riots, but to you and me."

"We'll do our best with what we have," he mumbled, and the hollow conviction in his tone was plain even to him."

Frank locked eyes with him.

"Captain Carter, are you aware that seven of your fellow officers are marked for death even as we speak?"

Carter reacted with a cop's outrage that the thought. "What? Why?"

"The murder of unarmed civilians at the Capital and Police Department riots, the latter in particular. If you recall, several of Columbia's citizens were actually chased down and shot, some of them while lying on the ground wounded. The Confederate Army Provisional represents the interests of those folks. It has put together a list of their names, and the Confederate Council has approved death sentences in absentia on those officers."

"You can't do that!"

"Yes we can, and you damned well know it."

"The courts –" he said reflexively, then stopped himself abruptly as quickly as he had said it. The courts, under orders from the Federal Government, had steadfastly refused to acknowledge the issue even existed. He shook his head.

335

"Is that why you brought me in here, to tell me you're going to kill my brother officers?"

"No, I brought you here to give you the chance to save their lives, and to ensure the safety of the people of Columbia."

Carter was utterly and completely lost now.

"I don't know what in the hell you're talking about."

"Captain, contrary to popular belief, we are not at war with the rank and file of the Columbia Police Department. Yes, there are certain people in the upper echelons – more politicians than policemen – who will be dealt with in time. You might as well accept that as a given, and we'll go on from there.

"As I said before, these seven men are killers: murderers, under sentence of death; however they are comparatively little fish in the scheme of things. We can kill them, yes, but to do so will put us at permanent odds in a very personal way with the Columbia PD. Do you understand my dilemma?"

"I understand you want something from me."

"Yes, I do. I'm willing to use my position to allow these men to live. They will have to resign or be fired and get out of the South, of course, but if they do that they can live, as will dozens of other officers who will otherwise die if the situation between the Confederate forces and the civilian powers in Columbia escalates further. If push comes to shove, we have both the capability and the will to utterly destroy the entire department and every man on it, and lay waste to half of Columbia in the process if necessary. Do you understand?"

Frank's calm delivery and direct stare made Carter believe he was telling the truth, which he was.

Frank continued. "What I want from you is a sort of unofficial armed truce with the Columbia PD. The Feds are handling everything to do with us anyway; you quietly spread the word to your men to leave us alone and we'll leave them alone. Concentrate on protecting and serving the citizenry of Columbia for a change, and stay out of this war. In return, we'll do our best not to run afoul of you."

It took Carter a while to close his mouth and get his breath back from the shock.

"Do you realize what you're asking?"

Frank nodded. "Do you realize what you're getting?"

The captain thought about that one for a bit.

"Okay, let's just say, for the sake of argument, I was willing to do this; it still wouldn't matter. I'm just a captain. I don't have the level of influence it would take to create that kind of climate. Hell, I'm not even back in the department yet. I'm still off on medical leave!"

"That can be changed. In fact, there are a great many things that are going to be changed, and you need to be ready to take advantage of them for both our sakes. You were always a good cop, John, and I think you'd make a good Chief. It's about time this city had one."

"What are you talking about?"

"This: we hear that you're in line for the chief's job, should Perkins and Frog-eyes leave, if someone powerful were to pull a few strings. We happen to know some folks are ready to do just that." Indeed, the Mayor of Columbia himself would do it at their behest, although he would never let Carter know that. "All you have to do is be there and be ready."

"Why would Perkins and Trigg leave? Do you know something I don't?" A sudden realization hit him like a bucket of cold water. "You're going to kill them, aren't you?"

"I never said that," Frank told him noncommittally. "That's not your concern right now. Frankly, we don't have to kill them. Whether we do anything to them or the Feds do, they're goners. They've been involved in this conspiracy from the beginning, and they know too much and have done too much for either side to let them keep running loose. You know Peters is going down; he's embarrassed Washington too many times, and when he falls, they'll fall with him...that is if the Feds even let them live. If not, no doubt we'll be the ones who get the blame for whatever happens, but it'll be a tossup as to which side actually does the deed. Either way, they're both dead men walking."

Carter swore at his brutally honest evaluation of the situation but Frank ignored it and went on.

"Here's what you need to worry about. One way or another, Columbia is going to explode, and then it's going to get one hell of a lot worse before it gets better. When that finally happens which side was at fault or who was right or wrong doesn't matter; what matters is that there's a stable man with no baggage ready to step in and run things here for the sake of the people."

"Do you really expect me to support you?"

Frank shook his head. "Of course not; I'm just asking you not to support the Feds either; as you've seen for yourself, that doesn't work out too well. What I'm asking is for you to stay out of the way and keep your people out of the way as much as humanly possible. This is between us and the United States Government, and it would be both to your advantage and to that of the people of Columbia if you'd keep it that way."

Carter thought about it carefully. Always an honorable man but a pragmatic one, he recognized much the same thing in Frank Gore, and looking into his former associate's eyes, he realized that he meant exactly what he said. Things were about to go straight to hell in a handcart, and if no one competent was left in charge when it did, then the whole city could very easily go right along with it. Whatever it took, he couldn't let that happen.

He didn't believe in the Confederate Cause, but since Federal 'law enforcement officers' had cold bloodedly shot not only him but dozens of unarmed citizens as well, he didn't believe in much of anything anymore. The only thing he had left was his duty, and that was to protect and serve the people of Columbia.

"All right. I don't like it, but I'll do it. It looks like I don't have one hell of a lot of choice."

As Frank thanked him and called the men back in to return him to where he had been picked up, he reflected that Carter was right; neither he, nor Frank, nor even the Feds for that matter had much choice in anything that was happening now. Everyone had to play the hand they were dealt, and play it out to the very end, because there was no going back for anybody.

The only way to go is forward.

DAY 128

CHAPTER 35

"I don't see how we're going to accomplish this," Frank declared, sighing in exasperation. He was assisting Tommy and Alpha Squad in planning the attack on the NABP, and they were getting nowhere fast. "There's no way we can get the explosives into the building and have them remain there undetected, and the closest we could leave a truck, the blast would be lucky to shatter a few windows and maybe cause a heart-attack or two." He looked around at the other members of the squad. "Any suggestions?"

The room was silent. They had turned, twisted, folded, stapled, and mutilated the scenario for days, and were no closer to a solution than before. Even the use of a stolen airplane as a make-shift bomber was discussed, but any craft would be likely to acquire would never hold enough of the mostly improvised low-grade explosives they had to do the job.

"I have a suggestion."

The others looked Arnel Scot. They were a little startled; since the murder of his family, he had barely said a dozen words to anyone. Of course, that meant, when he did speak, he was obviously worth listening to.

"We get a delivery truck: the biggest one we can find. We load it up with everything we've got that's explosive or flammable, get close enough to the building to make a run at it, punch it right through the front doors and keep going. Bury it as deep as it'll go inside, and then bail out and run for it. Touch her off and *Boom!* The job's done."

Frank had a sinking feeling about which way this was going, but he didn't let it show in his voice. "It would be kind of risky for the driver, don't you think?"

Scot shrugged. "I'm volunteering to be the one behind the wheel, sir, and it's a risk I'm willing to take."

The argument went on for some time, until it became apparent there was literally no other way to accomplish the task. Still, Frank balked.

"I'm not going to start sending my men on suicide missions!"

"You're not sending me, sir; like I said, I volunteer. Besides, it's not suicide, just a long shot. I might make it out before it blows; at least, I'll give it a try."

"I know horse manure when I hear it, too."

"Look, Captain; I want to do this. I *need* to do this; you of all people should be able to understand that. Weren't you willing to do pretty much the same thing to get your wife back, go on a mission you knew there wouldn't be any real chance of coming back from?"

Frank nodded, gathering his thoughts before he spoke again. That one had hit close to home.

"Arnel, this won't get them back."

"Alright then, what would you have done if she hadn't made it? Would your vengeance really have had *any* limitations? No? Well, neither does mine. Besides, vengeance is neither here nor there; this is something that needs to be done for the Cause. I'm not just throwing my life away. After the truck comes to a stop, I plan on running before it blows and getting away if I can. But if that doesn't work out, and I die during this mission, I'm laying down my life for something a lot more important, something a lot bigger than me. I'm laying it down for my country and my people, and I reckon God will take that into consideration. Someone is going to have to do it, and since I'm the only one here with nothing left to lose, it logically falls to me."

Frank just stared at him for a moment, silently considering his unspoken words that fell between the lines.

Besides, it hurts too damned much to live, and I miss them so very much!

Thinking about how easily the dead woman could have been his own wife, Frank came to a shuddering understanding. "Alright then, but understand this: I don't like it, and I want you to know, if you

342

change your mind, I don't care if it's five minutes before the operation begins, you can do it with no hard feelings and no shame. We'll try something else."

Scot smiled sadly. "Sure, Captain. If I change my mind, I'll let you know."

Every man in the room knew in his heart that would never happen.

Frank and Sam sat quietly, listening to Sergeant Thompson explain their plan to execute Judge Feldman.

"We decided to build on something that's already been proven effective. The Israeli Mossad carried out a series of assassinations against the Arabs involved with the massacre of their athletes during the Munich Olympics. They worked on the principle that two men or a lone man may arouse suspicion, but a couple seldom does; I mean' who's going to take his wife or girlfriend to a killing?

"It's done as a walk-by. The couple walk towards the target, then at point-blank range they draw and fire, emptying a pair of semi-auto silenced .22 pistols into him: subsonic ammunition, like .22 shorts. The whole thing is over in less than five seconds, and the two assassins get into a passing car and leave the area.

"So, what do you think?"

Frank thought about it before answering.

"Wouldn't it be simpler to just park there and nail him when he comes by?"

Thompson shook his head.

"We thought of that, but it would attract even more notice. This is a fairly exclusive neighborhood, and while you can drive through it without any problems, a strange car parked along the street for any length of time would definitely attract attention. People would think we were there to burgle a house, and they'd have the cops there checking us out within a few minutes. A lot of the residents run or walk through there for exercise though, so if someone is on the sidewalk dressed halfway decent, they won't raise any eyebrows."

Frank couldn't disagree with his assessment. "You've done your homework, I see; good job.

343

"I'm familiar with the original Israeli operation and I think you're probably right. This may be the best way to go about it, with one exception: you don't have any women on your squad."

"I was coming to that, sir," Thompson told him. "I was hoping to borrow one of the ladies who were at our special warfare school in North Carolina. They're not officially part of the First Columbia, but they've trained with us and know how we operate, and I've been around them long enough to believe they're competent to do the job. I'd trust them to watch my back any time."

Both the officers remained silent so long that the sergeant had to fight the urge to fidget. It was Frank who finally broke the silence.

"Kerrie's face is known, but she just doesn't have it in her, not at this point at any rate. Oh, she'd fight to defend herself or us, certainly, but there's no way I'd trust her to carry out a cold-blooded killing like this one. She been traumatized so much she's psychologically fragile, and we can't afford to have her freeze up or go to pieces during the operation.

"Samantha's the most qualified. You've seen her point shoot, and she's definitely developing the attitude. There are problems with that, though. First, since the Feds went to hunting us, her face is probably the best known in the country other than mine; it's not at all unlikely she would be recognized by the target or a bystander, and that would put your entire mission in jeopardy. Secondly, she hasn't recovered emotionally from what they did to her, and the Post Traumatic Stress has left her a little…unstable, as much as I hate to say it. Until she gets a handle on things, I wouldn't want to depend on her being able to carry out that kind of act without putting both the team and herself at risk."

The last thing Frank wanted to do was to send Samantha into combat, but he still felt like a traitor to his wife with his words. He couldn't deny what he had come to believe, however. He didn't know exactly what was wrong with Samantha lately, or what to do for her. From a commander's point of view, he couldn't justify the risk, not only to her, but also to the men she'd be working with, as well as to the success of the mission. This *had* to go right.

Nothing's simple anymore.

"To be honest, Captain," Thompson said, "I was thinking more of Donna Waddell. She seemed pretty capable and about as gung ho as they come."

Sam opened his mouth to deny Thompson's request out of hand, then was left speechless with horror when he saw Frank nodding his agreement.

"I won't force her, but I'll ask her if she'll volunteer. Tell Sergeant Caffary to send her in here on your way out."

It was only with the greatest of difficulty that Sam managed to contain himself until the sergeant closed the door behind him, then he exploded.

"Damn it, Frank! You're not sending her on this mission! I won't have it!"

Frank drummed his fingers on the table until Sam completed his tirade.

"I'm sorry to say this, Sam, but you're the liaison: Edge's observer. You and he put me in command, and as long as I am, I'll make the decisions as to who goes where."

"Donna is my Goddaughter!"

"I'm aware of that; I'm also aware she's a duly sworn-in soldier in the Confederate Army Provisional, and under my command. I don't like using women any more than you do, but when I need to, I'll do it. Right now, this mission's chances of success will be enhanced if she's a part of it. I still won't order her to do it, like I would a man, but you'd better believe I'm going to ask her."

The older man snorted derisively. "Coming from you, that'll be the same thing! She worships you, Frank!" *And I know she feels a whole lot more than that for you too, although I hope to God you and Sammie never see it,* he thought to himself. *We don't need any more complications.*

"I'm sorry to hear that – she shouldn't – but that doesn't affect the situation. I need a woman for this job, and she's the only one available other than Cynthia, who's not trained yet."

"You wouldn't ask Samantha –"

His accusation was cut off abruptly as Frank's fist slammed against the tabletop and he shot to his feet, leveling his finger at the end of Sam's nose.

"I'm going to tell you something right here and now; we may be friends, but don't accuse me of playing favorites! I've taken the oath and I know my duty! If I thought for one minute she was capable of carrying this out, she would be my *first* choice, and as God is my witness, I'd send her. It would break my heart in two, but I'd still send her.

"How about you telling me, Sam; is she normal? Is she stable enough to trust on a mission like this right now, with not only the mission itself at stake, but the lives of every man on it? You've known her almost as long as I have, so you tell me! With the Post-Traumatic Stress, and all these mood swings and strangeness, would you be confident in sending her out in her present condition?"

"No, but –"

"Then how about Kerrie?" Frank cut him off again. "You think she's ready to be trusted to kill a man in cold blood and not come apart herself?"

"Of course not, but what about Donna? She's not ready!"

Frank sat back down. "She's the most ready one I've got. I've seen her in action firsthand, and I'd trust her to watch my back anytime. I've done it before." He paused. "There's another reason as well. That girl wants action, Sam, and she's not going to stop until she gets in the thick of it. If we don't give it to her, she'll go off and find some on her own, and I can tell you for a fact, as tough as she *thinks* she is, she's *definitely* not ready for that. This way I can give her what she wants in a controlled, fairly safe way –"

It was Sam's turn to cut him off. "*Safe?* She's going to assassinate a man!"

"Yes, she is, with a partner there, backup on the scene, and another squad on standby, as opposed to a pitched firefight where anything can happen. Which would you rather see her in?"

"And how is *she* going to deal with it once it's over? What if we end up with three mental basket cases instead of just two?"

Sam was horrified as he watched the agonized look running over Frank's face and realized what he had just said.

"Oh Lord, Frank, I'm sorry! I didn't mean it like that!"

"It's okay, Sam. I know." Inside, he was thinking something else all together.

No, I don't know at all. What if he's right?

Sam sat in furious silence as Frank briefed Donna: a fury equaled only by the girl's enthusiasm at being personally asked by Frank to volunteer for a mission.

It such a thrill to be treated with respect for a change, like an adult – like a soldier – especially by him!

"Before you're so quick to accept, you'd better hear some of the details first. This is something you've never done before.

"If you're willing, I need you to take part in an assassination. We have an enemy who may need killing: the Federal Judge who we believe is going to turn loose the murderers of Bob Franklin. If he does that, I want you, along with your partner, to shoot him. Will you – or maybe I should ask *can* you – do it?"

"Yes; I can and I will." Despite her excitement, she chose her answer carefully; she instinctively knew that if her words were to the effect that she *thought* she could, the conversation would be over and someone else would be going on the mission.

"Private Waddell – oh hell, *Donna* – you need to understand this is not going to be a long range hit. You're going to be close enough to touch him and look into his eyes when you pull that trigger, as close as you and I are right now. You'll be close enough for his blood to splatter all over you.

"One more thing. You know what happened to Sammie when she was captured." Donna nodded solemnly. "*No one* on this mission will be captured, do you understand? No one else I'm responsible for will go through what she did, not to mention the fact that we, as a unit, are unlikely to survive an intelligence compromise of that level. There will be backup, but regardless, no one gets left behind alive – *no one!* If your partner is in immediate danger of capture and there is no other way to prevent it, you *will* shoot and kill him without

347

hesitation. If you are the one in that danger, he will do the same for you. Do you understand?"

He was pleased to see that she at least thought about the ramifications for a few moments instead of answering reflexively.

"I can do it. Dead's dead, isn't it, and killing's killing? The target would be just as dead if I shot him with a sniper rifle from a thousand yards or launched a missile at him from a thousand miles. I always thought it was kind of sick to pretend there's a real difference when the result will be just the same.

"As to the other, yes, I can do it, and I pray to God that if I'm the one they're about to take, my partner will do it for me. I'd rather die than go through what poor Sammie went through. I mean that, Frank; I'd rather die."

Much to her surprise, Frank reached out and took her left hand in his right, while looking deep into her eyes. She had the distinct feeling he was looking into her rather than at her, searching for something inside. She shivered at the contact of his skin like she had just received a mild electric shock. *If you only knew…*

"You're a smart girl, Donna, and you're absolutely right, up here," he told her as he pointed towards her forehead, then switched the direction of his finger until it was aimed at her heart. "In here though, you might find it a little harder to convince yourself, if not beforehand, then certainly afterwards."

She sighed before speaking. "Frank, I know how you feel about women in combat, so I know full well that if you didn't need me for this mission, you wouldn't even have suggested it. That's a good enough reason for me."

"It's the mission and thus the movement that needs you, not me personally. I'm not asking you to volunteer as a favor."

"I know, but that doesn't change my answer." Knowing how badly it would make him feel, she didn't articulate the rest of her thoughts into speech, thoughts that had filled her head ever since she went with him on the daring two-person raid that rescued Jim Reynolds, and had seen him in action.

To some of us, Frank Gore, you are the movement! And to me…you're even more.

DAY 131

CHAPTER 36

Newscast, Columbia

...There has been yet another surprising turn of events in what has become known as the Capital Riot Trial, where four African-Americans are charged with manslaughter in the death of White supremacist Robert Franklin. Both the prosecution and defense rested early this morning, and made their closing arguments this afternoon. Sources close to Judge Emmett Feldman indicate that a verdict may be reached within a couple of days.

Frank stood and looked out over the sea of expectant faces, carefully keeping his own features neutral, but inwardly, he wondered if Sam, standing behind him with Neil Larson, was right. This was certainly a motley-looking crew.

They ranged in age from what had to be at least seventy down to boys and girls still in high school – and one or two who looked even younger than that – and in physical conditions from excellent to non-existent; one had to walk with a crutch, and another was even in a wheelchair. Still, he reflected, they were believers and they were willing…and they were all he had. Carefully, he made eye contact with each one and finally nodded.

They had the fire, or they wouldn't be here, and they would do, if for no other reason than they had to.

He had intended to keep each of the new squads secret from the other, but now there was no time and no logistical way to do that, with the trial winding down and the sudden announcement that the verdict might be ready the next day. The best he could do was to keep their missions separate.

"Ladies and gentlemen, thank you for being here today. It's volunteers like you who will see our country free.

"There are a few things you need to know. To begin with, upon your acceptance for this mission, you joined the Confederate Army Provisional. You are now under military discipline in a time of extreme emergency. That means there is no going back.

"You are going to be divided into squads, with each squad given a particular mission which you will discuss with no one outside your squad with the exception of your assigned commanders, and that includes other squads. From this point on, until the mission is over, you will be incommunicado. You will not phone, email, post a letter, or send smoke signals to any other person whatsoever; I don't care if it's your mother. Treason is too great a risk. Each squad will be directly responsible for the enforcement of security within it, and each and every member is hereby *ordered*, under pain of death himself, to immediately shoot and kill anyone on his squad attempting to get any information out. No warning, no questions, no exceptions; just pull the trigger. If you fail to do so, not only you and your families, but the war itself could be put in jeopardy. Do you understand what I'm saying?"

The heads nodded, some with narrow, thoughtful eyes, most with frightened but determined eyes, and a couple that, unless Frank was mistaken, would actually look forward to doing so.

I reckon it takes all kinds.

"We'll provide you with the equipment you need to do your assigned jobs, and we'll arrange for certain picked groups to network together as necessary.

"Lieutenant?"

Rob stood up, ski mask in place. The anonymity of those not yet known to the enemy was too precious to compromise.

"I need the following people to go with Captain Gore and Councilman Larson into the briefing room. Go when your number is called." As a security measure, each individual had been assigned a number, one through forty-eight, to keep at least the bulk of the volunteers' identities out of Federal hands in case of capture. "Everyone else, sit tight and wait your turn. Numbers one, fourteen, fifteen…"

Frank settled on eight squads of six volunteers each. The oldest, youngest and less-physically capable members were assigned to three scout squads, each one to provide lookouts and backup communications for other teams while it carried out their respective operations. Three squads were made of the most capable individuals would be the ones doing the actual takedowns. Two more squads, armed to the teeth with automatic weapons, grenade launchers, and a few LAWS rockets, would be held in reserve in two separate locations, ready to move in at a moment's notice and shoot or blast a way out for the takedown squads should anything go wrong. He put the ones he had pegged as psychos in these reserves, because if they were needed, there would come in rolling hot, and there would be no time for niceties or finesse.

Always one to appreciate a fine weapon, Frank looked in admiration at the rifle Tommy had handed him. He had asked for a sniper's weapon that he could shoot from a confined space, and the biker had come through.

It was a Savage T110 FPS in .308 caliber, firing a 165-grain match boat tail. The stainless steel barrel was only eighteen inches long but very thick, and was fluted along its length, the long grooves lightening the weight and dissipating heat without appreciably affecting its stiffness. Topped with a Leopold 3x9 scope and nestled in a synthetic stock, it was almost made to order for the job at hand. In fact, it was almost made to order period; very few of them were ever built.

"Will that suit you?"

"Tommy, I don't know what to say..."

"Just say you'll take care of it and not let it get all scratched up before you give it back to me. And quit fondling it; you're making your wife jealous!"

Samantha, who had been quietly watching Frank examine the weapon, smiled at the irascible biker's entertaining rant. Reaching out, she took a 20 power Bushnell spotting scope off the table and peered at it and took a deep breath. *Well, here goes nothing.*

"This, along with my Smith & Wesson and one of the MP5s should do fine."

Both men turned towards her.

"Fine for what?" Frank asked.

"Fine for your spotter, which is going to be me."

Frank just looked at her, but it was Tommy who spoke. "Sammie, you can't do this, not in your con –" He stopped abruptly, both at the fire in her eyes, and at the sudden realization that she was in the process of drawing her arm back, apparently with the intent of propelling the heavy spotting scope in the direction of his head with great force. He took the hint.

"I think I'll leave and let you deal with this on your own, Frank." Slapping his captain on the arm while keeping a way eye on Samantha, he added, "Good luck, partner!"

Frank ignored his departure, and continued staring calmly at his wife, studying her until she began to become uncomfortable. She had expected an argument, probably the strongest one they had ever had, but what she hadn't expected was for him to just stand there and look at her. She decided to play it smart, and wait.

I really hope he's not building to a big blow-up. God knows I've pushed him far enough.

She needn't have feared; Frank had never really raised his voice to her, let alone his hand, and he didn't start now. His words were calm, matter of fact, and as brief as they came.

"Why?"

"Because I need closure. I need to be there when it happens. I need to be with you."

"Do you realize what you're asking me?"

"Yes I do. I want to go."

"You've only had three weeks of training."

"So has Donna."

"Sammie –"

"Please, Frank!" She laid her hand on her husband's arm, her voice pleading. "I can't continue to stay cooped up here while you're out there risking your life."

He shook his head.

Lord, she's making this hard!

"I don't want to risk *your* life!"

"Then take me with you where you can keep an eye on me!" She hated herself for what she was about to say, but she couldn't seem to stop. "It's less dangerous being wherever you are than being left behind!"

He almost staggered under the burden of guilt that had weighed down on him since her capture, and she was immediately disgusted with herself for flogging him with it.

You're being a total bitch, and your husband deserves a lot better than that!

"I'm sorry, Frank, I shouldn't have said that, but please; I need to be with you on this one. I'm your wife. When I took that vow for better or worse I meant it, and I belong by your side."

He set his lips in a thin line and looked her straight in the eyes. "What about the *'obey'* part? Does that count anymore?"

She swallowed hard. "You know it does; that's why I'm asking. If you tell me I have to stay here, then I'll stay. I'm just begging you not to tell me that, honey, not this time. *Please!*"

She braced herself for his answer, knowing in her heart of hearts he was going to order her to do just that.

Finally, he sighed.

"Alright. I love you, Sammie, more than I can tell you. If you say you need this, then I'll trust you and take you at your word. You'll be going with us."

She started to thank him, but he raised a finger to stop her. He was sterner than she had ever seen him.

"One thing; can I trust you to keep your word under *any* circumstances – *any at all?*"

"Yes."

"Okay then; if you want to go, you'll give me your word, right here and now, that you'll obey any order I give you with no hesitation and no argument, and you'll obey it to the letter. That means if I tell you to stay, you stay, and if I tell you to run, you run like the devil himself was on your heels, and you won't look back to see if I'm following."

353

"Frank, I can't –"

"That's my condition; take it or leave it. I love you, but if you don't accept it, so help me, I'll leave you here, under guard this time, to make sure you stay. The men in your class are already experienced, and so is Donna, at least to some degree; you're not, and three weeks of training is not sufficient to make a skilled fighter out of you. I love you too much to let you sacrifice yourself for a whim. I know you're willing to take that risk, but I'm not; I have to live with myself too."

She had always respected Frank, and even though she wasn't going to get her way as much as she wanted, she suddenly respected him even more now that she saw the depths of his strength. She had just found his limit, at least as far as she was concerned. He would only be manipulated so far, and there were some things he wouldn't back up on, even for her, even though it obviously hurt him to tell her 'no.' She had no doubt, if she didn't agree, he'd leave her here with a couple of heavily armed 'babysitters' who would politely but firmly make sure she stayed put, no matter how angry and hurt over it she would be.

And you know if he had a hint of what you're keeping from him, you wouldn't go at all! Neither would he; he'd want to sit and nursemaid you, and the whole unit would fall apart, and maybe the war.

She squared her shoulders. That wasn't going to happen, not until the time came anyway.

She met his gray eyes with her blue ones. "I promise, Frank. I give you my word."

"Good enough; go get your gear ready to go at a moment's notice. For you, running shoes, some loose, comfortable jeans, and take one of my shirts to wear over whatever top you put on; it'll be long and loose enough to hide your weapons."

"Thank you for letting me come."

"If I can't trust my own wife to watch my back, who can I trust? You might say you've got a vested interest in keeping me alive." He grinned, and then added, "at least, I hope so."

"I love you, Frank." She leaned forward, pulled his head down and kissed him. He rested his forehead against hers.

"And I love you too; maybe I can show you just how much tonight." She smiled and blushed becomingly. "In the meantime, go get your gun; we've got work to do."

And God help us!

Philip Silverstein rubbed his face furiously as he rode the elevator alone down to the parking garage. The pressure and fatigue were close to overcoming him. He caught a glimpse of his reflection in the polished stainless steel of the elevator door, and saw a stranger looking back. With gray hair, bagged eyes, and deep lines that hadn't been there just months ago, it was the face of a tired old man, sitting atop shoulders slumped with the weight of his responsibility. He shook his head.

What a mess.

He was a man caught between: between loyalties and between enemies, and the force they exerted was about to squeeze him to death.

The door slid open at the second level and he stepped out, feeling the faintest hint of the night breeze that had worked its way into the garage. Before he allowed the door to close behind him, he carefully scanned the area, which was nearly empty of vehicles; only half a dozen were there in addition to his own. Considering the circumstances, he felt imminently justified in being more than a little cautious. He was reminded of his father's old adage: *Just because you're paranoid, it doesn't mean there's not someone out to get you.*

DAY 132

CHAPTER 37

Big Jim Perkins sat at the desk in his study on the second floor of his home, staring at nothing. That was all his future held. The chief of police knew beyond doubt he was a dead man, dead and damned. He was on borrowed time; if the CAP rebels didn't assassinate him, he'd end up taking the fall for Peters and his bunch of Federal killers...that is, if they didn't decide to simply eliminate him out of hand as a loose end. After all the years of political maneuvering, arm twisting, and ass kissing, the paths of his life had narrowed down to two: death, which was the most likely, or Federal prison, which for a cop didn't even bear thinking about.

In the open drawer before him was his handgun; not one of the semi-automatic Glocks issued a few years back, but the old .357 magnum service revolver he had carried as a rookie nearly three decades ago. The blue had faded with years of holster wear, and he knew without picking it up that the worn checkering on the walnut grips would be as comfortable as an old friend. It was almost like it spoke to him.

I'm here for you, buddy.

So it had come down to this, the final option. He heard the faint sounds of his wife in the kitchen downstairs, and thought of all the lies he had told her and the untold number of adulteries he had committed against her over the years. Sheila might have been a ferociously ambitious social climber, but she was not a stupid woman. She had to know about at least some of his many infidelities, but had never said a word or given any indication besides a hurt glance when she thought he wasn't looking. She had stuck with him for twenty-eight years. He shook his head and put his right hand into the drawer.

Might be the best thing for everybody concerned.

357

As he reached for the weapon, his fingers bumped a little leather picture album, small enough to fit in a pocket. Distracted, he picked it up and studied the worn black surface a moment before opening it. Inside, a picture of his father in a Columbia PD uniform much like his own looked back at him accusingly.

Well Daddy, it looks like your boy's finally got himself into a mess he can't finagle his way out of this time. You always told me it would happen some day, and it looks like you were right. You were right when you said I'd wish I'd listened to you, too. God knows that's one thing I wish.

Paul Perkins had been a Columbia cop, one of the old school variety. *"I'm a peace officer first,"* he was fond of saying, *"and a law enforcement officer second. A policeman's job is to protect and serve the people, and you can't do that if you let blind obedience to the law get in the way of common damned sense!"* He'd always stressed to his son, and drummed it in with his belt when necessary, that the responsibility of a man was to be an example, and that honor, courage, and honesty were the only things anyone could accumulate that were of any real or lasting value.

Of course, with an attitude like that, he was lucky to retire a sergeant after thirty years of hard service, and the cancer took him nine years later. He was pleased at first, when his son followed in his footsteps, all full of dreams, but as he watched Jim's meteoric rise through the department and the methods he used to get there, their relationship became increasingly strained until the two hardly spoke by the time of the old man's death.

I finally understand, Daddy. For what little it's worth now, I finally understand.

"No you don't," he seemed to hear his father's gruff voice say from somewhere deep inside. *"Or you wouldn't be taking the coward's way out."*

He turned the album's page to get away from the accusing gaze of his father only to find a picture of himself in his rookie's uniform, fresh out of the academy. He'd actually had ideals then, and plans to change the world.

Perkins snorted with derision. He'd changed it, all right: helped turn it all to shit, that's what he'd done.

Sweet Jesus, I wish there was another way!

As if in response to his half-curse, half-prayer, the answer came to him.

Sheila Perkins was surprised when her husband slipped his arms around her waist from behind and kissed her on the back of the neck below her short, dyed blonde hair.

"When was the last time I told you I loved you?"

"I don't know," she said softly.

"I can tell you when: too damned long ago." Taking her by the shoulders, he turned her around to face him. "Honey, I've only done one thing right in my entire life, and that was marry you, and I've made a mockery out of that too many times to count. You know it and I know it."

"Jim, it's alright…"

"No, it's not alright. I've never been anything but a son of a bitch to you and to everyone else around me. I've been a coward, a bully, and an ass kisser to get where I am today, which, when you think about it, is nowhere. I've wasted my life, and the worst part of it is that I've wasted our time together." He swallowed hard. "I want you to understand something, Sheila; through it all, I never stopped loving you. I know I've hurt you time and time again, but I always loved you. I'm asking you to forgive me."

For the first time in her life, she saw the tears beginning to course down his jowls.

He means it! He really means it.

"I love you, Jim, and yes, I forgive you."

He kissed her gently. "I've got some things to straighten out that I should have taken care of a long time ago. Put on something nice and get ready to go out. I've got to make some calls."

"Mr. Peters!" The voice of his new secretary, Sandra Howard, came out of the intercom, her excitement evident despite the slight electronic distortion.

"Yes?"

"Sir, you'd better turn on the TV. Chief Perkins is holding an emergency news conference, and I think you need to hear this."

"Thanks." Eisner had been an efficient and talented employee, and Ms. Howard seemed to be cut from the same cloth. She was an experienced staffer whom the local FEMA head had known casually for years. If Peters didn't trust her judgment, he wouldn't have had her for a secretary.

He pushed the remote button, and Perkins' substantial uniformed bulk filled the screen behind a podium. It looked like they were on the steps of police headquarters.

How dare he hold a conference without clearing it with me first? I'll have his fat ass!

"I expect the CAP guerrillas would like to kill me," he was saying, "and I wouldn't be surprised if they manage it." A moment's hesitation, then, "I can't say I really blame them, because it's no more than I deserve."

What the hell? Peters wondered, a chill of premonition suddenly running up his spine.

"I doubt I have a whole lot of time left, and when a man gets towards the end of his days, it's time to shed some burdens. I've decided I owe it, not just to the people of Columbia, but also to myself to clear my conscience once and for all.

"Like every man, I've committed many wrongs in my life. Some are private," he glanced back at his wife, standing behind him, tears gleaming in her eyes, "but others are public. As the chief of police of this great city of Columbia, I had a duty to protect and serve the people: a duty I have failed, and a trust I have betrayed. Instead, in my cowardice, I chose to protect myself and serve the Federal Government and its agent, FEMA Advisor Ronald Peters: a man I now know to be a tyrant and a murderer.

"To begin with, the story told of the events at the Capital Riot by the rebel forces in the now infamous video is the true version, in every pertinent detail. I know, because I was there. My officers made a tragic mistake in the heat of the moment: a mistake that cost the lives of many of Columbia's citizens: a mistake that, as chief of police, I take full responsibility for. I wish to God I would've done it sooner.

"At the second riot, in front of the police department, the shooting was started neither by the crowd nor by the police; it was started by members of Ronald Peters own Federal goon squad, firing from the windows of the police department. For my own men's inexcusable actions during the aftermath, I, again, take full responsibility. Don't blame them – blame me. I allowed that kind of climate to develop, and I stood by and did nothing either to stop it or to correct it once it happened.

"Further, as to the matter of former Columbia Police Officer Franklin Gore and reporter Samantha Norris, they were framed, at least for the initial charges against them. I know, because I helped Ronald Peters do it, at his orders. Representative of the Federal Government or not, I should have told him to go to hell; but I didn't.

"To Officer Gore and Ms. Norris – Mrs. Gore now, I understand – I'm sorry. I won't ask for your forgiveness, because after what I helped do to you, I have no right. I just want you to know that I am truly sorry.

"To the good people of Columbia, I apologize as well. I misplaced my allegiance with a monolithic, tyrannical, murderous Federal Government rather than with the people of my city and my State. I have failed you, and I have betrayed you.

"When I was a young rookie, I had ideals: ideals I lost along the way in my lust for money, power and position. My greatest regret, and my greatest shame, is that it took me until now to find them again. I loved police work," he paused, choking a moment as his voice caught, and then went on, "but I have proven myself unfit to have the honor to wear this uniform. Here." Reaching to his breast, he took off his gold chief's badge and laid it reverently on the podium. "Please, the next time, pick a policeman instead of a politician to wear it. Tell him to let the Federal Government worry its own damned problems; his job should be to worry about the people of Columbia."

Turning, Perkins stumbled as he made his way from the podium. His wife caught his arm and held it tightly as she maneuvered him toward the waiting car. The reporters present were so stunned at his apocalyptic admission, they forgot to question him until the car door had already closed. Belatedly, they snapped their hanging jaws together and rushed the vehicle, shouting futile queries as it sped away.

Pale and feeling slightly sick, Peters pressed the intercom button.

"Sir?" Ms. Howard replied quietly.

"That was a live broadcast, wasn't it?" he uncharacteristically asked the obvious.

The secretary sighed heavily. *"Yes sir, on several stations. I-I suspect that it will, in all probability, hit at least some of the national media before our people can catch it, probably within the next hour."*

"Thank you. Hold my calls."

Peters slumped back into his chair as if he was a puppet and someone had abruptly cut his strings. After a lifetime in bureaucracy, everything was collapsing like a house of cards, and he realized, this time, he was going to fall with it. There was no way out.

He stared out the window, looking at nothing.

Across town in the basement of the old school turned CAP headquarters, two other people were watching the broadcast in equal amazement. Frank and Samantha both held their cleaning rags in one hand, their weapons dangling forgotten in the other. When the camera panned on Chief Perkins driving away, as one they turned their heads and looked at one another. This was not at all what they'd planned on.

Frank was the first to realize what it meant.

"Sergeant Kowalski!" he bellowed, tossing the rag aside and rising quickly to his feet. "Change of plans: Peters is going to be moving and he's going to be moving soon. We leave *now!*"

CHAPTER 38

Peters' footsteps were lonely echoes as he walked down the Capital hallway. He was alone; it almost seemed as if everyone else had either left or shut themselves away behind their office doors in instinctive avoidance, like he was a leper. If he had been given to fancy, he might have imagined himself ringing a bell and calling out, "Unclean! Unclean!" as he walked. Ronald Peters was not a fanciful man, however, just a failed one.

The phone call his secretary had no choice but to put through despite his orders made that abundantly clear. It wasn't the President this time, but the head of Homeland Security. His superior didn't rage or bluster; there was no point in wasting a good ass chewing on a man it was too late to save. All that needed to be said was relayed in clipped, precise tones, as cold and regular as ice cubes. Peters was to return to Washington immediately, if not sooner. He was also told to bring whatever personal belongings he had with him, because he wouldn't be coming back to Columbia.

Peters already knew that, of course. After the CAP forces had made their now-famous video available to the world, that his career was effectively over was pretty much a given. Now, though, following Perkins' airing of their mutual dirty laundry in the public eye – *Who would have ever thought that fat slob would have had the guts?* – that wouldn't be enough, not nearly. Someone was going to have to take the fall for the whole enchilada, and, probably unique in the history of the United States Government, the person doing it this time would actually be the one responsible for it: none other than Ronald Peters.

He was oblivious to the hiss of the elevator doors closing behind him or to the flashing numbers of the floors. All he could think of was a twenty-two year career shot to hell, and the prison cell that would be waiting for him. There was no question that everything that had happened in Columbia – a Red State Republican stronghold no less – would cost the President the election, so he could expect no sympathy either from the Administration, the Party, or the neo-conservative pundits who would throw him to the wolves as a renegade in a frantic attempt at damage control. As if that weren't bad enough, the change in administration would leave the Democrats in charge, and they would be licking their lips at the chance to set an example of someone who royally screwed up under the previous administration, even though the sanctimonious bastards wouldn't have done things any differently themselves. It wouldn't be a country club prison for him; it would probably be Leavenworth.

That's if he were lucky, if you could call it that. Ronald Peters knew a lot of things, maybe too many to be given even the slightest chance that he'd roll and turn state's evidence or write a tell-all book. Even alone in the elevator, he felt a painful tension between his shoulder blades as he realized he was now an officially certified loose end. He knew all about loose ends; he had taken care of enough of them himself over his career.

No, he corrected himself, thinking of Frank Gore, Samantha Norris, and Jim Perkins, *not enough after all.*

Numbly he stepped out of the elevator as the doors closed behind him a final time, and mechanically headed for the exit.

He had no sooner walked out the door of the Capital building when a very homely man with big ears mashed the buttons on his cell phone.

"Mommy?" Kowalski said in the prearranged code, feeling slightly silly. "Uncle's leaving the house just now; he should be there in about five minutes."

"Thanks son," Samantha told him, feeling even sillier. "We'll put something on the stove for him."

She looked over at Frank, lying beside her, and he nodded. They were about a block from Peters' hotel in an older model blue Ford LTD that had been especially modified for the occasion. Although the back seat looked stock, it was mere upholstered covering over a plywood box that would swing out of the way when a hidden latch was popped, giving access to the trunk and leg room for the two people lying inside it. The knocked out keyhole made a lookout point, and a broken taillight a firing port.

"Is he still driving that same car?"

"Yes ma'am; you'll know him when he pulls up."

"Okay, you come on home now. Bye"

She spoke loudly, so she could be heard in front.

"Get ready, Huey."

"Will do, *Mommy*." Huey Moore's disrespectful, irreverent, and utterly infectious good humor was clear in the voice that filtered through the upholstery. "I'll bang on the trunk when I see him."

Inside the confines of the trunk, they heard the door open and felt the car rise up on its springs as Huey's considerable weight left it. Closing the door, he went to the rear and they could tell when he leaned on the trunk, because the car sagged again.

"Hey Huey?" Frank called out.

"Yes sir?"

"As soon as you see him and let us know, get off the car until it's over. You're rocking it so bad I won't be able to hit anything."

"That's right, blame the fat guy," he replied just before lighting a cigarette while nonchalantly continuing to lean on the vehicle.

Frank smiled at Samantha in the darkness. He didn't have to say it, because she understood.

We've got some damned good men on our side.

Huey was impossible not to like. At six feet, two inches tall and three hundred pounds, with a smile as broad as the graying hair on his round head, the forty-nine year-old former Klansman could have been the poster boy for the stereotypical jolly fat man; in fact, he had even played Santa Claus a time or two. Still, he was much more fit than his appearance would indicate, and had been a former professional wrestler as well as a Marine in his youth. Through it all, or maybe because of it, he had never lost his sense of humor.

"Okay, Sammie, get your scope ready. Remember, don't speak to me or distract me when I get ready to shoot, and for goodness sakes, don't move. I didn't realize the shocks on this thing were so bad."

"If the car is rockin', I won't bother knockin'," came the teasing voice from outside, followed by, "I know, I know; shut up, Huey."

Samantha choked back an insane giggle at the big man's joke as she glued her eye to the spotting scope. Frank positioned his rifle and began breathing with a slow, carefully controlled rhythm while he emptied his mind of all extraneous thought and emotion. Why he was doing this may have been personal, but the act itself had to be coldly professional for it to have the best chance of succeeding.

The weight suddenly left the car and there was a quick *thump-thump-thump* on top of the trunk.

"Dark blue Lincoln, inside lane, about one block: possible." Huey was all business now, the clowning he was famous for evaporated as if it had never been. His higher vantage point had allowed him to spot the car first.

Fighting to remain calm, Samantha adjusted the scope, cursing inwardly because of another car in the way. Just ahead, a third car stopped, waiting to cross traffic in a left hand turn, and the car they sought changed lanes to the outside. She quickly glanced at the front plate.

"License confirmed."

She felt Frank shift slightly as she studied the windshield, trying to see through the glare. As if made to order, a cloud crossed the sun, and she finally saw the glasses and non-descript hair.

"Target confirmed," she said flatly, amazed at the calmness in her own voice.

She held her own breath and lay still as she felt her husband – her avenger – take a pair of deep, saturating breaths, then hold his respiration.

Even with their earplugs, the discharge of the high-powered firearm within the confines of the trunk was startling, and she jumped despite herself. Outside Huey played the part of a startled passerby, frantically looking around as if to see where the gunshot had come from.

Fifty yards away, Ronald Peters' windscreen suddenly spider-webbed and crumbled, and the bullet entered his upper chest, just below the knot of his tie, rocking him back in his seat. In shock, he lost control of the car and instinctively hit his brakes as the wheel began to drift to the left.

Behind him was a white Toyota being driven by a four hundred pound Black lady, who had time only to scream, *"Oh Lawdy!"*

before she slammed into his left rear bumper, knocking the Lincoln sideways.

Frank, who had already racked the bolt and had been desperately trying to see to get a second shot suddenly found himself with a clear side view through the passenger window and instantly squeezed the trigger.

The bullet shattered the glass, passed through Peters' head just behind the temple, and exited tumbling through the driver's window, carrying a brief comet's tail of glass fragments, blood and brains in its wake.

The FEMA chief's lifeless body collapsed on the steering wheel, activating the horn that sounded in a long, continuous dirge as the slowing vehicle rolled across the other lane of frantically braking traffic before coming to rest against the curb.

Huey threw the smoldering remains of his cigarette on the ground, got back in the car and started it up.

"Confirmed," he said.

The two were silent for several minutes as the Ford rumbled down the streets, the only other noise being the echoes from the radio that Huey had deliberately turned up in order to give them some privacy. Finally Samantha asked the question.

"So, how do you feel?"

"How do *you* feel?"

"I asked first."

Frank blew out his breath. "I've accomplished what I set out to do; this part of the mission is over."

"That's all?"

"Yeah, it is. I'm glad he's dead and it's only right that we were the ones to take him down. Justice has been served, but it wasn't, I don't know…"

"Satisfying?" she asked, and felt him nod beside her. "Me neither. Like you, I'm glad we did it, but I don't really *feel* anything; I just feel tired."

"So do I, and I don't know if that's good or bad." He paused, thinking deeply. "Now we've got Jim Perkins to deal with."

"Yeah," she said, and her voice didn't sound nearly as certain as before, "now we've got the Chief."

Deputy Chief of Police '*Frog-eyes*' Trigg – Acting Chief as of an hour ago – picked up the phone.
"Trigg."
It was the dispatcher. "Sir, Ronald Peters has been killed."
Trigg almost fell out of his chair.
"What! How?"
"It's not positive since the Medical Examiner isn't there yet, but a patrolman responding to a two vehicle accident on Main found Mr. Peters in the front seat with at least two gunshot wounds, one of them in the head."
Trigg's brain began working overtime, and he quickly came to the conclusion that he didn't want a damned thing to do with this particular situation.
"I'll call the FBI. Issue the orders to seal off the area, and don't do *anything* until they get there. I don't want anybody near that car. This is a Federal mess, so let them clean it up."

Newscast
Columbia, South Carolina

"The Federal Bureau of Investigation has confirmed that, contrary to earlier speculation, controversial FEMA District Manager Ronald Peters was not shot; I repeat, he was not shot. According to the Federal investigators, he died instantly from head injuries sustained in a car crash on Main Street. Witnesses state that he made an abrupt left turn without signaling and was struck from behind by Ms. Lucretia Simon who was unable to stop. Ms. Simon received only minor injuries and was treated at the scene. No charges have been filed at this point, but the investigation is continuing…"

Internet Blog

Contrary to the claims of the Federal Government, FEMA chief Ronald Peters was assassinated. Witnesses at the scene heard a pair of shots just before the wreck. No doubt this administration is cleaning up some loose ends in an attempt to silence the truth...

DAY 133

CHAPTER 39

"As I see it, the place where we're most likely to have problems is the big hit – the NABP party. A major complication is going to be the police presence; it will be heavy, without a doubt, but we've still got to get through it. Does anyone have any suggestions?"

Sam sipped his coffee as Frank looked at each of the other three men in turn, and Tommy, Rob and Caffary returned his gaze silently. Finally, the biker responded. "Can we get the explosives in there ahead of time?"

Frank shook his head. "They'll already have the building sealed off – standard operating procedure. They're not stupid, and they should expect us to try something like this."

"I think we could still manage it," Tommy put in, "if we had enough high order explosives to work with, we could make do with a smaller amount we could conceal inside of something, instead of needing a truckload of it. Is there any chance of laying hands on some Semtex or C4 – anything like that?"

"Huh!" Sam snorted. "When pigs fly maybe! We have some, but there's no way we can get the kind of amounts we'd need for this project. Ammonium Nitrate and gasoline mix with a little bit of dynamite is about it."

Rob finally added his two cents, while idly drawing invisible circles with his finger on the table. "I just don't see any practical way we can get that truck through the barricades and the armed cops. They can't afford to let anything happen there, and they'll be expecting us to try. Hell, they'll be ready to shoot at any white face that shows itself. Even with a suicide driver, he'd still be killed before he made it halfway to the building."

"Shit," Sam muttered. Rob was the most experienced of the group at this kind of operation, and his doubts were something to be taken seriously. "I just don't know how we're going to pull this off, realistically. We've got to do something; Edge personally ordered this part of the operation as a key point in his overall strategy."

"To hell with him!" Tommy growled with deep feeling. "I mean it; to hell with our precious Field Marshal. I know he's your friend and all, but I've had about enough of that high-handed son of a bitch's attitude."

"Tommy, we've been over all this before. I don't like his attitude either, or his command style for that matter, but he's still our leader. More importantly, there's no question he's competent. Hell, like Frank told us one time, who's going to replace him? Nobody else is qualified. Ain't that right, Frank? Frank?"

All eyes turned towards the ex-cop, but he didn't seem to hear them. Deep in thought, he stared at the tabletop without focus, obviously wrestling with a difficult decision. Suddenly, his right index finger tapped the wooden surface sharply as the answer came to him.

"When Samantha and the others were being held in the Columbia lock-up, how did we get them to move them where we could get to them?"

"You should know," Rob told him, "you're the one who came up with the plan to make them want to move them by making it appear to be too dangerous to keep them where they were."

Frank nodded absently. "Alright; we know the NABP has enormous political clout, particularly in perception. If they were to demand a minimal police presence in the vicinity their little shindig, I believe the department would be forced to accommodate them, no matter what the risk."

"True," Sam said, "but why on Earth would the NABP do that?"

Frank's face was grim at the thought of the hell he was about to unleash; he was about to start down a yet another bloody road there would be no going back from. "Because we'll make certain they don't want the cops anywhere around. Rob, do you have that information on Cynthia's attackers?"

Jamal Wright and Otis Crump weren't particularly surprised when the unmarked police cruiser with the blue bubble on the dash pulled to the curb beside them; they tended to attract cops for some reason. They proclaimed loudly and often it was because they were Black, but everyone, including them, knew it had more to do with the fact that the pair looked exactly like what they were: dangerous punks. They struck their best loose-limbed 'gangsta' poses as the other Negroes on the sidewalk stopped to watch the show.

Both cops got unhurriedly out of the cruiser, nightsticks in their hands.

"Hold it right there, boys," the larger of the two, a hugely muscled man with the smooth skin of a shaven head showing from under the edge of his cap. Despite the heat, he wore a long-sleeved shirt. His partner was shorter and lighter, with brown hair cut short. Mirrored sunglasses concealed their eyes and, not coincidently, much of Lieutenant Johnson's and Sergeant Hodges' identity.

Jamal and Otis bristled at the 'boys' appellation, despite the fact that only one of them had seen his nineteenth birthday, and him only just.

"Whatchu want?" Jamal demanded belligerently. "An' who you callin' 'boy'?"

Hodges pointed at them with his nightstick. "Were you two with those niggers who raped that White girl, Cynthia Dover, a couple of months back?"

Several of the growing crowd murmured dangerously and Jamal's wide-lipped mouth opened with shock at the thought that a White man would dare call him a nigger. One young Black boy their own age laughed at them from the crowd and called out, "You gonna take dat shit from him, Otis?"

Otis flexed his arms in aggressive street fashion and, in a jeering, bragging voice, loudly proclaimed to all within earshot, "Shit, ain't no rape; that White bitch wanted it."

Those were the last words he ever said. With no warning, Hodges' nightstick whipped backhanded across his mouth, sending blood and broken teeth flying several feet down the sidewalk. Before Otis even had time to stagger under the blow, a steel-toed boot drove upwards into his crotch, lifting him off the ground as it crushed his testicles and cracked his pelvis. As he bent forward and fell, the stick clubbed him once again, this time across the back of the neck where it joined his skull.

When the larger man struck, Rob was only a split second behind. Grasping the stick in both hands, he punched the end into the startled Jamal's solar plexus with enough force to rupture his internal organs. Still holding the baton two-handed like a chinning bar, he jerked it up as if performing a power lift with a heavy barbell. The high-impact plastic slammed under Jamal's chin, shattering his jaw and driving his teeth together so hard they crumbled. His tongue happened to be between them and they sheared almost an inch of it off; it fell on the concrete like a large pink slug, beating its former owner down by less than a second.

One of the crowd, a very muscular colored man, melodramatically ripped off his shirt and charged, screaming curses. An instant later, he was still screaming, only this time on his knees in pain. Hodges' stick had whipped expertly in a figure-8, the two rapid downward strikes snapping both the man's collarbones. A third blow, this time to the top of the head, silenced him, fracturing his skull in the process.

While the disguised skinhead was dealing with the interloper, a hard-eyed Rob drew his Glock and fired a pair of shots through the head of Jamal Wright as he lay on the ground. While the crowd watched aghast, he turned did the same to Otis. Their blood ran across the walk and into the gutter.

"Alright!" Hodges bellowed, waving his own pistol and thoroughly enjoying himself. *I've wanted to do this for so damned long!* "The rest of you Black apes listen up! *This* is what happens to any nigger that rapes a White woman – *any* nigger! No more rioting, no more burning, and no more raping! The Columbia Police Department is not going to put up with this bullshit from you coons any longer. Spread the word, and don't make me come back here." To put a final emphasis on his remarks, each of the two fired half a dozen rounds at the crowd. Their aim was careful; none of the slugs actually hit anyone, but they knocked dust from the brick walls and concrete walk, and shattered the windows of two cars and a barbershop. The panicked mob ran screaming for cover.

As the two got back in the cruiser, another White man – Private Doug Long from First Squad – on the other side of the street put his video camera away and hurriedly left the scene; he intended to be well clear before the crowd came out of its state of shock and went on a rampage. Just as he had been assigned to do, he turned north, heading straight for the NABP headquarters. He had a tape he wanted to give them, and he was sure they would appreciate it.

Meanwhile, three blocks away, two men identifying themselves as plain-clothes policemen took James Williams, a friend and rape partner of Otis and Jamal, from his roach-infested apartment and threw him off the fourth-floor balcony and onto the concrete sidewalk below. Another of their friends, Kalunda Smith, answered his door and was blasted in the stomach at point-blank range with a 12 gauge riot gun, the 00 pellets painting the inside of his apartment with blood. Another known only as "Shine," was crushed to death when a 'borrowed' police car suddenly mounted the curb and smeared him against the brick wall of a liquor store, then backed away and drove off, leaving him there for all to see.

British News Service Report, Columbia

The African American community was horrified today by what appears to be the vigilante murders of five young men by the Columbia Police Department. The five had been part of a group that was cleared of any wrongdoing in the alleged rape of a city high school senior about two months ago.

According to witnesses, the alleged officers used racial slurs and referred to the incident when these young men were killed. Several bystanders were also assaulted and seriously injured.

The police deny any knowledge or complicity in the incident, blaming it on a false flag operation by disguised Confederate terrorists, but not every member of the African American community is willing to believe them...

"It's done, Frank," Rob told his captain.

"Yeah, I've been listening to the news. Have you hit all of the targets involved in Cynthia's rape and Chucky's death?"

"We couldn't locate one of perpetrators, and the school principle and the local prosecutor who jointly facilitated the cover up are currently out of town."

Frank nodded. "They'll have to go on the list, I reckon, along with any we miss tonight, as targets of opportunity to be taken out whenever – if ever – we get the chance. Have Mike pass their specs around to the other states in case they show up there. Congratulate Alpha Squad for me; you all did an outstanding job and I think you've answered the purpose admirably. Intelligence is telling me that Bessant doesn't want a cop within a mile of the place. He's already called in a bunch of Black Warriors to provide security, which will also work to our advantage."

"How so? Less professional?"

"That, and it saves us collateral damage in the form of the officers who would otherwise be on site. It's going to be bad enough as it is."

Something in Frank's voice or demeanor got Rob's attention. "Is something wrong?"

"No," he said after thinking about it for a moment. "No, I just hate the thought of this becoming a full-blown race war, is all. I knew it was inevitable – hell, I suppose it was inevitable from the beginning, but I'll be damned if I have to like it."

"If it's any comfort, Frank, nobody else really likes it either, not even the hard core racists like Hodges and some of the other skins when you really get down to it. It's just one of those things, like in nature: sometimes one thing has to die so something else can live. Lord knows they've been killing us piecemeal long enough."

"I know; that's why I can accept it, regardless of how abhorrent it is. Like you said, it's nature, survival of the fittest. I don't hate colored people as individuals, Rob; some of them, like Jennie May Summers, I loved almost like my own family. Still, as a race they're among the enemies of my people, and it's my own people I'm responsible to first. I've got to see to it that they live, whatever the cost to those outside."

Unconsciously, his hand crept up and closed about the old locket hanging against his chest.

"Besides standing before God, some day I'll have to face my people that have gone on before. This may sound heathenish, but I firmly believe they'll ask me what I did with their legacy, and what I did to keep our line and the dreams they fought for alive. I reckon I'd better have a good answer ready, because a man who won't fight for his own isn't a man at all."

Rob put his hand on his shoulder, a rare gesture for the normally unemotional professional soldier.

"Then I don't think you'll have anything to worry about."

DAY 134

CHAPTER 40

Newscast
Columbia, South Carolina

"Jim, can you tell us what's happening?"

"Sylvia, the scene at the court house here in Columbia is pandemonium. We have just received word that all four defendants charged in the beating death of seventy-seven year-old Robert Franklin have been found "Not Guilty" on all charges. According to preliminary reports, Judge Emmett Feldman, while acknowledging that the defendants actions resulted in the death of Franklin, nevertheless accepted the defense council's argument that the act was brought on by a combination of self-defense and 'Black rage' at his actions in supporting the Confederate Flag; a symbol equated with racism."

"Jim, as we know, Robert Franklin was associated with several right-wing extremist groups who advocate a separate Southern nation, which, according to the Justice Department, is a code-word for racism. Some of these groups have been linked to an on-going series of terrorist attacks in all parts of the country.

"According to police reports, on May 3 of this year, Franklin had attacked the governor and State officials at the pole formerly holding the Confederate Flag in front of the Capital. He injured several people, some of them seriously, with a heavy cane that he habitually carried. Enraged by this offensive attack, the four defendants, Jerome Green, Muhammad Amin, Kahlid Porter, and Leroy Jackson, the brother of slain Columbia police officer Martin L. Jackson, rushed through the police line. Franklin attacked them and in turn they struck Franklin several times. He was later pronounced dead on arrival at a nearby hospital.

"What's happening now?"

"The defendants have just appeared in the company of their attorneys and the head of the NABP, Reverent James Bessant. The crowd is going wild."

"Jim, are there any protestors present?"

"Yes, there are a few, but the police are keeping them carefully to the rear in order to stop them from creating a racial incident...

"This is it. Tommy. Alpha Squad is under your command now. The NABP party will be your sole target because it's so high a priority. No pressure," Frank told him with a humorless smile, "but it's more important than all the other targets put together. Everything hinges on it; it has to be taken out."

Tommy answered in the affirmative, with a lot more confidence than he felt.

"Alright then, finalize the plan, tie up any loose ends, and then come back and run over it with me one more time when you're done. You've got the experience, but I'm responsible for the outcome." *Along with the lives of every man on that squad,* he thought grimly, *including the one who's going there to die.*

"Rob, you've got fourth squad. Your target is Judge Feldman. No option; he has to die."

Rob's lips barely moved.

"Consider it done."

"Sergeant Stock," he said to the slender, unprepossessing man you wouldn't look twice at, and would never have thought to have been an Army Pathfinder and a high ranking black belt in Tae Kwon Do, "Charlie Squad's assignment is the local DJP head, Herschel Zuckerman".

"You've just made my day; I've wanted that son of a bitch for years! You know," he said with a halfway grin, "Buchanan is going to be jealous when he finds out."

"Not too much, I don't think; I'm giving him and his squad my old friend Silverstein."

"That leaves Perkins, Trigg, and those cops."

"I'll use Fifth Squad to handle them."

"*All* of them?"

Frank shook his head. "No, just the chief and the assistant; the cops are minor targets that can be dealt with at another time if necessary."

Sergeant Stock shrugged and left, and as soon as they were alone, Sam whistled. "Edge isn't going to like that."

"Then Edge can come down here and damn well do it himself. I'm responsible for the success of this operation, and I'll make the decisions concerning it. I'm not going to jeopardize either it or my men by stretching them too thin.

"Besides, I've cut a deal – more like a mutual understanding – with the next one in line for the chief's chair. I traded the lives of those cops for more freedom of movement, without the concentrated interference of the Columbia Police Department once he's in place."

Sam's mouth widened in shock. "You never told me that!"

"Until now, you never asked. I figured, as important as this is, the fewer people know about this little secret, the longer it'll stay that way."

"Well, I can't argue with that."

Judge Emmett Feldman breathed deeply through his nose, his expensive running shoes slapping the sidewalk. His dyed hair gave no hint of his fifty-two years, but his body didn't lie. A year ago, his doctor told him, if he wanted to live, he would have to get some exercise, and Feldman was a man who considered his own life very valuable indeed. So every day without fail he pounded the pavement religiously, literally running for his life.

The stresses of the day were draining out of him; some times it was hard to operate with the public eye on him. Not too hard though: in releasing the three men, he had done the right thing. They were murderers, sure, and all had records a mile long, but they weren't the threat to society that the old man they killed was. Until the racists were gone by whatever means necessary, America would never be the truly multicultural society that people like the judge dreamed about.

There were some people who didn't see it that way of course, which was why, tucked into his waistband beneath his windbreaker, a diminutive .38 Smith & Wesson Chief's Special rode comfortably in its holster. That was just in case, though; the chances of anyone actually mustering the courage to attack a judge were slight. Still, you never knew.

As he rounded the corner, he saw the sidewalk was empty with the exception of a young couple half a block away, walking towards him, hand in hand. Giving them a quick once-over, he saw they were casually yet fashionably dressed with hair that was carefully styled; in short, they obviously fit into this up-scale neighborhood, so he paid them no more mind.

Further up the street behind them, near the end of the block, a white Dodge Grand Caravan was headed in his direction. Other than vaguely noticing, he paid no attention to it either; he had trouble picturing right-wing terrorists driving a mini-van.

Puffing and panting, he was within ten feet of the couple when he saw their hands move and guns appear in them.

George Cox and Donna Waddell simultaneously drew their weapons, a pair of Ruger .22 semi-automatics, specially modified by Tommy. Each of the barrels had been turned down and drilled multiple times, then covered with an integral silencer. Internally, he had also modified the springs to make the pistols function reliably with low-powered .22 Short ammunition, avoiding the ballistic crack of the slightly super-sonic .22 Long Rifle rounds the weapons were originally chambered for. The ammunition was equally non-standard; the bullets in Donna's gun were hollow-points, with each tiny cavity packed with as much cyanide as it would hold, while George's projectiles were cast of hard marine bronze to maximize the weak cartridges' penetration.

Before Feldman's mind fully recognized what was happening and he could decide to stop, flee, or reach for his own compact revolver, both pistols raised in his direction, were thrust out at arm's length, and began to spit death. Within two seconds half a dozen rounds punched into his chest at point-blank range, three spilling a fatal load of poison and three penetrating his heart and lungs. Inertia kept him moving forward even as his legs began to buckle, and the couple quickly moved aside as he collapsed at their feet. Without

382

hesitation, they emptied their remaining shots into the back of his head as he lay on the ground.

The mini-van stopped and both of them got in, less than fifteen seconds after they had first drawn their guns.

"Are you alright?" George asked her.

Donna, white as a sheet and dripping with sweat, gulped hard. "Yeah, I – I think so. It's just so…just…" She gagged, but managed to keep from vomiting.

"Yeah," he replied, "I know. Still, it had to be done."

Thinking back on her older sister lying dead at the base of a flagpole, Donna's lips set and she nodded.

Bill Wilson cut the steering wheel and pulled into the parking lot of a convenience store, ignoring the spaces in front and pulling behind by the dumpster. He left the ignition on and the key in place as he opened the door.

"Let's go, folks; time to swap rides." At the other end of the lot, Dean Yates was waiting in a late model Monte Carlo.

Just as they'd counted on, less than five minutes later one very hot Dodge Grand Caravan pulled away from the store in a hurry as a pair of unsuspecting Mexican car thieves seized a target of opportunity.

Philip Silverstein grumbled tiredly as he exited the elevator onto the fourth deck of the parking garage. These past months, particularly the past few hours, had been hard on him. Following Perkins' startling confession, the station had lost all credibility since it had backed the government line from the very beginning; indeed, Peters had orchestrated and approved their stories, to make certain they fit. Now this…

He shook his head. He had been on the phone with the station owners – a communications conglomerate based in his own hometown of New York – and his job was definitely in jeopardy. They wouldn't have done anything differently, but that didn't matter; it wouldn't save him. Someone would have to be the sacrificial goat to pacify the public, and it looked like he was the one who would have to learn to bleat.

He came to an abrupt halt. There were people around his car.

He was already turning in preparation for a desperate sprint back for the elevator in hopes it was still there when one of them called to him.

"Sir, is this your car?"

He relaxed, irritated with himself, as he saw the glint of badges and recognized one of the building's security guards standing there beside two Columbia cops. Hastily, as if to convince them as much as himself that his episode of panic had never taken place, he walked faster than usual across the concrete towards them.

"Good evening Mr. Silverstein; I was just about to call you." The guard subserviently showed the manager the cell phone in his hand as proof of his good intentions.

"Good evening Larry. What's going on?"

"Sir, these two officers want to ask you…"

One of the pair, a gangling, goofy-looking red head, interrupted him. "Sir, we have reason to believe this vehicle was involved in a hit and run accident this afternoon."

"Hit and run? That's ridiculous! I've been here all day!" The *"you dumb-ass pig"* was left unsaid, but nonetheless implied in his tone.

"I tried to tell them…"

The red haired cop ignored the guard. "Did anyone else use this car today or have access to the keys?"

"No; they've been in my pocket all day. Now look; I'm tired and I'm going home. Go harass someone else!"

Using his nightstick, the cop gestured towards the lower part of the left rear quarter panel. "Then how do you explain this paint-scrape, sir?"

"What?" the station manager almost shouted. The BMW was his pride and joy, and he was instantly so filled anger there was room in his mind for nothing else. Quickly he brushed past the officer and bent over to assess the damage. "Where?"

He was so interested in the car and the motion was so quick, he never saw the blur as the stick came down full-force across the juncture of the back of his neck and the base of his skull. He collapsed like an empty sack.

Before the guard could move or even open his mouth, the other cop, a deceptively pudgy-looking blonde with a crew cut, shot pepper spray into his eyes. Gasping in shock at the pain, he had just started to turn away when a shot-filled blackjack in his attacker's other hand smacked him smartly behind the left ear and knocked him into dreamland.

"Cuff him and gag him," grunted the first cop, actually Andy Buchanan in disguise, never taking his eyes off the unconscious Silverstein, "and stash him somewhere. Lay him face-down so he won't strangle."

"Teach your grandmother to suck eggs," Henry Toland grumbled, dragging his limp burden to a narrow space between a support column and a wall.

Andy Buchanan had a deep respect for Southern womanhood in general, and a deeper respect for Samantha in particular, even without his high regard for her husband. The thought of this fat Yankee Jew putting his hands on her, and intentionally trying to crush her face during the beating he was giving her when Frank Gore intervened in this very garage made doing his job that much easier. He wouldn't particularly enjoy it, but it wouldn't bother him too damned badly either!

Andy continued the assignment impersonally and ruthlessly, just as the Rangers had taught him – KISS: *Keep It Simple, Stupid!* His method was as simple as it got: he simply took the nightstick and beat Silverstein's head in with it.

Acting Police Chief Trigg grunted with exertion as he quickly made his way to his assigned car. From the calls the department was getting, the whole city seemed to be going crazy, and even though he knew there was nothing he could do, it wouldn't be a good move politically to be sitting in his office while it happened. No, his proper place was out in the public eye, putting on a show by delivering the reassurance his presence would bring.

Levering his bulk into the Chevrolet, he turned the key.

At least he didn't have to worry about car bombs; he kept the black vehicle parked right next to the building, under the constant watchful eye of the security cameras. Moving the gearshift to 'D', he pressed the gas pedal and went rolling towards the exit. He looked both ways, but saw nothing beyond a large overflowing trash bin on the sidewalk beside the drive.

Watching through his binoculars, Frank said, "Now!"

Sergeant Kowalski pressed the green dial button on his cell phone, sending the signal that triggered the bomb buried under the trash.

The device was a simple one: a Claymore mine with a five gallon jerry can of gasoline sitting right against the letters, '*FRONT TOWARD ENEMY*'. The trashcan split apart like a peeled banana, burning garbage was thrown for dozens of yards in all directions, and the Chevy was totally engulfed in storm of fire and flying steel shrapnel that turned it into a blazing sieve.

Uri Mayer looked up at the sound of the knocking coming from their motel room door.

"Are you expecting someone?" he asked the other three Israelis and received replies in the negative. Each man quickly slid pistols – and in one case an Uzi 9mm submachine gun – under whatever was close at hand, keeping them concealed but within easy reach. Mayer kept his own pistol in his hand as he went to the door and looked out through the peephole.

A pair of clean-cut men in dark suits gazed back at him, eyes invisible behind the dark sunglasses. The closer of the pair reached out and knocked again, rapping the door sharply with his knuckles. Evidently hearing Mayer's movement behind the door, he held up his identification to the tiny glass lens.

"FBI; open the door. We'd like to talk to you."

The Mossad agent turned back to his partners.

"It's the FBI," he said in Hebrew. "Keep the stuff out of sight." Before opening the door, he quickly slipped his pistol into a concealed holster at the back of his waistband.

386

"Yes sir?" he said through the crack just big enough to admit his head. He was somewhat reassured since, behind the agents, he could clearly see a black government Humvee parked in the lot, a masked, fully armed and armored agent standing behind it with his rifle at the ready. Most other people would have been greatly disturbed, but to the Mossad agent, it meant that the men at his door were who they claimed to be.

"We need to see your identification, sir."

"Here it is." Mayer produced a drivers license that would stand up to even close scrutiny, partly because the Israelis had excellent document forging technology, and partly because it originally belonged to an actual man whose name was listed on it; a man whose body had been weighted and dumped into the deepest reaches of the Gulf of Mexico off West Florida two weeks ago in order for Uri Mayer to assume his identity.

The agent gave it a cursory examination and handed it back.

"You gentlemen are going to have to come with us."

"Wait a minute; what's this all about?"

"It's a Homeland Security matter. Step out of the room one at a time and keep your hands in plain sight."

Uri looked back at the others and nodded. This meant an end to their mission, but they had operated in the US before and knew how it worked. They would be detained, questioned, and then quietly deported back to Israel in order to avoid embarrassment to both nations' governments. Because of that belief, they offered no resistance when Harrison, Steiner, and the rest of Tommy's dojo crew in Federal mufti took them to the Humvee Frank had stolen from the BATF months ago. After patting them down and confiscating their weapons, they put the cuffs on them and took them away.

Surprisingly to everyone concerned, the rest of the missions went off without much of a hitch. Neal Larson had modified Frank's plan and used the same fake Federal Agents on two more takedowns one right after another, those of the Sythian mercenaries. The first group surrendered immediately, but something raised the suspicions of the

387

members of the second. They began arguing and Steiner promptly gave the signal that sent the rest of his squad in black Federal uniforms pouring into the room, taking the front door with them. In the resulting melee, Harrison's left shoulder had a chunk knocked out of it by a bullet, one of the mercenaries was killed outright and a second wounded in the groin by the CAP guerrilla's MP5s. The other two were summarily beaten unconscious in an adrenaline-charged moment, probably with a good deal more force than absolutely necessary. The backup squad immediately arrived and secured the perimeter while Harrison's people loaded them up.

The real Federal Agents targeted by the other squads didn't go quite as easily. Both groups were taken out with no warning by grenades smashing through their windows, followed by the guerrillas performing their rapid entries, shooting anything that moved beyond raising its hands. Four agents, all of them wounded, were taken alive.

No one wanted to take a chance with the Delta Team. The CAP hit squad actually checked into the same motel under a false name. Parked a van beside their targets' rented car, they used the process of unloading their luggage to slip a package of C4 beneath the neighboring vehicle's chassis where a couple of attached magnets held it in place. The guerrillas simply waited in their room until the Delta crew got in, and pushed a button to activate the detonator. One of the squad was sliced badly across the forehead by flying glass when the resulting explosion shattered most of the motel windows in the process of turning the car and four men into a twisted, flaming pile. They left their suitcases full of thrift store clothes behind and walked away to be picked up by their backup squad.

As he turned the wheel, guiding the truck up the street that led to the front of the Multicultural Center, Arnel Scot was mildly surprised at how calm he was about the whole thing. Glancing at the pictures of his wife and son taped to the dashboard, he even smiled, knowing he'd be seeing them soon.

"I'm just glad y'all can't see me right now," he said aloud. "If you did, I bet you'd laugh."

Arnel was talking about his disguise; the others had really done a number on him. His hair was gone, shaved off, and his skin had been dyed the color of coffee with cream. Thin circles of spring wire inside his nose widened his nostrils, and he looked like what he was meant to: a light-skinned mulatto deliveryman.

His costume had been effective so far; he had passed through the police roadblocks a block away – as close as they dared come to the center after today's incident – with no more than a quick and cursory examination of his fake but very real-looking invoice for the food that was supposed to be in the back of the truck. Fearing more problems, the cops quickly apologized and sent him on his way.

This next stop, though, might be a little bit hairier. He reached down with his left hand and patted the MAC 10 submachine gun wedged between the seat and the door, ensuring its position so he could grab it in a hurry if need be.

Half a dozen armed Negroes in front of the building alerted at the truck's approach. Five of them instantly snapped to a port arms posture, shotguns and semiautomatic rifles across their chests. The sixth, obviously the leader, imperiously waved a hand for him to stop, and Arnel eased to a halt right in front of him.

The men were Black Warriors: a group of radical and violent Negro paramilitaries with origins that traced back into the 1960's. Berets, fatigues, and skin: all were Black. The NABP had brought them in to provide security. If it had been armed White men, the police would have immediately put a stop to it, yet in nearly every state, at least in the past twenty or so years, the Black Warriors was given free rein to march armed through the streets on occasion, lest law enforcement be charged with racism.

The face popped up in the driver's window as the athletic man jumped up on the running board.

"Whatchu' want?"

Arnel showed him the invoice and kept his voice slow and sloppy. "I got a delivery for the party; they're running out o' food. Where do I take it?"

"Yo' don't make deliveries through the front door, dumb-ass nigger! Take it roun' back!"

"I ain't never been here before; how do I get there?" he said, putting a whining note in his voice.

"Go roun' the block an' through the alley."

Arnel had been halfway expecting that, and had planned for it.

"Can't; police done blocked off the alley. Ain't lettin' nobody through."

"Shit! Then drive up cross the lot toward the front door, then turn left an' follow that fire lane roun' the building."

Well, Arnel thought as he pulled into the lot, *at least I'll be following half those directions.* Lining up on the front doors, he put the accelerator to the floor.

When the front tires hit the curb of the sidewalk in front of the entrance, the heavy truck almost went airborne. Inside, the Black Warrior security guards and everyone else in the lobby shrieked in terror and threw themselves to the side as the juggernaut of destruction tore through the doors and their adjacent windows, taking the steel framing with it and sending shards of glass flying through the air like whirling scythes. His windshield shattered into a blizzard of glass, but Arnel squinted his eyes and kept his foot pressed tightly to the floor, both hands holding the wheel steady. Like a charging elephant, the truck barreled across the lobby and slammed into the cinderblock wall on the opposite side, coming to a stop with the crushed engine compartment protruding through into the meeting hall.

Half stunned at the impact, Arnel tried to pull himself loose just as he had promised, but the steering wheel of the wrecked vehicle had been pushed backwards and was pressed tightly against his chest, pinning him in his seat. Reaching to his waist, he fumbled for his detonator switch as he heard the sounds of angry voices and running feet approaching. He knew his comrades outside had a remote detonator of their own, but he didn't fully trust them to use it in time.

Throwing back his head, he shouted the final words of Sampson:

"O Lord God, remember me and strengthen me, I pray thee, that I may be avenged!"

The operator sighed as she punched the button to answer the call. It never seemed to stop, but tonight was worse than usual. It was like the whole city had gone nuts.

"911; please state your name, location, and your emergency."

"This is Shahanna Banks at the Multicultural Center. Somebody just drove a truck through the building."

"Could you repeat that, please?"

"Can't you hear, bitch? Somebody just drove a delivery truck right through the front of our building, across the lobby, and halfway into the hall!"

"Are there any injuries?"

"I don't know. Security's trying to get to the driver now; he's some kind of a nut, yelling something about God avenging him or something."

The operator went cold. She had been through the required training, and she suddenly had a feeling that she knew exactly what this meant. Frantically she started mashing more buttons as she spoke.

"I'm dispatching units to your location. You need to evacuate the building *now*! Get everyone out immediately, and move them to a safe distance. Do it now!"

"Why? What the mother f-"

The call cut off with an abrupt click followed by a dial tone, and an instant later the echoes of the blast rattled the windows of the dispatcher's office. Staring through the glass with her jaw hanging in slack disbelief, the operator could see a glow rising in the sky.

Even at a mile away, the noise of the explosion echoed through Frank's headquarters in the abandoned school. He sat for a moment, unmoving, until his cell phone rang.

"Yes?"

"It's done," Tommy told him, and Frank heard his voice catch just slightly.

"Then get out like we planned before everything goes crazy. Head for the prearranged rendezvous. Arnel?"

"He won't be coming with us."

391

"Thanks."

He clicked off the phone and pressed the intercom button.

"All personnel please assemble in the briefing room."

They were all there by the time Frank arrived.

"That noise you just heard was the passing of the NABP, and the passing of the hero Private Arnel Scott of Alpha Squad, who willingly laid down his life for his people and his country. Hats off and bow your heads."

Not all the men were Christian, but they didn't object as Frank asked God to receive their fallen comrade in Jesus' name.

Afterwards they dipped the flags and saluted, holding it in silence through a recorded version of *Taps*.

As soon as it was over, they headed for the vehicles that would take them out of Columbia ahead of the massive Federal reaction they knew would be coming. On the way, though, Frank had one last stop to make.

Newscast: April 15, 10:09 PM, Columbia, SC

"We now go to Jim at the Multicultural Center in Columbia. Jim, can you hear us?"

"Yes, Sally. It's mass confusion here. Police, fire, and rescue vehicles are coming and going in a constant stream."

"Can you tell us what happened?"

"All we know for sure at present is that most of the Multicultural Center, including the lobby and the reception area, appears to have totally collapsed and is still burning. The smoke and darkness make it very difficult to see clearly."

"Is there anyone still inside?"

"Yes, it appears that there are at least several dozen people missing and still unaccounted for, including the four former defendants from today's trial, the national NABP head Saddam el'Amin, South Carolina NABP Chairman James Bessant, and New York Congressman Cecil Wilson. Firemen fear that they may still be trapped inside.

392

"The rescue teams are ready to go in just as soon as the fire department gets the flames under control, but due to the nature of the collapse and the resulting fire, the death-toll could run very high."

"Do they know the cause yet?"

"They have established that there was a large explosion; we have reports that it broke windows several blocks away and heavily damaged adjacent buildings. According to an anonymous law enforcement source, a witness said that just prior to the blast, a male subject crashed a delivery truck through the front door of Center. At this time, we don't know if he left the vehicle inside and fled on foot before the explosion or if he's still inside. No one has claimed responsibility for the blast, but the White Neo-Confederate terrorist group, the Confederate Army Provisional, is suspected."

"So is this is an racist act of domestic terrorism, Jim?"

"It's too early to tell, Sally, but it certainly looks that way..."

"We're going to cut away from Jim in Columbia for this late-breaking news. The Columbia Police Department has just reported that Judge Emmett Feldman, who presided over the Robert Franklin murder trial was shot multiple times while jogging in his suburban neighborhood and was pronounced dead at the scene..."

"Honey, it's the FBI," Sheila Perkins called over her shoulder, a tremble in her voice as the dark suited pair stepped in through the open door uninvited. They were a male and female team, he in a suit and she in a blazer and skirt, both charcoal gray and both wearing sunglasses despite the darkness.

Jim Perkins sighed, and came downstairs towards the foyer. He had known this was coming, but he still didn't regret doing what he had done to bring them here; for the first time in a long time, he knew he had finally done something right. He glanced first at his wife, nervously wringing her hands and on the verge of hysteria, then at the pair who were in the process of putting their ID's away. Somehow, they were both vaguely familiar. Seeing his look, the man took off his glasses, and the recognition hit him like a hammer.

393

"Oh," he said resignedly. He recognized his caller instantly, despite the hair dye and the goatee he had shaved his beard back to for the occasion: likewise the woman when she took off her own shades and regarded him coolly.

"Hello, Chief.

"Jim…" Sheila began uncertainly, but Perkins ignored her.

"Frank, Samantha." Everything seemed unnaturally calm and clear, as if he were separated from the action, a disinterested bystander watching from a safe distance. "I've been expecting someone, but it didn't occur to me it would be you two."

"Jim," Sheila said again, insistently, "do you know these agents?"

"They're not agents. This is Frank Gore and Samantha Norris-er, Gore now I guess." After a moment he lamely added, "Congratulations," because he didn't know else to say.

Sheila's eyes widened, and she fought for breath.

"No!" she gasped in a barely audible voice. "Oh God please no!"

The former Chief took her by the arms and gently moved her behind him. Turning back, he regarded the pair calmly. Surprisingly, even though he had been dreading was about to happen, he noticed he was unafraid.

Now that it's finally here, it's almost a relief.

"Look, I won't resist; do what you have to and get it over with. Just please don't hurt my wife, okay? She has nothing in this"

"We didn't come here to hurt anyone," Frank told him calmly. "Relax, Chief. As much as you deserve it, we are not here to kill you."

He couldn't believe what he was hearing.

"B-but, what are you here for then?"

"Chief," Samantha spoke up for the first time, her voice strained with the effort of what she was about to say. "We're here to forgive you."

"Why?"

"Anybody ever tell you not to look a gift horse in the mouth?" Frank asked dryly.

Perkins just stared at them.

"Look," Frank explained, "we have two reasons. First, you've done the movement a great service by coming clean publicly like you did. You did as much damage to Dixie's enemies in terms of publicity as we have.

"Secondly, you repented publicly and at great risk to yourself. We're not monsters. If someone sincerely repents and seeks forgiveness, we feel obligated to give it."

He gaped at them for a long time, and finally it was Samantha who spoke.

"For me there was a third reason, and she's standing behind you right now." She gestured at Sheila, clinging to her husband's arm. "I saw her with you during that press conference, and I saw the way she looks at you. She looks at you like I look at Frank. In spite of all you've done, she still loves you. You don't deserve her, *you son of a* –" She struggled for a moment. "You do know that?" She waited until he nodded before continuing. "If you want my forgiveness, you treat her right from now on."

"You can count on that," he told her, pausing to smile at Sheila and patting the hand she gripped his bicep with. "I've always loved her, but it took believing I was going to die to make me realize just how much."

"You came very close to dying, but you've got a new lease on life now. Make the most of it." Frank told him.

Perkins still couldn't believe his good fortune.

"It's over then, for me I mean? Just like that?"

"As far as we're concerned: however, that's just us. We didn't tell anyone else what we were coming here to do; as far as they know, we're here to execute you. There are still quite a few out there who have it in for you, and not just in the Confederate Army Provisional. The only reason the Feds haven't come for you already is they're still trying to sort things out after Peters' death. That won't last more than another day or two, however, and they'll be coming, them or some of the other CAP personnel, or maybe the families of the people your men killed during the riots. The best advice I can give you is to get out: cash out every credit card and bank account you've got *tonight* and go somewhere, preferably far, far away." He smiled, barely, for the first time, although it never reached his eyes. "After your little expose, I figure the Europeans will give you amnesty; I hear Paris is nice this time of year. A word to the wise; if you stay here, your life won't be worth a plugged nickel."

The two turned to leave, and the Chief stuck his hand out.

"Thank you."

Frank looked first at the proffered hand and then into Perkins' eyes. He made no effort to take it.

"Make no mistake, Perkins; after what you had a hand in doing to us, particularly what happened to my wife as a result of it, I don't have any use for you. I said I'd forgive you; I never said I'd like you."

"You're late, Sergeant Stock."

It was almost 3:00am and Charlie Squad was to last to arrive at their rendezvous point and temporary headquarters, a closed wholesale nursery in the rural area west of Conway. Frank had been more than a little concerned, despite their phone call reassuring him that they were running behind.

"Sorry, Captain," he told Frank with a grim smile, extending a piece of paper "but I brought a written excuse. Here you go."

Frank looked over what appeared to be a series of random letters and numbers.

"That's Zukerman's passwords for the PJP computer system, his credit card, his bank account, and their local organization's bank account. I thought they might come in handy."

Frank called out, "Cynthia!"

Frank had temporarily pulled her from Samantha and assigned her to himself as his secretary, company runner and general gopher. She immediately left the computer equipment she was helping to set up and came to the door.

"Yes, Frank…I mean Captain?"

He smiled at her. "Whichever, honey. Please transfer this information to Intelligence ASAP and tell them to access it *immediately* before it is discovered and blocked. It's urgent, top priority"

"Yes, sir!" With that, she grabbed the paper and left the room at a dead run, her athletic shoes slapping on the floor.

Frank smiled at her enthusiasm and turned back to the sergeant. "Is he dead?"

Stock nodded.

"He is now. Once we got the information we wanted, we shot him, dropped the body in a shallow grave in an illegal garbage dump along a back road, and kicked some stuff over it. He probably won't be found for at least a few days, if ever."

Frank didn't ask what they had done to Zukerman to get that intelligence. Whatever it was, it was over and done with now, and there was no point in going into it. Still, although he couldn't complain about the results, he wasn't entirely satisfied with the squad's actions for a number of reasons. He chose his next words carefully.

"Sergeant, that showed a lot of initiative on your part, and I can't fault your accomplishment. However, a kidnapping is much more complicated and risky than an assassination, and shouldn't have been attempted without prior planning and extra backup nearby."

"Sir, we didn't intend to kidnap him, but we caught him with no one looking – he actually came around a corner unexpectedly and physically ran into us – and we thought we shouldn't waste the opportunity. I'm sorry if we were mistaken; the responsibility is mine."

Frank realized that Stock wasn't afraid of the consequences of his actions; instead, he was worried about disappointing his Captain. That said a lot for his loyalty. He thought about his own relationship with General Edge and sighed, then softened the mood with a grin.

I'm not going to be a hypocrite.

"No apologies are necessary; the mission was a success and then some. I wasn't there so I don't know the situation. For all I know, I would have probably done the same thing. I'm not going to take away your flexibility to make improvised decisions in the field; you're obviously damned good at it. I just want to remind you to always make certain you use all due caution in exercising that flexibility. If it comes between a mission like this being successful

397

and my men coming back alive, I'll take my men every time. Fair enough?"

"Yes sir," Sergeant Stock told him, grinning widely and pleased with himself, and even more so with his commander.

Official US Government Communication:
15 July, 11:50 PM
Federal Emergency Management Agency
Press Release

The Department of Homeland Security, in accordance with today's Presidential Directive, has declared a state of emergency in the following states: Alabama, Arizona, Florida, Georgia, Kentucky, Louisiana, Mississippi, Missouri, New Mexico, North Carolina, Oklahoma, South Carolina, Tennessee, Texas, Virginia, and West Virginia. As of 12:00 AM 16 July, these states are officially under martial law. Units of the National Guard from California, Colorado, Connecticut, Illinois, Indiana, Kansas, Massachusetts, Nebraska, New Hampshire, New Jersey, New York, and Ohio are being deployed, and will assume the security of the affected areas. The civilian government is hereby suspended except to such extent as is required for cooperation with Homeland Security and the assigned military commanders. All state executive, legislative, judicial, administrative and other employees in the affected states are hereby ordered obey any and all directives under penalty of federal law. Police, fire, and emergency personnel shall remain at their posts under penalty of law until such time as they receive orders from the office of the military governor.

Effective immediately, a curfew from 6:00 Pm to 6:00 AM shall be immediately in effect for all non-essential personnel, with essential personnel to be determined on a case-by-case basis.

Live Newscast from the office of Senator Canady (D, Massachusetts)
1:03 AM

"The brave men of Massachusetts will do their duty, never fear. They were in the forefront of the fight to bring freedom to the South in 1861, and delivered a lesson the racists and traitors have apparently forgotten. Well, we're going to go down there again and give them another little 'Yankee spankee' to see to it they have reason to remember!"

British Broadcasting Service
7:00 AM

U.S. National Guard troops responding to this second American Civil War that some have been calling the Third Revolution have bogged down in the upper South after coming under scattered but heavy attacks by insurgent guerrilla forces in at least eight states during their first day of occupation. Five hundred twenty-eight soldiers are already confirmed dead and an unknown number wounded in several sniper incidents, roadside bomb attacks, and troop train derailments, although unofficial estimates place the death toll as much as three times higher. Also not known is the number of civilian casualties, or those of the Confederate Army Provisional insurgents...

Embedded Reporter
U.S. Newscast, East Tennessee

"Dozens of Indiana National Guardsmen are missing and feared dead following a cowardly attack by Confederate terrorists this morning. Official sources indicate the attack occurred when the terrorists, armed with stolen explosives, detonated an explosion that caused the collapse of a large cliff beside a road as the troop convoy was passing this morning. The resulting rockslide completely buried a section of road and an unknown number of military vehicles...

Local Newscast
Northern Virginia

"Rescue workers are desperately attempting to save the lives of what may be hundreds of Massachusetts National Guardsmen still trapped beneath the waters of the Potomac. Their troop train derailed when the trestle carrying it was apparently dynamited by Southern terrorists..."

Anonymous e-mail to the office of Senator Canady

"Who got the *"Yankee spankee"* this time, you blue-bellied son of a bitch? Y'all just come right on down; we've got plenty more where that came from!"

DAY 149

CHAPTER 41

"Sammie?"

Startled, she looked down at the man in the wheelchair as he rolled through their new headquarters door. Not only had she not heard him coming, but Mike Dayton almost never left his basement, let alone his house. Now here he was, almost halfway across the state, backed up by Billy and Jim Reynolds.

"Oh, hi guys. What's up?"

"Everything," he told her earnestly, and began filling her in on what he had finally pieced together.

After weeks of spying, bugging, hacking, occasionally blackmailing and threatening, and then reviewing it all in every moment he could spare from his primary intelligence work, he had finally figured it out. Neil Larson, with the complicity of Herdman and MacFie, had intentionally set Edge and Frank against each other in the hopes Frank would do their dirty work for them and eliminate their mutual rival. If he didn't, or if the General came out on top and managed to kill Frank, they intended to assassinate him themselves at the meeting. To make matters worse, Edge had taken the bait, hook, line and sinker, and had brought an armed squad of Virginians with him to enforce his will. Quite possibly they were there to kill her husband and most of the Council if he felt it was necessary, and he probably would. When Mike finished, he stared at her intently.

"Well?"

It took her awhile to answer. Her thoughts were a jumble of puzzle pieces, and it was as if someone was dumping them out of a box and she was trying to catch them and put them together in midair. Her experiences had left her with a healthy distrust of everyone but Frank, so she wasn't about to accept even Mike's information at face value. Still Frank was in the Council Chamber, and whatever was going to happen was going to happen there. She was going to have make a decision, and make it quickly.

Jim Reynolds and Billy Sprouse hustled Samantha out of the back of the van as Danny Drucci, on covert guard duty, abruptly straightened up in surprise from his position on the front porch of the safe house.

Grabbing him by the upper arm, she jerked him close and whispered in his ear, "Get a squad up here *now*! Frank's in danger!"

That was all Danny needed to hear. Not even taking time to acknowledge her beyond a quick nod of his head, he began speaking into his radio while she and her fierce two-man entourage barged through the front door. Sam looked up from his seat in the living room and instantly sprang to his feet.

"What in the hell do you think you're doing?"

The Palmetto Colonel's startled voice attracted the attention of Edge's driver, who was in the next room making a sandwich, and he stuck his head around the door to see what was going on. Billy saw the sudden movement and unfamiliar face and, as he was within arm's reach, reacted instinctively. His huge fist promptly connected with the side of the Virginian's jaw, catching the man's head between the blow and the hardwood doorframe. He dropped like a marionette whose strings had been cut.

"Who was that?" the big man asked with what sounded for all the world like mere idle curiosity.

Sam's eyes were already wide, but grew wider when Jim produced a 9mm Berretta.

"Who else is here?" he hissed, and before his Colonel and former commander could find his voice, he shifted his weapon's muzzle in his general direction. "Who else, damn it?"

"Just...the Council, and Frank...and Boggess from West Virginia. They're all in the dining room in the meeting right now." Seeing Billy staring at him impatiently, he gestured towards the unconscious Virginian lying in the doorway. "That's Edge's driver; he's the only one who came in with him." No sooner were the words out of his mouth than Billy dropped to one knee, relieved the fallen man of his holstered pistol, and proceeded to duct tape his hands and feet together before slapping a final strip across his mouth to keep him quiet.

Meanwhile, Samantha reached up and gently used her fingertips to move Jim's pistol aside, much to Sam's relief. After instructing the pair to secure the doors and allow no one to enter besides the irregulars, and to brief them when they arrived, she turned back to Sam, who couldn't wait any longer.

"Sammie, what's happening?"

Speaking rapidly in a low voice, she told him, adding, "You need to choose a side and choose it now; there's no more time!"

He looked into the eyes of the woman he had given away at her wedding and swallowed hard. "I've already chosen it. What do you want me to do?"

She explained what she needed as she headed towards the dining room's closed door.

"Get them together and get in here as quickly as you can," she called to them over her shoulder, "I don't know how long we have."

Quietly, she opened the door and stepped inside. The Council, her husband, and Jack Boggess – who had returned with Edge and was being introduced to the leadership – were seated around a large, rectangular oak table. Their conversation abruptly hushed as every eye turned in her direction – especially Frank's, who was shocked and not a little angry that she risked herself yet again in order to be with him, especially when the roads were crawling with soldiers.

Damn it! I'll...no, my wife might have some problems, but she's not an idiot and she's certainly not a liar. If she broke her promise to me, it must have been for a very good reason. I just wish I knew what the hell it is.

Jack Boggess raised his eyebrows slightly, the only reaction on his poker face. In her tight jeans and tee shirt and carrying only a zippered purse, Samantha was even more beautiful in person than in the pictures he had seen, but more than that, he sensed that something unexpected was about to happen here. The tension, already high, ratcheted up another notch.

She ignored them and took a vacant seat in an upholstered chair away from the table, against the wall. Larson had barely opened his mouth to object, but shut it with a snap when Nash smiled at her and nodded his approval of her presence. Neil mentally shrugged.

Her being here won't make that much difference; she's not even armed. Hell, it might even be advantageous having her present in the long run.

Council Chairman Nash turned his attention back to Jonathon Edge. If a lady – the Communications Officer for the Confederate Army Provisional no less – wanted to stand by her man while he was on trial, he wasn't going to interfere.

Besides, maybe her presence will make this pack of idiots at least try to keep it civil!

"General Edge, I understand that you have some charges to make."

"I do." He spoke to Nash, but fixed Frank with a cold stare, angered by what he saw as a deliberate ploy to physically introduce his beautiful and charismatic wife – a living martyr to the Cause no less – into the equation in order to gain sympathy. He wasn't about to let that happen. "I charge Captain Franklin Gore with mutiny, multiple counts of disobedience to direct orders, insubordination, and misappropriation of military supplies."

"Oh hell, not more of this." Edge glared at him and Nash sighed. *This was getting complicated.* "Alright. Captain Gore, you've heard the charges; how do you plead, or do you wish to hear the specifics?"

Frank had finally had enough, and his temper, long suppressed, began to take hold. He snorted in derision at Jonathon Edge. "Guilty on all counts."

"W-what?"

"You heard me, Mr. Chairman – guilty on all counts: guilty as hell. I admit it; I did what was necessary to protect the lives of my men and maintain at least some semblance of the justice we must have unless *we* are to become like the very people we're fighting against." He rose to his feet, anger clearly evident in his voice. "I admit that, with Mr. Boggess' expressed permission," he said,

404

looking toward the Mountaineer, who nodded his agreement, "I took enough of the weapons that *my men* captured during a raid *we* paid for out of *our own* state funds to replace the worn out and obsolete arms they had, to give them the best equipment available to fight with, in order for them to do their jobs and stay alive. I admit I saw justice done locally, taking care of our own problems in Columbia without seeking approval from some quasi-central, micro-managing authority. Contrary to direct orders, I also let some people live who, in my judgment, were not worthy of death, or whose deaths would have been detrimental to our Cause in the long run. I may have erred, but if I did so, it was on the side of mercy, duty to my men, and common sense.

"Finally," he said, returning Edge's glare with one of his own, "I defied my commander face to face when he was acting like a pompous, egomaniacal horse's ass. I used my men to force him to back down when he was going to *shoot me*, and I'd do it all again. I make no apologies for any of it."

Several things happened at once. Nash laughed until his substantial belly shook at Gore's open slam against Edge, who leapt to his feet in a rage, fists clenched and his eyes fixed on Frank, and in an instant both of them were nose to nose in the center of the floor. MacFie was stunned at the Commander's rhetorical power, and was rapidly realizing there was much more to this man than met the eye. Boggess' eyes widened slightly in admiration at Frank's audacity. Herdman looked to Larson, who ignored him and took the opportunity he had been waiting for while Edge was distracted. His right hand dropped and reached behind his back towards his belt. It came up with Berretta 9 mm.

MacFie came to a snap decision and changed his mind too late. He yelled a warning and lunged for Larson, but was too far away to reach him in time.

The movement was hidden from Edge due to his angle to it, but, alerted by MacFie's shout, Frank saw it, and, still unsure of exactly what was going on, acted instinctively according to his police training. While his right hand dropped for his .45, his left shot out with all his body torque behind it. His body was a bow and his palm

405

was an arrow. His feet twisted, weight shifted, hips and waist turned, shoulder and arm muscles came into play, and the heel of his palm sucker-punched the General in the center of the chest, bowing his ribcage inwards, driving the breath from his lungs, and knocking him back so hard he fell back against the table and onto its top, almost going head over heels off the far side of it.

A pair of shots echoed through the room, there were two meaty impacts, and Frank spun halfway around.

Hands reached for weapons, then froze as the door slammed open hard enough to drive the knob through the wall paneling behind it. Everyone in the room found themselves staring into a small forest of gun muzzles as Rob entered and swung to the left, Caffary to the right, and Tommy right up the middle, all with submachine guns, and followed closely by Sam with a Remington 870 12 gauge pump, Jim with an M16, and Billy with another shotgun that was a twin of Sam's. All the hands but one backed slowly away from what they had been reaching for. That hand belonged to Samantha and held her Smith and Wesson, a thin wisp of smoke curled up from its muzzle that still pointed toward the seat where Neil Larson was sitting.

Had been sitting; his body lay sprawled next to his overturned chair, the blood and brains from his shattered head draining freely onto the carpet as the nerves in his body made their final quiver. As soon as Larson made his move, even though the others weren't there yet, Samantha couldn't wait any longer. She knew it would be obvious to the men in the room that, with her tight clothing, if she were armed at all, the only place she could be carrying was in her purse. She had sat it on her lap and studiously kept her hands away from the zipper on top. However, her purse was a Coronado Hobo Bag given to her by her husband, with an almost invisible concealment holster within that accessed from the side. Having unobtrusively slipped her fingers inside it in preparation, she had drawn her Smith and Wesson and shot Neil Larson through the head. She stared numbly at his body for a moment, and then turned toward Frank.

He looked back at her and she saw his tanned face had taken on an unnatural pallor, and blood was staining his shirtfront. Her pistol thumped forgotten to the floor as she wailed and ran to him.

The armed men yelled loudly and profanely for no one else to move.

"Oh God no!" She stared at the large crimson blotch on his solar plexus and burst into tears as she felt her whole life coming apart. "Tommy! Frank's been shot!" She sobbed wildly as Tommy swore and ordered the others to watch the prisoners as he ran forward.

Frank poked gingerly at the center of attention, taking inventory, then smiled painfully.

"It's okay, Sammie. It's okay." He showed her the spreading stain on his punctured left sleeve. "It's from my forearm; when he hit it I jerked it up against me by reflex. That's what got the blood on my shirt" He gritted his teeth as he carefully tried to flex his fingers. "It hurts like hell, but I don't think anything's broken. It looks like it may have missed the artery when it went through."

Despite the blood, she clung to him desperately, ignoring the stain that was getting all over her.

Tommy didn't pause in fishing out the first aide gear he kept the cargo pockets of his pants filled with.

"Somebody get him a damned chair!" he shouted, knowing Frank too well to expect him to lie down. Shotgun dangling from one hand, Sam hastened to comply with his subordinate's command.

Frank was slightly giddy, running on an adrenaline overload, and the last thing he wanted to do was sit down just now.

"I don't need a chair."

"The hell you don't!" Tommy growled as Sam grabbed one and shoved it to them. "With all due respect, Captain, you've been shot and you're either going to sit your ass down while I check you out, or I'll tell Billy to sit on you and hold you down! Now which is it going to be?"

Frank sat.

"Good shot, by the way," Frank told Samantha, nodding at Larson's corpse. "Now, would you mind telling me just exactly what the hell is going on here?"

Fortunately, Larson had been using military hardball ammunition that had not expanded, but left a neat hole in and out through Frank's forearm, miraculously failing to do more than chip and crack the radius, nick the main artery, and had damaged but not destroyed the tendons. Frank sat grunting occasionally as Tommy worked, dealing with the pain that the medic's Lidocaine injections refused to completely kill by keeping his concentration on the ongoing explanation.

The surviving Council members, along with Bogess, sat with their hands in plain sight on the table through it all. They had little choice; Sam had ordered the others to shoot the first one who moved. Much to his shock and chagrin, Edge was included in that number. He sat there numb, torn with conflicting emotions.

Sam wanted to call in the rest of the troops, but Frank said no and his increasingly nominal commander deferred to his judgment. The Captain explained that they already had more than enough hardware to kill everyone present, and if that became necessary, the fewer people who knew about it the better. Caffary spoke into his radio, and then listened to the crackling return voice with a satisfied smile.

"The 1st Columbia has secured the house and perimeter, sir," he told Frank.

Tommy finished his bandaging, and Frank became more infuriated by the second as the story unfolded. Mike Dayton, assisted out of the van by some of the Irregulars, wheeled himself into the room and played his surveillance tapes, interspersed with his explanations, leaving the others in open-mouthed shock: some at what had been attempted, and others that they had been caught. When he finished, despite the medic's protests, Frank rose to his feet. He was lightheaded and weaving slightly, but his face was dark and twisted with anger.

"You," he said, pointing at Jonathon Edge, "were so paranoid, you convinced yourself I was determined to be in charge." He turned to Herdman and MacFie, both pale and trembling. "And you two, along with Larson, determined to put me in charge without even

408

asking me, by making me an accessory to treason and murder. Well people, your dreams have come true; I *am* in charge, and I hold all the cards."

Edge looked at Sam, and his friend shook his head sadly. The farmer had finally made his decision for the good of the movement, even though it was tearing him apart inside. Edge quietly resigned himself to his fate. He felt like praying but couldn't think of anything to say. He knew he had made this bed; now he would die in it. *There was still a chance...*

Caffary saw the General's expression and sneered, "Don't expect that squad you brought with you to come riding in to save your bacon, General. We knew about them even before Sammie – sorry, ma'am, I mean Lieutenant Gore – brought us the news, and they were already in the custody of the First Columbia Irregulars." He glanced at Frank. "I was going to report that as soon as I got the chance, sir, and since I knew you'd ask, we surprised the ones on the outside and took them down with no causalities to either side." *Nothing that won't heal up in a week or two anyway,* he silently amended. The men the Virginian had brought with him were good, but there were only six of them. A couple had tried to fight back, and gotten thumped pretty thoroughly, but it was nothing worth mentioning to the Captain, whom Caffary considered to be over-sensitive about such things.

Even without Mike's information, Frank had expected something from either Edge or Larson, so he had taken the precaution of covertly inserting the Irregulars in a pattern surrounding the building, with orders to pick up anyone suspicious and hold them. Obviously they had.

"Thank you, Sergeant, but I wasn't worried; I know I can always depend on my men to watch my back."

Caffary glowed and seemed to grow an inch or two as Frank continued.

"Mr. Nash, Mr. Boggess, please keep your hands where they are to avoid any misunderstandings, but you can relax. You two are innocent in this matter and will not be harmed." A look of relief crossed their faces. "Mr. Nash, is your heart alright? Do you need your pills or some water or something?"

"No, but thank you, Captain."

Frank nodded curtly and asked Tommy to take the senior Councilman's blood pressure anyway before turning towards the pair of conspirators.

"Gentlemen, do you have anything to say on your behalf?"

"Now wait just a minute," Herdman said, his voice breaking with fear. "This isn't a trial! I'm a member of the Confederate Council; you have no authority over me."

"On the contrary: this is a state of emergency in which at least two members – two surviving members that is – of this Council stand accused of conspiracy to commit treason and murder. One Councilman has been killed in the commission of attempted murder, and as a result of their actions, our General was conspiring to have his subordinate – myself – murdered. In a state of emergency, the military rules, Mr. Herdman."

"But you're not the highest ranking officer!" he said, looking pointedly at Sam Wirtz.

"Yes he is – I'm officially placing myself under his command as of now." Sam snapped.

"But – you can't –"

"Yes we can; we're the ones with the guns, remember?" He nodded at Frank. "Captain?"

"Thank you. Now that we have heard for Mr. Herdman's defense a mess of legalese, I would like to give Dr. MacFie the opportunity to explain himself."

MacFie gazed at him levelly. All the fear, all the ego, had been stripped away at last, revealing just a Southern man who, too late, was ashamed of his own actions.

"I have no excuse, Captain. I am guilty as charged and ready to accept what ever punishment you see fit to meet out."

Herdman was aghast.

"Now just a minute –"

"Shut up, Herdman; just shut the hell up. You and I have let our egos rule our actions for years, instead of concentrating on the good of the movement. You know as well as I do, down inside, we've considered ourselves to *be* the movement, and in doing so we've betrayed it."

He looked up at Frank. "You owe me nothing, Captain Gore, but might I ask you to please make it quick?"

In reply, Frank reached for the old .45 at his waist.

As Tommy removed the blood pressure cuff, Nash spoke up hastily. "Captain Gore – ah, the hell with it – *Frank*, I don't know if this is a good idea."

The wound had his left arm stiff and throbbing, and he grimaced as he rested his right hand on the butt of the pistol instead of drawing it. The strain sounded clearly in his voice.

"So what do you suggest? That we simply let it go?"

"No, we can't let it go; this is too big. But this action would be a severe blow to movement."

"Wouldn't leaving two conspirators together be an even greater risk? Can we afford to take the chance on something like this happening again? The next time, instead of General Edge, it might be you or me, or some one else. If that happens to the wrong one at the wrong time, both the struggle and the entire movement could collapse. I haven't come this far to lose this war, whatever the cost."

Nash mulled over the matter carefully, and came to a decision: not a pleasant one, but a necessary one. His normally jovial face set into a harder form.

"I can't argue with that. That could very well happen if *two* conspirators were able to plot. If one pays the price, the other will not only not have anyone left to conspire with, but will have a substantial deterrent not to do so."

Frank nodded as he caught the senior Councilman's drift. He hated this, even as angry as he was. Still, this was something that had to be done, and, as always, he'd do what he had to.

"Very well – which one is more valuable to the movement?"

Herdman and MacFie were horrified at their fates being coldly debated, but it was Herdman who interrupted.

"Now just a damned minute! You can't just kill us, just like that!"

Frank regarded him coldly.

"Yes we can. We can't afford the cost to morale of a formal trial, particularly not when your guilt has been established beyond any doubt and admitted to. Whatever is to be done must be done here and now, and the story will never leave this room. The movement is more important than any of us, gentlemen; I just wish you'd thought of that before, so…" He paused as he sought the words that wouldn't come, then shrugged meaningfully.

"But we did it for you – and for the movement!"

MacFie snorted.

"Bullshit!" He glanced at Samantha and reflexively said, "Pardon my language, Mrs. Gore, but that's just bullshit." He knew he was looking at his own death and was determined to face it like a man. "Herdman, you know as well as I do we did it for us. It shames me to admit it, but I'll be damned if I'm going to lie about it now. We did it all for us.

"Sure, I thought Edge and his dictatorial attitude was a threat to the movement," he said, glancing at the Virginian who was watching the proceedings with a blank expression, "and I still do, not to put too fine a point on it; he's a menace! But when it boils right down to it, we were jealous. *We* wanted to have that same power for ourselves. We're just like he is: there's not a dime's worth of difference between any of us."

"No!" Herdman shouted. "It wasn't like that!" He pointed an accusing finger towards MacFie. "For him, yes; but not for me! I always had the good of the movement at heart…"

"We're going to die, you idiot, and I'm not going to do that with this lie on my conscience. There's enough there already." The whole thing seemed surreal to the professor, but he continued. "I forgive you, Captain Gore, for what you are about to do. May I have a moment to pray?"

Frank looked to Nash. "Mr. Chairman, in your judgment, is Dr. MacFie is not only potentially redeemable, but is also of more importance to the Cause than Mr. Herdman?"

The answer was a no-brainer for Nash, who had never been particularly fond of either man, but Herdman least of all. He was too sneaking; at least with MacFie you generally knew where you stood.

"Certainly; not only has he admitted his error, but for all practical purposes, he has far more followers and influence…"

Herdman panicked and made a break for the door. At least he tried to; he had no more than leaped to his feet when both Billy and Rob, tense and as tightly wired as coiled springs, fired at the abrupt motion. A three round burst of 9mm slugs from the MP5 and load of #00 buckshot tore his chest and throat apart and spattered the wall behind him and the seated men to either side with blood. His lifeless body overturned the chair he was still straddling and took it to the floor with him.

Frank pursed his lips as the smell of burned powder filled the air once again.

"Okay, that's one item off the agenda…which brings us back to General Edge."

Edge locked eyes with him, and neither looked away.

"Shall I stand against the wall?"

"I sincerely hope that won't be necessary, since I doubt the movement will survive it. You're too valuable."

Edge was stunned, but his mind was racing toward the realization it had been dancing all around.

"You *intentionally* took that bullet for me! It wasn't an accident!"

Frank shrugged noncommittally, even though the motion hurt like hell. To be honest, he hadn't known what was happening or who was coming under attack and had reacted instinctively, without thought, striking Edge less to knock him out of the way for the General's sake than to momentarily stun a possible enemy, get him out of grabbing distance, and keep him from interfering as he addressed the immediate threat. Still, Frank had been with the movement long enough by now to know there was no reason to point that out. He wasn't going to lie, but if Edge wanted to come to that conclusion, he sure wasn't going to stand in his way either. He

413

grinned inside. *I reckon bringing this movement together is more important than nit picking over details.*

"The point is that you, like Dr. MacFie – who, by the way, you should remember finally tried to *stop* Larson from shooting *you* in the end – are too valuable to this struggle to lose, at least at this stage of the game. Unfortunately, like him, you also have a giant ego and a more than adequate dose of paranoia, and that is going to stop and stop right here and now, or we'll see just what this movement can survive.

"Despite my best efforts to reassure you to the contrary, you've convinced yourself I wanted to be in charge. Well, for the moment I am, and there are going to either be some changes here or there's going to be some more killing." He looked pointedly at each man in the room. "Do you all understand?"

Nash looked first to Edge and then towards MacFie and smiled like a cherub with satisfaction.

It's the first damned time one of our meetings has actually come to proper order!

"It looks like you have the floor, Captain."

"Thank you, Mr. Chairman. Since I first became involved in this movement and I suspect long before, it hasn't been a team; it's been a contest of egos. Those days are over, gentlemen, and they are over for good. We are at war, not to see who gets to sit in the catbird's seat, but for the independence and the very survival of our people. We are no longer scoring points at a cocktail party, and we are going to cease acting like it. There will be no more *me* in the struggle, only *we*.

"For the first order of business, there are currently two vacant seats on this Council. Congratulations, Mr. Wirtz and Mr. Boggess; you are now full members of the Confederate Council. I hope you can bring a little more common sense to it than it has displayed so far."

Boggess' jaw dropped in the first real expression any of them had seen since the initial shooting, and Sam exploded.

"I won't…"

"You *will*," Frank cut him off. "You asked me once if I wanted your job because you said I was better suited for it than you were. Does that assessment and offer still stand or not?"

"Yes – I mean no – I mean – damn it Frank, don't you do this to me!"

Frank gave him a look that said *paybacks are hell*, and then continued. "I'm taking you up on your offer, not because I'm better qualified for your job, but because you're better qualified for the Council than anyone else I know. You're a thinker who hasn't lost his ability to feel, and you're subtle and honest at the same time. Dixie needs you here, Sam. You told me once the only thing any of us owed anything to was the movement; well now it's your turn to pay up."

He turned his head to look at the West Virginian, still sitting open-mouthed.

"Mr. Boggess, you and your people have signed on and are now a part of this revolution, so it's only right that you all be represented. This isn't a deep-South thing; this is an *all*-South thing. You have a calm thoughtfulness that's been missing from this Council. Do you agree to serve?"

"Do I have a choice?"

Frank bared his teeth in a smile through the throbbing pain that seemed to be getting harder and harder to ignore.

"No, not really, but I thought it would be nicer to ask."

Abruptly the sandy-haired man threw back his head and laughed out loud.

"Alright then, so long as I can still go back home and continue to fight alongside my men. They need me up there."

"Done. We can keep in communication with you through the usual channels.

"General Edge, I hope you finally understand that everybody is *not* out to get you, and that I *do not* intend to replace you; I *never* intended it! I not only don't want your job, but I'm not qualified to do it – nobody here is! You are not only a military genius, at least when it comes to the big picture, but you are hard and experienced enough to lead our armies to victory, *if* you can manage to put your ego and paranoia behind you and put the movement first. Agree to do that, and you not only stay in charge of the Confederate Army Provisional and keep your seat on the Council, but you also get to live awhile longer too."

"You took a bullet for me…" he repeated, still awed by his sudden epiphany.

"Well, I wasn't sure just who he was shooting at and I was actually hoping it would miss both of us, but no such luck. At any rate, you're too important to lose at this point, at least *if* you're finally willing to get with the program. If not, then you will cease to be an asset and become a liability. This movement can't afford any more of those." He looked pointedly at the bodies of Larson and Herdman cooling on the blood-soaked carpet before pointing to the professor and adding, "You might also remember that, even though he conspired against you, in the end it was Dr. MacFie who really saved your life, not me. He did it even though he had good reason to believe you intended to kill him too, along with a lot to gain by you're being out of the way. If not for his warning, I would never have reacted and you'd be a dead man right now."

"Dr. MacFie, the same goes for you. You're this movement's greatest statesman, bar *none*, and it's time you started acting like it. Like you said, you and he," he said, gesturing first at MacFie and then at Edge, "are just alike: two peas in a pod. Both of you love the South, but from the way you act, it sure seems to me like you love yourselves a whole lot more. That's not good enough anymore, and will no longer be tolerated. There will be no second chance.

"You have the ability to speak, attract, and inflame the passions of our people, as great an ability at that as General Edge has with military matters. *Use it*, and you and he can worry about who gets to be President of the Confederacy *after* we win.

"As for you, Mr. Nash, I realize you've done your best for years to get the leaders of this movement pulling in the same direction. Now's your chance to actually do it, with Sam and Jack to help you, and all the guns of the 1st Columbia Irregulars to back you up if need be. Make it happen."

"Sam, Jack, you two have got both the experience and the good, common sense of those who have 'been there and done that,' but you haven't lost your humanity in the process. I'm depending on you both to make this a real Council, and not just a rubber stamp. Whether I agree with your decisions or not, both myself and my men will back them up 100% as long as they lead towards our independence."

"Sammie." She jerked, startled by his sudden address. "I know how much you're dedicated to the truth. However – and this goes for every one here, without exception – what happened here today cannot and *will not* leave this room – ever! We can't have the world know that we've reached the point of having to kill each other this early in the game or we are well and truly lost. Do you understand?"

She nodded, frustrated but realistic enough to accept it, something she wouldn't have even considered just months ago. Of course, then she hadn't realized what was at stake. *It's amazing how fast you become pragmatic in a war.*

Frank gestured at the two bodies.

"Remember this: Councilmen Larson and Herdman were not traitors killed by their own comrades. They are martyrs, heroes, shot down without warning in an ambush by the enemy. At least that is the way it will be portrayed, and no one in this room will say any different. Are we all in agreement?" He looked from one to another, and didn't stop until he had gotten an affirmative answer from all of them, including the armed men backing him up.

His vision was starting to tunnel, and he seemed to hear someone distant speaking with his voice from increasingly farther away.

"Good," he heard himself say. "Then the Council is back in session." He faced Edge and saluted. "I'm returning your command to you, sir."

Weak from shock, stress, and blood-loss, he never knew it when his knees buckled and he crumpled to the floor.

DAY 150

CHAPTER 42

Frank realized he was lying in a strange bed and had no earthly idea how he'd gotten there. It was comfortable, but his left arm ached fiercely. Strangely groggy, he wiggled his dry tongue and had the distinct impression that something had crawled into his mouth and died sometime back. He moved slightly, grunting as he adjusted his position, and a soft hand closed around his good one. He recognized its feel at once. His eyelids slowly came open, but took awhile to focus.

"Hi Sammie. What happened?"

She smiled that perfect smile at him and he thought she was beautiful, despite the fact her eyes were red from tears and fatigue.

"Oh, nothing much. You just did what no one else has ever been able to do: unite the leadership of the Southern Movement for the very first time. Oh yeah, and since you didn't listen to Tommy and sit back down, right at the height of your glory you passed out and fell flat on your face in the floor right there in front of everybody, frightening your wife half out of her wits."

He groaned, his face reddening.

"I did all that, huh?"

"Oh don't worry, there's more. It looked like we were in the middle of a Federal raid, with people running around and yelling out conflicting orders. I was squalling and Billy wasn't much better off. Sam was waving his arms around like a chicken, giving orders no one was listening to, Caffary was hovering over you like a mother hen, MacFie and Nash were actually holding each other up, Rob was waving his gun all over the place looking for someone to shoot, and as God is my witness, I swear Edge had tears in his eyes. I guess no one had ever risked their life to save his before." She snickered. "Tommy got so mad he had a cussing fit and fired a burst into the floor to get everybody calmed down."

"Mmm. Sorry I missed it. *Yuck!*" He worked his mouth and tongue some more, trying to rid it of the gummy feeling. "Doggone, I feel terrible!"

"Probably because of all that sack time. You've been out for almost sixteen hours."

"Sixteen hours! With just an arm wound?" *I'm becoming a wimp!*

She gave him a defiant look.

"That and the fact I had Tommy sedate you, and ordered Sergeant Caffary to post a guard outside the door to see to it you weren't disturbed." He opened his mouth but she laid her fingers firmly across his lips. "No; don't you even start! You know good and well you haven't been getting nearly enough sleep for weeks and it wore you down. I just decided to take the opportunity and see to it you caught up on it a little to give you and your arm a chance to start healing up. There's no use complaining about it now, because it's over and done with."

"But the Council…"

"Did just fine without you. You may not realize this Franklin Gore, but you're an inspiring man. They got the coffee pot going and stayed in there all night until they hammered out an agreement they could all live with. Edge fully runs the military and the Council runs everything else. We actually have a set of bylaws and a provisional constitution now, spelling out the responsibilities and separation of powers, and they're expanding the Council to eventually include a representative from our forces in each state. We've come a long way, and we couldn't have done it without you."

He finally gave up and grinned.

"Maybe I should sleep in more often."

"Not hardly. If you feel up to it, you'd better go the bathroom and get dressed – there are some people out in the parlor who want to see you in the worst way, and I'm afraid they're going to wear holes in the carpet pacing back and forth. I hung a fresh uniform on the back of the door."

As she helped him slip his injured arm into his sleeve before putting it back in the sling, he asked her something he had been wondering about. "How did you know which one to shoot?"

"I didn't. I knew Edge would like to kill you but didn't know if he would try it here in a Council meeting. Also, from Mike's information, I knew *why* Edge wanted to kill you, because Larson's scheme had convinced him he had to. As far as Larson goes, I remembered what you said: '*if Larson knows anything at all about me, he has to know I'd kill him if I ever found out he had used me in that way and turned me into a murderer*'. Worse than that, though, he called you his '*monkey on a stick*', and no one talks about my husband that way! Still, I couldn't make up my mind, so I just decided to shoot the first one that made a move if Sam and the others didn't get there in time, and then cover the other one until things got sorted out." She saw her husband's eyes widen in surprise and added, "I know now it was a silly decision."

Frank shook his head. "No, it was a pragmatic and perfectly logical decision, the same one I like to think I would have made myself under the same circumstances. I'm proud of you, honey."

He kissed her then, and kissed her again, and in the end it took quite a bit longer than expected for him to finish getting ready.

Finally, in his starched gray fatigues, spit-shined boots, and bandaged arm in a sling, Frank opened the door to the parlor, the largest room in the house, only to find the room wasn't nearly big enough. Not only was the entire Confederate Council there, along with Rob, Tommy and Billy, but so were the 1st Columbia Irregulars – *all* of them – and half a dozen somewhat battered Virginians whom they had treated to numerous beers to make up for the damage. Everyone was jammed almost shoulder to shoulder, and Frank reflected that it was a good thing the door opened outward instead of inward, or he wouldn't have been able to get it open at all.

They all started cheering, and the noise was deafening in the small space.

"Go on in, Frank," Samantha told him from behind.

"I can't; there's not room enough."

421

Caffary, realizing his predicament, bellowed loudly. "All right, people – fall out into the surrounding rooms and hallways. Make a hole for the Captain." They obeyed, those filing past Frank shaking his hand and slapping his back enthusiastically and leaving the door open as they left so they could hear the proceedings. Only the officers and the sergeants remained of his company.

Council Chairman Nash stepped forward and began reading from a piece of paper.

"Captain Franklin Gore, this Council and indeed, our country, has found in you the kind of valor, insight, and self-sacrifice I'd thought extinct among our people since the days of Jackson, Lee, and Forrest. You have accomplished what no one else ever has, and in doing so, you have single-handedly saved our movement and our nation from self-destruction. Even more importantly, you voluntarily laid down the power you had in your hands after you accomplished your purpose, something almost without precedent.

"In recognition of this, we have unanimously agreed to recognize your devotion by confirming your promotion as *personally* requested by General Jonathon Edge. Effective immediately, you are hereby promoted to second in command over the entire Confederate Army Provisional. Congratulations, General Gore."

Frank was speechless and Edge himself stepped forward, pinned a star on each collar with his own hands, and then saluted. Numbly, Frank returned the gesture and the General smiled and shook his hand.

"Thank you," the Virginian said. "Just – well, thank you. I look forward to working with you."

He was only the first. By the time they were all through, Frank's hand was red and raw and there were bruises on his back from the slapping.

Last of all, Sam took his hand.

"Congratulations, my good friend, on both counts. I can't think of anyone better suited to either job."

Frank looked at him warily. "What do you mean, 'both counts' and 'either job'? Have you promoted me to something else too while you had me unconscious?"

"You know."

"No," he assured Sam, shaking his head. "I don't know. What are you talking about?"

Sam rolled his eyes, looking around the room, and the whole place burst out laughing, except for Samantha, who blushed and elbowed Tommy hard in the ribs.

"You and your big, fat mouth!" she hissed.

In desperation, Frank turned to her for an answer.

"Sammie, will you please tell me what's going on here?"

"I wasn't planning on making the announcement until the ceremony was over and we were alone, but it seems our medic can't help gossiping like an old woman." She took a deep breath. "You're not just going to be a general, Frank; more importantly, you're going to be a father."

His eyes widened in surprise.

"You're…pregnant?"

"Uh-huh, a little over two months along."

He didn't know whether to sit down or fall down, so he settled for holding his wife and telling her he loved her.

EPILOGUE

Rear Admiral Fred Hardy committed the information on the computer screen in his ready room to memory before erasing it with a powerful electronic shredder program. Despite having well over five decades of life behind him, his mind was as sharp as ever, certainly sharp enough to retain the pertinent details. The information – a classified analysis of the latest news of what had truly become the Third Revolution along with other facts and figures and polls – clandestinely forwarded to him in the daily intelligence report told him all he needed to know.

Almost all: this new war of secession wasn't the only thing on his mind by any means. He wasn't the only one watching the violent events unfolding in the South. Other intelligence reports had come to him indicating the revolution also had the undivided attention of the European Union, Japan, and the Shanghai Co-operation Organization, among others.

The SCO had started out as a relatively loose organization of three nuclear powers – Russia, China, and India – along with several Central Asian countries. Following the implosion of the United States and the subsequent diminution of its place on the world stage, their power had grown exponentially, and with it their ambitions. Now they were courting both Koreas along with Japan, and if they convinced them to join, they would literally control everything east of Suez; they would be *the* power in the Pacific. Although it couldn't be proven, there was no question that one of them, China, was behind the latest announcement by a formerly unknown Hawaiian independence group, who had declared the island chain a sovereign kingdom a week ago, accompanying that declaration with a car bomb that devastated a Federal building in Honolulu. Russia, in the meantime, was playing its own game with its cards held impenetrably close to its national vest.

The EU was just as capable of smelling opportunity as the SCO, and they definitely had the scent. They didn't bay as loudly as the

Easterners on the trail, perhaps, but they were quietly gathering their resources to fill any vacuum the US might leave as it drew more and more of it's remaining forces home to deal with the insurgency. The growing power of the hard right parties, determined to restore their own countries to their former glory of empire, were becoming more and more of a driving force, even if they weren't fully in power themselves yet.

Japan was watching the revolution and everyone else closely, with an impenetrable, almost stereotypical inscrutability, fully realizing that whichever side they ultimately decided to take would make all the difference.

And then there was the Arab League and the Latin Americans, who were playing games all their own...

As if that weren't enough, all of them were making quiet, cautious overtures to the Confederates, who were now actively courting foreign assistance and diplomatic recognition.

He lowered his head for a moment and pinched the bridge of his nose as he felt a headache coming on. Everything was going straight to Hell in a handcart, maybe literally, because if this went on long enough, it would doubtless spread until someone inevitably made a wrong decision, and...

World War III, only this time all sides will have the bomb.

Snorting in disgust at his momentary weakness, Hardy deliberately straightened up. He had passed through the Naval Academy and BUDS training over thirty years ago, and there he had quickly learned that you dealt with situations as they were, not as you'd like them to be.

He was too disciplined to reach for the bottle in his desk drawer; instead he stood and crossed the room to his personal coffee maker. Pouring a cup, he sipped the strong black brew unadulterated as he stared at the world map that decorated his wall. Perhaps if he looked long enough and hard enough, he would make sense of the whole thing.

Inside, he knew better; it was too soon yet. Things were definitely happening, but many more probabilities and potentials were there, ready to fall into line in an as yet unknown order, and tip

426

the scales one way or another. That those scales would eventually be tipped was no longer a question, and the instinct that had kept him and the men under him alive throughout his career told him on which side the balance would fall.

Admiral Hardy had been through a stint in the SEAL Teams and had commanded ships in the theater of battle. He had been in tight places and spilled quantities of his own blood on more than one occasion. Despite all of that, he was suddenly more afraid than he had ever been in his life. There worst part was that there wasn't a damned thing he could do about it yet but wait and see.

COMING SOON!

The Confederate Army Provisional is tested as never before as regular Federal military troops are unleashed on Dixie with the full authority to stop the revolution by any means necessary. A series of tragedies leave Frank and Samantha faced with the choice of going beyond even the Feds' savage brutality, or losing their country, their lives, and everything they hold dear. It's a time of the unthinkable, when all sides raise

THE BLACK FLAG

3223154

Made in the USA